William Smethurst is a director of a television production company. His previous novels, NIGHT OF THE BEAR (written jointly with Julian Spilsbury) and BUKHARA EXPRESS, are both available from Headline.

The author lives in Warwickshire with his wife Carolynne and daughter Henrietta.

Praise for NIGHT OF THE BEAR:

'An action-packed story of human persistence against unthinkable odds ... A magnificent and moving story of vivid characters and high drama' – *Newtownards Chronicle*

'This moving and dramatic story is so very credible that it is at times hard to remember it is fiction' – *Dorset Evening Echo*

Praise for BUKHARA EXPRESS:

'An uncomfortably convincing glimpse of the future – and a classic of pace and tension' – *Daily Telegraph*

'First class thrills' – *Bolton Evening News*

Sinai

William Smethurst

HEADLINE
FEATURE

First published in 1996
by HEADLINE BOOK PUBLISHING

First published in paperback in 1996
by HEADLINE BOOK PUBLISHING

A HEADLINE FEATURE paperback

10 9 8 7 6 5

ISBN 0 7472 4816 8

Printed and bound in Great Britain by
Mackays of Chatham PLC, Chatham, Kent

HEADLINE BOOK PUBLISHING
A division of Hodder Headline PLC
338 Euston Road
LONDON NW1 3BH

For my father

My grateful thanks to Alison Cooper of the University of Warwick, who helped me with the quantum mechanics; and to Jonathan N. Tubb, the British Museum's curator of Syria-Palestine, who helped with the archaeology. Neither, I have to say, can be held responsible for the use I made of the information they provided.

The Truth Behind the Exodus

Many have argued that the Israelite tribes, fleeing Egypt in search of their ancestral home in Canaan, would have taken the ancient track along the Mediterranean coast called the Way of the Philistines. The 'Parting of the Waves' could have occurred on the shallow sandbars of Râs Burûn, a place where strong winds sometimes hold the sea back and then release it suddenly in what seems like a tidal wave. Chariots caught on the sands at the wrong time could easily have been overwhelmed. The Israelites would have detected in this the hand of God.

Others have noted the references to volcanic activity in Exodus and argue that the entire migration must have taken place in north-west Arabia. In Exodus 19 we read: 'And Mount Sinai was altogether on a smoke, because the Lord descended upon it in fire: and the smoke thereof ascended as the smoke of a furnace, and the whole mount quaked greatly.' This theory makes a nonsense of much of the Exodus story – the account of the flight from Egypt, the very clear description of how the tribes went south along the coast of the Red Sea. But the historical chapters of the Old Testament were not written down until centuries after the events supposedly took place, and it is now recognized by scholars that many elements were 'absorbed' from the cultures of other peoples. The laws handed down to Moses on Mount Sinai, for example, were already known and in use by many nations of the Middle East. The Book of Proverbs has been discovered, in modern times, to have been loosely based on the work of the Egyptian scribe Amenemope. The story of a great volcanic eruption could easily have mingled into the story of a great migration.

For this book I did not cross the Wilderness of Shur on foot, as the Israelites supposedly did, or on camel, as did Professor Palmer, the great Victorian explorer who tried to plot the desert wanderings of the Israelites. For much of my time I travelled by local Egyptian bus (of the three options, the least comfortable). It was a journey well rewarded. I stopped at waystations and desert oases. I stood where the Israelites must have stood, looking at mountains that would not have changed.

Professor Palmer, who tried to trace the path of the Exodus in the 1880s, believed that every word written in Exodus was literal fact. He rejected one possible site for the 'handing down of the laws' on the grounds that 600,000 Israelite men together with their women and children (2 million people plus perhaps 4 million animals) could not physically have fitted into the available space. But there is no reason to suppose that the figure of 600,000 men was regarded by Old Testament writers as literal truth. It would have been impossible for so large a number to have travelled together without dying of hunger, thirst and disease, even though the Sinai was undoubtedly more fertile in 1500 BC than it is today.

In the late twentieth century we are used to seeing

pictures of populations forced to flee or to be massacred. On our television screens we have seen it happen – in Bosnia, in Rwanda, in Kurdestan, in Cambodia. We can imagine how the Israelites fled from their homes as the King's militia swept through the eastern Delta. We can imagine the middle classes – lawyers, scribes, landowners – tramping the roads side by side with the peasants and brickmakers. Children would have been orphaned and swept away from their homes, their survival dependent on acts of individual kindness and compassion. There would have been shocking indifference to life, and many acts of courage. The Israelites may well have had a common destination – the fertile country of Canaan – but no clear idea of the best way of getting there. Once in the Wilderness they would have seeped through the Sinai mountains along many paths; groups of families travelling together, lending mutual aid, but never growing into so large a group that they could not find grazing for their animals.

In Sinai I went to the places where, according to bedouin legend, many events of Exodus took place. I went to the two traditional bedouin locations for the 'Parting of the Waves'. And in the second location, where the Wadi Gharandal comes down to the Gulf of Suez, close to where a small port existed in the days of Rameses the Great, I understood how the 'Parting of the Waves' might actually have happened.

And I saw with my own eyes what might have been the 'pillar of fire' that guided and comforted the refugees from Egypt so long ago.

O my father, O my brother, O my mother Isis, release me, look to me, for I am one of those who should be released. *Your limbs are the two children of Atyum, O imperishable one, you shall not perish and your ka shall not perish for you are a ka.* I have gone out. I have risen up. I am alive. O Horus, son of Isis, make me hale as you made yourself hale. Release me, loose me, put me on earth, cause me to be loved. *I am the weneb-flower of Naref, the nebheh-flower of the hidden horizon, so says Osiris.* My hair is Nun; my face is Re. My eyes are Hathor; my ears are Wapwawet; my lips are Anubis. My arms are the Ram, the Lord of Mendes; my breast is Neith, Lady of Saits; my back is Seth, my phallus is Osiris! My feet are Ptah, and Thoth is the protection of all my flesh.

Voices from the Ancient Egyptian Book of the Dead.

Part One

1
The Wilderness of Shur

In the Wilderness, there was no such thing as time.

Behind them there was time. Behind them, in the King's Lands, was a place where time had long been recognized, identified and ordered; a place where there were *hours* – twenty-four of them in every day – and eleven days in every *week* ('Ten days shalt thou labour,' the God-Pharaoh Akhenaten had said, 'and on the eleventh day thou shalt rest') and where it was known by the King's astronomers, who perched in silvery starlight on the cold white summits of the pyramids, that 365 days existed in every year (although they had not discovered the need for leap years, and farmers complained bitterly that winter was come in summer, and the months were turned backwards).

But time was now behind the travellers. Before them, in the Wilderness, there was no time. There was pretty well no anything, Ruth thought, opening her mouth and giving a great cry of sadness, a cry that was swallowed up by the emptiness, by the shimmering heat.

Her husband, Zuri, was with the harlots.

There he was, bouncing along in his litter, which was being carried by the four old Ethiopians, and by

him the harlots were singing and laughing as he
cackled obscenities that made them shriek.

'He is with the harlots again,' said Esther gloomily,
coming up behind her.

'Yes,' said Ruth.

She was tired and sat down in the sand. Esther,
who was fourteen, and was Zuri's daughter, sat down
beside her. Rebecca, pale Rebecca, was still walking
ahead of them, dragging herself forward across the
grey salt marsh towards the grey mountains, a thin
little figure all on her own in the Wilderness.

The harlots shrieked again.

'Oh, oh,' said Esther, shocked.

Zuri was singing. He was singing a rollicking
shanty, a fellaheen's song, a song of the Nile. Then
he broke off to shout at his Ethiopians, telling
them to trot along lively. It was terrible in a man so
ancient.

Ruth looked back, towards the flock, to see if Shelumiel could see his father's behaviour, but behind them
the air was thick with the dust from the hoofs of the
sheep. Shelumiel was Zuri's elder son. He might beat
the Ethiopians if he saw what was happening; but he
might just look stony and tell Ruth to be quiet and
mind her own business. She was only a young wife,
a new wife.

'When will we stop?' asked Esther.

'When we get to the hills.'

'This is a terrible place. A terrible, terrible place.'

Esther was trying to speak bravely, light-heartedly.

Ruth lay back on the grit and looked up at the sky.
It was the same sky that she had seen every day of
her life in Goshen. She tried to imagine the sounds
of home: the doves in the eaves, the creak of the water

wheel, the quiet thud of the wooden shovels of the men in the granary.

Esther said, 'Is that Ti?'

Ruth stared up at a thin wisp of golden cloud.

'Ruth, are those the Mountains of Ti?'

They had all heard of Ti. Beyond Ti were the Springs of Ophir. Beyond Ti was the King's Highway and the road to Canaan.

Ruth sighed and sat up. She looked at the small hill of broken rocks ahead of them. Rebecca, who had lived her life as a herdsman's daughter on the banks of the Nile, was still plodding forward towards the grey rocks, her head bent, a thin little wand in the vast desert.

'No,' said Ruth, 'that is not Ti.'

On the small hill sat a boy on a donkey. He was watching the herd and flock of her husband, Zuri, watching over them, she thought, protectively.

Esther said, 'It's your *bedu* again.'

'Yes,' said Ruth, romancing to herself.

The hill was called Raha, and the boy sitting on his donkey was watching the tribes that covered the plain – eleven, twelve tribes perhaps, split into groups of families, spreading into the far distance, with their herds of cattle and flocks of sheep, their oxen hauling sledges and hurdles, their strings of pack animals. In the distance he could see women driving a herd of hobbled gazelles. Looking another way he could see men driving milk-fed hyenas that waddled fatly.

They were a great mystery, a great wonder, were these Amorites. The Egyptian border guards at Baal-Zephon called them *hapiru*, meaning gypsy thieves; they themselves claimed to be called the Children of

Israel. The first tribe had appeared nearly three months ago, from Zaan in the north, scurrying across the sandbars of Lake Menzelah. Then other tribes had appeared, fleeing without leave, it was soon learned, from forced labour on the grainhouses of Kantarah, from Succoth and from the King's new city of Pi-Ramese. One tribe had been stopped by Egyptian soldiers, the Pharaoh's Own Regiment of Thebes, and had been forced to turn back, but in general the border guards had been concerned to recover as much plunder as possible (for the fleeing Isralites were laden with plunder) and then to let them go. They were bad luck, these *hapiru*; they poisoned the water, cursed the crops, and their magicians made frogs fall from the sky.

Below him, the first of the tribe of Simeon were approaching Raha, the women making their way ahead of the cattle through the spiky desert broom. He watched them find their way up into the gully. They were soft and intellectual and exclusive, these Israelites. Everyone said that they had left Kantarah and Pi-Ramese not because of indignity and slavery, as they claimed, but because the Egyptian public works officials had refused to grant them an extra public holiday to worship their God.

Well, their God would not guard them here in Sinai, which even the bedouin knew was ruled by Hathor, and where Isis flew hither and thither across the night skies, seeking the corpse of Osiris.

The sun's shadows were lengthening. Below him, on the Plain of Shur, tents were being raised. Most of them were of black and grey woollen stuff, but one, close under the hill, near to the families in the gully, was almost white and was made of linen, and had gold-painted posts, and was more of a pavilion than a tent of the desert – the sort of pavilion the bedouin boy (who had never been further west than Baal-Zephon) imagined being pitched among pomegranate groves or in the pleasure gardens of the Nile; the sort of tent an Egyptian queen might command to entertain her lovers. Round it he could see women. They wore bright clothes and had bare stomachs, and their arms were festooned with bangles of gold. He was watching them, incredulous and fascinated, when he heard chattering, city voices: people coming up through the scree from the camp in the gully, climbing the track made by badger and antelope. As they reached the summit a sand viper shot out from under a thorn bush and zigzagged away across the rocks, and his donkey moved uneasily.

There were four of them – a girl of his own age, perhaps, and three children, one a boy. They stopped, suddenly very still, although they must have recognized him – he had been guiding their tribe ever since they first tumbled through the salt marsh and across the great valley.

The girl called a greeting.

He ignored her. He looked over her head, towards the great rim of Ti that was now darkening into the eastern sky. His tribe had lived on Ti for a generation, ever since their camps on the plain had been destroyed by Egyptian cavalry. He had been born in Nakhi, an oasis so poor that as a child he ate worms.

The girl said, 'I am the wife of Zuri, of the house of Simeon.'

She spoke a Semitic tongue, as he did himself, though in a refined and sophisticated fashion, with the sing-song inflections of Lower Egypt.

'I am Ruth, the wife of Zuri-shaddai,' she repeated. 'Is it possible, I wonder, that you can understand what I am saying, *shasu*?'

Shasu was the Egyptian name for bedouin who were taken captive; it was a name of contempt. He looked at her coldly. She was plump, with brown curly hair. She turned and said something quietly to the children, who laughed.

She called, 'Listen, O horse-soldier. We are looking for wood. Can you help us to find wood for our fire?'

He stared out beyond them at the black rim of Ti. The children snorted.

She said, 'O soldier of the *bedu*, soldier most feared among the four divisions of the army of the Pharaoh – ' the children were laughing, open-mouthed – 'we are looking for wood for our fires. Perhaps you do not need warmth. Or perhaps you do not know about fires?'

The children roared.

'Perhaps you are a king? Perhaps you do not speak to us because you are a king of the bedouin? O king, my lord, the sun from the sky, my god, my sun!'

He decided that she was a season younger than he was. Fifteen, fourteen perhaps. When the Egyptians killed the Israelite men and he had plunder of his own, he would buy her. 'This is one little *hapiru*,' he told himself toughly, 'who won't be skewered by the Egyptian lancers, who won't be raped by the garrison troops of Araru.'

Suddenly she turned and led the children away towards the thorn bushes. They were the bushes the sand viper had darted into. He wondered if there was a viper's nest in the bushes, if any of the Israelites would be bitten. He wondered if it was true that

Egyptians had magical wands that would counter the effect of a viper's bite. It would be interesting to see it happen, or indeed to see it fail.

The serpent remained quiet. Eventually the Israelites set off back down through the rocks, dragging a dead broom bush behind them. Its branches would flare and die in a second, but its thick roots would burn for half the night. On the edge of the scree the girl turned.

'Good-night, *bedu*. Good-night, great horse-soldier.'

She smiled an unpleasant Egyptian smile, and disappeared back down through the rocks.

He walked his donkey over to the other side of the ridge and looked out across the Wilderness of Shur. Smoke was rising from the fires of the families of Benjamin and of Gershon and of Reuben – although he had not bothered to learn their names; they were all *hapiru*, all Egyptian Amorites. Further out in the desert were the campfires of the other tribes. It would soon be dark. He watched a great flock of quail sweeping south from the Great Sea, and the sun fall over the Bitter Lakes in a flash of gold. Then, in the dying light, he saw a small cloud of dust rising from a column of horsemen that was leaving the customs post of Araru.

It was the militia, coming out to harry the tribes.

Ruth was preparing the cakes when the horn sounded, spreading barley dough on the heated rock, on the olive oil and the salt, while on another stone she was roasting the pistachios that were such a favourite with her husband, Zuri, who was a gourmand when he was not singing shanties with harlots. Would they have pistachio nuts to eat, he had asked the Kenite, Moses, in the *Promised Land*? Would it be a Promised Land flowing with *milk* and *honey* and with pistachio nuts? The Kenite had laughed (Zuri said) and said that it was a good thing to enjoy a joke – which had puzzled Zuri, who had not been joking.

The horn sounded; the horn of the Benjaminites. Then Ruth heard the horn of Dan and the distant trumpets of the Levite priests. She heard Shelumiel shouting to the herdsmen. She jumped up and screamed to Esther, and to Giliad and Rebecca. They ran into the tent and pulled and tugged at Zuri, who was drooling over his goblet of wine. They dragged him out and pushed him towards the rocks. He bleated and howled. Ruth would have left him behind, but Shelumiel would have killed her. She told the four old Ethiopians to guard the sledges and the oxen; they looked round them helplessly, not daring to run. Rebecca was crying – she was always crying – there was something wrong with her; she had a *serpent* inside her, eating her, and that was why she was so thin. They dragged the old man up into the rocks. Soon Shelumiel came running up the gully, calling to his father. She shouted down to him, told him where they were. He ran off again. Soon the wives and children of the shepherds and the herdsmen came scrambling up the hillside.

They found a cleft in the rocks. Ruth peered down into the gully, calling out occasionally to make sure the old Ethiopians did not leave the sledges. She could just see the blur of their white kilts. Zuri crouched down on his haunches and rocked and moaned. Giliad, who was thirteen and hated to run and hide, was silently furious.

There was no telling how serious the attack would

14

be. Last time it had been a squad of garrison guards, riding out for fun, to see what they could steal. A week ago a Hurrian caravan had wandered into the camp of the Levites in the darkness, and the Levites had killed four Hurrians and the others had run off, leaving their goods behind them. These days the Levites made the world move, Zuri claimed, though nobody had heard of them in five generations, until they had been expelled from the King's Lands for sorcery and heresy, and all the other descendants of Abraham had been expelled with them, or killed, or put to the corvée.

Perhaps the Levites had caught another pack train. She could hear distant shouting. There was a trumpet – an Egyptian trumpet, an army trumpet. There was a terrible scream. Somewhere on the plain a fire flared and threw huge pale shadows against the side of the gully. Giliad wanted to climb to the place they had collected wood, to see what was happening, but Ruth would not let him go.

The distant fire flickered out. The darkness returned. A million stars were suspended from the roof of the world. Zuri slept and snored. He shivered uncontrollably but did not wake up. He was her husband. She took off her shawl and put it round his shoulders, then shivered, sorry for herself.

Esther whispered, 'Look.' The moon was rising over the rim of Ti. She said quietly, 'Glory to thee, thou who risest in the horizon. Praise to thee, thou beautiful beloved child.'

The sun and the moon were the eyes of the Sun God. It was with drops of water from his eyes that he had created man and woman. The Eye of Thoth was looking down on them. Ruth saw him, silver in

15

the sky. She wept with self-pity. She thought of her
father and mother, who had died in the same plague
that had taken Esther's mother, and Giliad and Shelumiel's mother, and a third of the population of
Goshen. *If our gods had brought the plague on the
land of Egypt*, the Israelites had cried to the Egyptians, *would our gods have killed so many of their own
people*? – but the Egyptians had not listened; the
plague had followed the frogs, and the frogs were
without doubt caused by Israelite magicians, and
Levite heresy, for the Levites believed in only one god
and were abhorred by all men.

It was after the plague had killed his wives that
Zuri had married Ruth. She had seen the contract,
written up by the scribe in Avaris. 'You are a wife,'
they had told her. Zuri had held a feast, and fed
her on skewered locusts dipped in honey. 'You are a
wife,' everybody had said, marvelling, giving her
pomegranate wine and beer made with blue lupins
and dates.

'A wife for the Wilderness,' she told herself now,
lost in self-pity, racked with cold; 'a wife for the
Wanderings!'

Esther and Giliad were cuddling each other for
warmth. Rebecca was asleep. She would sleep anywhere, she and her serpent. She was the daughter of
a herdsman who had been killed by Egyptians
enraged by the theft of their goods. Zuri had taken
her into his household, but had not taken her as a
wife or as a concubine. She was just there, neither
family nor bondswoman, dragging herself about, nur-
turing her secret snake. She cried a great deal – to
make Zuri sorry and marry her, said Esther, or
to make him give her as a concubine to Shelumiel.

16

They were all of the family of Zuri, of the house of Simeon.

Eventually Ruth heard the shepherds returning up the gully from the desert. 'Old man,' she said callously, shaking her husband. 'Old man.'

They helped him back down to the tent. He was bent and his limbs were stiff. The fire was out. Ruth shouted angrily at the dim white shapes of the old Ethiopians who had sat on their haunches in the dark all that time, uselessly.

Esther brought the fire to life. She had a skill with fires. She mumbled spells over the wood and it flared into life. Ruth took up the half-baked cakes and gave them to Zuri, and then to Giliad and to Esther and Rebecca. She gave a cake each to the old Ethiopians who, this time at least, had not run away to hide. The Ethiopians muttered their gratitude and shuffled away. They did not understand why they had had to leave the vineyards of Goshen. Like Zuri, their master, they chattered all the time about the barley fields they used to till, and the white wooden house by the canal.

Shelumiel came up the valley with the herdsmen. He flung himself down, his body streaked with sweat and dust. 'I only know part of what happened. The Zebulunites lost two pack horses loaded with grain. There was a family of Amram with a table – a big, heavy wooden table, a table with five legs – and they were trying to run through the desert away from the cavalry! They were trying to hide under it when the Egyptians killed them.'

Everybody laughed.

'What happened to the table?' asked Zuri, interested.

He was lying on his wooden bed, inside his tent, looking out at the world. His old limbs trembled and shook, but he dipped his cake eagerly into his wine, crumbling it up. He was old and his teeth were worn to the nerve ends; in Goshen he had screamed pitifully even as he scrunched the bones of the tiny green frogs. 'Did you hear what happened to the table?' he asked.

Around him, in the tent, were his own possessions, dragged up the gully on a sledge. His bed was his joy: it had carved gilt cobra legs, the cobras having green eyes. Then there was a chair inlaid with ebony and ivory that he had possessed for a hundred of his two hundred years (that in truth he had found in his neighbour's house when the neighbour had fled, at the time when the gifts of the Egyptians were being collected; the gifts that now were called the *belongings*); his cedar pot-stand with its mantle of soft Egyptian linen; his painted lamp-stand, fancifully shaped to imitate a column of papyrus (papyrus imitation had been the fashion two years ago, among the petty princes of Lower Egypt); his decorated wine jar set with lapis lazuli; and his small, black-wood carving of the Goddess Taweret, in her guise as a pregnant hippopotamus.

'I do not know,' said Shelumiel coldly, 'what happened to the table.'

'You must go and look in the morning.'

'There is something else I do not know,' said Shelumiel. 'I do not know what happened to the bedouin. The Egyptian cavalry were among us and the bedouin were nowhere to be seen. How much are we paying the bedouin?'

'The Levites are giving them five pieces of silver,

every ten days,' said Zuri, 'until we reach the Wells of Ophir or release them from their contract.'

'And for what do we pay them this money? To abandon us when Egyptian cavalry appear? And where are the Levites leading us? Where is anybody leading us?'

Zuri said, 'Who can say?'

'Listen,' said Shelumiel. 'Down in the desert there are a hundred women wailing round the tent of the Kenite. "Are there not graves in Egypt," they are wailing, "that you brought us to the Wilderness to die?" '

'Yes,' said Zuri, who was so very old, and would have wailed with the women himself if he could.

'And who made this Kenite the *lawgiver*? Who made this Kenite into the *prophet*? The men of Korah say he was only a scribe in the subprefect's office in Migdol. Sweet God!' said Shelumiel suddenly, his face cracked with weariness. 'Sweet Akhenaten!'

'Ah,' said Zuri, nodding his head, 'sweet Akhenaten.'

'Get me wine,' said Shelumiel.

Ruth had been sitting looking into the fire. She got up and went to fetch him wine from the sledge. Shelumiel was losing his fatness, losing his plump sheen; he was spending all his days running about after the sheep. She felt her way through the darkness, guided by the sound of the running stream that echoed under the rocks.

Occasional cries still came from the desert. She could hear the mournful howling of jackals, a sound she had heard often round the necropolis of Goshen, but here in the gully everything was quiet. There was no sound but the soft bleating of sheep, the tinkle of the goat-bell and the murmur of the water. The air was cold; this was not yet the end of the winter.

She poured wine from the goat sack, dark liquid, black in the starlight. When she got back to the tent a stranger, a Levite, was also sitting by the fire. He looked thin and hungry, his clothes were ragged. Nobody gave much to the priests these days, and they had no cattle or sheep of their own. He said, 'They took ten slaves from Judah, and fifty of the mules.'

Shelumiel said, 'Sweet Akhenaten!'

'Do not profane the name of Akhenaten,' said the Levite.

'Do not tell me,' said Shelumiel, who had become more irritable as he became thinner, 'which god I may or may not profane.'

The Levite made a gesture of peace, of submission almost. They were sad people, these priests, turned out of their temple, reduced to beggars – those that had not been caught and killed by the terrible priests of Amun.

Shelumiel passed him bread across the fire. The Levite ate slowly but with quiet intensity.

'Oh, he was sweet,' said Zuri suddenly.

'Yes,' said Shelumiel wearily.

Zuri said, 'So sweet!'

'Yes, yes,' said Ruth.

Zuri was famous for having seen Akhenaten when Akhenaten walked the earth. He had been there, as a boy, outside the temple at Memphis, when the beautiful young Pharaoh had stood on the throne steps and the brass bugles had sounded, and Akhenaten had put on his head the white crown of Upper Egypt – to show his contempt for the mortuary priests of Thebes, those terrible priests of Amun – and had declared: *There is only one God. There is only one*

20

God. In heaven and earth there is one God and he is not Amun.

'Akhenaten was sweet and he is dead, and so is Nefertiti, his most beautiful wife!' Zuri cried out. 'And the priests of Amun are taking their revenge! They are building a temple that will take 100,000 workers twenty years to finish, 100,000 workers on the corvée . . .'

'The people of Israel will no longer serve on the corvée,' said the Levite, quietly but with conviction.

'There are strangers in Goshen!'

'Yes, there are strangers in Goshen.'

'Strangers are sitting in my house . . .'

While here in the Wilderness was Zuri the Simeonite, in his declining years, yellow-bearded old Zuri, lost in the Wilderness because of those terrible words on that golden morning of flowers and sun: *There is only one God in heaven and earth and he is not Amun.*

But if the one God was not Amun, who was he?

Akhenaten himself?

Akhenaten the God-Pharaoh?

It was all too much for an old, old man.

'How many dead all told?' asked Shelumiel.

'Forty perhaps, all told,' said the Levite. 'Half of them boys.'

'Forty dead!' said Shelumiel bitterly. 'It will be in stone on the walls of Karnak. "I slew them all, none escaped me, the field of Raha was white with corpses of the *hapiru*." ' He laughed and poured wine down his throat. 'By Ashtoreth! By the Living Goddess of Asher!'

Zuri looked worriedly at the Levite, the messenger who carried tales in two directions. The Goddess of Asher was loathed by the Levites. They hated the way she sat bare-breasted outside her temple, enticing the poor shepherd men to prayer.

Shelumiel said, 'Well, we can't drift around Shur from watering place to watering place, being slaughtered by the garrison troops. What do we do when the pastures are bare and the stream is dry? Some of the families are going north. Do we all go north?'

'The Lord God has told Moses that we must not go north.'

'Perhaps we can find a god that says something different. You know there are seabirds to eat along the Way of the Philistines? And partridges, fat little partridges. What would you say to a dozen partridges roasted on a spit, eh?'

The Levite smiled wistfully. His bread was finished. Ruth passed him a cup of wine. He said, 'Brother, we must follow the prophet. We must follow the bones of Joseph.'

'There are many families,' said Shelumiel, 'who say the bones of Joseph are in the necropolis of Goshen. But if Moses will not have us go north, where will he have us go? And will his god remember, perhaps, that cattle and sheep need pasture?'

'He saved us from being slaughtered in Egypt, Shelumiel. He saved us from the corvée, he brought us safely out of the Black Lands.'

Certainly somebody had brought them out of Egypt. They had not *decided* to leave the Delta, to abandon their homes and grazing lands in Goshen, to take their herds and flocks on the long trek to Giza, to Succoth, to Baal-Zephon, out into the Wilderness, day after day following the black scaregull-flapping priests of Levi. A decision, somehow, had been taken for them.

22

'Well, personally,' said Shelumiel, drinking his wine, stretching, relaxing now, 'personally, I'll go where Miriam goes. I'll go whichever way Miriam and her lovelies decide to go.'

Zuri laughed. 'Ho, ho, ho,' he laughed. Shelumiel was his son, a chip off the old block, and he loved him.

Ruth felt sorry for the Levite. He had walked a long way up the gully. Somebody ought to give the Levite a donkey.

Zuri stopped laughing. He said, 'I am an old man.'

'Yes,' said Shelumiel, 'you are a hundred.'

'I am certainly an old man.'

They all nodded. He was an old man, they agreed, a hundred and fifty years old at least.

'Old man,' said Ruth sadly. 'Old, old man.'

'To be taken,' Zuri cried, 'from my house, when so old!'

He was not really, they knew, a hundred, or a hundred and fifty, nor were there 100,000 in the family of Simeon, or 400,000 in the tribes wandering the Wilderness of Shur. But he was truly old. He was one of the few that had ever seen Akhenaten the God-Pharaoh; even the Levites, the priests of Akhenaten, respected him for that.

The Levite stood up, stiffly, his muscles evidently causing him pain. He said gently, 'Fear not. Be strong. See the salvation of God.'

Zuri lay on his bed. Ruth pulled a blanket over him. It was a bedouin blanket of brightly dyed wool. A light burned in the brass bowl. In a linen bag, clutched in his hands, were his treasures, that he had brought out of Egypt. There was a scarab necklace and a gold amulet that Ruth coveted. Wrapped in a linen cloth there was a statue. Zuri took it out, as he did most nights. It was a likeness of an ancient priest of Ptah, made out of solid silver, about two hand's-breadths in length.

Ruth was afraid of the statue. They would be cursed, she thought, for bringing it out of the land of Misri, out of Egypt. She looked at it in the light of the lamp and thought, 'We are Egyptian. It is not our fault they call us *hapiru*. I know that the ka of the priest of Ptah wanders among us during the night, and that Isis will come across him on her relentless search for the body of Osiris, and take vengeance on the people who brought the ka of so great a priest out of the Civilized Lands, to suffer in the wilderness.'

Zuri said, 'It will make perhaps 1,000 silver shekels when we melt it down.'

'No,' said Ruth, frightened.

'He is only the priest of a god of Upper Egypt,' said Zuri, with false bravado.

'Old man,' said Ruth, 'do you believe in the Kenite's God?'

Zuri blinked evasively. 'Did Akhenaten not say on the temple steps at Memphis, "There is only one God and he is not Amun"?'

'And is this one God the God of the Levites?'

Zuri did not answer. Even in his thoughts he did not want to betray Renenutet, the green and gold Cobra Goddess of the Delta.

She said, 'When you are gone to the Otherworld, can I marry a bedouin?'

'Moses,' said Zuri, 'has married an Ethiopian.'

'The Kenite has married many women,' Ruth said. 'The bedouin take only one wife.'

'When I die, you are to go to Shelumiel.'

'Shelumiel only wants me,' said Ruth bravely, 'for a concubine.'

Zuri was gazing into the flickering flame of the lamp. She leaned over and snuffed it out. She said, 'I would rather marry a bedouin.'

'Don't,' said Zuri in the darkness, 'add to my troubles.'

He lay in the dark, as still as a mouse. He was a sad old creature, fit only to goggle at harlots. She went out of the tent. Giliad was asleep by the fire, wrapped in a woollen cloak like a soldier. Esther and Rebecca were curled under a blanket of skins.

She threw a bunch of broom on to the embers. The red sparks flew upwards, up into the gully. She crawled under the soft goatskin blanket, next to Esther, who was murmuring in her sleep for Eli, her toy hippopotamus. She listened to jackals barking, the *little jackals* of the night, and to the murmur of the stream. The air was cool but sweet; she could smell the scent of wild desert thyme. Distantly, she could hear the flutes and lyres and timbrels of the harlots, who were playing a lament for the dead outside their tent down in the valley. She looked up again at the stars, thinking that if she looked very quickly and suddenly she might see Isis, flying back and forth over Sinai, collecting up the torn limbs of Osiris. She thought she felt a drop of water on her arm, which would have been Isis weeping; but when she felt it, her arm was dry and cold.

She snuggled down under the blanket. In Egypt she had been very fat and desirable; she was distressed now, every day, to find her legs and arms becoming firm and hard.

She looked at the loom of the hills, wondering where her *bedu* was now.

What would happen to them all? The Levite priests said that Moses had had a dream in the night that they crossed from Baal-Zephon and left the land of Misri. In it, God had said they must go southwards along the Yam Suf. If they went south, said the God of Moses, they would find a safe passage through the great Mountains of Ti. And on the other side of Ti they would find the Wells of Ophir. And there would be a sea of azure blue, and the start of the King's Highway, which was the legendary road to Canaan.

A breath of night air made the tent walls flap in the darkness.

The ka of Ka-nefer, the priest of Ptah, irrevocably released from the dreamworld on the death of his master, was out and about.

She buried herself under the blanket. She tried to imagine the Wells of Ophir, with their date palms and mimosa, and the King's Highway stretching eastward along the coast of the azure sea.

2
A Death in Sinai

Wolfgang Gabriel had been climbing the hillside for nearly an hour, occasionally stopping to turn and look at the view out over the Gulf of Aqaba, but mostly scrambling grimly upwards, his head bowed, his vision restricted by the green shade of his baseball cap, so that he nearly fell into the barbed wire that was strung, gleaming, across the track. He put out a hand to save himself and a twisted barb of metal pierced his palm. He swore softly as a globule of blood formed. Standing upright and looking round, he saw that the wire was stretched in rolling loops, fixed into the ground at intervals on metal posts. In both directions it ran up the sides of the small wadi and then disappeared.

He looked down at his tourist map. It told him there was only one path up the hill, and he was on it. The path, said the brochure, led to the 'one true well' of St Onuphrios, the hermit of Sinai, who had spoken not a word during fifty years, but had lived naked in the barren mountains, and then, on the day of his death, had said: 'He who holds intercourse with his fellow men will never be able to speak with the angels.'

And then St Onuphrios died, said the brochure, *and*

*the young hermit buried him in his cell, and when he
stepped out of the cave it collapsed behind him and
the date palm by the well slowly disappeared and was
no more.*

Gabriel wiped sweat from his forehead and looked
back down the hillside. By the shore was the Desert
Oasis motel, with its white walls and drab-green
dusty palms. In the car park he could see the coach
that had brought them from Taba. People – tiny at
this distance – were milling round a family of bedouin
who were offering horse-rides in the desert. He smiled
faintly, reflecting that Sartre, a thousand or so years
after St Onuphrios, had noted that 'hell is other
people'.

Beyond the motel was the sea. It was azure and
lime green along the coral reef, a deep blue further
out. In the hazy distance he could see an Egyptian
navy patrol boat heading down the gulf towards Tiran
Island, and the tiny bobbing boats of snorkellers
round the wreck of the cargo ship *Jackson*.

He turned and looked up the wadi. According to his
map, the well of St Onuphrios was no more than 1,000
metres above him. It was described in his brochure as
being in a hidden valley, next to a small ninth-century
mosque.

He hesitated, glancing upwards. The sun burned
in a milky-white sky. It was an unusually hot
December this year and the heat pouring down over
him was almost liquid. He was used to the desert,
but had not calculated on having to climb quite so
far.

He would go to the next summit; if it proved to be
false, he would turn back. There were other 'true
wells' of St Onuphrios in Sinai; every crumbling ruin

28

had some bedouin legend attached to it.

The barbed wire was tricky to get through, but he was stubborn, not a man to give in easily, and although he grazed his leg and had to take off his shirt to wrap round the razor-sharp barbs, he finally won through to the other side and continued onwards up the mountainside.

'Sinai. A small, barren desert, arid and featureless in the north, rocky and mountainous in the south, smaller than Maine – so small you could lose it in Texas and never find it again. The place where Christ fasted in the Wilderness. The land of the Exodus.'

Richard Corrigan paused. The tour guests were looking at him attentively, with suitably awed expressions on their faces.

'But did the Exodus ever actually happen? Did a guy called Moses even exist – and if he did, what sort of man was he really? Manetho, in 250 BC, said that Moses wasn't a Jew but a renegade priest of Heliopolis. Karl Marx, for no obvious reason, decided that Moses was an Egyptian priest leading a Negro revolt. In the twentieth century, Freud declared, again without the slightest evidence, that Moses must have been a priest who had got his religious ideas from the sun cult of the Pharaoh Akhenaten. Well, yes, OK. It was Akhenaten who first propounded the heresy that there was only one God, and today it is Akhenaten, not Moses, who is widely recognized as the first modern man, the first individual with a modern mind, the person whose life marks the end of prehistory.'

Again he paused and looked round.

'All these theories. But is there a single shred of evidence that Moses ever walked the earth, or that the Exodus of Jewish tribes from Egypt ever took place?'

'There's the Bible.'

It was Mr Baker from Virginia. Richard had wondered who it would be.

'We have the word of the Bible,' said Mr Baker, polite but stiff, not a man to be seduced by subtle, weasel words just because he was in the Old World. 'I reckon that's good enough for me.'

'The problem with the Bible, Mr Baker, the problem with the Old Testament, is that the early chapters were written down several hundred years after the supposed events actually happened and many of the events described were borrowed from the folk-legends and folk-histories of other Middle Eastern tribal societies. In Egypt itself – and Egypt was a very civilized, well-organized, well-governed country with a written language and an extensive civil service – there is not a single reference to the ten terrible plagues: to the Nile turning to blood, frogs invading houses, locusts eating the crops, darkness falling over the land or the death of the nation's first-born. No reference anywhere to the departure of 600,000 men with their families, their herds and flocks, and all the loot that the Bible admits went out of Egypt with them. The Exodus has been variously dated to the reign of Akhenaten the heretic, Rameses the Second, or Rameses the Third – in other words some time between the mid-thirteenth century and the mid-eleventh century BC – but this event of such enormous significance in the history of Judaism and Christianity is nowhere mentioned in Egyptian histories of the times. As far as Egyptian history is concerned, it is as if the Exodus never even happened.'

They were looking at him warily. Telling folk who'd spent several thousand dollars to come on a 'Pathways of the Exodus' culture holiday that there was no Exodus after all was like telling visitors to Disneyworld that Mickey Mouse didn't exist.

'So is the Exodus just a Hebrew folk-legend? Was Moses a sort of religious King Arthur, with a tabernacle instead of a Round Table? Was he a Robin Hood, with the Pharaoh as the Sheriff of Nottingham?'

The analogies went down well at the University of Kent, where he taught a Continuing Education course in 'Facts behind the Bible'. Now, at the back of the tent, a retired professor of linguistics, Bill Dyson, grinned and clapped his hands silently.

'And if the Exodus did take place, if the biblical story is true, what did these two million people live on? What did they eat? OK, Sinai wasn't the desert it is now – we'll be going to the Pharaonic mines south of Sarabit el-Khâdem the day after tomorrow, and you'll see the evidence of smelting works that must have needed vast forests of wood to feed the furnaces – but it could not have been a fertile place—'

'I always understood, Richard,' said a voice, 'that they lived on quails and manna.'

'OK, let's talk about manna.'

He paused. They sat and waited for him to deconstruct manna.

'At first – when they were starving – the tribes of the Exodus were ecstatic about manna. They thought it tasted like wafers of honey. Then, after a bit, they got sick of it and complained. They said they really wanted cucumbers, and melons, and leeks, and onions, and garlic. They wanted flesh. They wanted the fish they ate of freely in Egypt – that is very interesting, by the way, most Egyptians regarded fish as impure. "Our soul is dried away," they said to Moses. "There is nothing at all besides this manna." Does anybody know what manna actually is?'

He looked round. It was dark now, but brass lamps had been lit, suspended from the roof of the mock-bedouin tent. His listeners were reclining on mattresses covered in colourful blankets, bedouin-style. They were sipping cups of Turkish coffee, or drinking beer. One of them was smoking a hookah pipe that had been lit for him, amid much amusement, by a waiter. There were nineteen of them in the group. There should have been twenty, but a German had gone walkabout.

'Oh, come on! Somebody say something, somebody please help me, please! Manna from heaven. What if you came across some and didn't realize what it was?'

They smiled. They were a good bunch, polite and interested. In Jerusalem, in Petra, in Taba, they had listened each evening to what he had to tell them. They were Timetravelers of Baltimore, with a respect for learning. Unlike first-year students at UCL and the University of Kent, they did not try to bunk off to the pub. At least, none of them had done so before tonight.

'I suppose you want us to say some sort of cookie,' said Miss Thorson, a retired Wilmington schoolteacher, now grimly determined on seeing the world, at whatever cost to her comfort, her digestion or the moral certainties that had sustained her for sixty years.

'A cookie. Yes, well, the Bible does tell us that manna was ground in mills and baked in pans—'

'I expect it was some sort of drug that made them

32

sexy,' said Eloise, an eighteen-year-old from Atlantic City. She was lying on her side on her bedouin mattress, wearing the harem trousers she had bought in Taba, resting her head in the crook of her arm. 'Is it true, Richard, that slave-girls to the Pharaohs had to be naked all the time as a mark of their servitude?'

'For Christ's sake, Eloise – ' said her father wearily.

Richard liked Eloise. He said, 'Very possibly, Eloise. Bondmaidens of the seventeenth to the twenty-first dynasties are usually depicted naked, or wearing only a leather thong around their waists.' He paused to let the image establish itself. 'I would recommend you to visit Gallery 62 in the British Museum, should you ever be in London, and look for the paintings from the tomb of Nebamun. These depictions that have come down to us, of course, are part of the tomb offerings, the grave goods, designed to provide the dead person's ka with everything it needed after death, and might not relate precisely to everyday life in Egypt, but you may be interested to know that the nineteen-year-old son of Ibn Tulun had an aviary of exotic birds, and in it, under palm trees, a lake of quicksilver on which he lay on an airbed, yes, an *airbed*, moored by silk cords to silver columns. And on this airbed he made love to a hundred bondmaidens in a hundred days.'

Another pause.

'Neat,' said Eloise.

'Jesus,' said a low male voice from the darkness.

'The girls were guarded,' added Richard, 'by a tame lion.'

'Manna,' said Miss Thorson grimly, 'you were telling us about manna.'

Celia, the tour leader, got up and slipped out of the

tent. Richard saw her go past the gift kiosk towards the manager's office. She was worrying about Herr Gabriel, who had been missing now for five hours. Earlier, she and Richard had walked along the beach for a kilometre in either direction, but had seen no sign of clothing or belongings, nothing to indicate that a portly middle-aged German had decided on a solitary snorkel. Over dinner she had wanted to call the police, but then discovered that to all intents and purposes there were no police, not civilian police, nearer than Sharm el-Sheikh. She didn't want to call Baltimore. She feared that she would either be blamed for letting the man stray off into the desert or given a black mark for panicking when there was no need. She was English and this was her first job as a tour hostess. She had spent two seasons as a ski-chalet girl in the Haute Savoie without losing a single punter. She was determined that when Herr Gabriel showed up she would leave him in no doubt about her feelings.

'Manna isn't a cake, it isn't a drug, it isn't a berry or a seed,' said Richard, after a further few minutes of speculation. It was getting late and he wanted a beer; he never drank before a lecture, but liked a glass or two when his work was done. 'It is, in fact, a deposit left by insects on the leaves of desert plants, most commonly the tamarisk, and most commonly found today to the north of Sinai in the Negev Desert.'

At this point in his 'Facts behind the Bible' lecture, girl students at the University of Kent generally went 'Yuck'.

'Yuck,' went Eloise.

'OK, it sounds revolting,' he said. 'But what we have here is a substance recorded as having saved

34

travellers in the desert from starvation some 3,500 years ago and it is a substance that we know exists. It thus gives a touch of corroboration to the Exodus story, and corroboration is sorely needed.'

'Richard?'

Celia was standing at the edge of the tent looking unhappy. 'I've spoken to Baltimore. You're not going to believe this, but I think they're calling out the army.'

They were UN Peacekeepers from Sharira Pass. At ten minutes past midnight their Land Rovers swerved into the courtyard and pulled up under the flood-lit palms. The commanding officer was a lieutenant in the Royal New Zealand Regiment. He came over to Richard and Celia and shook their hands, then said to Richard, 'We'll search out as far as we can, but it's a bloody mug's game crashing about in the dark.'

Richard said, 'We've already checked along the beach, one kilometre in either direction.'

Celia said, 'I'm the tour leader. My name's Celia Wilson. I'm sure you'll do everything possible.'

Tour guests milled round the mock-bedouin tent, worrying loudly. Herr Gabriel was the only non-American on the tour, and although most of them had tried to be friendly to him in the five days since they'd left Jerusalem, he had tended to keep himself to himself. The RNZR lieutenant went off up the hillside with his men. Richard and Celia sat out on the terrace, overlooking the sea. A waiter brought them coffee and a saucer of pistachios, and lit a small spirit lamp. Richard ordered a beer, a bottle of Stella local, the best bottled lager in the world, still only around a dollar a pint, and still, thank God, available – Cairo was virtually dry, according to the stories of distressed travellers. The moon was huge and yellow over the dark waters of the Gulf. From the bedouin café, a tin-roofed coffee and Pepsi-Cola stall on the dirt road next to the motel, came the sound of Radio Amman: a wailing, tortured love lament sung by Kaka, the Madonna of the Muslim world.

'Christ, I really needed this,' said Celia grimly, not referring to Kaka's love song.

They watched the UN Peacekeepers fan out along the beach and then up the scree slopes, calling out to each other at intervals. Torches danced in the darkness, will-o'-the-wisps in the Egyptian night. Richard had offered to go with them; his offer had been curtly refused.

After a while guests started to drift off to bed. It had been a long, hot day and staying up, they told each other, wasn't doing anybody any good. Richard suggested that Celia go to bed – to rest at least if she could not sleep – but she shook her head irritably. They sat and drank more coffee. It was two a.m. before the soldiers returned and sat round the terrace drinking tea from their flasks. The lieutenant came over, sat down heavily and took out his mobile phone. 'I'm calling up a Chinook,' he said, dialling the civilian airstrip at Gibeil.

'Calling up a what?' asked Celia.

'Rescue-command helicopter with a heat-seeking probe,' said the lieutenant, his khaki shirt soaked with sweat despite the desert chill. 'It was no use calling it up earlier. It can only show a body in the rocks once the ground surface has cooled.'

'What about goats?' asked Celia.

'It knows about goats. Goats are small.'

'Camels?' said Celia, who by now knew instinctively that Herr Gabriel was dead and her career as a tour guide finished.

'This device,' said the lieutenant, drinking thirstily from his flask, 'can do a DNA on the fat in a camel's hump.'

Celia said, 'It's not the first time somebody's gone missing. You remember the party of American tourists that disappeared in the late eighties? They were supposed to have gone off into the Zaghra Wadi and got caught in a sandstorm, but nobody's ever found a trace of them, and their relatives are still flying over and calling for government inquiries, even after all this time.' She was taking comfort in having lost only one Timetraveler, when others had lost so many more.

The lieutenant was reading a large notice stuck on the wall of the terrace. 'You don't suppose he's gone on one of those? You don't suppose he's out there bopping with the belly-dancers?' The notice advertised 'Nomad Evenings'. It promised an international buffet and live bedouin music for thirty US dollars. It read:

A ceiling of silver stars and a floor of golden sand.
Did you ever count the shining stars in an endless sky?
Did you ever listen to the sound of silence in the desert?
Did you ever have the feeling of being one with nature?

'They're only on on Fridays,' said Celia, 'and they only pick up from here if there's enough people booked in

37

Dahab. And they don't,' she added snootily, 'have belly-dancers.'

The lieutenant turned to Richard. 'How are you involved with this lot?'

'I'm the guest lecturer.'

'Dr Richard Corrigan, of University College, London,' said Celia. 'He's the acknowledged world expert on the Egyptian war machine of the nineteenth dynasty.' She was quite proud of him, even though they'd known each other for only a week.

Soon the helicopter could be heard. It swept slowly in from the Gulf, crossing the old-gold disc of the moon, turning and moving up the mountain. Suddenly a searchlight speared down on to the bare slopes.

'We can only overfly inland for five kilometres,' said the lieutenant. 'There's a restricted zone covering the Sinai Science Nature Park. They're trying to reintroduce wolves and leopards. Daft really. They'll snaffle a tourist one day and then there'll be trouble.'

Celia said, 'Is that a joke?'

'Sorry. Your chap can hardly have got more than five kilometres, I wouldn't have thought. What do we know about him?'

'He's a retired motor-caravan dealer from Dortmund,' Celia said. 'A widower. He joined the tour at Jerusalem. Most of the tour flew in directly from America, but there were a few spare places on the bus, and he took one of them. His personal form says he's fifty-seven years old, interested in Islamic and Coptic art and Old Kingdom funerary offerings. His next-of-kin is his only son, an accountant in Munich called Alex.'

'When he wandered off, did he have water? Did he

take a sleeping bag? Did he have warm clothes?'

'If we had seen him wandering up the mountain in the middle of the afternoon with water bottles and camping gear,' said Celia, in the very English voice that had proved so invaluable to her as chalet girl and tour hostess, 'we might have made some comment at the time, don't you think? If only to note his apparent dissatisfaction with Timetraveler Tours?'

The lieutenant looked at her thoughtfully, possibly feeling sorry for the poor sod who ended up marrying her. 'Perhaps,' he said, 'somebody could check his room? Perhaps he had a sweater or coat that you might remember, and perhaps we could see if it's there or not?'

Richard said, 'I'll go and look.'

As he left, the New Zealander was saying to Celia, 'Now, *Tour Leader*, I want you to tell me everything you know about this man. Did he seem to be in a normal mental state? Was he fit and healthy?'

'For Christ's sake, don't say *was*,' snapped Celia.

Herr Gabriel's warm pullover ('Be sure to bring a warm sweater,' tourists were advised. 'In the desert the temperature can drop at night to ten degrees centigrade or less and a frost is not unknown.') was in his suitcase, which had not been unpacked. By the case was a copy of Tubb and Chapman's *Archaeology and the Bible*, and Volume XX of the academic archaeology journal *Levant*, open at a report on the excavations at Tell-es-Sa'idiyeh in Jordan. There were several books on early Coptic art and Old Kingdom magic.

Richard went back to the terrace. Celia was staring out over the sea. The lieutenant was reading aloud from the Timetravelers of Baltimore tour brochure.

' "A morning visit to Mount Sinai and the Monastery of St Catherine, built on the site where Moses saw the Burning Bush. At the monastery see the basilica, the Chapel of the Burning Bush, the Library and Museum." You did all that, did you?'

'Yes.'

' "Also the delightful garden and shrine to the prophet Saheh . . . In the afternoon we travel to the three-star Desert Oasis motel, where bedouin tribesmen wait to show you their traditional handicrafts and invite you to camel-rides in the desert as the sun goes down." '

'Celia?' cried a tour guest, calling from the hotel entrance. 'Are you out there, Celia?' It was the voice of somebody who had found a spider in her bath.

'Oh, Christ.'

'You don't think,' said the lieutenant, 'Herr Gabriel might have gone off for a camel-ride in the desert as the sun went down? Or do they only have camel-rides on Fridays?'

'Celia! Celia!' said the plaintive voice.

Celia went.

The lieutenant said, 'If he's up in the hills, he'll show on the screen. When did you last see him?'

'About three o'clock,' said Richard. 'Just after we arrived. There was a late lunch, a buffet.'

'What did you do after that?'

'Personally, I went for a lie-down.'

'It's a pity Herr Gabriel didn't do the same. You don't suppose he could have taken a bus to Nuweiba?'

'We thought of that. There's only the East Delta bus, and that came through at two-thirty.'

The lieutenant went back to the brochure. 'If he doesn't turn up, he's going to miss an "awesome drive thru the Colored Canyon". Are you still allowed through the Biyar Wadi?'

'No. We heard in Taba that it's been sealed off by the army. Something to do with the Science Nature Park.'

Celia returned. A few minutes later the lieutenant was called to the radio. He came back and said, in an embarrassed voice, 'The Chinook's disgraced the service.' The aircraft's heat-seeking probe, he told them, had burst into life to show hundreds of hot little shapes swarming over the empty mountainside.

'Goats,' said Celia, 'that'll be bedouin goats.'

'It's not bloody goats,' said the lieutenant. 'I've told you, it knows goats. Well, if he's up there he's up there till the morning. My guess is that he's in the water. My guess is that he went snorkelling and got into difficulties, and nobody saw him, and he just drowned.'

'Oh, dear God, no,' said Celia, for this was her nightmare – the scenario in which maximum blame attached to herself.

Police from the Tourist and Antiquities Department arrived just after seven a.m. The tour should have departed for Sharm el-Sheikh at seven-thirty, but they wouldn't let it go until statements had been taken from everyone. The UN helicopter was again sweeping over the bare mountainside. Tourist Department policemen wandered along the beach, their submachine-guns held in the crook of their arms. Nobody really suspected a Muslim fundamentalist attack, but these days they carried their guns at all times, as a matter of course.

Richard found Celia drinking coffee and eating

cakes. She was a big girl, swallowing down sweet Egyptian pastries for comfort. She said, 'Baltimore are asleep now, thank Christ.'

Richard said, 'There's some sort of ninth-century mosque up in the hills. I'm going to climb up there and take a look.'

'The army say they checked it out last night.'

'Professor Dyson says he'd like to see it, and the Schofields say they'd like a walk. We'll be back down by lunchtime. You OK?'

She nodded. 'Take lots of water and don't lose them, for God's sake.'

He went. Celia hesitated, then took up another pastry, one with apricots and almonds and pistachios. The Egyptians were devils when it came to pastry. They could teach the French a thing or two, she thought, then remembered – a moment of solace – the *tartes au citron* she'd practically lived on in the Haute Savoie. Eloise came out into the sunshine, daisy-fresh in her harem trousers, with a bare midriff and a little sunflower-yellow top.

'No sign of Herr Gabriel?' she asked, sitting down. 'Where's Richard? You know what I dreamt last night, Celia? I dreamt that Richard was a Pharaoh in ancient Egypt.'

'And don't tell me,' said Celia, 'you were his bondmaiden, forced to go naked as a sign of your servitude?'

'Only one of his bondmaidens,' said Eloise modestly, 'but I had hopes of becoming his favourite. Wasn't that a weird dream?'

Richard led his small group up the track. He liked Dyson, a lean, humorous man in his early seventies, and the Schofield couple, who were just retired and genuinely interested in the history of Sinai. After an hour they stopped and looked back down the mountain. An Egyptian warship was on patrol, heading north to Taba from Tiran Island. There were several pleasure craft, snorkellers from Sharm, motorboats carrying out scuba-divers from Nuweiba to the coral reefs, far enough out for them to find turtles and shark.

It was getting hot. It wasn't supposed to be this hot in December.

'You all all right?' he asked. 'Say if you want to turn back.'

They were fine, they chorused; they were tough cookies.

'Do you really think Herr Gabriel came up here?'

'It's quite likely. He has an interest in archaeology,' said Richard.

There was a stillness now. The faint buzzing of insects in the wild myrtle suddenly stopped. The heat of the sun must have made them drowsy.

They all stared out over the Gulf, at the distant coastline of Saudi Arabia.

The navy patrol boat had disappeared.

Mrs Schofield said, 'Richard, do you really think the Exodus was just a myth?'

'I believe Amorite tribes, at some time or another, came wandering through the wilderness.'

'And what you said about the Bible – that it was really just copied from the writings of other contemporary cultures?'

'Well, I don't know if I'd call the Hittites a culture – don't tell anyone I ever said that, it's a heresy – but I do know that the Book of Proverbs was lifted straight from an Egyptian papyrus called *The Wisdom of Amenemope* – Amenemope was a witty scribe – which rather supports the Exodus story, if you think about it, although the Egyptian papyrus was written about 1000 BC, which dates the Exodus a bit late on.'

There was a pause. They had all been brought up to believe that the Bible, even when it needed fairly radical interpretation, was essentially the word of God and not the saws of an ancient Egyptian wit.

'You all OK to move on?'

They continued up the hillside. After 500 metres they reached a ridge summit. Beyond it was a small plateau leading into a rocky defile. At the entrance to the defile was a smudge of acid-green lichen on the rocks. Next to it, as muddy-brown as the rocks themselves, was the tiny mosque of St Onuphrios. The well of St Onuphrios had long since been filled in by the desert sands. Only the rough-hewn stones of its rim and a grey thorn bush marked the place where thousands of pilgrims, over a dozen centuries, had drunk, gratefully, before continuing their journey south towards Jebel Musa.

They went over to the mosque. It was a dome made of mud bricks, defaced and crumbling. There was a smell of urine and the buzz of flies around the small opening as Professor Dyson bent down to look inside. Herr Gabriel was lying on his back, unconscious but alive.

It took forty-five minutes for Richard to scramble down the mountain and another hour before Gabriel was brought down in the helicopter. His skin was swollen and puffy over all of his body but tightly contracted round his skull. He was carried into a bedroom. Towels filled with ice were wrapped round his head. An army doctor, also from the RNZR, suspended a saline drip over his head.

The lieutenant came in and said, 'I don't understand this. My men looked in that mosque, in it, round it, behind it, it was the bloody obvious place to look.'

The doctor said, 'Go away, Patrick. Now is not the time.'

'He was dumped in that mosque after we searched it, he must have been.'

'Just go away, Patrick.'

An hour later the doctor said, 'It's not working. What we have here is voluntary dehydration, the body refusing to accept liquid even though it is literally dying from lack of moisture.'

Celia said, 'You mean he's unconsciously committing suicide?'

'I mean that human blood cells can only stand 1.1 per cent salinity. If you pump in too much liquid too fast, the red blood vessels burst. A dehydrated camel can drink 400 pints of water in ten minutes, but humans were never designed for the desert.'

Richard said, 'He can't be that dehydrated. He was drinking beer, then water, then orange juice, yesterday afternoon.'

'No way.'

'I saw him.'

The doctor said, 'Look at this.'

He lifted Gabriel's hand. On it was a small cut caused when his arm had flopped over the side of the stretcher as they winched him up to the helicopter. The doctor gently opened the wound then squeezed

45

the flesh. Richard and Celia looked at the reluctant trickle of blood: it was dark, thick as treacle.

'Dehydration *in extremis*. This man has not taken liquid in significant quantity for three days.'

'Three o'clock yesterday,' said Richard stubbornly. 'A bottle of Stella beer, then a pint of mineral water and orange juice. He was thirsty after the journey. We all were.'

'The ice packs aren't bringing down his temperature,' said the doctor, not listening. 'The human body's a poor thing when it comes to survival. Our body temperature can only vary by three and a half degrees.'

'What about the camel?' asked Celia quietly, close to hysteria.

'Twelve and a half,' said the doctor. 'If this bloke's got Blue Cross insurance I'd like to get him out to Cairo.'

'He's a Timetraveler of Baltimore,' said Celia. 'He's got all the insurance he needs.'

Just like the Pharaohs, thought Richard, voyaging in the Underworld with insurance to pay the boatman, food for the journey and bondmaidens to pleasure them as they went.

The doctor went to the door and yelled for more ice. The hotel manager shouted back, upset, that the hotel's ice machine was small, it was producing ice as fast as it could. A boy came in with a bucket of ice slush. The doctor said, 'This is no fucking use', and strode out. Celia said, 'I'm going to ring Baltimore. I'm going to get Baltimore out of bed, it's seven a.m. over there now, it's time to tell them', but she did not move.

Herr Gabriel moved slightly. His mouth opened

46

then closed; he muttered something.

Celia said, 'Who speaks German? Shall I get somebody?'

Gabriel murmured again, his voice stronger. Suddenly he spoke with a guttural but sing-song voice, a high wail.

'That's not German,' said Richard.

'Well, what then?'

'Be quiet—'

Gabriel spoke again, then stopped. Richard said, 'It's a prayer to the Sun God. An ancient Egyptian prayer.'

Celia said, 'What? *What?*'

Richard said, 'Thou appearest resplendent on the horizon of the heavens, thy beam encompasses the lands.'

Herr Gabriel's mouth was swollen and cracked. Even as they looked, white veins were spreading a tracery over his mottled skin. They stared down at him, the retired widower, lonely, interested in Islamic and Coptic art, in Old Kingdom magic. Suddenly he moved his head fretfully, trying to free it of the packed ice-cubes. He spoke again, still in a high, sing-song voice.

Celia said, 'Well, what's he saying?'

Richard was staring down at Gabriel.

'Richard! For Christ's sake!'

The door opened. The doctor came back in. 'The helicopter's coming. Bugger the insurance, I've fixed a UN casevac to Eilat.'

Gabriel had stopped speaking. The doctor leant over him. He said, 'He's dead.'

There was a silence in the room. The flyscreen rattled gently in the breeze that came in, every morning, from the Gulf. The doctor said, 'Shit.' Celia said, 'Oh, dear God – ' but her distress was less acute than it might have been. She had lost a Timetraveler but he had not drowned in the sea, and it was difficult to see how she could be blamed.

The doctor said, 'What was he saying? What the hell sort of language was that?'

'Egyptian.'

'Egyptian? You mean Arabic?'

'No, something older, a sort of Coptic, a Semitic variation. At first he was talking German, talking about a statue, a silver statue of a priest of the fifth dynasty, then he started talking in an early Coptic tongue.'

'You speak it yourself?'

'No, but I recognized the words.'

'Will we have to stay here for an inquest or what?' said Celia, her mind on other things. 'We're booked in at the Sharm Aquamarine for the next two nights, but it's going to be hellish if they make us stay around after that. What do you think, Richard?'

Richard was still staring down at Herr Gabriel. Again the wind rattled against the shutters. She wondered what was the matter with him. Why he had to be so laid-back, so bloody far away. Were all academics like this?

'Richard, *Richard*!'

But Richard still looked down on Herr Gabriel, the retired motor-caravan salesman from Dortmund. After a moment he said, 'Rouse yourself, O King. Go, so that you may govern the mounds of Seth. Go, so that you may govern the mounds of Osiris.'

3
London

The Air Egypt Airbus came down to land at Gatwick, where the December temperature was eight Celsius and a thin drizzle was falling. Richard and Celia said goodbye. She was going home for Christmas. In a festive fax, Timetravelers of Baltimore had congratulated her on her calmness and level-headed handling of the situation at the Desert Oasis. Several tour guests had given her Christmas presents, bought in the giftshop at the Hotel Aquamarine in Sharm el-Sheikh; Eloise's family had invited her to stay with them if ever she was to fetch up in Atlantic City.

'Well, bye-bye then,' she said.

'Cheerio,' said Richard.

They were standing by the long-stay car-park bus stop, in a bleak and windy underpass.

'It's been great—'

'Yes,' said Richard.

Celia sighed. It was not a romantic spot. There had been a time – a place, a moment – in Taba, when they had sat drinking Campari sodas by the turquoise, softly floodlit pool and things had been different. The tour guests had all been in bed. The silver moon had risen over the date palms. The sky had been purple velvet. They had watched an Arab boy scoop the water with a net, catching the little frogs that hopped in each night from the desert. They had kissed. She had wondered, as his hand slid along her thigh and she moved to make things fractionally, though not significantly, harder for him, if a romance was beginning, and whether she would go to bed with him now, or later in Sharm el-Sheikh, and she had thought how funny it was that she should be contemplating sex with an American academic (it wasn't as if she was the type usually turned on by *brains*). Well, she hadn't gone to bed with him in Taba, he'd missed his chance there, and Herr Gabriel's death had put an end to any further thoughts of romance in the desert.

'Perhaps,' she said brightly, 'you'll be the guest lecturer for another of my groups.'

'You never know.'

Thank God nothing had happened in Sinai – sexually, emotionally, that was. He'd been useless over the German's death. He'd been worse than useless, actually, making a fuss, demanding an inquest, causing trouble when the Tourist and Antiquities Police were obviously doing everything they could. Herr Gabriel's corpse had been whisked away to Sharm airport in a police car – OK, they'd put it in the boot, but where the hell else would you put a corpse when you had four cops and four submachine-guns to fit in as well? Then two Interior Ministry officials had flown in specially from Cairo – it had all been sorted out so *smoothly* when you considered what it was usually like dealing with foreigners; and all Richard had been able to do was mutter weird rituals about sun gods and the mounds of Seth over Gabriel's body and demand a 'full post-mortem' and an inquest that would have kept them all in Egypt for a fortnight. It really did show you; the English really were the only people who knew how to stay calm in a crisis.

From a distant Tannoy Cliff Richard warbled, 'Christmas time, mistletoe and wine' – as he had warbled, it seemed to her, every Christmas since she was born, probably since the actual birth in the stable.

She peered out into the wet gloom, looking for the long-stay car-park bus.

She was going home to Morecambe, that seaside resort in Lancashire described as a graveyard with fairylights; the place they didn't bury the dead, but propped them up in bus shelters; where pleasure-boats left from the pier and were never seen again. Back to her family. The awfulness of it suddenly over-whelmed her.

'Oh, God,' she said. 'Christmas at home.'

The bus arrived. They hugged and pecked. He helped her get her case on board. She waved to him as the bus pulled away, out of the underpass, into the late afternoon drizzle. He waved in return, then hurried back into the warm concourse, heading towards the tube.

She was a big-boned girl, he thought; more vulnerable than she pretended to be.

It was after six when he reached his small, two-roomed flat in Islington. It was on the top floor of a late Victorian house, part of a terrace in a grim, bleak street behind St Pancras. A resident with community spirit had pinned tinsel round the mailboxes in the hall. In his flat the heating had been off for two weeks. It was dank and cold and unwelcoming. The milk he had left in the fridge was semi-solid. The only food in evidence was two thin slices of pastrami that were curling at the edges and had acquired a greenish tinge. The geranium on the window-ledge, given to him last summer by a female student at University College, was a sad sight, its moisture diverted by its lifeforce into one tiny, frail green shoot.

How much water could a geranium absorb in an hour, say, compared to a camel, or a human being?

He cut off its dead leaves and plunged the dry, gritty rootball into water. He watched the bubbles of air shoot out and hoped for the best. He made instant coffee and drank it black, looking through the post that had been piled on the mat. There was a lot of junk mail, his Visa card bill, and his subscribed *Chicago Military Warfare Quarterly*. There were four Christmas cards from his family home in South Dakota, and one from his first wife, Melanie, in Vermont, enclosing a Christmas card from herself, her second husband and their two boys, and the message 'God Bless You'. There was nothing from Weybridge, where his second wife, Kirsty, lived.

There was a letter from Cairo, forwarded by University College. Ms Elizabeth St George, managing a project for Drextel University's Department of Physics, would be in England in early January and would like a meeting. It was written on American University of Cairo notepaper. He looked at it, puzzled. What did a physicist from Drextel want with him?

He put his cards up over the gas-fire. It was two days to Christmas. He found and munched a cheese biscuit, looking out over the rooftops of Islington into the wet, black, dirty London night, and felt like a character out of Dickens. After a while he went out to his local supermarket and bought himself a load of chill-fresh prepared meals and a small free-range chicken. The staff were all wearing Santa Claus hats. The girl on the checkout smiled and hiccuped, told him to take care of himself, leant over and grabbed him and gave him a kiss that tasted of sherry wine. She knew from his purchases that he was going to spend a sad Christmas, eating sad, lonely TV dinners in a flat somewhere.

Ten days later he was lunching in a Bloomsbury sandwich bar with Worboys, an assistant curator in the British Museum's Western Asiatic Department.

Rain splattered against the windows. It had been raining, ceaselessly it seemed, since he had returned to England. 'Not for us all the pleasure-domes of Taba, or coral reefs of Sharm el-Sheikh,' said Worboys, wiping steam from his glasses. 'I couldn't help wondering – ' he lowered his voice and leant foxily across the table, his expression that of a man curious to know how one booked a tour of child-prostitute brothels in Bangkok – 'how you got into that sort of thing?'

'Actually, they approached me,' said Richard. 'Good Lord, there's Vronwy.' He banged on the glass window. The sandwich-bar man shouted angrily at him in Italian.

Vronwy Garthside was walking along the opposite pavement. She was a young anthropologist from University College, small and slender with large eyes, lusted over by every male in the Institute of Archaeology and the BM's Egyptology and Western Asiatic Departments – except, perhaps, Worboys.

'Don't, or she'll come in here and bother us,' said

Worboys, but Vronwy was already crossing the road. 'Now that's a girl for the perks,' Worboys went on, prodding his cheesecake. 'You know she's got a grant to go to the American Universities Conference at Tell el-Amarna next October? Sometimes I think I'd cut a more memorable figure if I were called Vronwy instead of Keith.'

He was joking. He laughed briskly. Richard said, 'Aren't you taking her to Sinai in March? I thought she was going as your anthropologist?'

'She might be,' said Worboys cautiously.

'Hi. Hi,' said Vronwy, coming in, wet and cold, kissing Richard on both cheeks, looking at Worboys and hastily making kissing noises as she sat down. 'How was it, you lucky bastard? Five-star hotels, swimming pools, loadsawomen?'

'There was one girl,' said Richard, 'an eighteen-year-old from Atlantic City.'

'Cor blimey, your worship,' said Vronwy, 'she threw herself at me. Came into my 'otel room wiv no knickers on.'

'Yes, very amusing,' said Worboys.

'Lucky sod. How are *you* then, Worboys?'

'I'm very well thank you, Vronwy.'

She ordered a cappuccino. Richard told her how a tourist had died on him, out in the Sinai; that it hadn't all been beer and skittles, Shangri-la and sunbeds. They chatted about departmental politics. She went to the loo. Worboys seized his opportunity.

'I just thought,' he said, 'that if I were to do a lecture tour, say next September, I might be able to stay on afterwards.'

'What for?'

'To get to the Amarna conference under my own steam.'

'I think it's lousy,' said Richard, meaning it, 'that a scholar with your reputation can't raise a thousand dollars for a plane ticket.'

'Yes, yes,' said Worboys, who was seeking more than ritual sympathy. 'But about your tourists. They want, presumably, to share our knowledge of ancient Egypt, to share our *enthusiasms*.'

Worboy's particular enthusiasm – apart from his job, which was Western Asiatic archaeology excluding Syria and Palestine – was for New Kingdom steles.

'Do you think,' he asked anxiously, 'I'd be able to keep them amused? Because I do appreciate that liveliness would be the name of the game.'

'I can give you the name and address of the company I went with. There are others.'

'Will you be going again yourself?'

'No. I don't think so.'

Vronwy reappeared. She established that Richard had spent a lonely Christmas in north London. 'You could have come to Shropshire,' she said.

They left the sandwich bar and walked up Museum Street. Leaves from the trees outside the British Museum were black and wet in the gutters. The roast-chestnut man shivered next to his hissing brazier. It was the first week of the school term; in the courtyard parties of schoolchildren were huddled over soggy packed lunches, or ran about in the rain trying to impale themselves on the railings. Teachers yelled, wild-eyed and grim.

'Have you been invited to Vronwy's party?' asked Richard as they went inside.

'Are you having a party, Vronwy?'

'Everybody's invited, it's a general invitation, nobody's been asked specially,' she said, blushing – or it may have been the rain and wind on her cheeks.

'Marian and I don't get asked to many parties,' said Worboys. It was a plain, unvarnished statement of fact.

Vronwy said, 'You are both very welcome.'

'Marian and the girls are away, as it happens,' said Worboys. He stood for a moment.

Richard said, 'I'll come down in a minute.'

Worboys nodded, then slipped behind a lion from the mausoleum at Halicarnassus, disappeared into the staff lift and sank down to the cellars where he had his den.

'Poor Worboys. Have you read Saltman's piece in the *Telegraph*?' asked Vronwy, mooching about, not wanting to be the first to say goodbye.

'That's what he wants to see me about.'

Worboys had recently published a paper proving that a neglected stele at Medinet Habu, long thought to show a sea battle from the reign of Rameses the Third, was actually from the reign of Rameses the Second, and was not of a sea battle at all, the 'ship' being in fact a covered Mycenaean battle chariot, the depiction of which conclusively proved the link (for so long debated) between Bronze Age Greece and New Kingdom Egypt. This stunning and sensational conjecture had been viciously attacked by Saltman of Pittsburgh.

'The argument apparently hinges on whether or not the men in the boat – or battle chariot, as Worboys has it – are Shardana. He wants me to declare myself. If we are not with him, it seems, we are against him.'

'You be with him. He's taking me to Sinai, Saltman doesn't even know I exist.'

'Right.'

'Why didn't you say you were back in London?'

'I didn't want to impose.'

She looked at him unfathomably.

'I'd better go,' he said. 'I'm seeing Worboys then meeting a visitor.'

'Here?'

'Why not.'

'Are you coming to my party?'

'Yes, but I'll be late. I'm showing this visitor round, and tonight she's taking me to dinner at the Connaught.'

'Bloody hell,' she said. 'My father used to take me there for lunch before packing me off to school.'

Richard remembered that she was from the fox-hunting aristocracy. Had he gone to Shropshire for Christmas, he would have ridden to hounds, no doubt, and eaten bloody haunches of venison, and gone a-wassailing.

'Who is she, an expedition sponsor?'

'She's some sort of project manager from Drextel.'

'And she needs showing round the British Museum?'

'She's a physicist.'

'What do you want with physicists?'

'Who knows. Do I bring a bottle?'

'Bring anything you like, except for Worboys.'

'He doesn't have much fun. He lives his days in the Papyrus Harris.'

'And that makes him different then, does it? Different from everybody else round here?'

She said she'd see him later and went, making her

way to the eyrie where the BM's anthropologists, he imagined, hung like bats. He went down to the old cellars, where so many dry and dusty objects were stored and where Worboys had a cubbyhole next to that of the Curator for Iberia and Latin America.

It was empty. Richard found a bottle of Bulgarian red that was a third full and poured a glass. There was a framed photograph of Worboy's wife, Marian, a primary school teacher, and his two little girls. Worboys came bustling in, carrying a blown-up photograph of his Medinet Habu stele. He put it down on his desk and angled his desk light over it.

'Right, here we are, here we are,' he said, trying to hide his nervousness.

It was a slab of inscribed stone, some two and a half metres high. It had been badly eroded, peppered by centuries of desert storms. The blown-up photograph was of part of the decorative frieze that had been buried in sand for much of its life, and was better preserved than the writing above it, which was virtually illegible. Richard looked at the outline of soldiers on the frieze. They were nineteenth or at the latest twentieth dynasty, seemingly in a boat, but a boat with some sort of protective shield, presumably against arrows, although it might have had a religious significance – it was not dissimilar to Cheops's solar barque, excavated at Giza, the boat made to carry the Great King on his celestial journey to the Other-world.

Worboys was rearranging bits of pottery on a shelf, humming quietly, apparently unconcerned. 'Saltman says,' he suddenly burst out, with a jocular laugh, 'that I should go and look at the Temple of Rameses in Thebes, with its relief of Shardana soldiers attacking in a boat! He says that I should examine the Uragit stele of Baal in the Louvre – not a difficult or obscure museum, he says. What an amusing man! – because it depicts Shardana with spikes between their horns just as they are on this stele. Well, I am saying to Saltman, have you never seen the wall-paintings from Pylos of Mycenaean chariots? Have you never been to the National Museum in Athens, not a *totally obscure* place, hm, hm?' He laughed, vastly amused to think of Saltman's stupidity.

'These are Shardana,' said Richard.

Worboys said, 'I know they are Shardana.'

He put down his bits of pottery. He sat down. He said, 'They are Shardana captives in a cart.'

'In the High Empire,' said Richard, 'the Shardana were mercenaries in the Egyptian army. They served in the Northern Corps.'

'Not always. Not all the time.'

Richard looked at him silently.

'By no means all the time,' said Worboys doggedly. 'There is evidence from the Papyrus Harris that Shardana were, on occasion, enemies of the Pharaoh.'

The phone went. Richard's visitor from Drextel had arrived.

Worboys said, 'I think I can argue a convincing case, don't you? You are the expert on military matters in the New Kingdom, not Saltman. What do you think?'

Richard looked at the figures on the frieze. They appeared to be waving weapons, short daggers like *khepesh* daggers from Syria, which made them unlikely captives. On the other hand, their helmets did not have the cheek protectors typical of Shardana; there was something odd about them.

There was something odd about the frieze entirely.

Worboys was staring at him anxiously over the Anglepoise lamp. Richard said, 'Yeah, you go for it.'

Elizabeth St George had wandered off from the information desk to look at Lindow Man. They described her. He went up the broad marble stairway. As always, gangs of schoolchildren buzzed ghoulishly round the corpse from the Cheshire peat bog, poring over the body that had been garrotted and ritually bled some two thousand years ago by priest-politicians – in the days, the curators often joked, before income tax. Elizabeth St George was looking intently at the green hologram of Lindow Man's face; the only face to have survived from British prehistory. She was in her early thirties, he guessed, slim, blonde and well dressed; a Jaeger silk scarf, a creamy white suit that might have come from the window of Harvey Nichols; not exactly a poor academic, not exactly a girl struggling on a project manager's fee.

He introduced himself. They went to the Egyptian galleries. She was nervous, willing to be impressed. She wanted to see weaponry from the New Kingdom Empire, but was distracted by a display of New Kingdom food – sun-dried fish, a cake of chopped dates, somebody's roast-duck dinner that was never eaten. He showed her an ivory-handled bronze mirror that had been highly polished by Museum staff. She looked down into it for a long time. She seemed to have forgotten about him, to have lost her nervousness. She said, 'Wouldn't you just like to see the face that first looked back from this metal? Wouldn't you just like to be able to recover it, to call it back? Her image is there, you know. Some rich man's daughter from Thebes or Memphis, looking at herself on her fourteenth or fifteenth birthday; her image is in the metal, a pattern of displaced electrons.'

A romantic physicist. He said, 'In that case, so is your image now.'

'Yeah.'

'Where are you working in Egypt?'

'Cairo.'

'Have you been there long?'

'Three months.'

'Cairo University?'

'We use the American University when we need to. We've rented a place out in Maadi.'

'You didn't say, in your letter, what exactly you thought I could do for you.'

She said, 'I'd rather not go into details until tonight. But I'm hoping you can tell me about the death of Herr Gabriel at the Desert Oasis motel.'

She stared down into the bright bronze, the circle of metal impregnated with the images of three thousand years.

She said, 'BSc from the University of Washington, PhD from the University of Warwick, five years lecturing in Kansas, now research fellow at UCL.'

It summed up seventeen years of poring over the bones.

'You are the world's number one expert on the Egyptian war machine of the eighteenth and nineteenth dynasties.'

Richard said, 'It's not a large field.'

'The Connaught Hotel,' she went on, this time speaking to the waiter, 'is noted for British cuisine at its very best.'

'We aim to please,' said the waiter, unfazed.

'OK, Jeeves,' she said brightly. She was still nervous, but trying to cover it up. She ordered whitebait followed by roast guinea fowl with juniper berries. Richard ordered whitebait and roast pheasant. She quickly finished her gin and tonic.

'Jeeves and Wooster,' she said. 'What a pair.'

They made small talk while they ate the tiny fish, scrunching up the little crumbly bones, the slivers of flesh. Did he enjoy working in London? He who is tired of London is tired of life, had he ever heard that before? The main courses came under silver-domed dishes. She started to tuck into her guinea fowl. He said, 'I don't want to rush you, and it's a great meal, but I have to go somewhere else after this.'

'Yeah, OK.' She ate some more. Suddenly she said, 'Herr Gabriel. You think he must have read that stuff somewhere, that prayer to the Sun God? You think it came out of his subconscious?'

He said, 'Obviously.'

'A motor-caravan salesman from Dortmund?'

'He was a very literate man, interested in Coptic art. He was climbing the hill to look at a ninth-century mosque.'

'That's not the same as showing an intimate knowledge of New Kingdom Egypt. You're two thousand years apart on this one, Rich. When he died he was saying something about a statue.'

'Was he?'

'You said so at the time. We've seen the UN Peace-keepers' report.'

So that was it. He had wondered, from the way she was talking, if perhaps she'd been chatting to Celia in Morecambe.

She was looking at him. He said, 'Gabriel was delirious.'

'Ka-nefer, the priest of Ptah.'

'A well-known high priest – not, by the way, nineteenth dynasty.'

'Solid silver. Fifty centimetres high. The wife and son kneeling at the priest's feet. It was stolen from the temple at Thebes or Saqqara. If it's turned up in Sinai, it's worth, what, five million dollars, ten million?'

'In theory it's worth any price you care to put on it. But you wouldn't be able to take it out of Egypt. If you did, you'd never be able to sell it.'

'There are people who'd buy.'

'Is that what this is all about?'

A waiter brought the dessert menu. She agonized between marmalade pudding with custard and Olde English trifle. She ordered the pudding.

'No,' she said. 'That's not at all what this is about.'

She sat and brooded, glancing at him occasionally. 'There were other strange features about Gabriel's death,' she said. 'The dehydration. What did you make of that?'

'The UN doctor was wrong.'

'Ah,' she said. 'Right. The UN doctor was wrong.'

The desserts arrived.

She said, 'Anyway, forget Gabriel. We need an adviser. We need somebody to go to Cairo and look at a nineteenth-dynasty body.'

'Who's we?'

'My project.'

'Which is?'

'I told you. A Drextel Department of Physics project.'

'Why not use one of your own people?'

'You're nineteenth dynasty.'

'Drextel has an excellent Egyptology department. If you're talking about a mummy, Minneapolis Institute of Arts is a leader in X-ray and CAT-scan. If you're talking nineteenth dynasty, New Haven even has the mummy of Rameses the Second's cook.'

'Rha,' she said. 'I've tried his recipe for stuffed quail. I couldn't get the larks tongues, so I used sweetbreads. I still find it amazing. A civilization with a complex and sophisticated cuisine all at a time when northern Europe was barely out of the Stone Age, when there was nobody in this place where we are now – ' she looked around at the rose mahogany panelling, the intricate plaster ceiling, the gleaming silver lid of the roast-beef trolley – 'but a few savages hacking at stone flints.'

Richard was also aware of time passing. 'This mummy—'

'I didn't say it was a mummy.'

'These skeletal remains. What condition are they in?'

'Excellent condition.'

'Where are they exactly?'

'I don't really want to tell you that.'

'Are they still *in situ*?'

'No.'

'Where then?'

'I'm not at liberty to talk about it.' Then, after a moment, she said, 'The Valley of the Kings.'

'When do you want me to go?'

'As soon as you can.'

There was a week before the beginning of the university term. He guessed the corpse was mummified, although it was true that some bodies had survived uncorrupted in the sands of the Western Desert – bodies buried in catacomb chambers away from the worms that gorged in the necropolises, until their skin was leathered and their flesh kippered by the dry, hot, moving air – and he guessed that it was *in situ* (she was lying about this) in a nineteenth-dynasty burial site and had weapons with it. It would be the weapons, and perhaps fragments of clothing, that they wanted him to see. He didn't think it was in the Valley of the Kings; she was putting him off the scent. How much, he wondered to himself, were Drextel offering to pay?

'A thousand dollars,' she said, peering, not remarkably, into his mind; nibbling a small square of chocolate fudge. 'Plus expenses. I'm sorry we can't go higher. Our project grant is not overly generous.'

No, he thought, not if we're having to buy dinners at the Connaught. It was the same the whole world over – you only had to see the overseas project directors, the UN World Heritage Site directors, the overseas aid ministers, all gorging themselves on pastries in the Cairo Hilton. So, a thousand dollars – seven hundred pounds sterling – as she said, not overly generous for the world's number one expert in the nineteenth-dynasty war machine.

But it was money that he could use. He contemplated this sad fact.

'How long would I be there?'

'Two days, three perhaps.'

'Tell me the connection,' he said, 'between this body and the death of Herr Gabriel. Tell me why an American physics project is digging up skeletal remains in Egypt.'

'I'm not at liberty to tell you the connection with the corpse, not at this stage. But you must be able to see our interest in Herr Gabriel, a man who recited a New Kingdom prayer to the Sun God *in an original Amorite, early Coptic language*! Have you read anything about research involving precognition and quantum physics?'

'No.'

'The problem of consciousness, what is *awareness* doing in a world described purely in terms of matter? You ought to look at the experiments done by the London Institute of Psychiatry. They've posed some really serious problems for the classical physicists, poor saps, but they fit the quantum model exactly – the brain and consciousness functioning at a quantum level, you know? Well, if you look beyond that to the possibilities for retrocognition—'

'I'm hearing this, I'm understanding nothing.'

'Drextel has a project relating Egyptology to recorded observations of the paranormal, and I'm its director.'

She put down her spoon. A waiter brought a pot of coffee.

He said, 'A project relating Egyptology to recorded observations of the paranormal?'

'That's it.'

'It's an interesting area of research.'

'I'm gratified to hear you say that.'

He would give it another five minutes, then make his excuses. He would cut through Grosvenor Square to Oxford Street and go to Bond Street Underground.

On second thoughts, he would make his excuses now.

'I don't think I'm your man.'

66

'You don't?'

'Ka-nefer was fifth dynasty, not nineteenth,' he said, 'of which I know about as much as I know about Chief Sitting Bull, but I'll gladly put you in touch with—'

'We're talking serious academic research here.' Her face was flushed.

'Yes, I'm sure—'

'We're talking about a project sponsored by Drextel University's Faculty of Sciences.'

'That doesn't make it something I want to get involved in.'

'Rich,' she said, leaning across the little table, 'what would you say if I told you the pyramids were homing beacons for spacecraft from the star Andromeda?'

In the first place he'd say that Andromeda was a galaxy not a star, and in the second place that she was stark staring crazy.

'I do know,' he said, 'that there's a lot of interesting research work going on.'

'Rich,' she sighed.

'And that,' he added, having eaten well and not wanting to seem impolite, 'there are more things in heaven and earth than this world dreams of.'

She drank her coffee. 'Thank you for giving me your time, Dr Corrigan,' she said. 'You've been very helpful.'

'Not really.'

'No, not really.'

She got up and walked out of the dining room. He looked at the second bottle of claret on the table. He had drunk half a glass from it, she had not touched it. He stood up, took hold of the bottle, went out of the dining room into a short corridor. He retrieved his coat. He draped his coat over the bottle. His action was observed by a headish sort of waiter, whose look indicated that nothing mankind could do in this world would shock or surprise him. Elizabeth was standing in the lobby, looking out into Carlos Place.

'I'm sorry I can't be of more use,' he said.

She looked at him.

'Herr Gabriel,' she said, 'had not taken in liquid for three days, despite what you saw with your own eyes, and his invocation to Ka-nefer, priest of Ptah, was of great significance; but the pyramids of Egypt are not, as far as I am aware, beacons for spaceships. Night, Dr Corrigan.'

Vronwy's flat was in Belsize Park. He arrived just after eleven. Vronwy was dancing in the gloom, but waved to him. The room was packed. British Museum staff, mainly from the Egyptology Department and the Greek and Roman Department, undergraduates from University College, Vronwy's students, eating taramasalata and worrying over their grants like dogs worry over bones. The undergraduates merged seamlessly into the research students, the junior fellows and assistant lecturers. They were bonded together by cultural riches and worldly poverty. Richard wandered about. He found some crisps and ate them thoughtlessly. An anaemic-looking girl who had herself wandered away in search of a drink came back and said, 'Oh, you haven't eaten them all?' and looked as though she might cry. He thought guiltily of the roast pheasant and trifle he had consumed. She said, 'It's all right, really,' in a sad voice. Vronwy came over, brushing aside her hair with her hand, her bosom heaving from her dancing, her dress clinging damply to her skin. 'Worboys is here,' she said. 'He's been telling one of my female students all about linguistic curiosities in the Papyrus Harris. She's had to go and hide in the loo. I don't know what there is left to drink.'

He found two glasses that had contained red wine, tipped their dregs into a potted plant, and poured the Connaught's claret. She gulped five or six quid's worth down. 'Jolly good,' she said absently.

He said, 'What do you know about Ka-nefer, the priest of Ptah, fifth dynasty?'

'Nothing at all.'

'My physicist from Drextel offered me a thousand dollars to ghost-hunt in the Valley of the Kings,' he said, exaggerating hardly at all.

'I trust you said yes?'

He wondered why he hadn't said yes. What was so wonderful about his reputation that he wanted to keep a million miles away from investigations into the paranormal? Abba was playing on the sound system. My God, it would be the Beatles next. Vronwy was looking round slightly awkwardly, as if she didn't quite know whether to stay or move somewhere else. The music changed. 'Michelle, my belle', words that had for a very long time gone together well. He said, 'Dance?' They moved closer together and he put his arms round her and she leant her head on his shoulders. It had been like this now for a couple of months, even though she supposedly had a boyfriend, a lover, a partner, called Maurice, who was something to do with computers. Perhaps he was on the way out. Lucy in the sky with diamonds; Richard on the rebound with Vronwy. Well, and why not?

'You should have come to Shropshire. You should have called me.'

'I didn't expect to be back.'

'Why were you back?'

'That man died, I told you.'

'That's no reason for you not to have called me. Why didn't you call me?'

There were his two ex-wives, of course, the fact that he was thirty-five and she was twenty-eight, and he'd already screwed up more than his share of personal relationships. That was why not, perhaps. A boring, very faintly grubby story, not untypical of our times.

A girl came up. 'He's after me again,' she said. 'It's not fair. I can't spend all evening in the loo. I want to have fun and enjoy myself. God knows it's not easy, you know. I work in a McDonalds from eight a.m. till six every Sunday. This is my only relaxation in five weeks, the only time I've been out—'

Richard found Worboys. He was standing by the door to the kitchen. Richard said, 'Tell me, Keith, what do you know about Ka-nefer, the priest of Ptah?'

'Oh, you're going back a bit there,' said Worboys. 'A bit before my time.'

Worboys belonged, like Corrigan, to the New Kingdom, the eighteenth and nineteenth dynasties, to the age of Rameses the Conqueror, who had had eight wives and a hundred concubines, and fathered well over a hundred children; all of which made Richard's own marital record seem less appalling.

'You must know about the statue of Saqqara.'

'Yes,' said Worboys, his eyes wandering round the gloom.

'I'm interested in when it was stolen.'

70

'Akhenaten's reign, or Tutankhamun's, but most likely Akhenaten's, and just as likely it was melted down in the religious purge. When the priests said stolen they might just as easily have meant taken away from them.'

'You don't think it still exists?'

Worboys looked surprised, then, instantly, cunning. 'Why? You haven't found a reference somewhere?'

'No, good grief. I'd hardly keep that to myself.'

But Worboys was looking foxily over his glass of cider. In the academic world men lied, cheated, deceived and destroyed. Saltman of Pittsburgh was out to destroy him, even now as he partied in Belsize Park.

The phone went. It was three a.m. He had to get out of bed to answer it. His head was thick with the effects of the wine he had drunk. She said, 'William Rees-Mogg.'

A pause. He said, 'Pardon?'

'Sometime editor of the London *Times*, OK, right?'

Hostility and fury seeped down the line.

'Chairman of the Arts Council. A lord. An English lord, OK, got it?'

'Yes.'

'It might interest you to know that he has experienced retrocognition. Experienced it personally. He has been taken back to a church in the eighteenth century. *I followed an eighteenth-century coffin*, he said – Lord Rees-Mogg said, this English lord – *I lived for that half-second a century and a half before my own*. Rees-Mogg has come clean on retrocognition, he's come out of the closet.'

'OK,' said Richard, speaking rapidly, 'OK, OK. You

take William Rees-Mogg to Cairo. You want to know where he lives? I'll tell you how to find out. You just ring the House of Lords, it'll be in the book, or look in *Who's Who*—'

'I don't want Rees-Mogg! Listen—'

'No, you listen. I have an academic reputation that has taken me many, many years to acquire—'

'Christ, you bastard—'

'And I am not going to Cairo to take part in psychic experiments or go looking for ectoplasm in the catacombs.'

'Reputation? Academic reputation? Listen, nobody had ever heard of you till you ponced off as a courier to a bunch of tourists. What am I saying? Nobody *has* heard of you except me—'

'Night, Ms St George—'

'My project is funded by Drextel's Department of Physics—'

'Good-night.'

He put the phone down. He went and made a large mug of tea. The phone rang again. He almost ran across the room to pick it up. 'Have you the slightest idea,' she was already saying, as he lifted the receiver, 'how important this is to me? How important this is for my future? Have you any idea what it is like to be project director of the biggest, most important thing you have ever been involved with—'

He put the phone down. After a moment it rang again. He suddenly felt weary. He picked it up.

There was silence. Then a faint sound of sobbing, the sobbing not of sorrow but frustration.

Then she said, 'I'll make it 1,500 dollars. I honestly cannot pay you more. I want you to look at my corpse, and give me your professional opinion as an expert on the nineteenth-dynasty Imperial army. That's it. That's all.'

He said, 'You keep saying corpse. Is it exposed skeletal remains or is it a mummy?'

There was silence. The rain thudded against his attic window.

He said, 'OK, when do you want me to go?'

'I'll call you back.'

It was nine o'clock when she called. He was eating warm croissants with butter and blackcurrant jam. She said, 'I phoned. Where were you?'

'Buying my breakfast.'

'You can't even make toast?'

'No.'

'I'm going today, but we can't get you on the flight. You're booked for tomorrow. The flight is at four-thirty from Heathrow. Is your visa OK?'

'No, but I can renew it this morning. I need to be back by Saturday.'

'No problem.'

'Listen, these remains. If it is a mummified corpse, you need to inform Cairo Museum and the Ministry of Antiquities—'

'It's all been done. Collect your ticket from the BA desk at three o'clock tomorrow. I'll meet you at the other end.'

He said to Vronwy, 'I need the money. I'm going. I'll be back on Saturday.'

She said, 'It all sounds a bit peculiar to me. Watch you don't get banged up in prison.'

'If I do, will you come and visit me?'

'I suppose I'll have to.' She looked at him fleetingly. She said, 'Have you remembered Melanie's birthday?'

'I remembered.' He'd sent the card to Vermont that very morning. What was Vronwy doing remembering the birthdays of his ex-wives? Perhaps the sending or otherwise of a card was some test of faithfulness and constancy.

'Saturday,' he said. 'I wondered if you wanted to go to a movie.'

'Spend your dollars? Yes, all right.' She added, 'You can come round to supper afterwards, if you want.'

He was back over Egypt, over the Delta. The lights in Club Class were dimmed, as they had been since they passed over Sicily. Outside, below, there was the solitary, lonely light of a ship out at sea. Soon he saw the lights of Alexandria in the darkness as they crossed the coastline. He imagined the Corniche now, at midnight, a salt wind blowing in from the Med; lovers still sitting drinking arak and coffee under café awnings, or walking hand in hand along the seawall.

'We are due to land at Cairo in just over twenty minutes' time,' the captain said. 'I've just been told that there will be a delay, hopefully not for long, but there are several planes queuing in front of us. Last week on this flight they sent us south round Giza, and the floodlit pyramids were a fine sight. I'll let you know if they send us down there again – ' He went on, chatty and calm, not saying that Cairo Airport had been closed because of a bomb attack, an outrage by Muslim fundamentalists. 'I've been flying into Cairo for, what must it be, twenty years, and I must say, it's extraordinary how the green carpet of cultivation has spread over the Delta—'

Yes, almost back to the way it was in the Middle Kingdom, when the black soil had been first irrigated;

or later, when Egypt was the corn basket of the Roman Empire.

The plane's engines were quiet, almost silent. The plane circled slowly, sleepily, in the black night. In Club Class many people were asleep, their courtesy blankets tucked up to their chins. The steward, who was called Crispin, passed along the aisles, peering down from side to side, inspecting his charges. The film was over; no more drinks were being served at the back of the plane, in World Traveller, but you could still have anything you liked in here: champagne, cognac, a glass of chilled white wine. 'Vodka and ice and tomato juice for the vitamins,' ordered the worldly American Evangelical Missionary sitting next to Richard, still reading his conference notes on the 'Future Strategy for the Coptic Church in the Face of the Threat of Muslim Fundamentalism'.

Richard's ears went dead. There was a sudden vibration that cut almost immediately. A woman in a seat across the aisle looked round, mildly startled. Richard looked out of the window. There were hardly any lights below them now. They were over the desert. Slowly the plane banked, turned, leaning ever so slightly, the missionary's drink at an angle in its plastic beaker, so that he lifted it and drank hastily.

They were circling over Sinai, slowly spiralling downwards. Below, in the darkness, he could just make out the dark mass of the south Sinai mountains, the plateau of El-Tîh.

'I'm pleased to say we now have clearance to land,' said the captain. 'We will arrive in Cairo in fifteen minutes – that is, ten minutes past midnight, local time.'

The plane curled back towards the Gulf of Suez.

They started to descend more steeply. The head steward said, 'On behalf of Captain Warner and the cabin crew, I'd like to thank you for travelling British Airways.'

Below them was dark, empty, arid plain that had once been known as the Wilderness of Shur.

There was a pinprick of light in the darkness, a sudden bright flare. A truck, perhaps, heading eastward towards the Khatmia Pass.

4
The Wilderness of Shur

The fire flared as the dry broom was thrown on it. A man stepped forward, into the light. He wore the long pleated skirt of an Egyptian army officer, knotted at the hips, his fringed red sash falling over his apron. His blue cloak was thrown carelessly over his shoulder. From the rocks at the side of the gorge, where the children and the women and the slaves watched, Giliad stared down at him in admiration. This was a most famous man, a most famous Israelite. He had served the Pharaoh at the fortress of Menzelah, where his company had won renown fighting the pirate ships of the Sea Tribes.

The Soldier looked round him, at the men of Reuben, of Simeon and of Gershon. He looked beyond – to the men on the fringe of the tribal meeting, the bricklayers, the men of Korah. The mad Benjaminites had not come; they had gone into the hills in the early afternoon, to the secret place where they fattened their hyenas.

The Soldier said, 'You know that God has come in a dream to Moses the Kenite, and has told him to lead us south along the shores of the Yam Suf. You also know that there are those who say we must go north, along the Way of the Philistines. Men of

Joseph, some families of Gad, men of Asher.'

There was a faint stirring. The cult of the Living Goddess Ashtoreth extended far beyond the tribe of Asher. 'The nakedness of thy son's daughter, or of thy daughter's daughter, thou shalt not uncover – ' cried the Levites, trying to stop worship at the Asherite temple, but the Asherites gave their girl children to the priesthood all the same, and if the Asherites went north, there would be those eager to follow.

'Well, what do you say?' asked the Soldier. 'Shall we go north along the Way of the Philistines?'

Nobody replied. The children were watching the huddle of Levites behind the soldier, trying to make out Moses, the Levites' *hawi*, waiting for some magic.

'It's a tempting prospect. There's good pasture along the sea road, particularly at this time of year. It's only a forty-day march to Canaan, driving the herds and the flocks; forty days, reckoned Abraham, forty days reckoned Joseph, and I doubt if it's become *more*. And there are quail to eat along the Way of the Philistines.' He went on, persuasively, but nobody was taken in. They knew rhetorical trickery when they heard it.

'Why, I've seen quail drop from the skies by the thousand, in the days when I was fighting the pirates, quail so exhausted when they reached the shore of the Great Sea that they fell into your outstretched hands – ' he held out his hands in the firelight – 'as soft and yielding as the breasts of Miriam's daughters.'

The shepherds and herdsmen roared. The vulgar men of Korah howled. Miriam's dancing girls, who were in a group next to the Levite priests, threw their arms over their faces so that their bangles flashed gold in the firelight.

'As soft as the plump warm breasts,' said the Soldier, cupping his hands and then holding them to his own chest, 'of the lovely Miriam herself.'

Miriam's girls shrieked. Their bangles danced in the air.

'Ho, ho, ho,' laughed Esther, who as yet had no breasts at all.

'Yes, yes, there are seabirds to eat along the Way of the Philistines,' shouted the Soldier, walking back and forth before the elders of Simeon, and Reuben, and Gershon. 'And there are fish from the sea for those whose gods will let them eat fish; and there are date palms and the sweet apple fruit of the acacia; and, for those who fancy it and have the silver, there are no doubt fat locusts on skewers, dipped in honey.'

Lips smacked in appreciation. Not one in a hundred had tasted locusts dipped in honey. Zuri had, though; they were an old favourite. He had had them at his wedding feast, at all of his wedding feasts – fat, juicy locusts, and little songbirds in a barley-crust pie.

'So why don't I advise the priests to take us north? Why don't I advise them to take us on the easy road, the sensible road, the road of our forefathers?'

He paused. They all waited for him to tell them why.

'I'll tell you – and no god has come in a dream to tell me this. The only voice that interrupts my dreams is the voice of my wife, or somebody's wife, and it doesn't say, "Get thee to the Wilderness".'

The men of Korah grinned and chuckled.

The Soldier suddenly shouted, 'It's because there are ten thousand Egyptian troops between Menzelah and Gaza, ten thousand troops including garrison hosts at Bahah and Zarw, and the First Division of Amun on the march somewhere. Can a hundred herdsmen with wooden staves fight the First Division of Amun? The division *rich of bows*, as their battle banner has it? Have any of you seen a phalanx of infantry, spearmen shoulder to shoulder, eight ranks deep, advance the way they advanced at Hebron? Will you go out, with your wooden staves, and put the Lion God of Judah or the Snake God of Dan against army regulars, or against the Sherden?'

He stared round. 'If you do, you'll be slaughtered. Those of you who live will be driven back to Egypt in chains. You will be put to the corvée and you will build grainstores and temples in Egypt until you rot. And your children and your grandchildren will be of the corvée and will be slaves for all of their lives. Well, I am going south. South along the Yam Suf, with Moses and with the bones of Joseph.'

He stopped. He turned and went over to the dancing girls, and sat down next to Miriam herself. There were murmurs of dismay, of discomfort.

A voice, a man of Korah, shouted, 'What about this God who talks to Moses? What about this *terrible* God who made the Nile run with Egyptian blood and brought down the green frogs?'

A man stood up from the huddle of Levite priests. He came forward into the firelight. He was not old – thirty perhaps, beardless, in the Egyptian fashion. He wore the leopardskin brevel of a priest, and over his shoulder was thrown the wine-red cloak that denoted high rank in the King's diplomatic office. He looked round nervously. He held up his staff and the people waited for him to turn it into a snake.

He said, 'We cannot stay in the Wilderness. We must find the road to Canaan. We must fulfil the prophecy of Joseph. We have a need for land. We do *not* have a need to be destroyed by the First Division of Amun.'

He paused for applause, but his words were not considered witty. He looked behind him, at the priests of Levi, for support. The priests were huddled miserably in their dirty robes. They were flockless and herdless, begging their bread, fleeing death at the hands of the terrible scribe-priests of Amun.

A voice said, 'Send to the consul at Mignol. Ask him to intercede with the King for us. You are a scribe, you know the words.'

There was a murmuring, voices saying, 'Yes, send to the King—'

Moses said suddenly, passionately, 'Will you worship a dog or a crocodile? Will your sons and daughters bow down before an animal? For sixty years we have worshipped our God in peace. Are our children now to worship false animal gods? Shall our women let snake gods suckle at their breasts?'

There was a ripple of excitement. This was a shaft aimed at the Danites, who worshipped Nehushtan the Snake. Ruth glanced at Rebecca, who sometimes mooned over a boy of the house of Dan, but she saw that Rebecca was smiling now at Shimi, a lad of the house of Gershon who had been kind to her.

'Listen, listen!' cried Moses. 'We have all made a great decision! We have abandoned the old false gods of our tribes! We have said that we will no longer build temples for the priests of Amun! We have said that we will no longer build grainstores for the mortuary priests, or pay religious fines in the court, or work

81

as common bondsmen! We have said that we will return to Canaan!'

He paused. His listeners were confused. Very few of them had said any of these things.

Moses said, 'Consider, oh consider, how many centuries have passed since first we were led into Egypt.'

There was a sigh then, like wind through fields of dry corn. It was the elders groaning. Ruth felt her eyes grow wet as she thought of the stories of her childhood. Stories of Joseph, who had been a land commissioner for the Pharaoh during the Great Famine, and had done so many clever land deals for the King when the Egyptian farmers were starving, and who had predicted that they would all go to Canaan and carry his bones with them.

'Well, we have left Egypt. We have left the Black Lands, and now we are in the hands of God. And God says that he will guide us to Canaan, which is a land of milk and honey.'

'Ah!' the elders sighed.

Ruth thought of the warm milk foaming from the pot, the brown honey bees of Goshen. She sat in the rocks, thinking of her mother telling her the story of Joseph, of the coat of many colours that his brothers stole from him, of the Ishmaelite merchants who came by the dungeon-pit on camels bearing spicery and balm and myrrh . . .

How Ruth had cried when Joseph had been sold to the merchants! How she had boiled with fury when Joseph's brothers had spilled kid's blood on the coat and showed it to Joseph's father, and told him that Joseph was dead! How she had wept when Jacob said, 'I will go to the grave mourning for my son.'

She jumped, startled. A man of Korah had pushed

his way forward, through the elders, and was standing by the fire, shouting, 'There is no road south but the road to the mines in the mountain! Ten thousand slaves a year are sent along that road. Ten thousand slaves are sent every year to Khadem. Ten slaves die for every ounce of turquoise, for every pannier of copper that is brought down to the sea. How will we escape the open mouths in the mountain, the open mouths of the mines of Khadem? Why will you take us south along the slave road, like lambs to the slaughter?'

'Because God is leading us,' said Moses, but his voice was faint, as though he was hoarse or had not eaten.

'South along the slave road!' shouted the men of Korah.

'No, no,' cried the Levites. 'God will provide!'

Aaron, the priest of priests of the Levites, came forward into the firelight. 'You have heard my brother, Moses! He has led you out of Egypt and will lead you to the Promised Land! God fights for us.' He raised his arms.

'Or we are dead men,' howled the Benjaminites, who had come down from the hills.

Then Miriam stood up. She cried out, 'We are going where the God of Moses takes us. To Canaan, to a land flowing with milk and honey.'

Around her, softly beating their timbrels, her dancing women sang, 'We are going home. We are going home.'

'Yes, we must go home,' sighed the women of the herdsmen, and the shepherds. 'Yes, yes!' cried the children in the rocks – home to the land of Canaan! Then Miriam, the dark-skinned, lovely Miriam came forward from among her dancing girls and began to dance in the firelight, which was better, in the opinion of many, than magic tricks by the prophet.

Moses sat back among the priests. In time, when the story-teller was describing the great drunkenness of Noah, and the disrespect of Ham, someone took pity on them and gave them food to eat and wine to drink.

Eventually the food and wine were gone, and the story-teller silent, and the fire left to die. The cavalcade went off into the darkness, down the gully, the Soldier on a donkey, the Levites stumbling in the dark on sore, bloody feet, the timbrels of the dancing girls still beating softly as they walked.

Shelumiel had disappeared with the herdsmen. Esther and Giliad were asleep. Rebecca woke them. She found Zuri, and led them all back up the gully, back to their camp, to the small brown goat-hair tent against the rocks.

'Let me tell you about this Levite, Moses,' said Shelumiel the next day, when he was drunk, 'who isn't really a Levite at all but a Kenite, whose actual father is unknown, who came from nowhere with a wife called Zipporah, and said that he had lived as a *shepherd* in Sinai – and did you ever see a less likely shepherd in your life? – who one day saw a strange thing, which was a bush of desert broom which was burning brightly with fire but which was not consumed. Moses, we are told, passed the bush and Akhenaten spoke to him from the flames, and said, "Moses, Moses", and told him to go to Egypt and save the people of his tribes, who were being forced by the little-Pharaoh of Pi-Ramese to carry stones in the corvée and worship the animal gods of Lower Egypt, which was terrible to the one God, whose name was Akhenaten. And so Moses was sent by this *one* God to Egypt, to be the prophet of the *one* God, and to lead the people of the families to the Promised Land of Canaan. "But who made you a prince and a judge over us?" he was asked by a wit in the wine shop at Mignol, and he replied, "The God of Akhenaten, the God of Abraham and of Isaac and of Jacob" – an answer which was unanswerable, said the wit.'

There was fighting among the tribes. Cattle were stolen from the Reubenites during the night. People were killed defending their *belongings*. A Levite girl ran off with a man from the house of Dan, and the Levites called her whore and decreed that she should be burned to death – it was a law of God that the daughter of a priest who played the whore should be burned – but the Danites would not give her up. Zuri spent his days with the old Benjaminite elder Gideon, who advised quietness. The Benjaminites were very cautious. They kept their hyenas hidden in the hills.

The Levites went from tribe to tribe, urging the elders to listen to the prophet Moses. But not everybody listened, not everyone was afraid of the Way of the Philistines. One morning men came up the gorge on donkeys, shouting farewell. They were men of Joseph, and of Dan and Gad.

'Which way will you go?'

They said they intended to skirt round the great fortress of Zarw that was now called Pi-Ramese, and find the old road to the east, the road of the bronze-workers and the seal-cutters and the spice merchants.

'Come with us,' they called.

Shelumiel looked at them silently.

'Come with us!'

Shelumiel shook his head, though without conviction. They laughed, and said, 'We will see you in Canaan!'

Rebecca looked anxiously for the boy of Dan who had been kind to her when they had fled through the night from the garrison troops of Baal-Zephon. 'Not all the families of Dan are going,' said Esther, but Rebecca sobbed. Life had taught her to fear the worst.

'The gods be with you,' the men on donkeys shouted. 'The God of the Levites protect you!' They were brave and bold and excited.

'Wait,' shouted Shelumiel. 'Take wine with us.'

No, no, they called. They had not time. But one of them, a man of Kohath, cousin to Izhar, who was 133 years old (almost as old as Zuri the Simeon) urged his donkey back up the path and leant down and said to Shelumiel, 'Watch out for the Levites. Aaron is become a *high priest*.'

'Watch out for chariots,' said Shelumiel. 'The chariots of Amun.'

'There are no chariots. It is a story of the Levites.'

The men of Dan and Gad trotted off back down the path. Rebecca sat over the fire and cried into the ash cakes. 'What about that Shimi, what about that boy of Gershom?' said Ruth severely. 'Wasn't that Shimi also kind to you?'

She and Esther and Giliad climbed the hill to the place where they had met Ruth's *bedu* on their first night in the gorge. Rebecca, they agreed, was in love with a boy from the house of Dan only because the God of Dan was Nehushtan, the Snake God, and she had a serpent in her stomach.

They stood on the hill and looked out over Shur. The pasture below was almost gone. It had been poor stuff to start with, pale, sickly green vegetation marking out the valley of Raha. Even up here, in the hills, sheep were scrabbling about in the rocks desperate for grass, and the stream that ran down the gorge was muddied and foul.

Perhaps, said Esther, they would all go back to Egypt. Perhaps they would give back the *belongings* and would be allowed back into the land of Misri.

'No,' said Ruth, blinking back the tears that swam in her eyes as she thought of the white-walled house at Goshen, of the bedroom with its bead curtains over the window, of her combs and her bronze mirror, of her little collection of Philistine decorated pots. She looked round for her *bedu*. It was over a week since she had seen him.

The hills were empty. Perhaps he had gone to Nakhi.

They watched the families of Joseph, and of Dan and Gad depart. Perhaps a third of the Danites and Gadites were on the move, their sledges pulled by mules, the old men and women walking in front, the herds and flocks following behind, the children running behind them with sticks. They had decided to avoid Zarw completely: they were going north-east across the desert, in a direction that would take them in four or five days to Bahah and the Great Sea. Ruth stood with Esther and Giliad and watched them go. They waved, and outriders from the families waved back. 'See you in Canaan,' one of them called, his voice coming up clearly from the desert below. Rebecca, who had followed them up to the hilltop, wept and said it was the boy of Dan who had been kind to her.

At nightfall they again went up the hill and looked out at the tiny lights of the campfires to the north.

The next night they looked but could see nothing.

Days passed. There were rain clouds in the mountains to the east, and they watched them and marvelled. One morning there was a strange watery smell on the wind, and a few drops of moisture fell from the sky, and many young children of the families screamed in hysteria, because they had been born in the worker village of Pi-Ramese, in the heart of the Delta, and in five years no drop of rain had fallen. At Goshen, though, it had rained three times – once when Ruth was five, again when she was ten, and again when she was fifteen.

It had been the third rainfall that had contained the little green frogs; the third rainfall that made the swollen Nile run red with the blood of Egyptians killed by Amorites in Kantarah, an event that had brought down on the tribes the malice of the priests of Amun, and from the civil authorities the cancellation of the public holiday for the Israelite corvée workers to worship the true God – or, as the priests of Amun put it, the heretic God.

It had been a terrible day for them all, said Zuri, when the frogs fell from the sky.

Now the remaining tribes were preparing to move. A few families were in a panic, setting off northwards after those who had gone towards Bahah, risking Egyptian soldiers rather than starvation in the desert. Most, though, were going south with Moses and the Levites. It was time for the family of Zuri-shaddai to decide.

Shelumiel said, 'I don't like the Levites and I don't trust Moses. But I trust the Soldier when he says there are chariots at Bahah. We can't face chariots. One day, but not yet. We all heard the Soldier. The Way of the Philistines has become the Way of Horus; it has become the Way of the Pharaoh's army. I say we go south.'

'Does the Living Goddess of Asher go south?' asked Ruth.

'Yes,' said Shelumiel coldly.

'Do Miriam and the harlots go south?' asked Ruth.

'Miriam and her musicians go south,' said Shelumiel.

'South, south,' said Zuri, thinking of his vines in the green fields of Goshen, a tired old man.

Ruth walked behind Zuri's litter, behind the four creaking old Ethiopians. The slaves were carrying the *belongings*, the mules were pulling the sledges. The bondsmen were driving the herd and the flock.

In the distance she saw a bedouin sitting his donkey on a desert dune.

'That's my *bedu*,' she said to Esther, thinking that perhaps it really was. 'It's all right, he'll look after us,' she added, thinking that perhaps he would.

Across the grey-dawn Wilderness, the sun came up over the Mountains of Ti. Somewhere, on the other side of those mountains, was the King's Highway; the road to Canaan, the land of milk and honey. In the meantime, they were moving south, south in search of a pass through the mountains, south by the Yam Suf, south towards the slave mines of Khadem.

Even so, her heart lifted and she sang, and Esther and Giliad sang with her.

5
The City of the Dead

A Narcotics Agency sign warned that drug smuggling in Egypt could result in death by hanging plus a fine of three-quarters of a million US dollars, a reminder that troubles never come singly. In London, Richard reflected, the equivalent sign had told him where to apply for a copy of the Traveller's Charter and promised a helpful service. A new notice warned in Arabic and English that the importation of alcoholic liquor was now an offence punishable by ten years in gaol. It was half-past midnight. In the banking cubicles clerks sat under low-watt bulbs and handed out thick wads of stinking, greasy banknotes – it was several years now since inflation had finally wiped out the coinage. He went past baggage reclaim. He had no suitcase. His stuff was in the rucksack that he'd bought in Tel Aviv when he was nineteen and hiking round the archaeological sites of the Negev Desert. It contained spare underpants, socks, and memories: student barbecues, oranges plucked straight from the tree, nights sleeping under the stars while a girl with a nice voice played her guitar and sang 'Michael, Row the Boat Ashore'.

There was a queue at immigration. Normally the bored, blank-eyed officials waved people through, but not tonight. The place buzzed with bad temper and stressed-out nerves.

Richard stood and waited. Next to him was a British brewer whose company had been funding a project to re-create the beer of Pharaonic Egypt. 'We've been growing ancient Egyptian emmer wheat outside Edinburgh, and using DNA tracking to find out the origins of the yeast. Did you know there used to be a beer in England called Pharaoh's Ale?' The brewer was a man interested in his trade. 'It's a crying shame, what these fundamentalists are doing. The Egyptians invented beer, even if it was a sort of alcoholic porridge.'

'Beer and spirits are still sold in tourist hotels, aren't they?'

'You're behind the times. It's as bad as Saudi. It's worse than Saudi. You're OK in Saudi if you know where to go. You're OK in Iran if you know where to go – I can take you to a place ten kilometres into the desert out of Mashhad where there's a beer stand all lit up with fairylights, and never less than a dozen air-force generals standing round drinking McEwan's Export.'

'I expect it'll be the same here.'

'Not for a bit, it won't. The mullahs chopped some bugger's hand off in a village outside Luxor last week, I heard about it from a Land Rover rep.'

They went through immigration. Taxi drivers held up signs – Hotel Ramses, Genoa Travel, Kuoni Worldwide, Movenpick Jolie Ville – but there were few tourists coming into Egypt these days, and most of those were flying directly to Sharm el-Sheikh and the other Red Sea resorts. Elizabeth stood in the middle of the reps, wearing a white linen suit and a broad-brimmed hat.

'Thank God! You know there's been a terrorist bomb? Let's get out of here. This all your luggage? This is Mac.'

Mac was in his early thirties, with a lean face, thinning red hair and not much time for false bonhomie. 'Hi,' he said, his gaze fixed somewhere over Richard's shoulder.

Elizabeth said, 'We've got a car. Jesus, have you tried driving a hire car round here?'

Richard wondered who Mac was. He tended, after two years in the UK, to view American academics through European eyes. There were those who aped Oxbridge gentility with college scarves and leather elbow patches on their Harris tweed jackets; and there were those who gave the impression they hadn't read a book since they'd left high school. This latter category wore check jackets and sweatshirts, ate hot dogs, talked loudly about baseball, and invariably turned out to be the most respected world scholars in their fields, publishing and knowing twice as much as anybody else, and becoming, at a frighteningly early age, faculty heads at the world's most prestigious English-speaking academic institutions.

Mac didn't seem to fit either category. Perhaps he was Elizabeth's lover.

They went out into the Cairo night. Taxi drivers enveloped them like moths. 'This way, this way!' they cried in tones of irritated authority. 'English? American? I am visiting Yorkshire soon, I have many friends in Yorkshire – ' a palpable untruth – 'Hotel Ramses? Twenty Egyptian pounds only.'

They pushed through.

The hire car was a Ford, new-looking but dented in several places. An Egyptian boy sat on the bonnet in the darkness. Mac had promised him money to guard it. 'Otherwise we'd have come out and somebody'd have stolen the wipers,' said Mac. 'You look round. Half the cars in Cairo have no wipers.'

Mac inspected his wipers. He gave the boy a five-pound note. The boy snatched it and said, '*Naharak, sa'id.*'

Richard said, '*Naharak, laban.*'

The boy disappeared.

Elizabeth said, 'What did you say?'

'I wished his day would be as white as milk.'

'Yeah, right.'

Elizabeth drove. Richard said, 'Where are we heading for?'

Nobody said anything.

Richard, tired, said, 'Look, do you mind telling me where we are heading—'

'We're booked into the Forte Grand at Giza,' said Elizabeth.

'All of us?'

'Yeah.'

'I thought you had a base at Maadi?'

'We're pulling out. Don't worry about it.'

'We're going the wrong way for Giza.'

'Our plans have had to change because of that bomb. We need to look at the body tonight. There's a lot of security people in this town getting very jumpy. Our contact is getting very jumpy.'

'This body, these remains, they're in Cairo?'

'Yes.'

'And you want me to look at them now, at one o' clock in the morning?'

'That's what the lady said,' said Mac toughly.

He shouldn't have come. He had assumed that Elizabeth was being secretive to guard an archaeological find, a series of late Bronze Age graves, perhaps. But if the contact was in Cairo he was a dealer, a fixer. Cairenes didn't wander round the Western Desert on camels, stumbling over Bronze Age cemeteries. Legitimate contacts, Ministry of Antiquities officials, American University staff, didn't have to be seen at one o'clock in the morning.

They passed the Commonwealth Cemetery. Egyptian Army APCs and fighter aircraft were floodlit outside the headquarters of the Arab Organization for Industrialization. Traffic was heavy: despite the hour, white-uniformed traffic police were on every junction; black-uniformed anti-terrorist police with Kalashnikovs sat in trucks down side-streets. They reached Central Station. Elizabeth swung the car round the statue of Rameses the Second, the massive column of carved stone that was the most valuable traffic roundabout sculpture in history, the most appalling desecration since Napoleon used the Sphinx for target practice. They were in the centre of a city half as big again as London; they passed a flock of sheep that were being driven, through the traffic, towards 6 October Bridge.

Mac turned on the radio, trying to find an English-language station. A pseudo-American newsreader voice, as sickly as warm milk chocolate, said, 'A statement issued in Tripoli by the Islamic Militant Front applauded the Egyptian Judicial Commission's move to incorporate more Islamic laws into the civil code—'

'Bastards,' said Elizabeth, turning the radio off. 'Do they really think they can buy off the fundamentalists? Did it stop them bombing the airport?'

Richard closed his eyes and dozed. When he woke up an illuminated sign said: MAADI DENTAL OFFERS A FULL SERVICE CENTER UTILIZING WESTERN STANDARDS OF STERILIZATION. LET OUR ORTHODONTICS PROFESSOR RESTORE YOUR SMILE. Mac was swearing quietly. He was trying to make a phone call but wasn't getting through; in Cairo mobiles often didn't. They looked for somewhere to phone from. Eventually Elizabeth pulled up outside the Maadi Petit Swiss Chalet Pei-Ching, which was still open, serving a solitary table of businessmen. She went into the restaurant. Richard got out of the car to stretch his legs. The night was clammy and humid, with no hint of a breeze. He looked in through the Pei-Ching's window. The businessmen were drinking out of little teapots. They looked both merry and furtive. A notice in the window read: THE FUNNIEST THING CONFUCIUS COULD IMAGINE WAS WATCHING SOMEBODY FALL OFF HIS OWN ROOF.

Mac got out of the car and mooched over. 'Curried duck and chips from Yip's carry-out on the Paisley Road,' he said, 'that's what you want.'

They both stared in at the businessmen. Mac said, confidentially, 'It's funny I don't seem to need a drink. I nearly passed out, no joke, when we came in to land and the steward said Egypt had gone dry and the mullahs were stringing boozers up by their bollocks. There'd been nothing about it in the *Sun*. But if it's not available, you don't need it, do you? A chance to sluice the old liver out, give it a rest, that's how I look at it.'

A man came walking along the pavement. He gave them both a card, then walked on. The card read: BEFRIENDERS CAIRO – SOMEONE TO TALK TO.

Mac looked at his card, puzzled.

Elizabeth came out. They piled back into the car. Ten minutes later they turned down a side-road.

'OK, this is it.'

They left the car and went through a narrow alleyway. The night had a thousand eyes, shining, yellow-green in the darkness, cruel, cold and predatory; the eyes of Bastet, the Cat Goddess of maternity, fertility and moonlight. There was the sudden howl of a tom, intent on adding to Cairo's half-million strays.

They walked between concrete-block buildings – not lavish, not the Western villas of Maadi, with their pools and palm trees – these were government agency buildings. There was a police control box, under the shelter of an acacia. The guard was anti-terrorist police: black uniform, dull black insignia, holding his submachine-gun in the crook of his arm.

They stopped. Mac said uneasily. 'They confirmed it would be OK?'

'Yes.'

'You want me to talk to him?'

'Yes.'

Mac went forward. He spoke in a low voice to the soldier. The soldier turned to look the other way, back up the street. Mac came back. He nodded.

They slipped past the checkpoint and into the building. A single electric light burned in the entrance hall. A clerk looked at them from behind his desk as though they were invisible, as though the wad of dollars Elizabeth placed carefully on the desk was invisible.

'That's not the full payment,' Elizabeth said to Richard, in a low voice. 'That is not,' she pointed at the money, 'the full payment by a long chalk.'

'Hurry up, for Christ's sake,' said Mac.

They went up two flights of concrete stairs, then down a corridor. They'd been here before, they knew their way around. They opened a wooden door that was half pebbled-glass and went into a room with white-tiled walls. There was a smell of antiseptic and something else, also chemical, that Richard could not identify, and then suddenly recognized.

From Cairo to LA, he thought, city mortuaries must be much of a muchness. Not that he had ever been in one before.

A boy appeared at an inner doorway. A small, dark boy, around sixteen but looking younger – the heir, maybe, to Anubis, Jackal God of embalming, lord, under Osiris, of the City of the Dead. He looked angry. Small but angry, a Jackal God with a problem, his face twisted and contorted. Elizabeth wearily held up a ten-dollar bill. The boy snatched it, unplacated. Richard remembered the magic spell to guard against Anubis cutting out and eating the heart of a traveller to the Underworld: *I live by truth, in which I exist; I live by saying what is in my heart, and it shall not be taken away; my heart is mine, and none shall be aggressive against it, no terrors shall subdue me.*

The boy led them into a smaller room. There was no window, no natural light. A bank of cabinets stood against the white-tiled wall, like metal coffins piled one on top of the other. There was a marble slab and a lamp suspended from the ceiling. There were two upright wooden chairs. The light was dim, the smell of antiseptic and formalin was overpowering. 'The VIP suite,' said Mac, in a low, awed voice, a Glaswegian with a taste for the dramatic. 'Nasser came here.

Sadat came here. Even the Shah of Iran finally step-ped this way.'

A click, as the boy locked the door.

'Can't we get any more light in here?' said Elizabeth.

'It's the bulb,' said Mac, 'it's only a forty-watt bulb. Give him some money, Liz, and say you want a hundred-watt bulb next time.'

'There'll be no next time,' said Elizabeth, 'he's made that clear enough.'

Mac stood on a chair and gingerly tipped the ceiling lamp so that the light fell more fully on the cabinets.

The boy attendant slowly eased the drawer open.

Elizabeth said quietly, 'Take a look, Rich.'

The corpse was perhaps 140 centimetres long. Amorite, the skin dull in death, male, early to mid-teens. Richard, from his watching of TV, had assumed all mortuary corpses to be naked or draped in some sort of shroud. This corpse wore a short-sleeved shirt of worn greyish-coloured linen, collarless, a leather skirt – but it wasn't leather, it was some sort of thick canvas, half a centimetre thick, stiff with a stain of what appeared to be tallow grease. He was barefoot. On one arm, high up, where they would normally be under his tunic, were dark-red tattoo markings: a bull hieroglyph and another Richard couldn't make out. The tip of his right index finger was missing, the tip and part of the nail, cleanly sliced away. He wore a wig, made of what Richard guessed to be palm fibre. Richard bent down over the tattoo markings.

Elizabeth said, 'Well?'

Richard said, 'He carries his food and water on his shoulders, like a donkey with a broken back. He drinks foul water. He trembles like a little bird in the face of the enemy. When he returns to Egypt he is nothing but a worm-eaten old faggot.'

Richard looked up.

Elizabeth said again, 'Well?'

'I don't understand.'

She was breathing quickly, staring at him. Her tongue moistened her dry lips.

Richard said, 'He's a boy soldier.'

'What dynasty?' she said.

He was bending down again, over the tattoo markings.

'Nineteenth dynasty?' she said. 'Would you say nineteenth dynasty?'

'Eighteenth or nineteenth.'

'You're sure about that?'

'No, it could be later.'

'How much later?'

'I don't know.'

'Christ,' said Mac, 'one Club Class air ticket and seven hundred quid and he doesn't know!'

Richard said, 'Have you a photograph of these markings?'

'Those things on his arm?' said Elizabeth. 'Yes.'

'The end of his index finger, it's missing—'

'It doesn't matter, it's not important.'

Richard looked down at the body in the mortuary drawer, at the Amorite's face. It had on it an expression of surprise and puzzlement.

Mac said, 'OK? We're OK, are we?'

Richard said, 'I don't understand.'

'Let's go and not understand somewhere else,' said Mac. 'Come on! Come on!' The boy attendant was already unlocking the door.

Elizabeth said, 'Rich? You OK? You seen enough?'

The corpse had a short sword, a falchion in a leather sheath. Richard leant over and pulled it out a couple of centimetres. The boy attendant shouted angrily, his voice filled with panic.

'For Christ's sake!' shouted Mac.

The dagger slid freely, as if it had been recently oiled.

They were in the Forte Grand, Giza. Mac poured miniature gin and tonics, already mixed, from his own private, secret minibar. 'Well, this is it,' he said, 'this is the end of the booze.' He looked at Richard, then with enormous reluctance passed him a glass. Elizabeth lay on the bed and kicked her shoes off. She said, 'I've got the autopsy report. You'll never know the cost of these four sheets of paper.' For a girl with an American University's budget and a taste for penthouse hotel life, she was curiously fascinated by the cost of living.

Richard said, 'There was one thing wrong.'

Elizabeth said, 'Wrong?

'The falchion. It was iron, not bronze. Macedonia, I think. I've a colleague who could tell you. That's why I thought it might be later.'

'So?'

'Egyptian infantry of the nineteenth dynasty, if it *is* nineteenth dynasty—'

'That's what you're here to tell us,' said Mac, looking at Richard's gin and tonic. 'That's what we keep asking you about, isn't it, sunbeam?'

'Listen,' said Richard. 'Call me sunbeam again and I will connect your teeth intravenously to your anus.'

'Boys, boys,' said Elizabeth. 'Please!'

Richard drank his gin.

101

'Rich?'

'The wig's right. The Amorite soldiers were like the Nubians and wore wigs instead of helmets. We know palm fibre was used – there's a report on a dig by Toronto University at Saqqara, a series of soldiers' graves behind the barracks, those were nineteenth dynasty, in fact they were precisely dated to Rameses the Second. The kilt is authentic, I should think, although of course I've never seen one in that condition before. They used to soak material in salted wine, then stick it together, layer on layer. It gave good protection against blunt weapons. The preservation in this case is incredible. The thing is, though, they didn't have iron falchions.'

'No?'

'You're a couple of centuries out.'

'Hear that, Mac?'

'I hear, Princess.'

'It's the little detail that trips up the best con, isn't it?' said Elizabeth, sitting up. 'You see why we needed you, Rich. We'll get the falchion taken off first thing tomorrow. Christ Almighty,' she screamed, 'you think you've been looking at some rich Egyptian kid run over on his way to a fancy-dress party? You still think we're going to try and sell you the pyramids?'

'Now Liz, baby,' said Mac. 'Now, Princess.'

'Listen,' she said. 'Just listen. That body has been in the morgue since 1973. It's been lying there in a secret government morgue, a security services morgue, since the night of 16 October 1973, precisely. On that night Egyptian Rangers went in behind the tanks at El-Garf, a place under the plateau of El-Tîh in Sinai, trying to break through the Israeli gun positions. Well, they didn't succeed. They didn't break through, and by morning the Israelis were back in force, round the passes of El-Tîh, starting the big counter-push on Third Army. When the Rangers finally pulled out, they brought with them around fifty dead or wounded and the squadron tank commander, who was unconscious but had shouted on the tank's radio that he was *surrounded by ghosts*. Back over the canal, about two hours ahead of the Israelis, they found that one of the dead was Elmer.'

'Elmer?'

'We call him Elmer,' said Mac.

'Dear God, why?' said Richard.

She said, 'He has the look of a guy called Elmer I knew in Connecticut. For fuck's sake, does it matter? Here, read this.'

She threw him the folder, then turned and stood looking out of the window, at the turquoise, illuminated pool below. There was a splash from the darkness, a girlish scream.

'Skinny-dipping,' said Mac, standing by her. 'Naughty, naughty.'

The folder contained an autopsy on corpse 609 showing that it was male, Amorite, aged around fourteen and had died of heart failure; 609's heart was over-large, due, the report suggested, to physical hardship and malnutrition during early childhood. He was already arthritic. Several of his teeth were already ground down, particularly the molars, due to sand in the food he ate. His last meal had been berries, eaten some four hours before his death.

'Carbon-dating?' said Richard.

Elizabeth shook her head sadly.

Mac said, 'Carbon-dating. It was what I said, too, didn't I, Princess?'

'In October 1973, Rich,' she said, 'that boy was four-teen years old. Since then he's been in a morgue.'

There was a pause.

'There are other ways.'

'Yes,' said Elizabeth, 'but they take time.'

'The tip of his finger?'

She didn't reply. There was the sound of more little screams from outside, laughs, then quietness. They'd have to watch it, those two out there, that the mullahs didn't catch them in the undergrowth, under the heavy, hose-pipe-drenched blossom of the frangipani. He could hear the hum of the air-conditioning. He said, 'You're trying to tell me that there's some sort of time transference going on in Sinai.'

Mac drank the last of his gin and tonic. He looked at the empty glass, a dog remembering a bone.

Elizabeth stared steadily at Richard.

He said, 'This is a project approved by Drextel? This is an American Universities-funded project?'

'Yes.'

'Have they got the index finger, the tip of the finger?'

'Perhaps.'

'It's nonsense.'

The knock on the door was quiet; the cleaners checking politely, making sure the room was ready to be serviced, except that it was the middle of the night.

Mac ambled across the room, opened the door a fraction. He closed the door and came back.

'They say he's there,' he said. 'They say the bugger's turned up.'

'OK,' said Elizabeth. 'Let's go.'

'Go where?' asked Richard.

'See a guy who can tell us about Elmer.'

On the way down in the lift Richard looked at his BEFRIENDERS CAIRO card. It was for people who were lonely or depressed, for people finding life hard to cope with.

They swung south past the Coptic cathedral and headed down El-Qala'a. This was Old Cairo, the bazaars and brothels still remembered by British Eighth Army veterans who had long forgotten the shitty sands of El Alamein. This was Richard's Cairo – an Islamic city, built in blood and splendour, in art and in faith; the capital of the Islamic world. They went past the towering menace of the Citadel, built by Saladin from stone salvaged from pyramids at Giza.

Elizabeth said, 'You know what happened in there?'

'Yes.' said Richard curtly.

In the Citadel, in 1811, the Mameluke dukes who ruled Egypt had been murdered, one by one, as they passed under the deep, dark arches of Pharaonic stone.

'What happened, Liz?' asked Mac, curious about life.

'Some French pop star threw a record launch party there two years back. Some Michael Jackson clone. They had ten thousand bottles of champagne flown in.'

'Bloody hell . . .' Mac wouldn't have minded some champagne.

A sign for Pepsi-Cola flickered, red and blue neon in the night. The car slowed.

'Shit, this indicator isn't working again,' said Mac. Elizabeth put her arm out and waved it up and down.

Mac, the cosmopolitan, said, 'Careful they don't steal your wristwatch.'

They turned slowly into a side-road. It was unpaved, and wide enough to take only one vehicle. On either side were dark, small houses made of mud.

They were in the necropolis. The City of the Dead.

'There's a mosque coming up. Turn right,' said Elizabeth, her voice strained.

The mortuary mosque, small, crumbling, its yellow paint flaking, loomed up. They turned into another narrow street. They moved slowly down between the half-sized houses. There was a smell. It seeped in through the air-conditioning.

'Oh, God,' said Elizabeth.

'Dead people don't crap,' said Mac succinctly. 'Nobody thought to lay sewers in a graveyard.'

They ought to have done. Cairo was a Third World city of 15 million souls, growing by 8,000 inhabitants every day. At first in a trickle, then in a flood, the homeless had crept into the City of the Dead. They had laid claim to the homes of the corpses. They had snuggled down with the coffins.

Elizabeth said, 'How was your flight?'

'What?'

A pause.

'Just trying to make conversation.'

'Drextel,' said Richard. 'If you're feeling chatty, tell me exactly where in Drextel's Faculty of Sciences this project has its home; where exactly it was nurtured. Tell me who exactly is in charge.'

'I'm in charge,' she said coldly. 'I've told you that I'm in charge.'

Mac said, 'OK, this is it,' and pulled up.

They got out. The necropolis lay all around them. From the main road, from the flyovers, it had appeared to be a vast pool of darkness. Only when

106

you were here, deep inside it, were you aware of the moving shadows, the dim oil lamps in the tiny ceremonial windows of the tomb-houses; aware that the City of the Dead was alive with people – filled with the roadsweepers, the beggars, the poor of Cairo.

Mac was looking round for a boy.

Elizabeth said, 'Never mind, it's not your car.'

'It's my car while I'm hiring it.'

Richard said, 'It's unlikely to rain now for another eight months.'

'If I'm here in eight months,' said Mac, 'it will be because I'm dead or in gaol.'

'Dead might be OK,' said Richard, 'but I'd keep out of an Egyptian gaol if I were you.'

'Let's go,' said Elizabeth. She led the way up a narrow alley. A standpipe dripped water and made the dirt muddy. A door opened and a man who had been watching from a window peered out and spoke, questioningly, in a low voice. Richard replied. The door closed quickly.

Richard said, 'He's a barber. He thought we had brought our daughter to be circumcised.'

'Daughter?' said Mac. 'Did you say "daughter"?'

'They slice off part of the external sex organ. The operation's illegal, but most Muslim girls are put through it. Circumcised wives are believed to be hygienic, feminine and faithful.'

Mac said, 'Perhaps I'll get my old girl done.'

Elizabeth said, 'This is it,' and knocked quietly on a door.

They waited. The smell deepened, penetrating their nostrils, seeping into their clothes, their hair, their heads. Mac swore, quietly and obscenely. Richard wondered about him: he was not your average academic, not your average Egyptologist, not even the sort of guy most university projects would take on as a minder.

Mac said,

'I'm Robbie Burns on the pier at Leith.
I've lost the key to ma arsehole,
So I'm shitting through ma teeth.'

Perhaps he was a lecturer from Drextel's English department.

The door opened a crack. Elizabeth said softly, 'It's me again. OK?' The door closed.

In the distance Richard could hear the roar of Cairo's traffic. At the end of the dark, fetid alleyway he could see red lights suspended in the black sky; the satellite communications dish and early-warning radar system on the Moqattam Hills. He thought about the dead boy in the morgue; the body, the corpse.

In the tomb-house an oil lamp was lit.

The door opened again. They crept inside. Stone coffins, decorated with flaking paint, were piled against two walls. There were a man and woman. There was a small child, a girl, around eight years old. There were dirty rubber foam mattresses on the floor, a cheap wooden table with a few pots and dishes piled on it. There was a plywood food cupboard with a wiremesh door. Against one of the coffins was a battered cardboard suitcase.

'This is Ali,' said Elizabeth tiredly, 'and this is his wife, and this is their daughter, Kareema. Hi, Kareema.'

Kareema said, in a quiet sing-song little voice, 'Hello.'

'See what I've got for you. Hey, look. You'll like this.'

She produced a bar of chocolate from her shoulder bag. Kareema took it in silence. The woman murmured her thanks.

Elizabeth said, 'Ali sells things in Midan el-Tahrir. Are you going to show us what you sell, Ali?'

Ali opened the suitcase. In the bottom of it were a few packets of hairgrips on a sheet of card. A dozen or so thick rubber, handpainted balloons. Shiny silver-bright bracelets. Ali held one up to Richard. On it, stamped in English on the thin, silver-bright cheap alloy plaque: I LOVE YOU. The entire stock wasn't worth five dollars.

Elizabeth said, 'They've got two grown-up sons, so they don't think they're that badly off. Kareema was a bit of an afterthought, weren't you, sweetheart? An afterthought from heaven, from Allah, OK?'

Kareema, not understanding, nodded, her dark-brown hair bobbing, and grinned.

'Kareema goes with her daddy every day. She lends a hand to the other traders by getting them drinks and food. You ought to see her run about all day with glasses of crushed ice and plates of rice and stuff—'

Serving the poorest of the poor. A child Madonna in the realm of the Jackal God.

Mac said, 'I think I'll wait in the car, make sure the bastards don't steal the wheels.'

The man said, '*Bismillah*.' He extended his hands, as if to stop Mac leaving, and spoke in rapid Arabic.

Richard said, 'He wants us to eat.'

'Oh, Christ!' Elizabeth said, dismayed.

109

Bismillah . . .

The woman was already taking things out of the cupboard.

There was melon, soft and overripe, alive with the promise of dysentery. There were cold potatoes in livid orange grease. There was a segment, in its foil wrapper, of Laughing Cow cheese. There was water from a Bakaka plastic mineral-water bottle, but it didn't look a very clean or new bottle. Was it drinking water? *'Di mayyua lil shurb?'* But of course. Drink, drink . . .

Mac said decisively, 'Yeah, I'll wait with the car, make sure we don't block somebody in', and left.

The water was poured into plastic cups. Richard said, 'They say that anyone who drinks water from the Nile will return to Egypt.'

'Yeah?' said Elizabeth.

'Others say drink from the Nile and you'll never leave. It's alive with tiny worms – some that grow into the muscles and heart and others that affect the brain and spinal cord.'

'That right?'

'It's also alive with parasites, typhoid, cholera and epidemic typhoid.'

'Cheers,' said Elizabeth, swallowing a number of mouthfuls, then dipping dark brown bread into the red-rust gravy.

'Cheers,' Richard said, impressed.

'I have to say, Rich,' she said, masticating with appetite, 'I am ceaselessly amazed by your breadth, not to say depth, of knowledge.'

Ali started speaking, quietly but insistently.

'He thinks it reasonable that we should pay him

110

something to tell his story. It is a story of his ruin, the ruin of his hopes. He wants,' said Richard, 'one hundred dollars.'

'No way.'

'It's not a lot.'

'It's a fucking fortune. Do you know what you can buy here with a hundred bucks?'

'What I don't know,' said Richard, 'is what you expect him to tell us.'

'*He* knows,' said Elizabeth. '*He* knows, because we've been here twice already. The first time he claimed he didn't know anything at all, the second time he wanted a thousand bucks.'

The man said, in English, 'One hundred. *One hundred dollars.*'

'OK, OK, don't get excited. Jesus. Fifty dollars and you tell us everything. Everything, understand? No holding back, no saving things up. Fifty American dollars, Dollars US. OK?'

Ali cried out in despair and shock.

It took ten minutes for him to come down to seventy-five dollars. Richard said, 'For God's sake, give it to him.'

Elizabeth was steely. 'Listen,' she said, 'if you've fought the American Universities Physics Council's Board of Finance for an overseas research grant and *won*, you can deal with these guys in your sleep. He gets sixty dollars or I walk.'

They settled on seventy.

'What exactly,' said Richard, 'do you want him to tell us?'

'I want to know what happened,' said Elizabeth, sitting, because there was nowhere else to sit, on the edge of Ali's wife's mattress, 'to tank 109 of the 44th

Egyptian Tank Corps, at Wadi el-Garf, Sinai, on the night of 16 October 1973.'

He was radio operator in a T-55 battle tank. He had been in the army eighteen months, and had done a radio engineer's course at Port Said tank school, graduating in August. He was just married, his wife was living with him in barracks. By August, when he graduated, assault training had already been going on for several months. He had done exercises with troops who were training on canals branching off from the Nile, working in the late afternoon when the smog was thick and they were told the American spy satellites would be at too low an angle to be able to see them.

Mac knocked quietly at the door, poked his head in.

'You OK?'

'We're getting there,' said Elizabeth, 'slowly.'

Kareema's black eyes were open as she lay curled on the mattress, her back against the stacked coffins.

'Tank 109 of the 44th Tank Corps,' said Elizabeth. 'You went over the Sweetwater Canal. You went into Sinai. You beat shit out of the Israelis, yeah?'

Yes, they beat shit out of the Israelis.

'You were at Wadi el-Garf?'

They chased the Israelis up into the mountains, back up the wadi, up the Gharandal, through the passes.

'What happened to your tank at Wadi el-Garf?'

His radio equipment jammed. The tank's new, Soviet-fitted experimental heat-seeking target locators went berserk.

Elizabeth said, 'What exactly, what *exactly* did you see?'

Ali looked at her in the lamplight. He was nervous. His wife was looking anxious. He spoke very quietly.

Richard said, 'He saw ghosts. Ghosts of old soldiers.'

He looked at Elizabeth. Her eyes were fixed on Ali. She said, 'What kind of soldiers?'

Ali spoke again.

'Ancient soldiers. Soldiers with spears.'

Now Elizabeth looked at Richard.

'OK, Rich,' she said quietly.

Richard asked questions. Ali was hesitant, his eyes flicking round the room. His voice became lower, more indistinct. Richard asked more questions, speaking more rapidly. Ali shrugged, shook his head as if in irritation. Richard said, 'He's making it up. He's inventing descriptions of soldiers. He's describing stuff he's seen in books. There were no soldiers with bows, not the kind that he describes. They were using composite bows by the nineteenth dynasty. His uniforms are Saracen, nearly two thousand years later – it's out of books, out of religious tracts, stuff he's seen in the mosque. He's making it up to get the seventy bucks.'

'Shit,' said Elizabeth wearily. She got up. Ali spoke loudly, vehemently.

Richard said, 'He was the radio operator in a T-55. He couldn't see anything. Only his screen, his little screen, and that was covered in red dots. It was his tank commander who saw the ghosts. His tank commander had his head up out of the turret. His tank commander saw the ghosts and went mad.'

'His tank commander,' said Elizabeth, 'was sentenced to death by military court.'

113

'No use offering him seventy dollars, then.'

'It was commuted. He was sent to the funny farm.'

Ali spoke again.

Richard said, 'He wants his money.'

'He wants *what*?'

Ali was staring intently at Elizabeth.

So was Ali's wife.

So was Kareema.

Elizabeth looked at Kareema, sighed, and handed the money over.

They were back in Giza by five-thirty a.m. The first dawn light was showing the outline of the pyramids, a denser darkness against the sky. They went into the hotel, past the cordon of anti-terrorist police, through the airport-type security. Mac's car keys triggered the alarm. He was frisked. He put up his arms with professional sang-froid; a man used to being frisked. They passed through into the foyer.

Richard said, 'The tank commander. You have the name of the asylum?'

'He's not there any more.'

'Where is he?'

'Somewhere in Sinai.'

6
The Wells of Marah

It was called Marah, which meant bitter. The tribes had travelled three days south through the Wilderness of Shur, and then had come to this place, where ten springs bubbled from a salt marsh. The springs were brackish – fouled over the years by Egyptian soldiery and Nubian slaves – but Miriam cast a spell and the waters became pure. 'Moses has made the water pure,' said the priests of Levi, insinuating themselves among the families, establishing credit, and everybody said, 'Praise to the prophet Moses', but they all knew that it had really been the witch Miriam. The tent of her dancing girls was set under a grove of date palms where the mimosa was in full bloom. The tribes camped along the shore of the Yam Suf, their flocks grazing on the salt marsh, all except for the Benjaminites, who camped far out in the desert, wary for the safety of their hyenas.

Zuri's black goat-hair tent was raised in the gritty sand next to the tents of Reuben and Gershon. These were the families from Goshen, and already they had travelled far together; from Tikwe to Giza, and then to Baal-Zephon and over the frontier. At night they set a guard to stop other tribes stealing their cattle. Nearby were the herdless families, people from

Pi-Ramese and Migdol; many had been labourers on the gates to the Pharaoh's house or brick-makers at Kantarah. These were the people who had been refused a public holiday or an allowance of sweet oil, or of ointments for the skin (the story changed with every telling – sometimes they said they had been ordered to *make bricks without straw*), and had finally refused to work.

Zuri called out at them angrily from the door of his tent. They were nothing but shiftless idlers! If it had not been for the shiftless, idle brick-makers of Pi-Ramese, he would still be in Goshen!

They told him to sod off.

When the old Ethiopians first put up Zuri's goat-hair tent, Ruth went behind it (she would not sleep inside, not with the displaced ka of Ka-nefer), curled up in the sand and slept for twelve hours; the sleep of exhaustion. When she woke up she could see clusters of tiny green buds over her head, the fruit of a date palm that had not yet set, and little green bee-eaters chattered in the branches, just as they did at home. Later, in the evening, fetching water, she saw gazelles; silent shadows on the edge of the camp, flitting backwards and forwards, unable to reach their waterhole.

Going back, struggling under the weight of the waterskins, she heard Zuri singing in his tent. 'O Re, O Atum, O Shu,' he sang, in his shrill, quavering old voice. 'O Tefnut, O Geb, O Nut, O Anubis before the divine shrine, O Horus, O Seth.'

He said his head ached. His forehead was mottled red and dry, and burned to the touch. Before him, on his coverlet, was a crocodile of clay with grain stuffed in its mouth.

Ruth said, 'Poor old man. Poor old man.'

Zuri chanted, 'O Isis, O Nephthys!'

She lay down on the sand of the tent's floor, too tired to move.

'O great Ennead,' Zuri howled. 'O little Ennead!'

He held up his small wooden statue of Bes, who was dancing and waving a little sword. In his other hand he held up a bronze of Taweret.

'Come and see your father, dead man or dead woman.'

'In Sinai there is only one God,' Ruth said, not because she believed it but because it would annoy him.

Zuri stopped howling.

'And I do not think the *One God* is Bes, the home-maker, or Taweret, the pregnant hippopotamus.'

Zuri blinked at her.

'I do not think,' Ruth said, 'that a pregnant hippopotamus is guiding us to Canaan!'

Zuri grinned. 'Ho, ho, ho,' he cackled.

'Ho, ho, ho,' chortled Ruth, pleased with her wit.

Zuri reached into his silver dish and threw her a dried fig cake. He was a generous old man, for there were hardly any fig cakes left. But it was also true that his one sound tooth, his great yellow incisor, had been broken by biting a fig cake with a stone in it.

'Keep quiet about your gods,' said Shelumiel, when he came from the flocks. 'The Levites have destroyed the Bull God image of Joseph. They pulled it down and burnt it while the men of Joseph were out with the flocks.'

Only two families of Joseph had come south; the remainder had gone north on the road to Bahah and the Great Sea.

'The Levites,' said Zuri irritably. 'The Levites!'

All the Levites were to be priests, and, just like the priests of Egypt, they were to be the only ones allowed to approach the temple, and only Moses and Aaron, his brother (his brother in the Egyptian sense, but by no means a Kenite), were to go into the land where Akhenaten lived as a God and talk to him.

Akhenaten who was now to be called *Yahweh the Thunderer*.

Shelumiel said, 'The gold lamp-snuffers of the Naphtali have been taken for a tabernacle. Old Enan's wife screamed when they took them.'

'Better a life in the Wilderness,' quoted Zuri sagely, 'than marry a shrill woman.'

'He's got both,' said Shelumiel.

They both sniggered. Ruth lay on the sand, as if dead.

'The lamp-snuffers of Naphtali,' said Shelumiel, 'had on them a device that Enan's wife said reminded her of the Eye of Horus.'

'Wives are notoriously superstitious,' said Zuri.

Ruth's eyes rolled. 'O Tefnut, O Geb, O Nut, O Anubis before the divine shrine,' she said.

Zuri said, 'I'm ill.'

That night Zuri dreamt that the Cobra Goddess, Renenutet, had come looking for him, in his vineyard in Goshen, sliding gold-green between the vines, calling out, 'Zuri, Zuri – ' seeking out her thanks-offering for the ripening of the fruit, puzzled to know why he was not there. Then he dreamt that Renenutet had slithered into his house, gliding from room to room, from the granary to the chamber of his wives, seeking him, calling, 'Zuri, Zuri – ' and finally coiling herself on his bed in loneliness and sadness.

In the morning he said, 'Bring to me Gideon the Benjaminite. I want him to interpret my dream.'

They went and fetched Gideon from the desert. When he came, Zuri said, 'How are your hyenas?' out of politeness, and recalled how he himself had once force-fed a herd of hyena for two years. He had planned to start a business selling hyena meat to the people of Kaal, who could not eat dogmeat since making dogs into their god. Nobody, Zuri said, had made the hyena into a god, no bands of hyena priests ever threatened to burn houses and slit throats, the way the dog priests did in Kaal!

'Horubis,' said Gideon the Benjaminite, an authority on hyena matters, 'is a hyena god worshipped in Pi-Ramese.'

'Ah, well,' said Zuri, not really interested – there was always some cult or other in the back-streets of Pi-Ramese, among the ignorant brick-makers. He told Gideon of his dream. Gideon said, 'Tell me of your house in Goshen.'

Ruth sighed and shook her head. The Benjaminites had never lived in houses. They were reckoned too mad to live in houses. As a result they were always curious about house life. She poured purple wine from the goatskin. It was thin, vinegary stuff; frontier wine, not the golden wine of Goshen.

Gideon said, wheedling, 'Zuri-shaddai, Zuri-shaddai, tell me about your house.'

Zuri said, 'It is a house to last for five generations. It is of Nile mud and straw, and thick-walled and cool.'

Gideon nodded and drank his wine, a far-away look in his eyes.

'It is a better house,' Zuri said, 'than the house of the scribe Nakhte!'

Ruth sat and listened. Esther and Giliad came into the tent, and sat and listened. Rebecca was away somewhere, mooning after a boy.

'The walls of the hall,' said Zuri, 'are inlaid with lapis lazuli. The domed ceiling is white and gold, and the shutters are of sweet-scented Lebanese cedar—'

How often in that cool, white hall had he greeted his guests! How often had his bondmaidens given out garlands and scented wax cones for his visitors to place in their hair to melt during the banquet!

'Ah, yes. Ah, yes,' nodded Gideon, though everyone knew him as an unsophisticate who would not have known what to do with a wax cone to save his life, and would probably have tried to eat it.

And the food, the food! It had been heaped on stands and tables, and musicians had played – the famous female musicians of Tikwe, with their lute and double oboe and tambourines, and that little singing girl whose name he could not remember now ('The Little Skylark,' said Ruth grumpily) – one of Miriam's girls at any rate – and, oh, what times they had had! Outside he had planted sycamores, figs and pomegranates and in the yard he had planted a date palm. Behind his house, in the courtyard, he had an aviary, an aviary with ro-geese.

Gideon nodded and exclaimed in wonder. Tears fell down Esther's cheeks as she remembered the ro-geese.

In front of the house, said Zuri, there was a channel of blue water dug from the great irrigation ditch of the Pharaoh Seti. 'At night you could hear only the splashing of the waves,' he said, 'the little waves of the blue Nile water, splash splash splash against the bank of the canal. It was only ever unpeaceful,' he added, 'when the drunken badger-worshippers went past in their barges, playing on flutes and castanets, their priests bending over and hitching up their robes to reveal their arses.'

'A truly wonderful house!' cried Gideon.

'Yes,' cried Zuri.

'Your house has been burned down!' cried Gideon.

'Yes, it has burned down!' cried Zuri.

'It has been burned down by the Egyptians.'

'Oh, it was a house that one could not tire of!' cried Zuri. 'It was a house where a man could be gay at the portal' – he wept – 'and drunk in the hall!'

Esther wept, Ruth wept. Giliad wept.

When Shelumiel returned, Ruth said, 'The house in Goshen is burned down', but Shelumiel was not interested. He said, 'Don't talk about Goshen. The Levites are offended that people still worship gods other than the God Yahweh. Tell him to keep hidden his statues and images. I'm going back to the flock. Make sure a watch is kept on the oxen.'

That night Zuri said to her, 'My house is burned down and there is nothing to see me into the Afterworld.'

Ruth said nothing.

Zuri said, 'Where does the God of the Levites say we will go to after death? If Osiris is not a god, then how can we go to the Land of Osiris when we die? Oh, we are mad to follow the Levites into the Wilderness! The Egyptians always gave us shelter. Joseph was a high steward to Potiphar. Where are we to go to after death? Where are we to go to if we die in the Wilderness? I want to see Shelumiel.'

121

Ruth looked at him. She felt lost, desolate. She went out of the tent and down to the salt marsh. Shelumiel was with the shepherds, worrying about the lack of pasture. He was tense with worry, his face white with dust. He was gulping down his wine and calling for more, tipping up the goatskin and squeezing it dry. Soon, she thought, there would be no more wine, however loudly he called. Where would they find wine at Marah? How could they brew beer without bread and barley? She told Shelumiel that his father wanted to see him, then followed him back.

Esther was tending the fire. Giliad was grinding barley grain, but for cakes not for beer. Ruth started to prepare a stew of lentils and beans and garlic.

'He is living in the past, your husband,' said Shelumiel later, coming out of the tent.

'How are the sheep?'

'We had four-score fat sheep when we left Baal-Zephon. Now we have four-score creatures of skin and bone.'

He sat by the fire. He was watching her, but perhaps he was thinking of other things. She stirred the stew, showing him her wifeliness. None of Zuri's other wives were here to take care of him in the Wilderness. His other wives had died of the plague, but she had not died.

'Your husband is living in the past,' repeated Shelumiel, sighing.

Yes, he was living in the past. He was sitting in his tent, looking out over the palms of Marah, the salt marsh and the distant Yam Suf, but in reality, the reality of his mind, he was living in the days of his youth, when he was superintendent of the granary, measuring the standing crops before the harvest, reporting to the Vizier of Goshen. He was remembering how his father's father was superintendent of absenteeism in the Valley of the Dead, at the time of Akhenaten. Night after night he sat over his thin wine with Shedeur the Reubenite. They talked about the things that they had left, the leavened bread and strong, thick beer – beer so sustaining that you had to strain it into the mug, or eat it with a spoon. They spoke of the fresh, shining fish of Goshen, the fish with oily flesh that the true Egyptians would not eat. They talked of the salt cakes and the wines of Ethiopia. They talked about their treasures, their *belongings* brought from the Black Lands, and about the *belongings* of the other tribes.

Old Enan of the house of Naphtali, he of the shrewish wife, had seven snuff dishes made out of pure gold, which was a scandal, for the Naphtali had always been poor – mere brick-makers, like the men of Korah (made out of the clay they worked with, said the wits). 'These are our *belongings*,' said the people of Naphtali, but everybody knew they had stolen their belongings from the Egyptians. Old Enan, it was said, had gone to the house of a scribe and the scribe's wife had given him the snuff dishes so that he would not make frogs fall from the sky.

Zuri and Shedeur laughed at that, but it was a bitter joke. Frightening Egyptian housewives had been the downfall of them all.

Ruth lay by the fire, half dozing, half dreaming, listening to their tales of woe. In Memphis, she knew, frogs had once truly fallen from the sky. The sky had truly rained small green frogs, frogs no bigger than a thumbnail. Many people had gone crazy with fear.

Everybody knew that this had happened. But why the Egyptians blamed the Israelites for making frogs fall from the sky, she did not know.

A boy from Gad, Wolf, the son of Eli, appeared at the hearth. A lock of his hair was braided, bound with gold wire, falling over his face in the high fashion. Rebecca nearly swooned. Wolf sat and talked to Giliad and did not look anybody else in the face or acknowledge their existence. When he had gone, Rebecca said, 'That Wolf was kind to me once on the road from Goshen.'

'The boy who was kind to you,' said Ruth, remembering the serpent, 'was a Danite, the son of Ahiezer.'

'Wolf was kind to me as well,' said Rebecca.

Zuri was offended because the boy had not spoken to him, not offered the greetings of his father or even his grandfather, Deuel. The boy had no manners, said Zuri, and should have been beaten more when he was small. 'The ear of a boy is situated on his back,' he said to Ruth. She said, 'What do you expect from Gadites? What do you expect from common ignorant people who wear gold wire in their hair and call their children after animals and birds?'

It was something the Egyptian lower-class people were always doing. Wolf, Lion, Crocodile for boys; Lark, Rabbit, Butterfly for girls.

Rebecca's lip trembled. She had been called Mouse when she was small. Her family, who were ordinary herdsmen, had called her Mouse. 'You are our Mouse,' they had said to her, 'our little lovely Mouse.'

Next day she was ill and lay clutching her stomach. A Levite priest spoke to her gently, then sent the midwife Puah to see her. The midwife examined her and put her hand on her stomach and peered into her eyes and examined the skin of her hands and felt her ankles.

Esther cried, 'Is it a serpent?'

Puah replied. 'Of course it's a serpent. She has a snake in her belly.'

They got thick bread beer from the Reubenites and squeezed date juice into it. They put in dried carob beans and castor oil. When the beans were swollen they made Rebecca, Mouse, drink it up.

For two days she lay by some rocks, shaded from the sun, and groaned. Once Wolf came and looked at her, from a distance, with Giliad, and she stopped groaning when he was there. Once, during the night, they heard her scream, and Esther went to her with more beer seething with carob beans and date juice. Then, on the third day, in the first light of morning, they found her back sitting by the fire. Esther said she had given birth to the snake. The snake had come out of her dead, said Esther – it had been a thin, smudgy snake with grey-white coils and Rebecca had buried it in the sand.

After that Rebecca sat by the fire, exhausted, for a long time. Esther said she was mourning the death of her snake child.

They spent two weeks at Marah; twenty-two days. At dusk, every night, Ruth watched the sand antelope. The creatures came so close, in their desperation for water, that Shelumiel led men to shoot them with arrows; but they were too cunning to be caught.

One morning, when Giliad was grinding the flour and Ruth was making the cakes, the air smelled of water, and the sky was grey and heavy over Ti. Ruth wondered about the families who had gone north on the Way of the Philistines. She wondered if they had been attacked by the Egyptians, or were even now drinking the milk and eating the honey of Canaan.

Another morning, as she made the cakes in the ashes, she saw her *bedu*, sitting on his donkey on a sand dune.

'There is nothing to say it is your *bedu*,' said Esther.

'Do not tell me it is not my *bedu*,' Ruth said.

The moon had died. The wells were dry. Tomorrow they would set out again on their journey to the Springs of Ophir. Some families said they wanted to go east, along the Way of the Hajji, into the Mountains of Ti. The bedouin, they said, knew of a path through the mountains. Again the Levite priests scurried around the campfires of the tribes – some said they had threatened to kill the elders of families who wanted to go along the Way of the Hajji, or send them into the mountains without oxen. But in the night twelve of the families went.

Some of the elders of Reuben also wanted to go along the Way of the Hajji. They said they feared the slave road to Khadem, with its wells and date palms, and sweet flowering mimosa. They said they feared that the slave road would take them all to Khadem whether they wanted to go there or not. Some said that Moses' God, Yahweh, was an Egyptian god, and was taking them all to the slave mines.

Nevertheless, when the time came, they packed their tents and loaded their sledges, and began to move south along the slave road – the families of Simeon, and of Reuben, and of Gershon and, some distance behind them, of Benjamin. South with the other tribes of Israel; with Judah and Zebulun, with Gad and Dan, with the brick-makers of Korah, with the Asherites, who still had their *Living Goddess*; and with Miriam and her beauties. With the Soldier. With the Levites, who carried Joseph's bones.

'Who is like to thee, O Yahweh, among the Gods? Who is like to thee, glorious in holiness, fearful in praises, doing wonders?' cried the Levites, running back and forth, thin and ragged, but seemingly the more passionate the more ragged and thin and hungry they got. Yahweh would save them! They had only to trust him!

South they went, along the coast of the Yam Suf.

7
Cabaret at Giza

She was lying by the pool, wearing a white one-piece that showed off her tan. Mac, lying next to her, was skinny but muscular. Beyond the hotel a massive grey triangle hung in the haze of smog. It was the Great Pyramid of Cheops, the first of the seven wonders of the ancient world, now providing a Disneyworld backdrop for the luxury hotels of Giza.

'Hi,' said Elizabeth. 'You had something to eat?'

He nodded and lay down on a sun lounger. She sat up and looked gloomily across the pool. She had a good figure, he thought; firm muscles, curvy and all-American where it mattered. A curtain of water was falling over an ice-blue concrete ledge, sending up a sparkling mist with a rainbow inside it. Two small children splashed and screamed in a restrained, self-conscious manner. Somewhere a mother shouted, 'Tasmin, Rupert, come out of the sun *now*.'

Elizabeth looked weary.

'I've got a week to crack this,' she said. 'One week and the dough runs out.'

'You can only do your best, Princess,' said Mac.

Richard still hadn't worked out where Mac fitted into the scheme of things. He had long since stopped wondering if he was a Harvard academic – reader, perhaps, in Byzantine Diplomacy? No, Mac was a mobster. But what was the Glasgow Mafia doing attached to an American physics project in Egypt, even a bizarre project like this?

'You ought to put some cream on, honey,' said Elizabeth solicitously. 'You need to get some of the high-protection baby stuff.'

'Yes,' said Mac, 'the sun's always more powerful than you think. They said that when I was a kid, and they hadn't even got round to stripping the ozone layer in those days.'

He put on his shirt. It was Hawaiian, covered in pineapples. A waiter came past. Mac said, 'What about a beer, then? A beer, a Stella beer?'

The waiter looked alarmed and backed away.

Elizabeth said, 'Chuck it, Mac.'

Mac said, 'They must have some stuff hidden away. It's only been a week. What must it have been like on the last night, eh? I'll bet half Cairo was pissed to buggery.'

He got up and wandered off into the hotel, perhaps to sniff out the last miniature Scotch whisky, the last dregs of bourbon. The woman, a diplomat's wife, Richard guessed, took her children in. The pool was empty, the water settled, bright and clear as glass.

Richard said, 'What happens now?'

She said, 'We're trying to trace the tank commander. We know he's in Sinai; we don't know exactly where.'

'You think he can tell you anything useful? Anything he didn't come out with at the debriefing or at his court martial, or tell the psychiatrists?'

'We don't know what he said to the army people or the psychiatrists. There's been a cover-up. A cover-up that's been going on for over twenty years.'

'The conspiracy theory of history,' said Richard. 'I've always inclined to the cock-up theory myself.'

'Don't be clever, Rich,' she said evenly. 'I've enough to cope with.' She inspected her toenails. 'Thanks for looking at Elmer.'

'That's OK.'

'You've seen the copy of the tattoo markings I gave you?'

'I'll need to check them out in London.'

'A Child of the Kap, yeah?'

'It could be.'

They sat in silence. It wasn't the tattoo marking that most puzzled him. It was the autopsy report on the corpse's teeth erosion. OK, if it was a genuine corpse from the nineteenth dynasty it made sense – in Pharaonic Egypt they ground their corn on stone saddle querns and ate vast quantities of sand with their food; even a boy of thirteen of fourteen might expect damage to the enamel of his teeth – but a late twentieth-century youth couldn't possibly get his teeth in that state, not by dressing up and living like an ancient Egyptian soldier for a couple of weeks.

If it was a hoax, it was a very elaborate hoax.

But how could it be genuine? How could a body have been preserved, in that state, for over three thousand years?

He thought of Lindow Man, now resident in the British Museum, of the skeletal arms, the kippered leathery skin that had become as one with the flesh-less bones. Elmer, according to Elizabeth, was older than Lindow Man, but his muscles were still set in the paralysis of rigor mortis. His skin, though dulled by twentieth-century preservatives, was entire.

A waiter brought coffee that Mac must have ordered. Richard said, 'OK. This tank commander, tell me what you know about him.'

She looked at him foxily. Then she said, 'You're not flying back to London?'

'We agreed three days.'

'Great. Rich, that's great.' She smiled warmly.

'Anyway,' he said, 'I haven't been paid.'

'His name is Sayed El-Prince,' she said, not reaching for a cheque book. 'He was twenty-seven years old in 1973, a major on General Ismail's headquarters staff, a high-flyer who transferred from the élite Fourteenth Mechanized Infantry Corps at Alexandria. He'd done a year at Sandhurst and would have done a tank school at West Point if US military cooperation hadn't been cut in '72. On the afternoon of 6 October he led a tank squadron over the first bridge thrown over the canal at El-Shalufa, following directly behind the Egyptian commandos. At some point in the next few days he penetrated down the coast. He led his squadron into action in the Somar Wadi and forced the Israelis to retreat. They were having trouble with fuel by this time. They had to hole up for twelve hours till a leaguer could catch up – is that right, a leaguer?'

'I wouldn't know.'

'Anyway, a fuel compound. On 16 October we know that he was pushing eastward. In the early evening, at a location we haven't been able to establish precisely, he led his tanks in an attack on an Israeli gun position. Ali says it was somewhere in a pass called El-Garf, up the Wadi Gharandal, but I'm beginning to believe he's not that reliable, I'm beginning to think he'd say anything for five bucks. We know they were definitely south of the Mitla Pass, and they can't have been further east than El-Tîh, because that was the extent of Egyptian penetration. Wherever it was, El-Prince claims that he was going into attack in column formation when his cannon suddenly started firing without any order having been given. A moment after that he ran his T-55 into an Israeli anti-tank ditch that wasn't actually there. The six other T-55s behind him were thrown into confusion. The Israeli guns had them in range. Two tanks were taken out by HEAT missiles. Another ran into an anti-tank mine. El-Prince claims he tried to send a signal "break contact" but no other tank admits to having received it; we don't know, nobody was keeping a tape of localized radio traffic. The other tanks managed to retreat. Immediately after the incident El-Prince was said to have babbled incoherently about *ghosts*. That was what did for him. Three tanks had been lost. Fourteen tank crew had died. A second attempt on the Israeli position, later that day, failed. As far as that sector of the front was concerned, it was the turning point. From that moment in time, in central Sinai, *the Israelis stopped running.*'

'All this,' said Richard, 'is a matter of public record?'

'Like shit it is. You think in October 1973 the Egyptians were going to announce that one of their tank squadrons had stopped fighting because they'd seen ghosts? My God, they didn't dare let a story like that get out. It was red hot, it's still red hot *now* – 6 October is about the only day of national pride in the Egyptian calendar. It was the day they licked the Israelis, and would have gone on licking them if the US hadn't piled in with the hardware and the ammo – that's what they think anyway.'

'I know what the Egyptians think.'

'El-Prince was court-martialled in secret, saved from death by family influence, sentenced to thirty years. After a few months he was moved to an asylum; classifying him insane was the safest option. As for the rest of his tank crew, the trouble was they didn't think fast enough. They supported his story. They said the gun's firing mechanism worked of its own accord. They said their weapons-ranging equipment went haywire. They swore the experimental thermal-imaging radar screen was covered in red heat dots. One crew member claimed to have heard a weird noise like *trumpets*, despite his earpads and the noise of the tank's engine. The radio operator – well, you've heard what the radio operator had to say. They were all quietly thrown out of the army. Think about it, Rich. Dismissed without honour from the army of Egypt in October '73. Think what a very terrible thing that must have been.'

Ali, more than twenty years later, living with his family in the City of the Dead.

'Ali's the lucky one,' said Elizabeth, reading his mind. 'The other three members of his crew have disappeared.'

Again they sat in silence. A barman walked across a little bridge to the bar, which was on an island in the middle of the pool. He put out brightly coloured fruit-juice drinks to tempt customers: mango, pomegranate, pineapple; their icy-coldness frosting the glass. The trouble was, there were no customers about.

Elizabeth said quietly, 'This thing, whatever it is, happening in Sinai. Some people say it goes back a long way.'

She was watching him cautiously.

134

'Go on.'

'Right back to the mystics, who set themselves up in caves round the Jebel Musa and levitated, disappeared, spoke with tongues, existed on air. Then in Victorian times – you've heard of Professor Edward Palmer, who mapped out the route of the Exodus, then disappeared with his companions in Sinai in 1882?'

'Yes. He was a British secret service agent, carrying twenty thousand gold sovereigns for the bedouin.'

'Maybe, but those bodies disappeared for *weeks* and those skeletons they finally brought back to London, well I'd like to dig those skeletons out of the crypt of St Paul's and do a DNA test. I'd be very interested in that. Strutt was Cavendish Professor of Physics at Cambridge at the time and he didn't like it.'

Richard said, 'Yeah, right', in a noncommittal sort of way.

'You know what Strutt said to the Society for Psychical Research? Scientists, he said, should concern themselves with phenomena which lie *just outside* convention's boundaries. Well, that's where I am, Rich. But I'm not going back to Palmer's day, or to the nuts in the cave. I'm talking the last thirty years. I'm talking physical phenomena since the Israelis put down a blanket of sound sensors after the Six Day War, right down the west coast and the mountains. There are files in Tel Aviv I'd like to get my hands on. There are files with the UN Peacekeepers who were put into Sinai in '73. The thing you have to remember, Rich, is that Sinai was ignored from Pharaonic times till the Six Day War. Armies passed along the north coastal plain, nobody went south. Who knew, or cared, if a few bedouin disappeared, *vanished* into thin air; who cared if nuts living in caves round the Jebel Musa *levitated* themselves or spoke in tongues? But listen, Rich, has it never struck you as strange that Sinai, this little desert of rocks and sand, is holy to three of the world's greatest religions? Has it never struck you that there must be something very special, something *supernatural* about the place?'

Well, no, it hadn't struck him, not for a moment. But it wasn't worth arguing about. 'You don't need to convince me,' he said. 'I'm on the payroll, I'm not worth convincing. There's no point in expending the energy.'

'It's just easier, that's all,' she said. 'It's just that bit easier when you've such a fight on your hands, if the people actually with you are actually on your side. I don't think the pyramids are beacons for spaceships, Rich, but I do think that the behaviour, the *behavioural possibilities* of subatomic particles are still very little understood. I think ghosts are leaving prints in the sands of Sinai.'

He was expected to say something. He said, 'Yeah, right.'

'Footprints in the sands of time.'

It was amazing, of course, how many physicists from reputable universities were getting mixed up in this sort of paranormal stuff. But, on the other hand, who could tell? The Great Pyramid of Cheops was a grey phantasm in the smog behind Elizabeth's head; and behind it, even fainter but virtually as large, loomed the Pyramid of Chephren, its summit still enrobed in its original white-cement casing. Who was to say that Cheops and Chephren had not, originally, had flashing red lights on their summits and lasers

136

beaming out into the galaxy? Perhaps there had been another hotel, here, on this very spot, an *intergalactic spaceport hotel* with specially designed beds for travellers with two heads and a large number of legs. Perhaps the animal gods of the ancient Egyptian world – Anubis, with his human body and jackal head; Thoth, the Moon God, with his baboon features; Sobek, with his bloody crocodile jaws; Bes, the ghastly cat-skinned squatting dwarf that guarded the ancient Egyptian marriage chamber – were no more than Holiday Inn guests of 2500 BC, passing travellers on the interplanetary trade.

She was staring at him.

'Yeah, right,' he said again.

'Oh,' she said, 'you unbeliever.'

'Honest sceptic,' he said.

Mac came wandering back.

'No news,' he said.

'Shit,' said Elizabeth St George. 'I'm running out of money. I hope you guys don't eat too much.'

'When I say no news, I mean no news about our friend from the funny farm. There's plenty of other news. There's been a rocket attack on Jerusalem that's killed twenty Jews.'

He sat down, taking off his Hawaiian shirt, opening a plastic bottle of baby cream.

Richard slept through the afternoon, stretched out on his bed with the air-conditioning full on. He woke around six and turned on the TV. NBC's world news showed Arab bodies on the West Bank after Israeli reprisals. In the States the Los Angeles Dodgers had pulled out an exciting 5–4 win over the San Francisco Giants. A Cairo English-language station was struggling to reconcile Muslim fundamentalism with the Egyptian government's stance over the past two decades. *What the world calls religious fanaticism and terrorism can now clearly be seen as an unfortunate response to the universal need for man to reunite with God. This is a global message. We must challenge Israel to reintegrate itself as a people of the Book, as a member of a larger family, not a prisoner of an isolated ghetto.*

He phoned Vronwy at the British Museum. He said, 'You were right.'

'What? You're in prison?'

'No, but it's all highly peculiar.'

He told her about Elmer. She said, 'Forget the thousand dollars. Get on the next plane. You can't afford to have your name linked to that sort of stuff.'

'My name's not going to be linked to anything.'

'Oh yeah? And what when she publishes a paper in some cranky American pseudo-scientific magazine with your name down as adviser?'

'As far as that goes the damage is done. I'm staying two more days. There's a guy she wants to talk to, if she can find out where he is. A guy who's had some experience of retrocognition.'

'Of what?'

'Retrocognition. Knowledge of the past, supernaturally acquired. I'll see you on Saturday, OK?'

She told him he was mad.

He called room service for some tea. He showered. He got a call on his phone. They wanted him down in the bar.

Mac was sitting over a Coke listening to a fat blonde singing 'Autumn Leaves'. Next to the bar a poster read: 'Rick and Cleo'. Cleo was singing of Sep-

138

tember, when leaves start to fall, in a soulful, consti-
pated voice. Rick, younger and more beautiful, in a
white dinner jacket, accompanied her on an electric
organ. She finished; the last note died away. She said,
'Thank you' with sincerity and dignity, although
nobody had clapped; indeed Mac was the only person
there apart from a middle-aged Arab in a suit.

Richard sat down and Mac said, 'Cheers, laddie',
which made him wonder if Mac was actually Scottish
at all. Cleo came down from her tiny stage and sat
with the Arab, who bought her a coffee. Her pink-
powdered bust trembled over her spangly dress like
Turkish delight. She looked fed up; so did Rick, who
remained on the little stage and drearily played on.
The poster promised that they would sing nightly and
announced in large letters that they were DIRECT FROM
LONDON. It didn't say that when they got back to
London they'd be booked into some big pub on the
river, some naff country club in Surrey, and a poster
would say 'Rick and Cleo. DIRECT FROM CAIRO.' Which
just went to show, thought Richard, that the grass
was always greener.

Mac said, 'She's a nice voice, very nice, and I'm
a connoisseur. I've worked with the greats. Barbra
Streisand, Madonna – you won't believe this, but
Madonna only revived "Material Girl" on my say-so.
I once escorted Richard Gere and his lady to Le Cap-
rice. They ask for me personally, some of them, when
they're in the UK.'

'You're a bodyguard?' said Richard, disappointed
that Mac wasn't a Harvard man after all.

'Surprised?' He looked pleased. 'It's a different
world these days, laddie. It's brain before brawn.
Forget about muscle-bound nightclub bouncers –

nobody hires boneheads unless they want to make a big splash, get their face in the papers. The best people want a cool professional, a guy who doesn't mix it with the paparazzi. Listen, what happens when you push a camera in some snapper's face these days, eh?'

'You knock the snapper's teeth out?'

'You end up on an assault charge. You end up in the nick and your employer is not best pleased. No, the best people want a protector with a good operational plan, a guy with a diploma in risk assessment. A guy with a good *vocational qualification*.'

He felt in his pocket, Richard wondered if he was going to produce his diploma. Instead he waved money at the barman, signalling for another Coke. He said, 'We're moving out.'

'Are you?' said Richard.

'The Princess,' said Mac, 'is packing.'

'I'm not going anywhere on your say-so.'

'Pack your trunk,' said Mac, amused, not upset, the very model of a gunman with a vocational qualification, 'like Nellie the Elephant did. The Princess'll call you.'

Richard ordered a mango-juice cocktail. On stage, Rick stopped playing and drank a coffee. Cleo, at the next table, was talking in a low monotone to the Arab: 'Some places treat you terribly. Some places don't even let you eat in the restaurant. Even if they do, it's the basic set meal and you can get really sick of ribs and salmon steaks and paw-paws after three weeks. This place is better than most. I'm not grumbling.'

Ah, but she was. Nobody made Barbra Streisand grab her evening bite in the staff canteen.

'At least it's not like North Korea,' said Cleo, 'where you go to do a cabaret for the President's son and find you're all alone with a fat boy who's got more hands than a centipede has legs.'

The Arab tutted, no, no, this was not like North Korea.

Cleo said, 'Mind you, he's the President now, has been for ages. He can have anything he likes. He had this weakness for young blonde girls, you know what I mean?'

The Arab looked politely puzzled, as if he couldn't imagine.

She said, 'Are you staying for a while?'

Yes, the Arab was staying. Cleo smiled, got up and went back on to the stage.

Elizabeth came into the bar, wandered over to them, sat down. She said quietly. 'He's working in Dahab, up the coast from Sharm el-Sheikh. He's under some sort of arrest; he can't leave south Sinai.'

Richard said, 'How did you find this out?'

'My guy in the police department.'

'Can we talk to him?'

'My police guy?' She was startled.

'The tank commander.'

'Nobody's *allowed* to talk to him. Anybody caught talking to him and he gets banged up in the asylum again. What's the Mukhabarat?'

'Egyptian Security Service,' said Mac. 'Nasty as the KGB, wicked as the Bulgars. Oh, they're a cruel race, the Egyptians.'

'The Mukhabarat apparently monitor flights into Sharm. Not just for our guy's benefit, I don't suppose. My police contact says there's a lot of military stuff at Râs Umm Sid. We'll have to drive down. Tonight.

You'll have to get the hire car back, Mac.'

'OK, Princess,' said Mac equably.

Richard said, 'So you're going to talk to El-Prince?'

'We've *got* to talk to him. He's the only one who actually saw anything.'

'Even if it gets him banged up in an asylum again?'

'We're not going to broadcast our visit, we're not going to announce it nationwide on TV.'

'What if he says fuck off?'

'Watch your language in front of the ladies,' said Mac.

'Fucking shut up, Mac.'

'Sure, Princess.'

'Rich, listen, please. You haven't quite got this yet. You haven't quite understood. We're not a bunch of cranks obsessed by psychokinesis and ESP. El-Prince will talk because he's been asked to talk, and because if he talks he'll get a US visa and work permit.'

'Your guy in the Cairo police department fixed that, did he?'

'Don't worry,' she said, 'your pretty little head.'

Richard wondered again about Drextel University's Department of Physics, its influence and its interests. He ought to have put a call through to the States; he ought to have checked it all out. He said, 'OK, but there are at least ten police traffic control points on the Sinai coast road, and passports are vetted at the Ahmed Hamdi tunnel.'

'But not by the Mukhabarat. We're tourists, we're going scuba-diving. Jesus, what is *that?*'

It was Cleo singing 'My Way'.

'Now, Ol' Blue Eyes,' said Mac fondly, 'is one star I never did work for.'

Elizabeth was harassed. She ran her hands

through her honey-blonde hair. She was wearing a tight-fitting sheath dress. Cleo, on the little stage, was looking down at her sourly.

'God knows, I don't want to cause El-Prince any trouble,' said Elizabeth. 'God knows he's had enough trouble in his life.'

Richard waited for Mac to say that man was born to trouble as the sparks flew upwards, or quote some incomprehensible dialect wisdom from his Glaswegian grandmother. Mac said nothing. He was staring at Cleo, entranced.

Elizabeth said sincerely, 'But we'll get him out, Rich. Whatever happens, we'll get him out, get him on a plane. Florida, Miami. He'll be OK in Miami.'

Richard looked at his watch: it was just after seven p.m. They'd get through to Sharm all right, but a dozen police posts would note their passing, note their passport numbers, feed their details into a Security Services computer, which wouldn't be any help to El-Prince at all.

'There's a better way to get to Sharm,' he said, 'if you want to be unobtrusive.'

'Yeah?'

'And it's cheaper.'

8
Nightbus to Sharm

It would soon be dark. Richard went out into the road and flagged down one of the old, battered taxis that cruised between the pyramids and the Cairo Hilton with a meter that didn't work. The driver insisted on showing him a postcard he'd been sent by some Norwegians. *To Muhammad*, it read, *the friendliest, nicest, honestest, driver in Cairo*. Mac came out of the hotel and went round the front of the car, checking up on things. He said, 'This guy's had his wipers pinched. I don't believe this city.' Elizabeth came out, tossing her hair back, sniffing the evening air, swatting at the official taxi drivers who were buzzing round her, complaining volubly and screaming that she would end up in a car *without air-conditioning*.

'We've got just over an hour,' Richard said. 'Let's go.'

They got in the car and moved off. Traffic was still heavy, long queues of vehicles caught behind donkey carts piled high with green fodder. Lights were coming on in open-fronted shops, bare bulbs dangling from dangerous-looking ropes of flex. Men stood on the pavement smoking cigarettes, or sat in the dust sucking on hookahs. On one street corner blue-uniformed, middle-class schoolgirls stood in a group, laughing and eating melon and pitta bread stuffed with meat. 'These crazy fundamentalists,' remarked Elizabeth, making her first disinterested observation on the politics of modern Egypt, 'will soon have those kids banged up indoors with scarves over their faces.' Small boys ran between the slow-moving cars selling bottles of Egyptian cola. There was a red haze, the sun's last rays caught in the dust of the city. They crossed the Nile over El-Tahir Bridge. A woman was curled up on the pavement; her two small children sat by her staring at the traffic, as they would sit and stare all night, unless they too curled up on the pavement and slept. The Nile was molten metal, dark pewter, the Nile Queen floating restaurant moored where Cleopatra's barge might once have moored. They passed the Mugamma Building, the Egyptian Civil Service headquarters, the place where Egyptians claimed there were more souls at rest than in the City of the Dead.

Mac said, 'How long have we got?'

Richard said, 'Just over twenty minutes.'

Soon they were on the flyover that crossed the necropolis, looking down on a land in deep shadows, the sun touching only the very top of the minarets of the funerary mosques.

Elizabeth said, 'That little girl, that little Kareema, it's not right a kid growing up in a place like that. I'm going to fix some more money for her dad, see if the embassy can't do something, get her on a Unicef training scheme of some kind.'

The taxi driver, Muhammad, offered to sell them two lucky gold amulets from the chamber of Queen Hatsheput, twenty dollars each or thirty-five dollars the pair, a special price only because they were his very good friends; OK, twenty dollars the pair, *no problem*.

'Tell him to be quiet,' said Elizabeth.

'OK, OK,' said Muhammad, 'five dollars just for the one.'

'Shut up,' said Elizabeth.

'We're on the road to the airport,' said Richard, after a moment. 'We're going the wrong way.'

'What?' said Elizabeth. 'What did you say?'

The taxi driver said, 'Airport. International terminal. Airport.'

'No, we didn't say airport,' said Richard. 'We've already talked this one through.'

'The airport?' shouted Elizabeth. 'What do you mean we're going to the airport?'

'You don't want the airport?'

'We don't want the airport.'

'Sharm el-Sheikh? We go to Sharm el-Sheikh? Yeah, OK, we go to Sharm el-Sheikh.'

'No, not Sharm el-Sheikh,' said Richard.

'Sharm el-Sheikh, *no problem.*'

'If he says no problem one more time I'll fucking kill him,' said Elizabeth.

Richard spoke in Arabic. The taxi driver was impressed. The taxi turned into the traffic. Horns blared. 'Oh, Christ,' said Mac.

They headed east. Mac stared out of the window, counting cars with their wipers missing. The last of the sun was shining on the Moqattam Hills, the radar mast was a sliver of shining silver, spearing the dark-blue sky. They were in the eastern suburbs beyond the necropolis and the Citadel; the poor suburbs where tourists never came. They pulled into a compound. There was a dusty concrete block building.

Armed police patrolled the wire fence. They were five kilometres and a world away from the cool marble and fountains of the Forte Grand hotel at Giza. A sign, in flaking paint, said EAST DELTA BUS CO.

The bus had once been painted in cream and green, and these colours could just, but only just, be discerned through the thick dust. The casing had been taken off its engine, which was rattling noisily and spewing out fumes.

'Is that the transportation?' said Elizabeth, awed.

They went to the ticket office. They were told that the bus was fully booked. The next bust to Sharm would depart at six a.m. and tickets would be ten US dollars each. After only token haggling Richard paid sixty dollars and three men obligingly agreed to spend another night in the big city.

They climbed on board. A damp, leaden heat enveloped them. Curtains were drawn against all the windows. Men were asleep, their feet sprawled across the central aisle, several of them already snoring. They found their seats, which were widely separated. Richard squeezed himself down. There was less leg room than on an economy charter flight. As his eyes grew accustomed to the gloom, he saw that the plastic cup holder on the seatback in front of him was broken and the upholstery was thick with grease and dotted with cigarette burns. Flies buzzed in the darkness. Most of the passengers, he guessed, were construction workers heading for Sharm el-Sheikh. Some might be military – private soldiers going to their units.

Time passed. Eventually the bus driver climbed on board, the door was closed and the bus pulled out into the night traffic, heading due east on the Suez highway.

It should have been cooler, but it wasn[...] [...]
engine made a dull blanket of sound.

Richard dozed, but his mind worked at [...]
time.

What, exactly, was he being asked to acce[...]

Forget for a moment about the corpse in the Cairo morgue. Forget time transference, he'd bend his mind round time transference later. Forget the 'experiences of retrocognition' claimed by this ex-tank commander, Sayed El-Prince. His mind went back to the Desert Oasis, to the last, dying moments of Herr Gabriel; to those words gasped out in a high-pitched Amorite, early Coptic tongue, a language that Richard had never before heard spoken.

The eye of Horus is your protection; it spreads its protection over you, it fells all your enemies for you, and your enemies have indeed fallen to you.

To your ka, O Osiris!

Richard moved uneasily.

A theory that might have sounded absurd in a London hotel sounded less implausible here in the Egyptian night, here in the fetid, tomb-stench heat, in the place where the spirits of dead men and women had been released to roam for four thousand years.

The ka was not only the spiritual but the physical double. It could be released during life in dreams – but it was firmly, irrevocably, released at death by the Ceremony of the Opening of the Mouth, a ceremony carried out by the priests of Ptah.

How was it that Herr Gabriel, in his last moments on earth, had been suddenly able to speak so fluently in a language that was dying out in the time of the Romans, that had not been commonly used since the days of Herodotus?

149

here was the ka of Ka-nefer now?

The bus had stopped, the engine still running. Eyes opened. He leant over the sleeping man next to him and pulled aside the curtain. Outside was a vast park of empty concrete. A solitary donkey stood under the floodlights. They were going through a military checkpoint. A red and white striped barrier was raised, a policeman with a Maadi AK47 waved them through.

The faint lights of the last Cairo suburb fell behind them. Ahead, lay the blackness of the desert. He dropped the curtain. He closed his eyes again. In his mind, unbidden, came the words of the *Book of the Dead*, the spells against oblivion, against the dying of the light.

O Horus, son of Isis, make me hale as you made yourself hale. Release me, loose me, put me on earth, cause me to be loved. I am the weneb-flower of Naref, the nebheh-flower of the hidden horizon, so says Osiris.

My hair is Nun; my face is Re!

My eyes are Hathor; my ears are Wapwawet; my lips are Anubis!

My arms are the Ram, the Lord of Mendes; my breast is Neith, Lady of Saits; my back is Seth!

My phallus is Osiris!

My feet are Ptah, and Thoth is the protection of all my flesh.

Ka-nefer was alive. Ka-nefer was alive and it was the voice of Ka-nefer that had spoken.

I am he in whom is the Sacred Eye, namely the Closed Eye. I am under its protection. I have gone out. I have risen up. I am alive.

I am alive.

I am alive.

There was a blast of sound, a flash of light, a massive wail. Richard's eyes shot open. Lurid colours leapt
from a television perched up over the driver's head.
On the screen came the caption, EGYPT VIDEO SERVICES.

Travellers stirred, sat up, opened little packages by
the flashing psychedelic light of the screen, started
to eat bread and hard-boiled eggs.

The film was an Egyptian musical comedy. A
middle-aged man with a stout and apparently cor-
seted stomach was wandering through Cairo's Botan-
ical Gardens singing about love.

Elizabeth came down the aisle.

'Rich?' she said. 'Rich?'

'Yes.'

'For just how long are we in this bus?'

'Seven hours.'

She stood for a few moments. She was blocking the
aisle, blocking off the view, but nobody complained,
they peered round her, tolerant of foreigners. She
turned and walked back up the aisle.

Richard closed his eyes. At the Ahmed Hamdi
tunnel the police gave only a cursory look at passports. Just after midnight they crossed under the
canal into Sinai. The video had finished. People dozed.
As they set off again down the coast road a new video
came on. It was a comedy about an Egyptian Laurel
and Hardy couple who had unaccountably been put in
charge of a suitcase full of money and were wandering
round Cairo with it, getting into incredibly funny
situations.

Travellers chuckled and roared. Flies buzzed. The
air was full of cigarette smoke and a sweet stench
that Richard put down, at first, to hard-boiled eggs.
Elizabeth came back down the aisle again.

151

Richard said, 'We're crossing the Wilderness of Shur. Are you by a window? Can you pull back the curtain? In Pharaonic times a road ran down to the slave mines at Sarabit el-Khâdem. We'll soon pass Uyûn Mûsa, the Springs of Moses. There used to be ten springs at Uyûn Mûsa, back in Palmer's day, although only two of them had drinking water. None of them has water now. It might well have been the biblical Marah, though I'm not convinced myself. This is the only road south, though. This is the way your Elmer must have come.'

She said, 'Never mind Elmer.'

He hoped she wasn't going to complain about the film.

'A man has come out of the washroom,' she said in a calm voice, 'with a black plastic bag full of shit. Even the most backward peasant ought to know that the toilet should be emptied from the outside, preferably when the bus is not moving. This is a Third World country, it is not a Third World bus.'

He said, 'What do you want me to do?'

She stood silent.

After some moments Richard stood up. She promptly sat down in his seat. He went to the back of the bus. He passed Mac, who was dead to the world, missing the video, missing the really funny bits. An Egyptian was sitting with a black plastic sack wedged in the open lavatory door, presumably because he could find nowhere else to put it. There was no reason to think it contained anything other than his worldly belongings, although Elizabeth could have been right, he could have been helping himself to a bag of free fertilizer.

He sat in Elizabeth's place.

152

At two a.m. the bus pulled off the road. They were at Sudr, a dozen single-storey concrete blockhouses half a kilometre from the sea, grouped round a couple of weary palm trees. Everybody got out, stretched. The air was cool. There was a coffee stall lit by a naked bulb. A dozen bedouin women, veiled, sat in the sand; the Cairo bus, even the night-service Cairo bus, was an event not to be missed. A bedouin served Turkish coffee and cola drinks.

Richard got himself a coffee. The smell on the night air brought back memories – the Pennsylvania University dig in the East Central Jordan Valley when he was a nineteen-year-old student. It had been his first visit to the Middle East, his first experience of the desert, his first taste of Turkish coffee, of kebabs and bean soup and smoky green tea brewed over a fire of thorn bushes; his first experience of many things, he thought, reflecting on a girl from Maryland called Suzy.

The British Museum had taken over the dig now; in the cubby-hole next to Worboys's in the bowels of the British Museum, Richard sometimes looked at the latest finds brought home from Jordan by the curator for Syria and Palestine.

He wandered away from the bus passengers, away from the lighted coffee stall, out into the desert, towards the sea. This was the mouth of the Wadi Lahata. He stumbled across a trickle of water, a red-rust pipe jutting out of the sandy bank. There were palms here, three of them, and a sad, tired tamarisk with empty cola cans round its roots. There was a misty moon over the Gulf of Suez, lights of a ship out at sea, seen across an area of swamp.

Elizabeth's voice called, 'Rich?'

She was stumbling about, looking for him. He stood still, in the darkness, under the weary, barren palm.

She called, 'Oh, for Christ's sake.'

She really ought not to keep saying that. For every hundred Muslims schooled in the gentle, philosophic teachings of the faith, there was one consumed by the burning creed of the ayatollahs, trembling to stick a knife in the back of the blasphemer.

He called. 'Over here.'

She was shivering. A cool wind was blowing down from the mountains of central Sinai, from the plateau of El-Tîh.

'Rich?'

'Yes?'

'You do realize –' the voice of someone breaking the news that his entire family, including his dog, is missing, believed dead – 'that we are less than half-way to Sharm el-Sheikh?'

'That's right.'

'We've been travelling for four hours,' she said, 'and a man back there says there is another five hours to go.'

'Look at it this way. It took the tribes of the Exodus a month to get this far.'

'They did not,' she said, 'have to watch Egyptian musicals on video. The Pharaohs might have ordered the killing of the Israelites' first-born and whipped their menfolk into slavery, Rich, but they did not go in for cruel and unusual punishments.'

She laughed suddenly. 'Hey, Rich!' She put her arms round his neck and kissed him. The wind blew her hair into his eyes like wet straw.

He kissed her back, politely.

'Elizabeth? Princess?'

A call on the wind. In a moment Mac would call 'Princess Elizabeth?' and they'd come and lock him up in the funny farm.

'Where the frigging hell are you? Elizabeth –' jealousy, suspicion, professional concern, a bodyguard without a body. 'Princess, the bus goes in two minutes.'

'Yeah. OK, Mac. We're coming.'

They headed back across the gritty sand, back up the Wadi Lahata towards the petrol station.

9
Dinkas

Chariots were coming. The bedouin boy could see the dust from their wheels. They were coming from Baal-Zephon, pounding down the slave road that led to the turquoise and copper mines of Khadem. They were coming after the Israelites who were camped at Laha, between the slave road and the Yam Suf. The bedouin leaders had warned the Israelites that the chariots would come. The Israelites had said 'Stay with us and help us to fight', but the bedouin had been hired as guides, not as cavalry, and five pieces of silver to the Springs of Ophir was poor payment for being slaughtered (not that the bedouin would truly go to the Springs of Ophir, which did not, as far as they knew, exist and which they privately understood to be whatever place they chose finally to abandon the Israelites.)

The chariots were coming. The boy, who was sitting on his donkey in the protection of the dunes, could see their dust rising in a cloud. They were the chariots of Najim, the consul of Migdol. Perhaps a royal messenger had been sent to Najim, from the Pharaoh in Memphis, telling him to sweep the border lands of vagrants and outlaw tribes. The bedouin boy had seen a royal messenger once, when his tribe had camped at Bahah by the coast of the Great Sea; he had seen the messenger ride his huge brown horse along the Way of the Philistines (that the Egyptian Army called the Way of Horus), carrying dispatches to the commander of the Army of Egypt in Ugarit. The bedouin boy had thought how glorious it would be, to be a royal messenger.

There were shouts, now, from the camps of the Israelites. He could hear screams from the tents. He could see women and children running towards the rocks. Men were driving the cattle and the sheep away, towards the foothills of Soh and the mountain called Budhi.

Where would the Pharaoh's charioteers strike? The camps of the tribes were spread over the plain, spread out over a huge area to gain what pasture there was – which was precious little, tough spindle grass along the coast, sickly green stuff along the wide valley and the stony banks of the Laha stream. The boy looked round, trying to identify the camp of the family of Zuri, of the tribe of Simeon. In the distance he saw the girl, the girl Ruth, hurry the young children into the old man's tent, which was a stupid thing to do – the tent would be no protection against the arrows of the bowmen who stood on the chariot platforms behind the charioteers.

The Pharaoh must have written to the sub prefect of Migdol. He must have said: 'Bring back the gold and jewellery plundered from Egypt!' The Israelites called it their *belongings*, but the Pharaoh in faraway Memphis had said: 'Bring back my *belongings*' and that was why the chariots were coming.

The girl should not have gone into the tent! She should have hidden in the rocks by the river, where the chariots could not go! But the boy did not think the Egyptians would get as far as the tents of the house of Zuri. They would come, before then, to the camps huddled by the track, and if they did wheel eastward they would first hit the camp of the Benjaminites; and the Benjaminites' hyenas were howling and shrieking like their owners, who were standing on rocks and waving and jumping up and down.

He turned back to watch the chariots. They were coming closer. Then he saw that they were not chariots at all but Dinkas; tall, thin, black-skinned Dinkas, who ran in a phalanx whilst their Egyptian officers rode on horses beside them.

He felt his heart thump with excitement. Dinkas regiments could run all day without resting. They killed without mercy. No men – not even the regiments of the Hittites – could withstand them.

The Dinkas stopped. They stood, panting for breath. They were coated with white desert grit, and sweat made black rivers down their bodies. Behind them stretched the road from Baal-Zephon, but they could not have come from so far – not on one march. Perhaps, thought the boy, they had come running through the night from the fort at Suz. Perhaps they had camped at Uyun, that the Israelites had called Marah – perhaps they had found the wells dry, and had come chasing after the Israelites, the *hapiru*, in fury.

He watched the senior officers ride forward.

There were two of them. They sat on their horses and pointed, casually, at the different families – at the herds of cattle and sheep being driven, still, towards the foothills of the mountain of Soh, and beyond that to the high fastness of Budhi. The boy thought how wonderful it would be to be an officer! Even an officer of Dinkas, he saw, wore a white kilt and a cape of dark blue.

The officers rode back to their troops. They shouted an order. The first two platoons of Dinkas spread out in a line. They beat on their shields.

There were screams of fear from the Israelites.

The Dinkas were forming a battle line. It was the first time the boy had seen men preparing to attack, preparing to attack and kill. He breathed quickly, his heart thumping faster than ever. Behind him – much further back into the dunes – were the other bedouin guides, but he was not worried, not frightened; the Dinkas, he thought, were not interested in a boy on a donkey. Suddenly he saw that the Dinkas were moving forward towards the Israelites, chanting as they beat on their shields, their officers riding in front of them.

Again they stopped.

From the nearest of the Israelite camps a man came riding forward on a mule. He was wearing Egyptian dress and a soldier's cloak. Soon he was alone in the open ground. He turned to look at the tribes behind him. Over the plain, stretching into the distance – stretching to the distant camp of the Levites – there must have been hundreds of Israelite men armed with staves and bows, and there were perhaps just two hundred Dinkas attacking them – a company, no more, and an under-strength company at that – two hundred men with two senior officers and four platoon commanders and a standard bearer.

But the Israelites were scattered in small groups.

The Dinkas were a compact, deadly force. A snake waiting to strike.

Everything was silent.

The man on the mule was looking at the Dinkas, then back at the Israelite men.

There was the distant bleat of sheep.

Overhead were ravens, turning slowly. They were looking to pick off weak members of the flocks, sickly lambs – for the lambs had begun to be born at Marah. The ravens had followed the tribes down the road by the Yam Suf. They would remain faithful, more faithful (a bitter shepherd of Naphtali had told the boy) than the black-cloaked bedouin.

In their camps, the Israelites waited.

Somewhere a child screamed.

The chief officers of Dinkas ignored the man on the mule. They looked round again at the camps nearest to the road. Then one of them pointed with his staff, pointed out the chosen prey, the family that was to be attacked.

The Dinkas wheeled. On a word of command they advanced, slowly, beating their shields. The boy waited for the men of the tribe to scatter, as they had at Raha – but this time the men of the tribe moved out to meet the Dinkas, to stand in front of their kraal.

The Egyptian officer yelled an order.

The Dinkas lowered their spears. They ran, silent and swift. Their spears rammed into the crude shields of the defenders. A small Israelite boy was raised, screaming, on the end of a spear, and the bedouin boy laughed.

The defenders were slaughtered. The Dinkas sliced through them, then jumped into the kraal. The Israelite soldier on the mule was shouting to the men of the other tribes. Some men were leaving their families and running towards him; but others were staying where they were, and from some tribes there were no men running forward at all.

Egyptian orders were being shouted. The Dinkas were reluctant to leave the kraal, the killing, but the Egyptian platoon commanders rode amongst them, and slowly the Dinkas retreated, loping back to the desert, carrying blankets, clothes, pots, waving their plunder in the air.

Behind them, now, Israelite men were forming up in a body, two, perhaps three hundred of them, facing the Dinkas.

The two senior Egyptian officers looked at the Israelites for a moment. They conferred.

Would they attack the Israelite men?

One of the senior officers gave a signal. The Dinkas closed ranks and moved slowly off to the Laha, where it ran down to the Yam Suf.

The men of Israel stood and watched as the Dinkas drank at the stream and filled their waterskins. It did not take them long. Before it was possible for even the bedouin to think of poisoning the waters of the Laha, they formed ranks and continued on their way, south down the slave road. They sang as they went.

Hurru is become a widow for Egypt.
Hurru is become a widow for Egypt.
Hurru is become a widow for Egypt.
Desolated is the Tehenu. Plundered is the Canaan.
The princes are prostrate saying mercy!

It was the campaign song of the First Regiment of the First division of Amun, of the Pharaoh's royal guard. Trust Dinkas, thought the boy with contempt, to sing such a song after killing the women of gypsies!

The Israelite men were now waving their wooden staves and shouting; making a brave show.

The Soldier had got down from his mule, and was walking among the dead.

The ravens were circling, lower and lower.

In the evening he saw the Simeonite girl leave her tent, the children behind her. He watched them walk along the bank of the Laha, searching for wood. They were not laughing and joking, not this time. He watched as they tugged feebly at thorn bushes, dragged branches listlessly across the sand, made a show of collecting fuel. The girl was thin, much thinnner than she had been at Raha. At Raha she had been plump and fat-cheeked. Eventually the children sat down, and the girl sat down with them. He splashed towards them through the muddy stream churned by the flocks of the tribes. The girl saw him but did not stand up.

'They have killed many of us,' she said. 'They have killed a family of Manmuleeh and a family of Amram; they have killed more than thirty of us. The men stood and did not flinch. The men stood firm and did not flinch against the Dinkas and the Dinkas killed them, and killed the women and children of the sons of Manmuleeh and the men and boys of the family of Amram.'

He said nothing.

'Well?' she said. '*Well*, O horse soldier, O slayer of Hittites?'

'Why do you go so slowly?' he asked, angrily. 'Where do you think you will find water that is free from Egyptians?'

She stood up. She turned away, bending down to collect wood. The Israelite children stared up at him accusingly. He said: 'Why do you say I have fought the Hittites? I have never said to you that I fought the Hittites.'

'No,' she said, not turning round, 'I don't think you have ever fought anybody.'

'I have fought many people!'

She turned and stared at him for a moment, then started pulling at a thorn bush. The children stared up at him reproachfully. He said: 'We are not in treaty with you. The bedouin have no treaty with the *hapiru*. We are guides, only guides.'

'Yes, you are only guides.'

One of the girls lay down on the rocks. She curled up with her hands between her knees, crying softly. It was the girl they had banished out into the desert for two days at Marah, the girl who had screamed in the night, and had given birth to a stillborn child.

Ruth turned wearily and said, 'Rebecca . . .'

From over the stream a woman of the camp – a woman with a *hapiru* woman's shriek – shouted angrily. The girl lying on the rocks did not move. She was shaking in all her limbs. The other small girl said, 'Come on, Mouse. Come on, Mouse.'

The boy said, 'It will be all right, Mouse.'

Ruth said, sharply: 'Rebecca!'

Rebecca, Mouse, stood up. She started to collect fuel, to pull at live, wiry branches of wild thyme. The other children got up to help her. It was stupid – they were in the wrong place. Here, down by the water, most of the wood was green and would not burn even if they did twist it from the branches; this was the end of winter, and many slaves going to Khadem had camped at the valley and stripped it of the easy dead wood.

Ruth had gathered an armful of twigs. She said: 'Listen, you can carry my wood, O horse soldier who has not killed a hundred Hittites.'

He stared at her. In the bedouin tribes it was the women who carried wood and drew water. It had always been so, and it would always be so; for as long as the sun and moon rose in the east of the world and fell in the west of the world, no man would be seen doing the job of a woman.

She was looking up at him. 'Well, O horse soldier?'

The children also had bundles of fuel, even Mouse now had armfuls of dead thistle. He was afraid that he would be seen carrying wood, or be asked to carry the wood of the children. But he was afraid, also, that the girl would fall over in the desert and die.

'What use are green branches?' he said. 'You need the roots of the dead tree.'

'I am not able,' she said, 'to pull out the roots of the dead tree.'

In the end he dismounted from his donkey, and pulled out a thorn bush. It took a long time, and he was soon drenched with sweat. She sat on a stone while he did it. Sometimes, glancing at her, he thought that she was watching him, sometimes he thought that she was far away, almost asleep.

'I hope,' she said, suddenly, 'that the Dinkas do not come again.'

He tugged at the thornbush. It was long dead, but its roots curled down under the stones of the desert. He finally pulled it out. Then he sat down, next to her on a rock, panting for breath.

'The Dinkas will not come back, surely?' she asked.

'No, they will not come back.'

Soon it would start to go dark. Even now red streaks were blazed across the sky over Misri. By the rocky shore of the Yam Suf men were digging a hole to bury the dead in the manner of the Israelites. Fires were being lit. He could see smoke rising from the distant camp of the Levites, the priests.

They were the clever ones, he thought. The Levites would not be lighting fires, cooking their meat, if the Dinkas were still in the area. The Levites sent out scouts, men they called Spies.

'Where do you come from?'

It was the boy, the boy called Giliad, the boy with the solemn, thin face and the refined, Egyptian accent.

'Where do I come from?' the bedouin boy repeated, warily. Then he said, 'Nakhi.'

'Is that in Ugarit?'

He shook his head, spitting contemptuously.

In due course he told them about Nakhi. He told them that he had once been to the Great Sea and had seen Lake Sirbonis, and had lived in a bedouin camp outside the fort of Bahah, which was the great way-station on the Way of Horus. He told them his ambition. It was to become an officer in the Egyptian Army, with a cloak of the King's blue, and to ride a brown horse.

'Would you order your Dinkas to kill us?' Ruth asked.

'I would not be an officer of Dinkas,' he told her. 'I would be an officer in the Division of Re, an officer in the Pharaoh's Own Regiment of Thebes.'

She laughed.

He stood up, got back on his donkey and rode away.

'Thank you, O horse soldier,' she called after him. 'O strong arm of women.'

He splashed his way back up the valley. When he looked back, he saw that she and the children were dragging the bush towards the tents of Simeon.

The tribes were settling for the night. The cattle had been brought back down from the foothills. Women and men were wailing at the camp the Dinkas had attacked. A cold wind was blowing down from Ti, and the Yam Suf was grey.

Just before darkness, sitting in the sand next to his donkey, the boy saw the man they called Lawgiver leave his tent and disappear along the valley and into the rocks on the slopes of Soh Mountain. The sun had gone, soon in the blackness Isis would be flying to and fro, seeking the parts of the body of Osiris torn apart by the jackal-god. The boy shivered, as he had when he saw the Dinkas. The Lawgiver was an Egyptian wizard, when all was said.

He rode his donkey back to the black tents of his tribe. He wondered how much longer he would be guiding the Israelites. How much longer it would be before the Israelites were too weak to defend themselves, and the bedouin took what they wanted and went back up into the mountains, back to Nakhi.

Ruth lay by the fire, next to Esther. Zuri called plaintively. He wanted her to sleep with him, in the tent, but she would not. He called out louder but she ignored him. Eventually he was quiet. She guessed that he was offering up a prayer to Bes the homemaker, or looking at his silver statue. She would not go in with him, not again, not while he possessed the image of a great priest. If Shelumiel knew she had disobeyed Zuri he would beat her. Although perhaps, on this occasion, he would not.

Again Zuri called, moaning sadly like an old billy goat for its mate.

After a while he slept.

Her *bedu* was called Jaha. His tribe came once from Ugarit, but lived now at a place called Nakhi. He had told her he had seen a camel. Was he telling the truth? He had told her there were camels in the mountains, but this could not be – camel were beasts of Canaan. Could Jaha have been to Canaan? Perhaps he had, thought Ruth. Perhaps she would see camels in Canaan, perhaps she would ride on a camel's back with her arms round its hump, and would drink milk from a gold cup and eat honey from a golden plate.

She told Esther what she thought might happen.

'You are in love,' said Esther, another Israelite whose head was stuffed with Egyptian stories of romance, 'with your *bedu*.'

In the night, the hyenas of the Benjaminites pulled many of the corpses from their pits and ate them. Next day the Benjaminites blamed Horubis, the Hyena God, worshipped by the people of the City of Migdol, and went round saying that nobody henceforth must eat the flesh of the hyena – hoping, as everyone knew, to keep the milk-fed hyena-flesh for themselves. Then word went round that camels, not hyena, had come during the night to drink at the stream of Laha, and had found and eaten the corpses of the Israelites.

The tribes moved their camps, from the sand dunes by the sea, to the rocks of the foothills of Soh.

A law came from Levites, saying that no son or daughter of the tribes of Israel might henceforth eat the flesh of the camel.

10
Snorkelling off Sharm

Jackson was a cargo ship caught fast on the reefs, a war victim, its sides massive and rust-stained, a landmark for the snorkelling boats and the scuba-diving boats from Sharm and Dahab. Over to the south, as they approached, they could see Tiran Island, home of mosquitoes, land mines and secretive Egyptian army units. An Egyptian navy patrol boat was edging round its isthmus. North of them, over the blue choppy waters, they could see the runway of Sharm's international airport. An Alitalia plane was slowly coming in to land, a tiny silver shape against the mountains of south Sinai. A second plane was circling over the mountains, on a path that would take it round over Mount Sinai itself, over the Jebel Musa and then back down to the Gulf of Aqaba.

The death toll on the West Bank was now over forty. Jericho was under dusk-to-dawn curfew, Gaza was in flames, and Arafat was in Israeli protective custody. Charter planes come to take the tourists home were queuing over Sharm el-Sheikh, Luxor and Hurghada.

The snorkellers from *Lady Carol* dropped over the side into the blue, clear water, yelling as the cold hit them, treading water as they spat into their goggles, then powering away, heads down, towards the shifting acid green and turquoise of the reef. This was their last day. They were due to be flown back home to Genoa at four p.m. They were making the most of their final hours.

'OK, in half an hour they're back. They sunbathe on deck; we give them lunch.'

El-Prince was whippet-thin. His hair was grey, his face deeply lined. He wore filthy jeans and a torn jersey, just like the bedouin sailor who was messing about in the galley. 'Until then sit down. Tell me how I can help you. Tell me what you want to know.'

He spoke lightly. But he already knew what they wanted to know. They wanted to know what he had seen on the night of 16 October 1973, that had led to his dismissal in disgrace from the élite Egyptian Tank Corps, his court-martial, his sentence of death.

He lit a cigarette. He stared at them, puffing blue-grey smoke. Eventually he said, 'And you can get me a visa to go to America?'

'We can get you a visa,' said Elizabeth. 'A work visa, a residence permit. It might classify you as a Cuban, but that's just to do with the quota.'

He inhaled carefully, then slowly exhaled the smoke, a man who had escaped one sentence of death, not afraid of another. The boat swung jerkily; it was choppy today out in the Straits of Tiran, even in the lee of the *Jackson*. The cabin stank of marine diesel oil and garlic. The bedouin hand was frying something up on the stove, throwing slices of yellow pepper into a meaty stewpot. Elizabeth, not a good sailor, looked round uneasily. She said, 'Does the chef speak English?'

El-Prince shook his head.

'OK,' said Elizabeth. 'Let's go back to 1973. You were a squadron commander in the 44th Tank Corps.'

El-Prince smiled faintly. Richard felt a sudden embarrassment. This man had been a *blood*, a soldier of the élite, of the cream of the officer corps. At the supreme moment, his life had been shattered. It was as if Patton had been falsely accused of some terrible, cowardly blunder in 1943 and been put into a lunatic asylum – reading in the newspapers about US Seventh Army taking Sicily; or Bradley had been tried for cowardice and treason, disgraced and dismissed, spending 1944 as a garage mechanic in Utah while US First Army was landing on the Normandy beaches.

'October 1973,' said Elizabeth. 'You were Headquarters Staff. You asked to be transferred to an active unit. You were sent back to your tank squadron on the night of 5 October.'

'No.'

'We've been through the records.'

'On the night of the fifth I was a reconnaissance observer with the Rangers that went across the canal to take out Israel's "secret weapon". A weapon the Russians had told us about, the Russian *James Bonds* had told us about, you know?'

'KGB,' said Mac, 'Fourth Directorate.'

'Yeah, KGB. You're a guy that knows these things?'

'He's a security expert,' said Elizabeth. 'He'll catch you out if you're not careful.'

'You think I'll tell you lies?'

'I wouldn't know,' said Elizabeth. 'I'm a Connecticut girl a long way from home.'

Richard said, 'What was this Israeli secret weapon,

173

so secret you and the Egyptian Corps knew all about it?'

'Thirty-nine storage tanks, each one containing two hundred gallons of spiked kerosene, a cocktail mixture that *fizzed*, specially prepared by Jewish scientists, with pipes running down to the canal, all ready and waiting to be turned on and ignited with thermite bombs. They planned to turn that oil on when we were half-way across the canal. They expected that oil to burn with temperatures of 700 degrees. They were going to fry us like sardines.'

'War's hell,' said Elizabeth.

'They must have got the idea off us,' said Mac modestly.

'Us?' said Elizabeth. 'Who's us?'

'The British. We were going to pour oil on the Channel in 1940, if the Germans invaded.'

'What happened?' asked Elizabeth, turning back to El-Prince. 'What happened to the fuel oil?'

'We cut the pipes or blocked the outlets with wet cement. Half of them wouldn't have worked anyway, the valves had been overtightened and rusted. You know, those Israeli kids didn't like being out there on the sharp end. Kids from university, kids from school, middle-class kids from Tel-Aviv. We took one of their patrols prisoner – know what they were?'

'Kids,' said Elizabeth. 'Let's try and keep to the story.'

'It's a myth, the Israeli soldier. They don't like fighting, they're no good at fighting. You know the only thing they have going for them?'

'American money, American technology,' Elizabeth said wearily. 'The night of 5 October 1973.'

'I was summoned back to Supreme Headquarters.'

He was staring down between his legs. His grizzled hair was thinning; he was starting to go bald. He said after a moment, 'I remember driving back towards Cairo, through the night, passing the convoys of bridging equipment heading east, passing the SAM missiles that were being taken up the canal. Nobody had told us what was happening, but nobody doubted what was happening! In Cairo, the last of the Soviet personnel were pulling out. We passed a line of coaches going from Gjizera Island to the airport. Brezhnev had sent twenty planes, down through Syria and Jordan, after dark when the satellites were blind. These were the diplomats, the scientists, the families of the advisers. I reached Supreme Headquarters just before o-four-hundred hours. The Headquarters staff of the assault division were called together by General Ismail. I was there. We were told that we were going to attack. I was one of those officers who vowed to succeed or die. To drive the Israelis from Egypt. I made that vow.'

'Yes,' said Elizabeth uneasily, her eyes flickering to the pan of beans and unidentifiable stuff stewing in oil. 'What happened then?'

'We all went out. We stood outside for a few moments. Then we rejoined our units.'

A last moment of camaraderie as the flush of dawn spread across the Delta. So it must have been, thought Richard, when the Pharaoh's commanders went out to meet the invading Hittites, the Hyskos raiders, the Sea Peoples.

'OK,' said Elizabeth, 'what then?'

The boat's radio came to life. A voice, young, male, Texan accent, said, 'This is a US warship. Our course and position are as follows – '

Joshua was sounding his trumpets and Jericho was falling. The PLO was holed up in the cellars, the fundamentalists were running riot, the Syrians were poised to cross the Jordan, and the US Navy was in the Gulf of Aqaba, keeping open the sea-lanes. It was as if The Stones were still singing 'Angie' and Nixon was in the White House, and Kissinger at the Department of State.

Elizabeth said, 'We haven't much time. You joined your unit.'

'I joined my unit.'

More cigarette smoke.

'Go on.'

'That was around fourteen hundred hours, when Sadat and Ismail were entering General Command Operations Centre. We were dug in five kilometres back from the Sweetwater Canal. During the early morning the water level had been lowered to prevent flooding if Israeli shells broke its banks. We were issued with chemically treated uniforms to reduce the effects of Israeli napalm.'

There were shouts from outside, from the water outside the portholes. People were clambering aboard.

Elizabeth said, 'Oh, shit. . .'

El-Prince rose, swung himself up and out through the hatchway. He was strong; he moved like a young man.

Richard said, 'Is this his boat?'

'No, he operates it for a firm in Eilat.'

'It's an Israeli boat?'

'There's a lot of Israeli money in Sinai.'

Richard looked out through the porthole. Other boats in the flotilla already had their passengers on board and were starting up their engines, turning towards Sharm el-Sheikh or Shark's Bay or Dahab. The sun was bright in a clear blue sky. Egyptian flags were stiff in the breeze. Some of the snorkellers were coming back to the *Lady Carol*, although others could still be seen nosing around among the shallow waters of the reef. The wind was getting stronger.

'OK, so what do you think?' said Elizabeth quietly.

'He's playing over the video,' said Richard, 'he's playing it over in his mind, re-running it for the million millionth time, trying to find the place the plot went wrong.'

'Does that matter?'

'The trouble is, the colours can change, subtly, only a little bit each time, until it's not quite the video it was. The little details, then the big details. He runs it so often the little confusions get ironed out. He ends up running the video as it ought to have been – not going through what actually happened but what he *thinks* ought to have happened. Then he can't figure out what he's doing on a Dahab fishing boat.'

'What's with the amateur psychiatry?' said Mac rudely.

'Memory plays false. It plays false for everybody. People swear that certain events happened in the summer, they can *see* the leaves on the trees and flowers in the gardens – but records show they happened in winter. Nobody can explain it. The mind assembles its own pictures, creates its own stories.'

'I would like to hear his story, the story he believes in,' said Elizabeth, stressed. 'I would just like to hear his story once before you debunk it, OK, Rich?'

'Brezhnev sent those planes on the night of the fourth,' said Mac. 'Our friend got the day wrong on that one. The Soviets were all scarpered by the night of the fifth.'

'They could have been the rearguard, the last out.'

'No,' said Mac.

'How would you know?' said Elizabeth.

'I read it up on the plane. You gave me the book to read,' said Mac.

Elizabeth looked as though she might start to cry, or might break something. Her eyes flickered over the huge pan of bean stew slopping about on the stove just inside the galley.

'God,' she said. 'God, I feel awful.'

El-Prince swung back into the cabin, shouting something to the bedouin in the galley. 'They're coming to eat,' he said, 'they're very excited. They say there's a shark down there, lying on the bottom.'

Elizabeth was dabbing at her mouth with a tissue.

'You OK?' said El-Prince.

'No.'

Richard said, 'How big is it? The shark?'

El-Prince shouted up the hatch in Italian. A bronzed girl leaned down into the cabin and held out her arms wide, like a fisherwoman boasting of her catch, her bikini top straining over her nipples.

'Very impressive,' said Richard politely.

'Yes,' said Mac.

'For fuck's sake,' said Elizabeth.

There were more excited shouts from outside, from the water. The Italian girl turned and went back on the deck. Everybody was shouting. Some snorkellers were splashing back down into the water again. Elizabeth said, 'I don't know if I'm believing this. Has nobody on this boat ever seen *Jaws*? Does nobody on this boat know what happens when you annoy one of those things? Does nobody know that Red Sea sharks are totally *vicious?*'

The cabin was rolling now; out of the window Richard could see white flecks on the waves.

'God, I feel ill.'

El-Prince said, 'You want to eat?'

She shook her head.

'In a few minutes we go back to Dahab.'

'But you won't talk to us in Dahab. You made us come on this boat.'

'We'll talk in Dahab.'

The last of the snorkellers came back on board. They all piled into the cabin to eat garlicky bean stew, chicken bits cooked in the ubiquitous red sauce of Sinai, sliced melon. They joked about the shark. From the ship's radio the US warship, which did not give its name or any indication of its size, was still calling out at intervals, alerting international shipping of its position, keeping open the sea-way to Israel.

Richard borrowed a mask. He went up on deck, slipped off his jeans and dropped over the side, keeping his shirt on to avoid sunburn. He paddled out from the boat, round in a circle. He saw no shark, but a school of turtles, stately as Spanish galleons, sailing through the green depths.

Half an hour later the *Lady Carol* was heading back to Dahab. The Italians sprawled over the deck, drinking in the sun, their suntans buffed and polished by the salty wind. One of them had a transistor radio and picked up a news summary: several foreign airlines had suspended flights to both Egypt and Israel. The Italians shouted to each other excitedly; perhaps they'd be stuck in Sharm for the duration of the war! Hey, what a shame, *what a shame.*

The boat slapped its way through the brisk waters. Elizabeth lay on the deck, face down, and rested her head on a towel, groaning. As they approached the shore the seas grew calmer. Eventually she went back down into the cabin, which still reeked of garlic and oil. She said doggedly, 'They'd lowered the level of the Sweetwater Canal. You'd been issued with chemically treated uniforms. What then?'

El-Prince gave her a cold, irritated look, then turned away.

'What if we can't talk to you tonight? What if something happens?'

He went up on deck, calling out to the bedouin, joking with the Italians.

She went up on deck after him. He was chatting in fluent Italian to the girl who had first reported the shark. He said, 'Hey, come and say hello to Maria.'

The girl said, 'Maria, Maria, you call all Italian girls Maria, yeah?'

'I'm a busy man.'

'So many girls to remember,' she said in a fine, ironic, tragic voice, 'so many names to forget.'

El-Prince grinned. 'Look, you see over there – on the other side of the helipad?' he said to Elizabeth. 'That's the bedouin hippie village. They smoke hash and make cheap souvenirs for the tourist trade. The Israelis built shacks for them to live in, those grey boxes you can see on the hillside made of breeze blocks, but the bedouin have put their black tents up behind each shack, and it's the tents they live in.'

Elizabeth said, 'You like the bedouin?'

'I am a bedouin. I am El-Prince.'

'El-Prince,' said the girl who might have been called

Maria. 'El-Prince. I'll call all the bedouin I ever meet El-Prince.'

'Ha, ha, ha,' laughed Mac, joining in the fun.

'Are there many bedouin,' said Elizabeth quietly, so that the girl could not hear, 'in the armed forces of Egypt?'

El-Prince looked tense. 'Have you never heard of the Desert Army?'

'That's Jordanian.'

'The bedouin don't take as much note of borders as some.' He pointed. 'If you look at the lighthouse at the edge of the village, that's the entrance to the dive site. But the best place is the Blue Hole, that right, Maria?'

'Yeah, that's right.'

'It's a deep pool in the coral. It goes down eighty metres, and at sixty-two metres there's an archway through the reef, into the open sea. It's deep and dangerous, and you can only go down at midday, when the sun is shining directly down.'

'There's something you can tell me, something I've always wanted to know,' said Mac, interestedly, to Maria. 'Scuba-diving is said to be better than sex and last a hell of a lot longer. Is that right, would you say?'

Maria looked at him. 'Well now,' she said, 'it depends on the sort of sex you have. Why don't you come down the Blue Hole with me and find out?'

She went to get her gear together. The *Lady Carol* was approaching the jetty. Mac said, 'Bloody hell, these Italians. You don't think she was making me some sort of offer there, do you?'

'Where can we talk?' asked Elizabeth.

El-Prince said, a statement not a question, 'We'll go to Sharm.'

'You OK to go to Sharm? Won't the cops see you with us?'

'You're tourists, you want to hire my boat. We'll go and walk along the promenade, take a meal. It looks good. It looks innocent.'

Mac watched as the Italian girls jumped up on to the jetty.

'Bloody hell,' he said, still musing about this and that.

They drove down the coast road. It was getting dark. Lights spangled both sides of Na'ama Bay, a necklace extending out round each headland. They parked and walked through the narrow alleyway of designer boutiques. People were strolling along the promenade, riding hire bikes, sitting drinking coffee and smoking hubble-bubble pipes under the huge banana palms that were laden with thick clusters of young green fruit. It was Italian Barbecue Night at the Hilton Village – smoky meat-juice smells and a live band – and it was Bedouin Night at the Movenpick Jolie Ville. At the Aquamarine they were offering grilled beef tenderloin, or, if that didn't tempt you, the *authentic Italian restaurant* offered stuffed baby chicken followed by Coupe Arabia, which comprised pistachio and chocolate ice-cream, with dates and whipped cream.

Tour leader Celia, Richard remembered, had gone for Coupe Arabia in a big way.

He looked into the Aquamarine's bar. Only three weeks ago he had sat here with his Timetravelers, drinking Sun'n'Surf cocktails. One of the vacation hostesses, a girl from Seattle working her way round the world, spotted him and looked slightly confused, trying to remember who he was.

They walked on. Elizabeth said, 'They reckon this is the most unspoilt place on the Red Sea.'

Unspoilt meaning only one Benetton shop, and not more than a dozen designer jewellery stores, and only the occasional pop star or politician walking the promenade as the sun went down over the headland.

But it still had a lot of charm, thought Richard. It was still a pleasure to walk the pedestrianized promenade, with its palms and bougainvillaea and occasional sweet smells of sewerage on the night air. A second wave of hotels was being built inland behind the coast road, but had not been built *yet*. Sharm el-Sheikh was still OK. It was St Tropez in the fifties, before the yobs caught on.

El-Prince led them away from the bay and across the desert road. They went to the outdoor bar of the Ibex hotel, the place where Sharm aficionados stayed, where old scuba-diving hands who remembered Sharm when it was a bunch of Israeli army huts and a wireless listening post still came back to sit over their coffees and reminisce about the good times. The Ibex was a series of bedroom chalets built round an open bedouin-tent restaurant and coffee shop. Backpackers came here when they got off the public bus, world travellers from Australia and New Zealand, big-bottomed girls from scuba-diving clubs in Manchester. It was Sharm el-Sheikh's greasy-spoon café. 'This is the place where the Mukhabarat hang out,' said El-Prince, 'when they leave the military base at Râs Umm Sid.'

'So what are we doing here?' said Elizabeth.

'Eating grilled pigeon. Listen, this is better food than anywhere else in Sharm el-Sheikh. Am I going to let the Mukhabarat eat it all?'

An Australian girl brought them Cokes. She brought El-Prince a hookah. She said, 'How are you, Sayed? How's business?'

El-Prince rolled his eyes.

'Yeah, it's a real pain. My mum and dad have been on the phone twice. I told them, for God's sake, it's not going to get down here. Even if there is a war, no way is it going to get to Sharm. You all OK for pigeon? Otherwise there's lamb and okra stew.'

They ordered pigeon.

El-Prince said, 'And four beers.'

She shrugged. When she brought them the labels had been removed.

Mac said 'Cheers' brightly.

'OK,' said Elizabeth, a girl for business. 'You attacked over the Sweetwater Canal.'

El-Prince took a swig of beer. He said, 'The Basr-Levi line they called it. It was said to be impregnable. We went through it like butter. The Jews were in their bunkers, praying. Nine days later we launched another attack—'

'Nine days? What were you doing?'

'Failing to take advantage, fucking everything up. You want the story?'

'No,' said Elizabeth. 'Skip the nine days.'

'We launched an attack a hundred thousand strong, east into Sinai, one of the biggest tank battles ever fought in the history of the world. You know that? Egyptian Third Army would have been in Jerusalem in a month if we'd moved earlier. If we hadn't given the Americans the chance to airlift arms into Israel, we'd have been taking our tanks into Jerusalem in a week—'

'Not you,' said Elizabeth. 'Others perhaps, but not you, Sayed.'

'No,' said El-Prince. 'No, not me.'

He drank, but sparingly, in a disciplined way.

Mac said, 'I'll get some more beer', and disappeared.

El-Prince said, 'You're sure about the visa? You're certain you can fix it?'

Two jeeps pulled in; divers from the Southern Oasis, calling for food, talking of the sea horses and Spanish dancers they had photographed on the sandy sea-bed.

'Don't worry about the visa. Tell us about the night of 16 October. The night after the big offensive by Third Army. The night after the tanks rolled east.'

One hand was stroking his forehead. He was sweating, but then they were all sweating. A heatwave in January, a hot wind from the hills – it was still too soon for the sea breeze to come flooding inland.

'My unit pushed down past Râs el-Sudr. We were winning, we were doing OK. We knew that behind us American planes were helping the Israelis take Chinese Farm, but south of Suez we were forging ahead, wiping out the resistance. We turned inland at Gharandal, up the track behind Sarabit el-Khâdem. Not the dirt road – we were north of the dirt road – it was a bedouin path we were following, up the Debbet el-Ramlch and the Wadi el-Garf. The Israelis had put construction gangs in, making it just passable by jeep. They had a listening post on El-Garf and gun positions at the top of the wadi, at a pass up on to El-Tîh, up to the plateau. We were moving so fast they were stunned. I had orders to take the guns, not so much take them as roll over them. Keep moving, fuel up and keep moving! We could hear the big battle further north, the tanks of Third Army. We could see the Israeli planes coming in, coming in waves, bombing our soldiers. Then we heard that the Israelis had got across the canal, that they'd cut the Cairo road. We didn't dare get bogged down! We knew that every Israeli tank we knocked out would be replaced or repaired by America, but not for days, not for a week perhaps – in the meantime we had to keep moving, every hour, every minute was vital, if only we could break through to the plateau, to El-Tîh, sweep round behind the Israeli forces—'

He stopped.

Mac had brought fresh bottles of beer.

Elizabeth said gently, 'You were heading up the Wadi el-Garf.'

'We were heading directly up towards the Israeli gun emplacements. Once we'd broken through our path would have been clear down the Wadi Ghabiyeh and out on to the northern plains. At nineteen hundred hours we held an O Group – an Orders Group – and I gave the other tank commanders their orders. At nineteen-fifteen hours we moved out of cover, out into the Wadi el-Garf, moving towards the narrow pass at Nagb er-Rakineh. I signalled the squadron to pull out, a hundred metres between each tank, into line formation, maximum power to the front and the best way to cross an open area. We reached the base of the ridge. It narrowed. We went into column formation. The Israelis still hadn't opened up – I thought perhaps there were no guns up there, perhaps they were cardboard guns, perhaps it was just a pretend battery – but then they started firing. I was in the lead. We had thermal-imagers, the first versions, or nearly the first, for picking out enemy infantry, but we had no infantry support ourselves; we were moving too fast. I was worried about Israeli infantry dug in at the base of the rocks, worried because we had a ten-metre dead space on either side from the gunner's station, but there was nothing I could do except hope they hadn't had time to take up anti-tank positions. By now they were firing phosphorus grenades and 84mm anti-tank guns. It was starting to go dark. We were approaching the defile, moving upwards, when the Israeli tanks opened up. Four of them, Israeli Centurions in echelon formation against our seven T-55s. I was getting the range of the furthest to the left and the radio operator was calling up our other tanks to warn them when the electronics went.'

He paused. Then he said, 'The comms went haywire. The thermal-imager was going berserk, red dots scattered over it like a fever. Then the cannon fired. It locked in on a target and fired. I opened the turret and stood up and looked out.'

He drank his beer.

There was a sea wind now, coming over the concrete road, bringing the sound of music from the beach barbecues.

'What happened?'

'I had a mental breakdown,' said El-Prince.

Silence.

'Or perhaps you didn't,' said Elizabeth quietly.

He shook his head.

'No, I had a breakdown.'

He lit another cigarette. The scuba-divers, lying on the mattresses under the black tent's awning, their

187

backs against cushions, were eating kebabs and salad. One of them said, 'Hey, it's Sayed. Hi, Sayed!'

'Hiya, Sayed,' called the others, their mouths full of kebab. 'You fancy taking us to the Blue Lagoon again, Sayed?'

'Any time you like,' Sayed called.

Mac said, 'There's two guys watching us.'

'Shit,' said Elizabeth, turning on him in suppressed fury.

'I couldn't keep quiet any longer,' said Mac. 'I'm a professional.'

Richard said, 'You had a breakdown – what sort of breakdown?'

El-Prince said, 'Mental overload. They explained it in the hospital. It's happened to guys before. The doctors explained it.'

Elizabeth said, 'No way does he get a visa to the States for telling me he's had a mental breakdown. Listen, listen, Sayed, unwipe your mind. You're blocking off your memories. OK, I understand why you're doing it, I understand and I sympathize, but it's not the *answer*, it's not the way to help.'

To help whom? thought Richard.

'Listen, Sayed, I do not believe you had a breakdown. Something happened. We both know something happened. What did you see in the pass of El-Garf, in the pass of – What is it?'

'Nagb er-Rakineh,' said Richard.

Mac said, 'They're just sitting watching us. They're not even drinking a beer or a coffee or anything. They're not so flaming clever. Don't go looking round suddenly. Just keep talking as normal, I'm going for a stroll.' He got up. Richard watched him go over to the giftshop, start looking through postcards.

In the corner of his eye he saw the two men, the watchers. They were at the back of the black tent, behind the scuba-divers.

Elizabeth said, 'I know what's in the mortuary at Maadi.'

El-Prince looked up.

'I've been there, Sayed. I've seen what's in the mortuary at Maadi.'

'I don't know what you're talking about.'

'They didn't tell you about the corpse, eh?'

Mac was holding up a T-shirt. It had RED SEA DIVERS written on it. He held it up and turned it round, keeping an eye on the watchers.

Elizabeth looked down into her beer. 'Never mind Maadi. What did you see, Sayed?'

'I saw ghosts.'

'Ghosts of what?'

El-Prince said nothing.

She said, 'Please.' Then quietly, softly, 'Think of the States. Think of being somewhere you don't have to run a boat for Israelis. Think of being someplace you can start all over again.'

'Soldiers. Ancient soldiers.' He spoke calmly. 'Soldiers from the time of the Pharaohs. Soldiers from the First Division of Amun.'

'You knew that?' said Richard. 'You knew that much?'

'Yes.'

'What were their weapons?'

'Javelins. Axes.'

'What were they doing, these soldiers?'

'They would have marched with me. They would have killed the tank-hunters, axed the skulls of the Israelis, destroyed their 84mm anti-tank weapons.'

'The First Division of Amun,' said Richard, 'a division of the army of the Pharaoh Rameses the Second, was coming to Egypt's aid in the Yom Kippur War?'

El-Prince looked puzzled.

'Was that what the psychiatrists said? Was that how they accounted for what you saw?'

'Maybe.'

'But you saw them?'

'Yes.'

'What else?'

'Savages, half-naked savages, with the yellow lion banner and the moon banner.'

Elizabeth said, 'Maybe that part was some sort of hallucination.'

'Maybe *that* part was an hallucination?' said El-Prince, amused.

'Forget the banners. Tell Rich here about the ghosts. Tell him what they were like. Tell him what they were wearing, these guys in the First Division of Amun.'

Three hundred rounds in ninety seconds, the muzzle glowing slowly red as the thermal-imager confirmed target after target, and he knew that the screen below was showing hit! hit! hit! though it could not possibly be true, for there was nothing to hit, nothing to strike, but still the infra-red target-finder was sending out warning! warning! target! target! and the muzzle spat, and he dodged back down again, back down from the turret, and looked at Ahmed, who was calm and matter-of-fact and carrying out his orders, and he didn't know how to say that the targets being thrown up by the computer and moving one oh four then one oh two and then all round the tank were simply not there, were not around him, were not, as

190

he later described to the cold and disbelieving major in Cairo, were not flesh, blood or steel *but were ghosts, and the rounds that Ahmed was firing were shedding flesh in a cause that was not his own, and in a war that was long long gone.*

Richard said, 'The axes. Can you describe to me the axes?'

El-Prince laughed. He said, 'Who are we kidding? No way will I ever get to America.' He stood up.

'Sayed? Sayed, listen—'

'When I was a young man, a young officer in the army, I had an electric storm in my brain. People have had worse things in life.'

'Think of the States, Sayed.'

He walked out, past the divers. One said, 'Bye, then, Sayed,' and he said, 'See you guys.'

The two watchers, sitting at their empty table at the back of the bedouin tent, got up and followed him. They made no pretence at secrecy.

Elizabeth's head was in her hands. Mac came back. 'OK, Princess, let's get back to the hotel. Let's figure out what to do.'

Richard said, 'Nothing he said was conclusive. Nothing he said was conclusive of *anything*.'

Elizabeth stood up. 'What do you want, Rich? What do you need to be convinced? You want me to send you back there in person?'

'Come on,' said Mac, crisply. 'Let's *move*.'

They hurried through the alleyways, past the designer clothes shops and the patisserie and out on to the promenade. Richard said, 'You reckon he'll be OK?'

'No way,' said Mac, 'is he going to be OK.'

Elizabeth said, 'Why shouldn't he be OK? As far as those guys were concerned, we're just tourists. Rich Yanks eating pigeon, talking about hiring his boat.'

'Don't kid yourself, Princess. He took us to that place because he wanted to *commit suicide*.'

'Don't say that.'

'You'll know it when he takes us with him.'

'Shit, Mac—'

'Shut up and keep moving.'

They turned into the Movenpick Jolie Ville hotel, under the huge arch and into the floodlit gardens, then into a glass-plated EgyptAir office. It was after eight o'clock but there was a queue at the desk. An Italian mamma, wrinkled and gravel-voiced, panicking to get back to Genoa, was saying in an American accent, 'Oh, my God. Oh, my God.' There was a plane out at ten p.m. It was full. It was full and overbooked, and there was a waiting list a mile long.

'It's cheque-book time,' said Mac.

Bumping hysterical Italian holidaymakers off their flight was more expensive than bumping construction workers off the Sinai coach, but being the Middle East all things were possible. They paid Club Class for Economy. They gave the guy a big tip. They took a taxi to the airport. Their passports were given only the most cursory look.

'They're not after us,' said Elizabeth. 'We're OK. I told you we'd be OK.'

'It's because we're on an internal flight,' said Richard. 'Internal passport checks are only meant to stop Israelis infiltrating Egypt proper from Sinai, stop them flying into Cairo.'

'Cairo? We're not going to Cairo. We're on a flight to Genoa. Three Club Class to Genoa.'

They were on a flight to Cairo.

'I don't believe this.'

'It's for the best, the Cairo flight goes first,' said Mac. 'We might make it. We might just get out of this place tonight. It depends on how long it takes those bastards to finish with El-Prince.'

'I still reckon Sayed will be OK,' said Elizabeth judiciously. 'I don't think they were after him at all.'

'Oh, good,' said Richard. 'Well, that's all right then, that's a relief.'

She ignored him. 'You reckon they were using directional mikes?'

'Yes,' said Mac.

Over the shoulder-high glass barrier, in the international departure lounge, a hundred or so Italians were making a human pyramid to have their photos taken. Mac looked at his watch, at the clock on the wall. He said, 'Don't go away', and wandered off.

Richard said quietly, 'El-Garf, Nagb er-Rakineh. They're not far from the Coloured Canyon. It's in this new exclusion zone, this Sinai Science Nature Park.'

'Yeah, Rich,' said Elizabeth. 'You see, perhaps, the reason for my interest in Sayed El-Prince.'

Mac came back. He had a bottle. It was in his jacket pocket. He showed them the top of it and winked. He had been swigging it in the gents.

'Oh, God, Mac,' said Elizabeth, 'Don't you think we're in enough shit? You want forty lashes from the mad mullahs?'

Their flight was called. They were bussed out into the cool night. They sat in the shiny Boeing 747 (Elizabeth said, 'Who says the Egyptian economy is on the point of collapse?') and waited for the captain to say, 'Could passengers McGlade, St George and

193

Corrigan please come to the exit at the front of the aircraft to talk to immigration officers', or a stewardess to come and whisper discreetly that there was a slight problem over their passports. The captain said, 'Welcome to AirEgypt Flight 916 to Cairo', and they took off. The plane circled over Tiran Island, gaining height, then set a course over the mountains of southern Sinai. Richard looked down on the moonlit peaks; Mount Sinai, Jebel Musa, the Jebel Serbal with its triple peaks, the red granite of Jebel Catherina, now nearly black in colour, the pinprick of lights at St Catherine's Monastery and along the cultivated oasis of the Firan Valley.

The plane crossed the Coloured Canyon at 20,000 feet. Richard looked down into total blackness. They crossed the moonscape of the Wadi el-Garf, flowing down from the long escarpment of the El-Tîh plateau, and, in the time it took him to drink a small plastic beaker of orange juice, they had reached the coast at El-Gharandal, a small cluster of lights, and turned up the Gulf towards Suez.

'What's the betting,' said Mac, coming down the aisle, leaning over him, 'they're waiting to grab us when we get off at Cairo?'

He was cheery, the film of sweat over his forehead was dry, his voice firm; he'd been in the toilets, having a little swig. 'What's the betting,' he said, 'they're waiting to grab us at the airport?'

11
A Lightshow at the Pyramids

They grabbed them in Giza. They might have grabbed them at the airport, but Mac had sneaked them out through the crew exit, hustling them efficiently past the airport security men, leading them coolly down the corridor with its little crew offices – Air France, Alitalia, Virgin – out to the taxi rank, and nobody could have followed them, not through that traffic, not the way their maniac taxi driver was swinging from lane to lane. Elizabeth was talking about getting on to her police-department chums and fixing Club Class tickets back to Heathrow. They were almost at the traffic island at the end of the Shari el-Haram when the traffic suddenly cut off behind them.

Then it cut on either side.

The taxi driver glanced round, startled, his neck swivelling from one side to the other. He had the look of a man who had prayed to Allah – *clear this filthy traffic* – once too often. He was just starting to say something when two gold-coloured Toyota Land Cruisers with black-tinted windows moved up alongside them, then forced them to a standstill in the gutter. The taxi driver's hand jammed on his horn. Then he saw the black uniforms, the submachine guns. His mouth turned into a sort of smile, an expression of great mildness and humility that did not save him from being yanked from his seat and dragged into the road, face down, with a boot in his back. Then the AK47s were pushing their aerated snouts through the open door into Elizabeth's cleavage; and Richard remembered reading how the Kalashnikov was the third-best-known brand name in Lebanon after Coca-Cola and Sony. He noticed that the policemen had dark-tinted sunglasses, even though it was the middle of the night, and they did not have the expression of bovine boredom that most Cairo policemen had.

'Don't argue, don't complain, don't do anything to annoy them,' said Mac, whose Glaswegian accent seemed to have gone, 'or they'll take it out on all of us. OK, we're coming out my friends. Relax, OK, no problem. And don't,' he said quietly to Elizabeth, 'call them fucking bastards.'

They were pulled out of the taxi. The road was still completely empty. Already the traffic snarl-up had to be stretching back to 6 October Bridge, back to the presidential palace. This was deadly serious, thought Richard. You didn't bring the centre of Cairo to a standstill to give three foreigners a verbal warning. You didn't go to all this trouble just to give a guy a motoring-offence ticket.

You had to be state security to get away with this.

You had to be very powerful, very nasty and very angry.

A crowd was gathering on the pavement. Two policemen were holding Mac, guns jabbing into his stomach, twisting his arms behind his back. Policemen were holding Elizabeth. For the moment Richard's own arms were free. He started speaking in Arabic, complaining in a loud voice, a voice loud enough for the crowd to hear, that he was an American citizen working for the British Museum. Two policemen were pointing guns at his chest and not looking impressed. Suddenly the taxi driver, who had been lying doggo with his face in the dust, lost his reason. He squirmed from under the policeman's boot, jumped up and headed across the road, his feet flying so fast he nearly tripped over. The crowd on the pavement shouted. The police gunmen yelled and raised their submachine-guns. Richard took a pace backwards as a short burst of fire rang out, aimed into the sky. The taxi driver collapsed, inert, like a toy with its battery cut off. Richard took another pace backwards, to the very edge of the crowd. The onlookers fell back, away from him, which was not what he wanted. Elizabeth was turning towards him. The police gunmen were turning towards him. He turned and plunged into the crowd.

He was a good fifty metres down a side-street, with children scattering away from him screaming excitedly, when something thudded into his back with a searing pain and his face was smashed down on to the road with such force that he did not notice the skin torn from his hands as they hit the gravel, or feel the boot in his ribs.

Wednesday night, six-thirty, was Japanese night at the Great Pyramids Sound and Light show. Japanese consumer goods were in all the shops of downtown Cairo, Japanese trucks were on all the roads, and Japanese voices boomed out over the desert, which made you wonder why the Japanese felt the psychological need to rewrite recent history by inventing parallel worlds – but there was no doubt about it, thought Mac (who was creeping through the graves of the Old Kingdom dynasties, through the broken tomb-scape, wriggling his way towards the Pyramid of Cheops), the book *Rising Sun Fleet* had made the Tokyo best-seller list – and not in the fiction section either, but in the technical section called *strategic simulation*; and millions of readers in Tokyo were now aware that in a parallel world the Nazis in 1940 had made themselves masters of England as far north as the River Mersey, and Churchill had headed a Vichy government in Edinburgh, and Admiral Yamamoto had bravely sailed the Imperial fleet half-way round the globe to liberate Britain and restore democracy to the planet Earth.

Dream on . . .

Or was there, perhaps, a world where it had all happened like that?

Were there worlds without number? Worlds where your dreams all came true?

Worlds populated by girls with big tits and Aberdeen accents who won the National Lottery every week and were mesmerized, slain, by chaps like Mac?

'There is a man in California,' Elizabeth had told him solemnly, when they were drunk one night in the little house in Maadi, 'who will tell you that all this is so, that all this is true, that all these worlds exist.'

Even the Aberdeen accent?

Even that, she had told him, fondly.

He crossed the concrete slab road. He slipped over it in a second, in the blink of an eye, bent double, moving very fast. In the distance he could see the lights of construction gangs on the new pyramids bypass, the 'road of desecration' that the UN World Heritage lot were wringing their hands over.

He paused, his back against the wall of a tomb-maker's house. There was a faint rustle, a faint swishing noise, a tiny movement in sand and gravel . . . a snake, a mouse, a scorpion perhaps.

He breathed slowly, silently, waiting for his pulse to quieten. After a few moments he quietly pulled a bottle from his pocket and took a swig.

Suddenly there was a snake in the sky. A huge, curling, writhing, green snake with a tongue that flickered like lightning over the low cloudbase of city pollution. It was supposed, actually, to be a little asp. Mac knew this from having watched the Sound and Light show in English.

From beyond the Sphinx came a round of applause.

And so, Cleopatra died. She died as Mark Antony had died. And Octavian was mad with anger that he could not parade her, his bound captive, his slave, through the streets of Rome.

Not in this world, perhaps, but who could tell? Perhaps in some other world Octavian had a real ball with tied-up Cleo, in the streets of Rome and anywhere else that took his fancy.

Mac snorted, coughed, took another quiet swig of Metaxa.

Was there a special world for the French, he wondered – a world in which the Germans had been repulsed on the Maginot Line and soundly thrashed by the magnificent French army? That would be a world worth living in – not just for the Frogs, but for everybody. It wasn't the fact that they'd surrendered to the Germans that bugged them, mind you, it was the fact that the British *hadn't*.

A world for the British – yes, let's make a world for the British! A world where there wasn't actually anybody else! No Yanks, no Germans, no Japs – just a few French peasants making cheese, a few Italians being romantic and amusingly corrupt; no other countries at all except, possibly, for New Zealand.

Vehicles were coming up the dirt road from the camel park.

There were four of them. They were being driven slowly, steadily. You'd hardly think they were being driven by Egyptians at all.

He sank quietly to the ground. He guessed that they were State Security Land Cruisers; those gold-metallic vehicles with tinted windows, air-conditioning, four-wheel drive and the very latest in security-forces weaponry.

He watched their headlights bobbing slowly up and down. Then he slipped out of the faint, reflected light, round a corner and into the deep shadows of the Great Pyramid itself. On his left was a long, modern building, seemingly on stilts. A searchlight from the Sound and Light show swept down the pyramids, illuminating for a moment a sign saying that the building contained the solar barque that 4,500 years ago had ferried Cheops from Memphis to his tomb.

Mac felt his way cautiously in the darkness, along the edge of the pyramid, along the worn stones. Behind him, when he glanced round, he saw the lights of the first Land Cruiser playing over the Pyramid of Chephren.

He told himself that they were guessing, just checking things out; they couldn't actually know he was here.

He had lost them over an hour ago in the camel park. They'd been close on his heels before that, chasing him on foot but not daring, thank Christ, to shoot,

as he raced through the dark gardens of the Movenpick Jolie Ville and out again into the backstreets of
Giza, over a wall, into a small house that was, it
transpired, the Cairo Children's Free Hospital for
Rheumatism and Heart Disease – how you got rheumatism in a dry husk of a city where it rained once
a year was but one of so many mysteries. They'd been
still on his trail as he ran between the neat, tidy pine
bunk-beds, each with its bright counterpane, each
with a big-eyed child who sat and watched in terrified
but wonderful silence as he ran past, jumped out
through a window at the front of the hospital, and
vanished across the road into the camel park.

That was when he had lost them. They'd assumed
that he had gone back down the road to Giza, to the
bright lights, to the hotels and the telephones.

He had hidden for some time under a pile of green
fodder, listening to the wicked snarling of dreaming
camels.

The first Land Cruiser was at the corner. He shrank
back against the stones.

He looked up at the sky, the loom of the night sky
behind the Great Pyramid of Cheops and the Pyramid
of Chephren. The satellite would be winking away up
there, beyond the smog, its transponders ready to
receive, store, route his message, but it was no use
to him – his miniaturized powerpack and transmitter
had been deemed too much of a give-away for this
particular job.

He tried his mobile again. No use. The Cairo network transmitter on the Moqattam Hills had been
hit by a fundamentalist bomb six months ago; it was
still operating on a back-up system that was weak

and overloaded. Perhaps Elizabeth could get a message through on her mobile, perhaps she wouldn't be searched.

Some chance . . .

Music swelled. A Japanese voice raised to high drama; lights and laser beams played dazzlingly over the pyramids – then silence and darkness.

The Japanese Sound and Light show was over.

Well, thank Christ for that.

Another Land Cruiser, this time to his left. It stopped.

They were at either end of his dark alley. He was trapped between the Great Pyramid and Cheops's solar barque. They were on to him.

He started to climb the pyramid.

Signs, every few steps upwards, warned him in Arabic and English not to do so. They reproached him for playing on a World Heritage Site. They threatened him with gaol.

After a while he stopped and gulped a mouthful of Metaxa. He was sweating – he was, let's face it, one very unfit and unhappy soldier.

Where would they take Elizabeth and the Yank professor? Back to the security detention centre in Maadi? To the Police Hospital in Agauza?

No, it would be Siwa, he guessed.

Out in the Western Desert.

The *State Security Hotel* with its five-star interrogation room – would that anything else in Egypt worked as efficiently as State Security!

He had a bit of a view now. He sat down for a moment. From a distance, from below, the stones of the pyramid had looked small and neatly laid; they'd looked as if you ought to be able to walk up the outside as if you were walking up some stairs. But it wasn't really like that. In reality they were rather large blocks, and they were jumbled at odd angles, and you had to pull yourself up from one to the next with considerable effort.

He drank again: it was three-star Metaxa, the stuff that seared the back of your throat, the good stuff.

A light, a torch, flashed for a moment across the house of the solar barque. They were welcome to search for him there. He took out his mobile, tried it again, but it was no use. He rested for a few moments, then carried on upwards. He had a view now, all the way across the city, all the way across to the Moqattam Hills.

Below him, illuminated, he could see a huge lion with the head of a Pharaoh.

How long had he been climbing? Half an hour, maybe longer. Would those buggers think to look upwards, to look up here?

A light, a torch – a powerful beam but not powerful enough.

He lay quietly. Perhaps they'd bring in a chopper. That was what he would have done, if it had been him. A chopper with a searchlight, a gunship with heat-seeking probes – but that might be a bit obvious, a bit over the top, might lead to a few questions being asked.

They were angling one of the Land Cruisers, angling it against some rocks on an incline so that its headlights would shine upwards. That was all very well, but you couldn't swivel it about, could you, not a bloody great Land Cruiser.

He lay and looked down at the lion, and laughed.

Oh, the sexual life of a camel,
Is greater than anyone thinks.
At the height of the mating season
He tried to get off with the Sphinx.

He tried his mobile again. No go.

The boys below would think he had gone out into the desert, or perhaps down into the tourist crowds milling round the Sphinx. They wouldn't mess about climbing pyramids in the dark, not if they could help it.

They'd wait at the bottom, though. Look out for him at dawn. Well, he'd wait till the tour buses were rolling up before he made a run for it. He'd make sure they all saw him, make sure there were a dozen camcorders on him, the wild man of Cheops. He'd surrender to the Tourist and Antiquities Police if he got half a chance. Christ, he hoped they'd have a couple of aspirins.

He drank.

A noise from below. A dog's bark, short and excited; more barks, a shout of command. So that was how they had tracked him.

They were coming up. They knew he was up here, breaking the by-laws, desecrating ancient buildings.

He pulled out his mobile again and pressed the tit and pointed it up into the air towards the Moqattam Hills.

Now you know that the Sphinx's back passage
Is blocked up by the sands of the Nile,
Which accounts for the hump on the camel,
And the Sphinx's inscrutable—

204

The burst of fire was from an RPK Automatic. He registered that much as he threw himself backwards—

– *smile*.

What the hell was happening? What the hell were they doing shooting fucking guns, for Christ's sake? What were the bastards playing at? Did they want to kill him? Did they want to *maim* him, the fucking foreign turds?

He rolled over, hugging the cool stone.

OK, what had Liz stumbled on that was so important that they were going round killing people? What had she found out? 'It's a watching brief, just a watching brief,' they'd said to him in London. Jesus.

He thought through the past two days: the body in the morgue, the radio-ops guy who hadn't seen a thing, knew nothing, El-Prince and his ghosts. The American from London – perhaps it was him. Mac had been watching him when the Security thugs grabbed them in Giza, had seen the alert look in his eyes, the way he buggered off into the crowd, giving Mac the chance to make his own getaway and leaving Liz to pay the taxi fare—

Was the American CIA?

What had been revealed that was so important, that was so vital, that was so explosive that these bastards were going round *executing people*?

It had to be El-Prince, they must have been talking to him. Talking to him? They must have had him on the rack. They must have brought him back to Cairo, flown him into the military airfield beyond Mahmasha, given him the third degree in the grey Mukhabarat headquarters in Maadi, the concrete windowless tower behind the English Club tennis court.

He must be there now; what was left of him.

Mac stood up. He stood up, knowing he was making a target against the luminescent sky. He held up the mobile again. Pressed 'send' again.

A connection. A voice said, 'British Embassy.'

He said, 'They've got Delta, maybe Corrigan. They'll have taken them to Siwa.'

'British Embassy.'

'They've got Delta and maybe Corrigan. They've got Delta and maybe Corrigan. They've got Delta—'

'British Embassy, hello?'

Music filled the skies. A voice said: *Four and a half thousand years have passed. Come back with me, now, to the very dawn of civilization.*

'They've got Delta. They've—'

He was bathed in light.

'You are very faint—'

Come back to the days when Egypt was ruled by the Lord of the Two Lands . . .

He threw himself down as a burst of fire sent bullets ricocheting around him and out into the night. He heard a warning yell, an angry cry from a man who was nearly level with him and was objecting, not unreasonably, to being shot at. He turned, scrambled upwards, filled with wild energy. He kept climbing, ignoring the sweat pouring down his face, the thudding of his heart, his lungs rasping for oxygen. He went on upwards for another five, ten minutes, scrambling up and round the narrowing height of the pyramid, getting away from the lights of the English-language laser show – then suddenly there was nothing left to climb.

He was at the top, on the apex. The booming English voice – *a hundred thousand men slaved for one-*

206

third of the year for thirty years to build the Pyramid of Cheops – was faint and far away. Looking the other way, away from Cairo, he could see, quite close, the summit of the Pyramid of Chephren. Beyond that was the darkness of a desert that stretched all the way to Libya.

They were coming up towards him on all sides. They weren't firing, just climbing, quietly, steadily in the darkness. Occasionally they shone torches to make sure he didn't slip down between them or lie concealed in the masonry.

They would soon be at the top. He could see their silhouettes. If he'd had a US Marine Corps M40 sniper rifle (his favourite) with starlight scope night vision he could have taken them all out; potted the fuckers like rabbits.

But they knew he was unarmed. They knew they had got him. That he had nowhere left to go.

He tried his mobile again. Whatever happened, security was now shattered. His call would have been recorded by the Egyptians, the embassy would be totally implicated. The head of Cairo Station would be having a fit; it might very well have put him off his dinner.

Static. He dropped the phone with a clatter.

A man, only a few feet below him, stopped for a moment. Then he continued climbing.

Mac looked up at the sky.

'Beam me up,' he said, 'Scottie.'

The world went on turning. The pyramids weren't transponders for space travellers after all. He sighed. Nothing, apart perhaps from Metaxa, was what it was cracked up to be.

12
Siwa

Alexander the Great was here. Some 2,500 years ago he came along the caravan track – already 2,000 years old itself – through the Wadi el-Raml and over the Kanayis Pass, taking a break from building his very own, personal city of Alexandria. He came to consult Amun, the Oracle of Siwa. He came to peer into the future and receive the assurance that he was the Son of God. When he got here, the excited peasants placed a ram's horn crown on his head and the place must have buzzed for a day or two, excited to find itself the centre of the civilized world.

They'd had little reason since then to hang out the bunting. Today Siwa was a tiny splat of green on the desert grit, a smear of penicillin on the laboratory slide. Its only visitors were army conscripts, who came up from the coast to fester in the barracks for three months, manning the chain of radar and sound-surveillance stations along the border with Libya.

Siwa Oasis.

A thirteenth-century crumbling fort that looked as though it was made out of melting chocolate ice-cream; 200,000 palm trees; 5,000 date-industry workers. Date-palm capital of the Western world – but dates, they would tell you in the fly-infested cafés of Siwa, were not what they used to be; the trade not what it was. Old date pickers could remember the days when every house in Olde England had a wooden box of Siwa dates on the table at Christmas – the days when Siwa dates were the most prized, succulent delicacy of post-war Britain. But not any more.

Siwa Oasis.

Intelligence HQ for Egyptian Second Army, Western Command.

For two days they were held at a barracks in the desert, kept apart, questioned by officers of State Security.

What was their purpose in visiting Egypt? Why had they gone to Sinai? Why had they sought out a former Egyptian army officer who had been court-martialled for treason? What was the name of the ship they had contacted in the Straits of Tiran? Not the US warship, they knew all about the US warship, but the Israeli ship? What was the name of their bedouin contact in Dahab?

What were the places they had visited in Cairo – a cunning question this, the word Maadi was slipped in, unobtrusively, to get a reaction. The interrogators weren't sure about that one. They didn't know everything.

'I am an academic at University College, London, currently attached to a project for Drextel University's Department of Physics.'

'No project with Drextel University is listed by the Department of Culture or the Department of Antiquities.'

'This is a physics project.'

'You are not a physicist, you are an Egyptologist.'

'Well, yes—'

'What sort of physics project?'

'Well, to be honest—'

'Radar? Air defences?'

'No!'

'Low-frequency microwave interception beams?'

'No!'

'No? We have very advanced stuff here at Siwa. All along the Libyan border. We could have showed it to you, if you'd come to us.'

'It's nothing to do with air-defence radar.'

'Then what?'

What indeed.

His head hurt.

'What is this physics project about?'

He said, 'Observed occurrences of the paranormal in the South Sinai Desert' – which was the end of his career, if ever it got out. He wondered why they didn't reply *You expect us to believe that?* in an incredulous voice, but they just wrote down everything he said.

Two days, two nights. His forehead throbbed mercilessly. One side of his face was livid to the touch, one side of his mouth swollen. The palms of his hands were raw; he thought they were becoming infected.

'OK, we've checked you out. You are an Egyptologist at University College, London.'

'Yes.'

'You are also connected with Intelligence.'

'I am not in any way connected with Intelligence.'

'All English academics work for Intelligence.'

'I am not English and in no way am I connected with Intelligence.'

'You will talk to MI6 when you go home.'

When you go home? Had his interrogator really

used the word 'when'? He clutched at straws. His heart lightened.

'No.'

'You will talk to the Foreign Office.'

'No.'

'After every visit to Egypt you have gone to White-hall to talk to the British Foreign Office.'

'No.'

'It doesn't really matter. We have no quarrel with Britain.'

'I am American.'

'CIA?'

'No.'

'No, MI6. We have spoken about you to the head of Cairo Station. We have spoken to Mr Piper. He is expecting you to cooperate.'

'I don't know what you're talking about.'

A second man, a man in uniform, said, 'You are a military expert.'

'I am a research fellow at UCL, my specialist field is the New Kingdom nineteenth-dynasty war machine.'

'Explain to us your involvement in a physics project.'

How much did he dare tell them? How much did they know already? A corpse kept for over twenty years in a government morgue in Maadi – if he admit-ted he'd seen it, would he end up incarcerated in some desert hell-hole for the rest of his life?

'How can a physics project,' said the second interrogator, 'need an Egyptologist, an expert on ancient Egypt?'

'I've explained it, it was a project related to the paranormal—'

The first man spoke. 'Tell us why you went to Sinai.

212

Tell us why you went to talk to a man who was dishonourably discharged from the army.'

He told them.

They listened. They looked at him. The second man said, 'You believed that stuff?'

Richard sat looking at his hands, which were puffy and raw and dirty. He suspected that insects were already laying eggs in his wounds. He had been given no water to wash them.

'I want a doctor.'

They sat for a while, smoking, looking at him. It seemed to him that they were puzzled.

'Sayed El-Prince is dead,' said the first. 'He knew that we were looking for him. He drowned himself in a place called the Blue Hole. His body was found only this morning.'

Richard said nothing.

They sent an army doctor to look at his hands, and his bruised ribs.

Early on the third morning he was taken from the barracks in the desert to the second-best hotel in Siwa – a move which showed deep malice on somebody's part. He was frogmarched up the stairs, into the sort of room holiday companies describe as basic. The security police went. A fly-blown notice behind the door said the room rent was a dollar a night. There was no bed linen, added the notice, and no restaurant. Well, no, thought Richard, there was no anything really.

Alcohol was forbidden.

His wallet was returned to him. In it was his British Library Reading Room pass. His English credit card. His passport. They had taken all his money.

After a while he opened the door, went into the corridor and knocked on the door of the next room.

Elizabeth was sitting on her bed, looking exhausted.

In the café nearby they ate bread and tomatoes, and Elizabeth tried to pay with American Express.

They walked to the edge of the village. The desert stretched out before them. There were 1,700 empty kilometres of it, southwards, to the nearest town. Behind them were 200,000 date palms, in plantations with springs bubbling up out of the sand.

He said, 'There are things, Elizabeth, that you have not told me.'

She said nothing. She looked out over the rolling dunes. Then she said, 'You know there are huge lakes of water under this desert? Vast reservoirs trapped in the sediment for millions of years, ancient seas that are sort of cocooned in sand and rock. It's by drilling down and tapping the water that they can create these oases. You drink water here and you're drinking stuff that's millions of years old. That means parts of you, of your personal chemical make-up, are also millions of years old. Just think about that.'

'Tell me what's going on.'

She stared out over the desert.

'Tell me why were we arrested.'

A pause. She said, 'Jealousy.'

He said, 'Jealousy.'

'There's a lot of academic jealousy, Rich, you should know that; perhaps things are different in England, but in the US academic jealousy is *vicious*, oh boy—'

'I have been arrested and beaten up by the secret police on the orders of your academic rivals at Drextel?'

'Sounds incredible, right?'

A moment later she said, 'How are you, by the way?'

'Bloody awful.'

'*Bloody awful* – you sound really English.' A pause. 'Yeah, you look bad.'

'Where's Mac?'

'He ran off. You did him a good turn.'

'That's OK, then.'

Nobody seemed to be watching them. Perhaps they were free to leave Siwa; to get a good night's sleep, get up early, take the morning bus. On the other hand, perhaps not.

He said, 'El-Prince has committed suicide.'

'Yeah, he dived in the Blue Hole. They told me. He dived at the wrong time of the day, in the early morning.'

'He thought he was mental. He thought he was insane.'

'No.'

'Tell me about Mac. Tell me what this is all about.'

She nodded. 'OK.'

They sat down, by some olives, in the shade of the pale-green leaves.

She said, 'The project's not funded by Drextel.'

He closed his eyes.

'It was to start with. I had a PhD research grant.'

His eyes opened. 'This is your PhD?'

'That's how it started.'

'You are actually doing a physics PhD on "Observed Occurrences of the Paranormal in the South Sinai"?'

'I am.'

'You actually got that accepted as a proper research subject—'

215

'Christ, Christ, you are just so blinkered. People have won Nobel Prizes for this sort of project. You do realize Rayleigh of the Society for Psychical Research was also Cavendish Professor of Physics at Cambridge? Have you looked at some of the prerecognition stuff of Nostradamus?'

'Fuck Nostradamus.'

'Oh yeah, yeah—'

'OK, go on.'

'I spent a year at Drextel, and at Harvard, most of the time looking through stuff left by William McDougall, a guy who held the chair of Psychology before World War Two and helped start the *Journal of Parapsychology*. He was working on Zollner. You know about Zollner?'

'No.'

'Johann Zollner, Professor of Physics and Astronomy, one of the very first to come up with the theory of the fourth dimension, because that's what this is all about. Rich, this is about time – and Zollner was the first at something else, he was the first to link psychical phenomena to physics, and call it transcendental physics. All this, Rich, in 1882, and you know what happened to him? He was reviled. They laughed at him and reviled him, and hounded him to his death.'

He said, 'They've hounded us to Siwa, which is marginally worse.'

'I'm laughing, Rich. I like it. Listen, this was what set me off. Palmer disappeared in south Sinai in 1882, coincidentally the same year Zollner came up with the theory of the fourth dimension—'

'We've talked about Palmer. Palmer was a British agent who got himself murdered.'

'Was he hell murdered—'

'Murdered on El-Kaah, which translates as "the plain", and lies behind El-Tur –'

'Rich, you look at the legends, the folk-stories of Sinai, the bedouin stories. People have been disappearing for centuries – *places* have been disappearing for centuries: *And the palm tree and the chapel were no more . . . and the well of St Onuphrios disappeared*. Gabriel picked a real hot spot, believe me, when he went wandering off into the hills behind that motel.'

'I know all about the legend of St Onuphrios. This is just the stuff you gave me by the pool in Giza. Give me some facts. Give me some evidence. Tell me why Drextel pulled your PhD research grant.'

'The money ran out. This is a big project – nobody seemed to realize how big. I managed to get backing from somewhere else.'

A pause. He said, 'Go on.'

'From another source.'

He was getting there.

'That was when Mac came in. He's looking after the sponsor's interest.'

'The sponsor?'

'Yeah.'

Another pause.

'Who is the sponsor?'

She was looking furtive, smirking a little.

'What is this source?'

'You don't think they've got directional mikes back there? You don't think that date palm moved just then?'

'I think if they wanted us to tell them anything, we'd have told them. I don't think that you or I would have resisted more than ten minutes, not if they'd been serious.'

'Big hero, huh?'

'Sorry.'

She glanced round her. She said, 'CIA.'

A pause.

'The CIA is funding your research project?'

She nodded.

'Mac's a CIA agent?'

'Yes.'

'A Scottish CIA agent?'

'You must have noticed his accent. It was *unreal*.'

'Mac's accent,' said Richard, 'was in my view the only thing about him that was not unreal.'

She said, 'I'm sorry, Rich. I'm truly sorry you got beaten up. And I'm so sorry that Sayed is dead. Oh, Christ.'

She put her head in her hands. He saw that her pink nail varnish was chipped and scuffed and her suntan was looking yellow and dingy.

The call to prayer could be heard from the mosque. It would soon be dark.

He said, 'You've got a physics degree? Tell me the physics part of all this.'

If the CIA were involved, he thought, it wasn't because of bedouin legends and psychic manifestations.

A car was outside the hotel. It belonged to the Tourist and Antiquities Police. The police officer got out of it as they approached and said, 'You cannot stay overnight in Siwa without written permission from the Governor in Mersa Matruh or the Frontier Corps in Cairo.'

'OK,' said Elizabeth. 'We'll leave. Just lay a car on, Jeeves.'

'You cannot leave Siwa,' said the Tourist cop, ready for that one, 'unless you are travelling in convoy. It is forbidden to travel the desert track except in a convoy of at least two vehicles. The desert is dangerous.'

They went and sat outside the café. They drank coffee. It went dark. The men of Siwa smoked their hookahs, the charcoal flaring in the gloom, sparks flying upwards. Elizabeth tried to phone Cairo using her Amex card. No way. He wondered how they would pay for the coffee, or the tomatoes they had eaten at lunchtime. Nobody seemed bothered. Another car drove up. An Interior Ministry police car.

A man in a shiny suit said, 'Get your bags, please.'

They had no bags. They got into the car. There was a second man in the front passenger seat.

'We are taking you to Alexandria. It is forbidden for vehicles to travel the desert track through Wadi el-Raml except in convoy—'

'Yes,' said Richard, 'we know.'

They waited in Siwa's central square for other vehicles. It was sticky and hot, even though it was still early January. The air would not start to get cold until the early hours of the morning. An hour before dawn it would be close to freezing.

'I told you we'd get out of this OK,' whispered Elizabeth.

'You did?'

'We have friends. We have friends who have *influence*.'

He looked at the police officers, the backs of their heads in the gloom. He said, 'Just be quiet, OK?'

219

'We'll be back in London by tomorrow night.'

London. He thought of Vronwy in her flat in Belsize Park. He was overcome with nostalgia for the little cafés in Museum Street, for the sodden black leaves in the gutters, for London buses in the rain.

A bus appeared, a very old Egyptian bus, a bus that made the night bus from Cairo to Sharm look like a brand-new luxury intercontinental sort of bus. The police car took its place behind it. Then an army truck also appeared and stopped behind them.

They were a convoy. The uniformed policeman from the Tourist and Antiquities Police counted the vehicles carefully, concluded that there were more than two, pondered for a few moments in the hope of a bribe that did not appear, then waved for them to proceed.

It was midnight as they pulled out of the square, which was fine, because they would avoid the heat by travelling through the night, even though they would not be able to admire the scenery along the road once taken by Alexander the Great, the Son of God. They both dozed. After a while, Elizabeth's head fell over against his shoulder, and he put his arm round her. She slept. Occasionally, when the car heaved more violently than usual and he opened his eyes, he saw in the car's lights the bones of dead, abandoned vehicles by the track. Two hours passed. His shoulder was hurting, and his ribs, but he did not like to disturb Elizabeth, who was snoring softly. Finally he slept himself.

He woke up as she was wrenched away from him, screaming in pain.

She was being dragged out of the far door. There was a burst of automatic fire and the police officers, who were turning, reaching for their guns, slumped forward in a spray of blood. Richard dropped to the floor, pressing himself down into the narrow tight space. Bullets smashed the side-windows into a million shards. They tore into metal and upholstery and flesh.

He was in Cairo. A man said, 'These are difficult times.'

He had been saved by soldiers, by conscripts in the army truck. They hadn't had live rounds for their AK47s, but they had fired blanks with wild abandon. They had pulled him out from the back of the car, a bullet through the fleshy part of his forearm, bits of glass stuck in the back of his neck like porcupine needles.

'Where is Elizabeth?'

The man shook his head, weary, perhaps embarrassed.

'Who were they?'

Terrorists. Fundamentalists.

'Don't,' said Richard, 'give me that shit. They let us out of the prison so that they could jump us in the desert. They let us out so that we could run. When we didn't run they laid on a fucking car. What are you doing to find the bastards?'

The man shook his head again. Life wasn't that simple.

They put coffee in front of him, thick with sugar. The man was looking through his passport. He said, 'You have been to Egypt many times before, always under the approval of the Ministry of Culture. Who do you really work for?'

Christ, not again, not all that, not all over again.

He said: 'I want to phone the American Embassy.'

221

'You have a second passport? Another passport as well as this one?'

'Yes.'

'Why is that?'

'Because I need to travel to the Jordan Valley.'

'You go to Israel?'

'To Israel and to Jordan.'

'You have a separate passport you use to visit Israel?'

It was a mechanical question. There was nothing new here. He didn't pretend to be excited.

'I want,' said Richard, 'to phone the American Embassy.'

Another man came in and sat down, a big man, a fat man. He said, 'Two policemen are dead. I am a detective superintendent. The more you can tell us, the more we can help you.'

Richard said, 'Where is Elizabeth?'

The detective superintendent said, 'Just tell us everything you know.'

They were in Maadi, back in the British garden suburb, back among the mangoes and the flame trees, driving past the massive, fantastic villa on Canal Street. They were travelling in a convoy of three vehicles again, but this time the vehicles were Interior Ministry Land Rovers. They turned by the Petit Swiss Chalet Pei-Ching restaurant.

'You think the woman Elizabeth St George is crazy? You think she is out of her mind?'

'No more than anybody else.'

The Egyptian detective pondered, then nodded.

They were driving past the tennis courts, past figures in white shorts and singlets. There would be jugs of lemon barley water, tea with sandwiches. Diplomats' lives didn't change much, not even when the world's foundations trembled. They turned down a road lined with flame trees and acacia, past villas that had been the quarters of senior British and New Zealand officers in the Second World War, villas where the defence of Tobruk, the stand at El Alamein, had been planned. Another turning. A police pillbox. A grey concrete building.

The superintendent said, 'Is this it?'

'Yes.'

'You recognize it? It is the place you came to before?'

'Yes.'

The Land Rovers pulled up. The door of the mortuary was closed, the glass dusty and forbidding. The soldier in the pillbox was looking at them.

The superintendent said again, 'You think Miss St George is crazy?'

'I just want to think she's OK.'

The man looked at him through soft, emotional eyes. He was a city detective. His daughter was getting married in two weeks. He repeated, 'You just want to think she's OK.'

It sounded like a line from a Cary Grant film.

'Yes.'

'I think she'll be OK,' said the detective. 'She's American. A foreigner.'

'There have been dead Americans.'

Two Interior Ministry soldiers from the first Land Rover were arguing with the guard in the pillbox. The soldiers were getting angry. The guard was shouting. Papers were produced. A call was made on a mobile. The guard listened for a moment, waved his arms in the air and walked away.

'Quickly,' said the detective. 'Quickly.'

They went into the building. The same clerk was behind the counter. He looked at Richard, startled. A soldier took the phone from its cradle.

They went up the two flights of bare concrete stairs and down the anonymous corridor. They went through the wooden door and into the room with white-tiled walls. There was the same smell of antiseptic and chemicals.

The boy attendant came out of the inner room and froze.

The detective questioned him. The boy kept glancing, terrified, at Richard. The detective shouted. Richard was aware of the urgency, the tension of passing time – elsewhere in the city phones would be ringing now, messages would be being passed. Presently the boy led them back into the inner room, into the body bank.

The detective said to Richard, 'This was the place?'

The same forty-watt bulb.

The same rows of metal drawers.

The same heavy smell of formaldehyde.

'This was the place.'

The soldiers were looking round them, curiously. The detective turned to the attendant and asked a question. Suddenly he shouted; the attendant shouted back, sweat on his forehead. A soldier hit him, but only for show, a token beating. The attendant looked at Richard angrily, reproachfully, then pulled open a drawer.

The detective motioned Richard forward.

Richard looked down. The face was blotched. Red blotches against grey-white skin.

The detective was asking him if this was it, if this was the body.

Mac's red hair seemed sparser than it had in life; the cheeks shrunk. The mortuary priests will have to stuff out those cheeks, thought Richard, as they had stuffed the cheeks of Henttawy, wife of the high priest of Amun; pad out that skin with resin, carmine those dull, inlaid eyes, to make them see into the Netherworld, send him fat and sleek on his journey.

Behind him the attendant was being beaten again. This was not the corpse the Interior Police detectives wanted to see. They wanted to see the corpse of the *boy soldier*.

The attendant was Anubis, God of the Underworld, disposer of corpses – but he was also an employee of State Security. Telephones would be ringing now all over Cairo, in ministries, in the presidential palace, in barracks perhaps. The corpse was the friend of the prisoner, the boy attendant was saying; the corpse was the prisoner's friend. What other corpse would he want to see in a Cairo morgue?

What other corpse?

They hit him again. There was a dull thud, a snap of bone, a childish scream. Richard closed his eyes, wishing he could blank out his ears. He was suffocating, he was sweating. The room was spinning, then righting itself, then spinning gently again, moving like a ship at sea. A soldier grabbed him and shouted. He blinked and focused his eyes.

The boy attendant was opening a second drawer.

There was the thin metallic sound of the overtight runners.

Richard was motioned forward. He had a split second's premonition before he looked down. Then he hit the soldier who was helping to steady him – hit him a massive swipe with the back of his fist, and the soldier grunted in pain and fell. Then Richard slammed his fist into the boy attendant, who already had blood running down one side of his face, and who cried a piercing cry at this new outrage. Two soldiers grabbed at him. The detective superintendent shouted in anger. Richard thrust the soldiers off and staggered out into the large mortuary room, and then flung himself down the corridor and down the stairs, falling down the second flight, stumbling up with a searing pain in his knee. A solitary soldier drew his pistol but dared not fire because he had no orders. Richard ran outside the mortuary. Everything was spinning and there was red film behind his eyes. He fell to his knees. He was aware of soldiers and police around him, yelling but not touching him, letting him crawl round in a circle; then the detective superintendent was pushing them aside, and another figure was bending down over him, crouching beside him, and an English voice was telling him it was going to be all right.

Part Two

13
London

Each morning he went to University College Hospital, a short walk down sad, litter-strewn streets from his flat behind St Pancras. They treated his minor injuries, probing carefully for shards of glass, telling him that some of the tiny fragments would have to work their own way out, advising him on how to avoid infection. In Surgical, the gunshot wound in his arm was displayed to medical students, who did not get to see wounds made by an AK47 from one month to the next, or indeed any kind of gunshot wound, London still being a civilized place compared to just about everywhere else.

The wound in his arm ached. The doctor who examined him advised paracetamol or common aspirin and told him to avoid alcohol. Whatever was the matter with you in England, they always told you to avoid alcohol.

He phoned the US Embassy three times. He received a letter, asking him to call a Mr Martin any time after 2 February. No urgency there.

Despite the aspirin his arm hurt; a dull, persistent pain. His neck stung and itched as the shards of glass worked their way to the surface. His ribs still hurt from being kicked in Giza, and his raw hands still throbbed. A nurse had cleaned them and said, 'Well, you *have* been in the wars', in a brisk, unsympathetic way, a woman used to cleaning up drunks after pub brawls.

He looked each day in the English papers, but there was nothing. He bought the *Herald Tribune* and *Wall Street Journal*'s European editions, from the stand outside Russell Square Underground that catered for tourists, but there was nothing.

Nothing until today. Today in the *Wall Street Journal*'s "world round-up" was a single paragraph:

US woman slain by Islamic Terrorists
Elizabeth Ford (34) of Connecticut on vacation in Egypt was killed on the 19th in an attack on a hire-car in the Western Desert near Siwa. Responsibility has been claimed by Libyan-backed armed Islamic Fundamentalist Group GIA in a fax to London-based Arabic daily *al-Hayat*

So she was called Ford, not St George. She really had been a dreamer of dreams, a girl living in a fantasy world. But she had not been killed by GIA. She had not been killed by freelance terrorists. Richard was no expert on Middle East terrorist organizations, but he did not believe that GIA, or Hizb ut-Tahrir, had access to State Security mortuaries in Maadi. Not yet. Not quite yet. GIA was doing what it had been told to do: putting up a screen.

And what about Mac? No mention of Mac anywhere. What was his surname? McGlade? Was there a widow McGlade somewhere, waiting for her husband in some Glasgow tenement, or in some crofter's cottage in the Highland glens? Were there little sandy-haired Macs looking out for their dad, little Miss McGlades in McGlade tartan kilts?

He read the paragraph again. Drizzling rain fell lightly on the newspaper; sooty city tears staining Elizabeth's epitaph: *US woman slain*.

After the pyramids, another monument to Empire. A towering dome. The busy clatter of a thousand tourists who must pay to come in, and must not use flash. Flags that once flew under India's hot sun, now decaying in the cathedral gloom. *The meteor flag of England shall yet terrific burn* . . . But this building was not a monument to the English – there was an abbey in Westminster for those who thought of the English – this was St Paul's, and it was a monument to Britain. Slim of Burma. Kitchener. Wellington. Roberts. Gordon – 'He saved an Empire by his warlike genius, he ruled vast provinces.' Collingwood, Vice-Admiral of the Blue, commander of the Larboard Division at Trafalgar, sailing here in a boat of white marble on a white marble sea, close to the bones of Richard Rundle Burgess, commander of the *Ardent*, who sacrificed his life to maintain his country's naval superiority and her 'exalted rank among nations'.

Richard was in the crypt, looking at Nelson's memorial, when Vronwy came behind him and said, 'Hi.'

'Cold marble,' said Richard. 'For so warm a man.'

'Ah, yes, Lady Hamilton,' said Vronwy, and added, a truism, 'All men are bastards.'

Richard said, 'He loved her devotedly.'

'He said he was warmed by love of his country,' said Vronwy. 'The women of blokes like that have a lot to put up with. Every time he came home there was a bit missing. An arm. An eye. A leg.'

'No,' said Richard. 'Two legs, always two legs.'

'Yeah, with their toes turned up.'

It had taken three days for him to tell her the full story of the corpse of the boy soldier. About the family in the City of the Dead, the nightbus to Sharm el-Sheikh, and the meeting with Sayed El-Prince. About Siwa.

About Mac, and about Elizabeth, in the morgue at Maadi.

She said, 'Richard, what are we doing here?'

'I want to take a look at something.'

They walked round the crypt, past the small bust of George Washington, soldier and statesman, past the memorial to the South Atlantic Task Force, and the memorial to the Air Transport Auxiliary with its inscription: *Remember then that also we in a Moon's course are history.* Egypt loomed large in the crypt of St Paul's. Harry Holdsworth Rawlinson, Principal Transport Officer, Egyptian War of 1882. Lawrence of Arabia, 1888–1935.

A Victorian inscription.

In memory of three brave men. Professor Edward Palmer, Fellow of S. John's college, Cambridge, Lord Almoner's Reader in Arabic and linguist of rare genius.
Captain William John Gill, R.E., an ardent and accomplished soldier and a distinguished explorer.
Lieutenant Harold Charrington, R.N. of H.M.S. Euryalus, a young officer of high promise.
who while travelling on public duty in the Sinai

desert were treacherously and cruelly slain in the Wadi Sadr

August 11 MDCCCLXXXII

Their remains after a lapse of many weeks, having been partially recovered and brought to England were deposited here with Christian rites, April 6 MDCCCLXXXIII

This tablet has been erected by the Country in whose service they perished, to commemorate their names, their worth, and their fate.

That tragic fate was shared by two faithful attendants, the Syrian Khalil Atik and the Hebrew Bakhor Hassun whose remains lie with theirs.

Vronwy read, 'Our bones lie scattered before the Pit as when one breaketh and cleaveth wood upon the Earth, but our eyes look unto thee, O Lord God.'

They stood for a moment. She said, 'I suppose the Syrian Khalil Atik and the Hebrew Bakhor Hassun appreciated being deposited here with Christian rites. What were a captain in the Royal Engineers and a Royal Navy officer doing in Sinai?'

'You have to consider the public duty for which they were so treacherously and cruelly slain. Professor Edward Palmer, Fellow of St John's College, Cambridge, Lord Almoner's Reader in Arabic and linguist of rare genius, was in reality a spy carrying 20,000 gold sovereigns to bribe the bedouin.'

'He was?'

Richard nodded.

'A complicated cover. What if somebody had come up to him and demanded to know the Arabic for "I want a banana"?'

'Oh, he was genuinely Lord Almoner's Reader in Arabic. And his survey of Sinai was a genuine attempt to make the connection – as he put it – between sacred history and sacred geography, and it really was done on behalf of the Palestine Exploration Society, and various biblical societies, and it was followed with interest by many pious old ladies in England.'

'But we know something else?'

'We know it was also sponsored by the British Army, and the Royal Engineers provided manpower, and the Ordnance Survey were there – they'd just finished doing the Lake District – and, at the end of the day, the expedition came back with a set of two-inch to the mile maps that were invaluable in the First World War when Allenby smashed his army through into the Negev and shattered the Ottoman Empire.'

'Ah, well,' said Vronwy after a moment. 'That's how we did things in those days.'

'Let us go,' said Richard, 'and have some tea.'

They went out into Paternoster Square. The wind struck damp in his wounded arm, but cooled the burning pinpricks of his sores. The drizzle had started again. A newspaper billboard read, 'Muslim Leaders Interned', but didn't say – because few in England would buy a newspaper to read about foreigners – that it was France, not the UK, that had locked up 1,500 Algerian Muslim dissidents. They took a taxi to Museum Street.

'Why are you interested in Palmer?' asked Vronwy.

'Elizabeth didn't believe that his actual bodily remains were brought back from Sinai. She thought that some other remains, odd bones, bits of camel perhaps, were interred in St Paul's. She believed that Palmer was actually the victim of some form of time transference. She believed a lot of people – things even – in Sinai have been the victim of time transference.'

'Right.'

Vronwy's eyes flicked to the back of the taxi driver's head, but the taxi driver was listening to a sixties rock and roll station.

'You and Worboys,' said Richard, 'might come across some evidence of Palmer's second expedition if you go from Nakhi south towards Sarabit el-Khâdem. They left whitewashed cairns all over the place.'

'What, with the sovereigns buried under them?'

'The sovereigns came later. His first two expeditions, when he mapped out the Sinai peninsula, were successful.'

'Ah.'

So logical. So rational.

They went into a café, the one where Worboys liked to take his coffee-break. There was a billow of steam as they opened the door. Vronwy said heartily, 'What sort of cake would you like?' He hesitated. She was looking at him tensely. Eating cakes would make him better. It would stop him talking about time transference.

'Carrot cake,' he said.

She smiled, and ordered Earl Grey tea. Her brown eyes looked at him over the teapot. After a moment or two she said, 'About Elizabeth.'

He said, 'What about her?'

'Was she crazy?'

'You ought to be a policeman in Cairo,' said Richard. 'You'd fit in, you'd get on. How would I know if she

235

was crazy? She thought she'd stumbled on some sort of paranormal psychic recurrence, some sort of physical instability in the desert that was distorting time. She thought it was being covered up by the Egyptian government, by the scientists. She thought that a corpse found in Sinai during the Yom Kippur War had somehow travelled forward from the nineteenth dynasty.'

'Yes.' A pause. 'Yes, that's what you said.' Another pause. 'And now you say she thought the same of Professor Palmer, except that he went backwards?'

'Crazier things have happened.'

'No,' she said. 'No, Richard, they haven't. We need to be clear about this.'

'I don't know if she was crazy or not. Why should anybody go to all the trouble of killing somebody who was crazy?'

'They were terrorists, weren't they? Terrorists don't run personality checks. They nearly killed you, for God's sake! They nearly gunned you to death!' She drank tea, seeking refuge from unfamiliar words and deeply foreign ideas.

He said, 'When do you go?'

'A week Monday, if we go at all.'

'You'll be safe enough in Sinai, out in the desert.'

She glanced at him, then glanced away. He wondered what she was thinking. He wondered about Maurice the computer man, who never seemed to get invited to her parties. Had she finally chucked him?

She ate her cake, deep in thought. She said, 'Well, it'll teach you to go flying off for adventures with strange blondes!'

She was trying to write it all off, put a line under it all.

He said, 'OK. I don't believe that Elizabeth was mad.'

'Oh, Christ.'

She turned and stared out at people hurrying along the street, a crocodile of children heading towards the British Museum from Tottenham Court Road Underground. She said, 'What are you going to do?'

He drank tea, his hands, still lightly bandaged, carefully holding the cup. 'Try to check things out. Try to get to the truth. Can you find out what tests are possible to determine whether a body, a piece of human tissue, was grown in the present day or, say three thousand years ago? And don't say carbon-dating.'

'I wasn't going to say carbon-dating, but how the hell would I find out that sort of thing?'

'You're an anthropologist.'

'The study of man as an animal. I never claimed to be a forensic scientist, but I've a friend in St Mary's Hospital. I can ask him if you like.'

In his flat, he watered his geranium and read his computer for messages. University College confirmed that he had four weeks' sick leave. A colleague at Wyoming State University, the only other authority he knew of, apart from himself, on the secrets of the Kap, would e-mail some stuff within twenty-four hours. From the British Library there was the two-volume published account of Palmer's Sinai expeditions of 1869–70. He opened it at random:

> The Viceroy of Egypt had given orders that our baggage should be passed unopened through the Custom-House, and that every assistance should be given us by the officials. The Peninsular and Oriental Company kindly allowed us to purchase provisions from their stores . . .

Those were the days to be British, he thought; Vronwy would like that. He took the last tablets in his course of antibiotics and went to bed, but slept badly, pictures of Herr Gabriel troubling his mind; Elizabeth at Siwa, saying, 'I guess I'm funded by the CIA.'

Elizabeth and Mac in the morgue.

Elmer.

Elmer was the key. Elmer had been flesh and blood, not the crazed imaginings of a disgraced soldier, the fantasizing of a mature student – and 'mature student' he had discovered, during so many years of university teaching, was so often just another way of saying 'immature person'. Elmer had part of an index finger missing and the missing bit was somewhere in a Western lab. Elmer had the insignia of a Child of the Kap on his forearm. Yes, Elmer was the key.

The quiet bleep of his computer woke him. It was two o'clock in the morning in London, afternoon in Wyoming. He blinked eagerly over the pages that were scrolling down the screen, then sat down and went through them again, disappointed.

His colleague gave him one ray of hope, a reference to a document in the British Library depository at Clerkenwell. It was a document Richard remembered having read some two years previously; he could not, now, remember having seen any references to the Kap. He went back to bed. When he awoke there was another message on the computer. It was from the British Museum. Worboys wanted to see him urgently.

14
The British Museum

'My God,' Worboys cried, jumping up, coming round the desk. 'Did you know the Trustees are threatening to stop my expedition to El-Misheili because of what happened to you?'

'I'm sorry,' Richard apologized.

Worboys was in the thick of it. He had just unpacked a telescopic carbon-fibre mast that would eventually be rigged over the graves at El-Misheili to support an overhead camera. Equipment lay all over the floor – photographic equipment, video-monitoring equipment, packs of dental tools and brushes. On his desk was a jumble of kettles and tin mugs, ten-metre cloth tapes, record books and pencils.

'They've even been on to the BSA in Jerusalem, asking their advice. It's outrageous, them dragging in the BSA.'

The British School of Archaeology was giving Worboys logistical support, providing him with his two vehicles.

'They don't want you to get into trouble,' said Richard, looking round for the usual bottle of Bulgarian red. 'They don't want their Western Asiatic assistant curator shot full of holes. It would lie heav-

241

ily on their conscience, and besides, you would not be an easy man to replace.'

'Ha!' said Worboys dismissively, not entirely displeased. 'What did it feel like being shot?'

'It didn't feel like much. Have you got a drink?'

Worboys looked round vaguely. The phone rang. He snatched it up, then grimaced at Richard. He spoke slowly with heavy good humour, unsuccessfully trying to mask his deep fear and loathing of the person he was talking to. 'You must understand, indeed I must rely on you to make the Trustees understand, that the Egyptian road-building project will not be delayed beyond the first week in April. The road building is vital, we are told, to service the climatology research station that is part of the new Science Nature Park. Building work has already caused damage to what is clearly an extensive late Bronze Age cemetery, a site more important, I might add, than anything so far found by the EES mission to north Sinai. No, no, I fear it is just not possible for my expedition to be postponed – ' his grin was as wide as the Cheshire Cat's. He chuckled good-humouredly. 'I have *just told you* why it cannot be postponed. Excavation cannot wait because the building work is not going to wait, and there is a *grave* risk, therefore, that these *graves* will be destroyed.' Again a high, good-humoured laugh. 'Will you please also make clear to the Trustees that my good friend Muhammad Garfi of the Egyptian Antiquities Organization approached me *directly*, in person, because of our excellent relationship, built up in the Abydos dig. You know he could so easily have gone to the Pennsylvania-Yale people, and if we pull out for no reason I fear he might still do so. No,' he said abruptly, his smile disappearing. 'No, I'm not prepared to consider any delay. You must tell the Trustees I see no reason at all for a delay, that in fact I regard a postponement as fatal. I beg your pardon?'

His face was turning red.

'No, I do not think we should let Pittsburgh take over. I think that would be a quite ludicrous thing to suggest.'

He put the phone down. 'Oh, my God, Oh, my God,' he said. He pounded his skull silently with both fists. He yelled, 'Aaarhg!' Two girls came in. They were his archaeologists, both Institute of Archaeology post-graduate students, both long-legged, bronzed Australians, although Worboys, it could be assumed, had not noticed this.

'Pittsburgh are trying to take over the dig!'

Richard found the bottle of Bulgarian red, tucked behind the photo of Marian and the girls.

'Saltman wants to take over my dig!'

It was Saltman of Pittsburgh who had savaged his article in *Egyptian Archaeology*. Pittsburgh's Egyptology Department was now, Worboys told them, pulling out its expedition team at Bernice Panchrysos in the Eastern Desert because of the political situation in Egypt proper, and offering to move them over to Sinai to make a preliminary survey of El-Misheili.

'Once they're there that will be it. My funding will be gone.'

Richard said, 'Is Vronwy here today? I was hoping to have a word with her.'

One of the girls, whose name was Di, said that Vronwy was buying curtains.

'Curtains?'

'Curtains for some guy.'

243

'Her bloke,' said the other girl, Jo.

'Oh. Right.'

'You know the one? The one who's always been knocking around?' said Di, watching him carefully.

'Maurice,' said Jo.

'They made things up,' said Di.

So that was why she had been peculiar.

Worboys said, 'When does our stuff fly out to Cairo?'

'Tomorrow at five a.m. The carriers are coming to pick it up this afternoon.'

'Let's get on with it then. Let's get it all packed.'

Jo went. Di started packing Worboys's emergency supplies. Medical stuff, a tin of Colman's mustard, Cadbury's drinking chocolate. Worboys sat rigid, his jaw working strangely. 'I only hope we're not wasting our time here,' said Di, wrapping several jars of Marmite in bubble-plastic.

Again the phone rang. Worboys snatched up the receiver. Richard could hear confident, satisfied tones at the other end. He poured Worboys a drink and waved the bottle at Di, who smiled radiantly and said, 'Please.'

Worboys said, 'I see.' He put the phone down. He said, 'We cannot fly into Cairo. The Heritage Office has been talking to the Foreign Office. Advice has been given to the Trustees. Well, that's that.' He sat, squat, hunched, dignified. Before him on his desk was his personal handpick and his personal trowel.

'Oh, Keith,' said Di.

'Do you know,' he said, 'how long it is since I put in my logistic proposal? Eighteen months. But it is always fight, fight, fight. It is always too many people chasing too few funds. I say nothing against the Trustees. But a Ministry of Heritage that cannot

244

appreciate the importance of late Bronze Age coffins in central Sinai! We are led by ignorant men. We live in an ignorant age. We must learn to kowtow to ignorance and vulgarity.'

'It's awful, Keith,' said Di.

'No decent sponsorship – not in these *post-Thatcher* years, not for something as *unsexy* as late Bronze Age graves. No brand-new Ford trucks shipped out for me. No Kelloggs Cornflakes Hot Air Balloon photography. No multi-packs of Newcastle Brown Ale. No free supplies of Kendal Mint Cake!'

'You weren't planning on climbing the Himalayas,' said Richard. 'What did you say the Egyptian road-building project was for, the one at El-Misheili?'

'I have no idea.'

'You were talking about it, on the phone.'

'There's a climatology research station at Sarabit el-Khâdem, in the new Science Nature Park.'

'That's a long way from El-Misheili—'

'I do not know. I do not care.'

Fair enough.

'Where are your vehicles?'

'They are being . . . they were to have been driven over to Suez.'

'From Beersheba?'

Worboys nodded.

'Why don't you fly straight to Tel Aviv? You can still get Sinai visas on the border.'

Worboys blinked at him. He grabbed again at the phone.

Richard left him. He went up in the lift to the Egyptology Department's document room. He checked in the catalogue, then phoned through to the depository at Clerkenwell. He went outside, took a taxi. The BM's Clerkenwell depository was in an old brewery warehouse building. In the Egyptology Department section were stored some 14,000 papyrus rolls, or fragments, largely unsorted, quite separate and distinct from those stored on microfilm and available to the public. An assistant brought him the documents he had ordered. He sat at a bare desk, under the electric light and carefully turned the clear plastic envelopes, which were in a folder marked 'TELL EL-ARMANA B4C'. Unknown. Pharaoh to petty king. Military district commander Gazru to Foreign Office. Foreign Office to King's Office.'

There were some thirty sheets. Richard had first read them when seeking information about Ay, a king's general. He had become convinced, at the time, that the fragments were part of the records of the Pharaonic Secret Service, the eighteenth- and nineteenth-dynasty intelligence network that not only served the King but – dangerously, corruptly – drew into its web information on the faults and vices of its royal master.

Spies for the priests of Amun?

Why else the hurried copy of a royal letter, a letter from the Pharaoh's private office to Adda-danu, a petty king?

Thus the King. He herewith dispatches to you this tablet by hand of Hanya, overseer of Archers—

Hanya, the King's chief whoremaster and pimp.

And also with everything needed for the acquisition of beautiful female cupbearers. Herewith are silver and gold and linen garments and carmelian and an ebony chair to the value of 160 diban. This to purchase 40 female cupbearers, 40 shekels of silver being the price of a female cupbearer. Send extremely beautiful female cupbearers in whom there is no defect, so that the King, your Lord, will say to you, 'This is excellent, in accordance with the order he sent to you.' And know that the King is hale like the Sun. For his troops, his chariots, his horses, all goes well. Amun has put the Upper Land, the Lower Land, where the sun rises, where the sun sets, under the feet of the King . . .

A reply:

May the King, my Lord, take cognizance of his servant and his city. The King, my Lord, the Sun from the Sky, sent Hanya to me, and I have indeed listened to the words of the King, my Lord, very carefully. I have heard the sweet breath of the King. It has come to me and I am very content. And I herewith give 10 oxen and 20 girls.

The King, the Pharaoh who had demanded forty beautiful girls, but received only twenty (and ten beasts) was Akhenaten, the heretic Pharaoh, who had as his wife the lovely Nefertiti.

Richard read on carefully. The papyrus was faded: even under the powerful light the once jet-black inscriptions were only dimly to be made out. There was the standard opening of a letter to the Pharaoh from one of his spies:

To the King, my Lord, the Sun from the Sky, my God, my Sun, the message of your servant, the dirt at your feet, the groom of your horses, I indeed prostrate myself on the stomach and on the back, at the feet of the King, my Lord, the Sun from the Sky, Seven times and Seven times . . .

The body of the letter itself was more difficult. The roll, B4c, was perhaps only twenty per cent complete, and most of it was the gossip of spies.

. . . like a bird in a trap, so are they in Gittipadella,

*for lack of a cultivator their field is like a woman
without a husband. Irsappa will not fight the Apiru
and cries, 'May the King my Lord know that the
Apiru are more powerful than we. May the King take
cognizance of his lands', but in truth Irsappa should
not be listened to, for he has archers that he will not
use, and the two sons of Labau keep saying to Irsappa,
'Wage war against the King, your Lord, as our father
did when he attacked the King's archers and departed
the evil ones', so, O King, may the King turn his attention to the chariots, so that chariots of the King, my
Lord, come forth to punish . . .*

And had they? Had a regiment of chariots
descended on the bewildered, scheming minor
king?

Time passed. He knew what he was looking for,
knew the document, the passage it was within, even
though it was some two years since he had read it.
He was deep in the diplomatic section, the most secret
reports on the fight between state and religion,
between the King and the Theban priesthood, that
had not began with Akhenaten, as generally believed,
but in the reign of Amenophis the Third, who had
married Tiye, a black woman and the daughter of two
provincial nobles.

The scandal among the priesthood!

The confounding of the most holy, divine, devout
article of faith – that the God Amun took the place
of the Pharaoh on his wedding night, and impregnated the new queen.

How could the priests of Amun proclaim on their
temple walls that the God Amun had impregnated a
commoner?

A black woman?

And now in the reign of Akhenaten here was Nefertiti, also black, *black and comely* – this was where those Exodus romancers got the phrase from, stolen from Egypt, like nearly everything else – *black and comely* Nefertiti, and the entire court crazy over Nubian fashions, Nubian manners; even the wigs of the royal ladies at Amarna were inspired by the short coiffures of the Nubians, and here was the Nubian influence spreading ever further through the Children of the Kap—

Here it was!

May your prosperity and the prosperity of your household, your sons, your wives, your horses, your chariots, your country, be very great . . .

A report to Ay, Akhenaten's man, the commander of the King's Horse, the Lord General of Chariots, the fan-bearer and personal scribe to the King, on the growing influence of the Kap, that secret organization made up of the sons of Nubian princes.

And of the many secrets of the Kap, of the servants of the viceroy of Nubia, of the sons of the kings of Wawat and Kush, of the King's servants who bear the title Child of the Kap, the secret insignia of such a child is reported to be of twisted flax below the bull, as denoting strength and constancy . . .

A mark, a twist of flax – that was what had been below the bull hieroglyph on the arm of the boy soldier in the morgue at Maadi.

His eyes were weary. He went to the registrar and asked how many people had withdrawn Papyrus Amarna B4c in the last two years, since it had been brought to London.

Two academics – himself and his colleague from Wyoming – and four students, two American, one French, one Dutch.

None called Elizabeth St George. Or Elizabeth Ford. Not that that meant anything; she could have used yet another false name. But he did not think she had done so. A deception so elaborate, so subtle – what could be the point? In many ways she had lied to him, over the funding, the involvement of Drextel . . . *but that was in another country*, he told himself, handing back the sheets of papyrus and going out into the dark afternoon, *and besides, the wench is dead*.

He did not think she had lied about Elmer.

He went back to the British Museum, to the canteen to eat. Di and Jo, Worboys's archaeologists, came and sat on either side of him. 'Hi, Di,' he said. ''Lo, Jo.'

Jo said, 'Keith says we're not sexy enough.'

'Tell him,' said Richard, 'that he's out of his mind.'

'The expedition,' said Di. 'He says the expedition isn't sexy.'

'Ah, yes,' said Richard, 'so he does.'

'But listen. We've been thinking. Late Bronze Age Sinai puts us into Exodus territory, right? The lost tribes, the parting of the Red Sea. Why don't we call ourselves Expedition 'Ark of the Covenant'. We ought to get the *Sunday Times* to sponsor that one. What do you think?'

'You're the Exodus man,' said Di.

'Why would the tribes of Israel,' said Richard, looking round for Vronwy, 'who were struggling desperately to survive in the Sinai Desert, go to all the trouble of building an ark – an ark covered in silver and gold and lapis lazuli, the sacred ark – and then just abandon it in the desert?'

'Because the Egyptian army was after them?'

'OK, right.'

'The host of Egypt, led by Amarek, the Pharaoh's commander-in-chief—'

'Amarek, if he existed, was a petty king, a sheikh, probably a Midionite.'

'These are details, Corrigan.'

'Yeah, Corrigan, don't get bogged down.'

'You think the Ark of the Covenant was buried in a late Bronze Age cemetery?'

'Why not?'

'Well, it would be a bit big, I'd have thought.'

'This is a *tell*, Richard. There's no saying what's under there, under all that rubbish, under all those ruins. Imagine a great cavern—'

'Its entrance disguised, the way the entrances to the pyramids were disguised. Think of the royal tombs in the Valley of the Kings—'

'Remember, Richard, that those Hebrews had been working on the pyramids. They were dodging the corvée. They were skilled tomb-makers and brickmakers. They'd been working in the Valley of the Dead, it even says so in Numbers—'

'They had the skills to build a cavern. A stone cavern, undisturbed for over three thousand years. A cavern temple with, lying in its centre—'

'The Ark—' breathed Jo.

'Of the Covenant.' Di's eyes shone.

'With just a single shaft of sunlight—'

'Falling on the snakes.'

They fell about. Di punched him on the shoulder, the way Australian girls did when they were not skydiving or arm-wrestling. He yelled and dropped his cup.

Vronwy was in the doorway, a big plastic bag from Heal's under her arm. Curtain material, presumably, for Maurice.

Di reached over and touched him lightly on his arm. 'Does it hurt?' she asked. 'Did I hurt you?'

'Only a bit,' he said, his arm throbbing unmercifully.

Every so often, like a shower of cold water, there came, with the physical pain, the knowledge that Elizabeth and Mac were both dead, that a just over a week ago they had been alive.

15
US Embassy, Grosvenor Square

On the desk lay a thin blue file without a label, the sort that could be used for other things once its temporary contents had been binned. Bill Martin, who sat behind the desk reading it, was perhaps thirty. He looked up and said, 'Sorry I couldn't see you sooner. I was in the country. Ever been beagling?'

'No.'

'It's like fox-hunting, but the huntsmen run along on foot, and wear blue coats instead of red ones. You ought to try to get out to the country and see them.'

'I must do that.'

'How can I help you?'

'Elizabeth St George.'

'We're calling her that?'

'She told me it was her name.'

'She gave us a lot of trouble. So did you, for that matter.'

He looked down again at the temporary file. They were in a small room, thickly carpeted but with no furniture except for the desk and two chairs. It was very hot. The window, triple-glazed, allowed no sound to enter. Martin said, 'OK. On 15 January we received formal complaints from the Egyptian government about two US citizens and one British subject breaking interior travel laws and contacting persons regarded as a security risk, presumably for media interview. We were asked if these three persons had media status and warned that the Egyptian authorities could not be responsible for their safety.'

He looked up at the bruise on the right side of Richard's face, the bandaged hands. He looked down again.

'Later that day we were informed that the same three people were suspected by Security Services of breaking and entering government buildings in Cairo. We were formally warned that when arrested no account would be taken of their nationality and that they would be subject to the full rigours of the law. We were warned in advance that media campaigns on their behalf in the UK or US would be disregarded. It might not seem so to you,' Martin looked up again, 'but these warnings were friendly. They were the only way pro-Western officials in the Egyptian Foreign Office could let us know what was happening. They were a way of telling us that you were in trouble.'

'I'm grateful to them.'

Martin looked down again.

'On 17 January, in the early hours of the morning, we learned through other sources that you'd been arrested in Cairo by Security Police. Considerable diplomatic effort over forty-eight hours by ourselves and the British resulted in your being transferred into the custody of the regular Interior Ministry Police.'

'The Mukhabarat released us,' said Richard, 'in order to kill us.'

'If you didn't like playing rough, you should've

stayed in South Dakota. You think you're all we've got to worry about?'

'No, I don't think that.'

Martin's eyes had not moved from the file.

'This wasn't the first time you'd come to our notice. Some four weeks previously you were in Sinai when a German citizen died. The man, Herr Gabriel, was in the care of a UN doctor when it happened. His body was taken by Egyptian police to Cairo for post-mortem examination. You telephoned the German Embassy in Cairo and advised them to get their own doctor present. The Germans ran a check on you. Have you ever,' he said, looking up from the file, 'been involved with intelligence work?'

'No.'

'A surprisingly large number of British academics have been.'

'That was what the Egyptians said. I told them I wasn't British.'

'It's a puzzle why the Brits recruit so many academics. Academics are not reliable. They defect just to show how clever they are, what an aristocratic élite they belong to, how easily they can fool the plebs who run the country. You'd think the Brits would have learned their lesson.'

'According to Cline,' said Richard, 'respect for scholarship is one of the distinguishing features that has given the CIA a marked superiority over other intelligence organizations.'

'I'm not talking about scholarship, I'm talking about useless British academics. Cambridge queers. Oxford dons quaffing port wine at the High Table. If you've ever been involved with CIA or with the SIS, tell me now. Don't waste my time.'

'I've never been involved with CIA or British Intelligence. If I had been, why would I be phoning you?'

'How would I know?'

'You telling me you're not CIA?'

'It's a big organization,' said Martin noncommittally. He looked back at the file. 'Richard Corrigan. Born Hot Springs, South Dakota. Mother a school teacher, father an archaeo-zoologist – an archaeozoologist in Hot Springs, South Dakota?'

'There's a place on 19th Street where mammoths once called by to take a drink. Ten-ton mammoths that didn't notice they were sinking into the swampy ground while they drank their fill. They disappeared, one on top of the other in the sink hole.'

'The things you learn. Married Melanie Plapp of Saugatuck, Michigan, and second Kirsty Candlish of Whitehaven, Cumbria.'

Richard said, 'You've got the story of my life.'

Mel was an innkeeper; she had remarried a man called Dale and they had a bed and breakfast in Vermont, called Whispering Pines, and two kids, and Richard was welcome to stay any time. Kirsty had come a long way from Whitehaven, Cumbria. She was a dealer in the City, a foreign exchange broker, a real ball-breaker. When they spoke on the phone she said, 'Hi, Richard', in a sad voice, sharing their common mourning for a marriage inexplicably shattered by an act of fate, which was how she rationalized her infatuation with a pinstriped gorilla from the money market.

'No children.'

'No,' said Richard.

'The world's number one expert on the Egyptian war machine of the nineteenth dynasty.'

256

He said, wearily, what he always said, 'It's not a large field.'

Martin put the file down. He glanced discreetly at his watch. 'OK,' he said, 'so what's your problem?'

'I want to know what happened.'

'Of the two of us, Richard, you were the one out there.'

'Was Mac a CIA agent?'

'No.'

'Elizabeth?'

'No.'

'She thought she was being funded by you.'

'She thought a lot of things.'

'So who was funding her?'

Martin shrugged.

'The British?'

'Could be.'

'You know what she was working on?'

'Paranormal stuff. Mummies coming back to life. The curse of Tutankhamun. Am I right?'

'It's one way of putting it.'

Martin said, 'She gave us a lot of trouble. We're straining a gut to stop a Middle East conflagration and she went to Cairo and started breaking and entering. Most people think she was out of her mind.'

'So why did they need to kill her?'

'One crazy dame,' said Martin, as if he hadn't heard. 'Come on now. Seeing ghosts in central Sinai? Taping conversations with psychiatric patients? Carving up corpses in a Cairo morgue?'

So they knew about the index finger.

'I wasn't there when that happened.'

'It doesn't matter,' said Martin. 'We weren't going to tell anybody.'

Richard said, 'Mac. Who killed Mac?'

'How would we know?'

'Who told you we had been arrested?'

'Sources.'

'I must write to Elizabeth's people, her family. Have you got an address?'

'No.'

'In that case I'll fax Drextel.'

Martin shrugged slightly.

'She's dead,' said Richard. 'She's dead and you don't seem interested.'

Martin said, 'We're not.'

'An American citizen, right?'

'Mixed up in somebody else's war.'

'Bullshit.'

'If that's it, the door's behind you.'

'The corpse in Maadi, the corpse of an ancient Egyptian boy soldier found in the middle of the Yom Kippur War.'

'A fake.'

'You know that?'

'No. Neither have I personally seen Hitler's diaries.'

'Elizabeth sent a sample of human tissue, flesh and nail, to a university medical department in the US.'

He was guessing.

'Could be.'

'Has it been analysed?'

'If she sent the money, I expect so.'

'OK, you think she was crazy, or you're pretending to think she was crazy. But I'm not crazy. I was with Herr Gabriel when he died. The UN doctor said Gabriel was severely dehydrated. He said he could not have taken in any significant amount of liquid during the previous three days. But I saw Gabriel drink coffee and iced water and orange juice at breakfast at Taba, I saw him drink coffee and Coke, I saw him drink a beer and a litre of water before he went up the mountain. Those are the facts. Right?'

Martin said again, 'Could be.'

'There are two possibilities. One is that on the mountain Gabriel was exposed to something that dehydrated his blood at an abnormally fast rate. At Washington I worked with some guys involved in CAT-scan X-ray utilizing microwave technology. CAT-scan is a development of medical scanners now being used by archaeologists to look inside mummies without actually unwrapping them – reproducing three-dimensional images of the bodies, even reconstructing the faces, putting flesh back on the bones. Microwave technology was a new development. They were moving towards a portable CAT-scan, one that could be used in the field. It was experimental, and in the end the development went ahead at Imperial College, here in London, without the microwave element. But these guys at Washington had a joint research programme with the army. With the Pentagon.'

Martin said, 'I'm listening.'

'You know the apocryphal story, from the early days of kitchen microwaves? The story about the kid who put his wet hamster in the microwave to dry, result one half-cooked hamster? Well, I saw Herr Gabriel's blood when the vein was cut open.'

Martin was looking at him attentively.

'You can look through the Washington Institute bulletin. There was a piece called something like "CAT-scan: the second option", but I'm going back more than ten years. You must have experts here who know a hell of a lot more than I do, or archaeologists in Washington do, about military microwave application.'

Martin said, 'That was the first possibility. What was the second?'

'That Gabriel had not, as the UN medic declared was the case, consumed liquid for three days.'

'But you saw him do so. You saw him consume liquid only hours before he went missing.'

Richard said, 'Yes, I saw him drink liquid.'

Martin said, 'I'm in Intelligence Directorate, and I'm in the Office of European Analysis. Microwave technology is way above my head, and so, for that matter, is detailed policy regarding the Middle East. But I hear what you're saying. Germans are one thing, but we don't want American tourists turning into microwaved hamsters. I'll pass on what you've told me.'

He pressed a switch. He said, 'You shouldn't have gone to Egypt to break the law. It's crassly stupid of Americans to think they can just go where they like and the marines'll come and get them out of trouble. Egypt is in one hell of a crisis situation. The government is trying to cling to power by appeasing the fundamentalists. There are colonels in the army who support Hizb ut-Tahrir and the Muslim Front, colonels who'd love to see a re-run of Yom Kippur. There are two hundred dead now in Gaza and the West Bank. A busload of Israeli schoolkids are maimed or dead. The only importance Elizabeth St George or Elizabeth Ford possesses is that she stays off the front pages of the newspapers, that we don't wake up one morning, during this crisis situation, to read "US woman tortured and killed in desert by Egyptian army" and find the White House telephone

lines jammed with callers demanding that we bomb
Cairo. Her folks know she got mixed up in a terrorist
incident and was killed. You go to the Third World
and that's what sometimes happens. Her body is
being shipped home. Stay clear of Egypt, Libya,
Algeria and Syria. You'll be arrested if you go to any
of those countries. Be grateful you've still got a resident's permit for the UK and remember it can always
be taken away from you.'

'It was the British who got me out of Egypt,' said
Richard. 'There were no fucking US marines came for
me.'

'Thanks for dropping by. Call us if you have any
more problems.'

Richard went out, under the security cameras, into
Grosvenor Square. He could see the turning to Carlos
Place and the Connaught Hotel, where he had dined
with Elizabeth. In his mind there came a fleeting
picture of her getting into a taxi, after their meal, the
light from the Connaught's lobby falling on her hair.
He went past Eisenhower's statue and crossed the
road and went into Grosvenor Square itself. Snow-
drops were pushing up through the dark wet earth;
daffodils and crocuses would soon be out. He leant on
the iron rail. Franklin D. Roosevelt looked down at
him. He was tired and stressed. He was a too-clever-
by-half academic. He knew that Bill Martin had told
a lot of lies, hidden a lot of truths.

He did not know that the security cameras high
above the carved stone eagle, moving and whirring
incessantly, homed in on him as he stood with his
swollen, hot, bandaged hands gripping the cold iron,
and then tracked him past the Canadian High Com-

mission and into Brook Street, on his way to Bond Street Underground; or that a security guard in the embassy basement operations room noted (but without knowing who he was) that he was being followed.

But Richard suspected that he was being followed anyway. It was something else that fretted him. The feeling that he was losing touch with reality.

That he, perhaps like Elizabeth, was going crazy.

16
Oxford

They were too clever for him on the Northern Line, but not on the Thames Valley Turbo. He spotted her instantly: dark, neat, mid-thirties, a faintly academic look, reading Samuel Butler's *The Way of All Flesh*, buying a cup of tea when the trolley came round. How did he know it was her? Well, really he didn't, of course; she might well have been travelling on beyond Oxford, on to Vronwy's Shropshire perhaps, if the train went that far. She was self-absorbed, intent on Butler's destruction of middle-class Victorian values. What was she then, if not a spy or a traveller to the West? A lecturer from Hertford College, possibly, or Lincoln – nothing too trendy, she didn't look as if she'd fit in with the New College lot, the intense, self-important novelists, the mad poets.

No, she was his follower, his companion for the afternoon, his 'tail'. There was nobody else possible. Opposite him was a fat, shell-suited mother with two small, fat children. Half a dozen anaemic students slouched in their seats looking tired and depressed. A businessman talked into his mobile.

The Thames was in flood, fields of glass reflecting the yellow afternoon sky. The train approached Reading, slowing past the water meadows, the sunset reflected in shining dark-glass buildings; the redbrick Victorian gaol where Oscar Wilde wrote:

> *Yet each man kills the thing he loves,*
> *By each let this be heard,*
> *Some do it with a bitter look,*
> *Some with a flattering word.*

Vronwy had said casually on the phone, 'By the way, did I tell you I'm back with Maurice.'

No, Vronwy, you didn't.

Now they were rattling along by the water meadows, past Caversham, where BBC monitoring staff listened to the agonies and excitements of the world, their receivers tuned to Cairo National, to Amman, to Damascus, to the cold voices of GIA and Hizb ut-Tahrir, and the Islamic New Brotherhood stations in the Gulf. Listening and analysing and summarizing.

At Pangbourne a woman walking two Labrador dogs glanced up at the train, then threw a stick into the floodwater and the dogs went splashing in to retrieve it. Vronwy was always talking about the two retrievers back at her family home; large, stupid dogs called Benbow and Hardy.

'I'm giving the sod one last chance,' she had explained, trying to sound both casual and jolly, making it clear that she and Richard could still be close friends. 'One last chance, and then that's it.'

Didcot. It was going dark now, as they swept past the cooling towers. Twenty minutes to go. He took out and re-read a letter from Celia, posted ten days ago in Taba. 'Hell, I've decided, is Christmas Day afternoon in Poolmeadow Road, Morecambe. Four o'clock when you're full of turkey and pudding, and people are trying to make you eat cold turkey sandwiches and trifle, and saying, "Are you all right? What's the matter?" because you're not hooting with laughter at the four millionth repeat of *It'll be All Right on the Night*, or they're saying, "Come and help with the washing-up then, Celia. You're not in one of your posh hotels now, you know." Christ, Richard, I knew, I knew. Anyway, I escaped on Boxing Day and stayed with some friends in Chelmsford and we watched bungee-jumping in the car park next to Sainsbury's. Before Christmas I'd tried for a ski resort and got put on a list – five seasons I've done in St Anton and they just shove me on a bloody list! Thank God for Timetravelers of Baltimore, or I'd be back in Morecambe doing bar work and phoning the Samaritans every night. Anyway, here I am in Eilat. The border's still closed with Taba, and Israeli soldiers with wicked-looking submachine-guns are all over the place, but we expect them to let us through tomorrow. I'm booked for three Sinai tours, taking me through till mid-March, but there's a rumour that Baltimore will pull out after this one. Some of the punters are beginning to realize that Sinai and Egypt are closely related. Who knows, I might get sent to Bali or Hawaii. Dreams, eh? The tour lecturer's called Tony Matthews. He's from Liverpool University. He says he knows you by reputation – what can he mean? The punters are OK. They were in Scotland for hogmanay and they're all wearing tartan caps. You should see all these tartan caps bobbing about on camels. Unbelievable! The temperature's in the seventies, and the moon's shining on the sea, and Tony's just bringing out two iced Campari sodas. Don't you

265

really wish you were here, Richard? See you some time. Love, Celia.'

He was touched. He would never have thought of writing to Celia, friendly, warm-hearted girl though she was.

'PS. I still can't get over that German guy. We're due at the Desert Oasis in two days. I wish we weren't going there. I'm determined that none of this lot will leave my sight for a second.'

At Oxford he stood in the aisle, politely, to let the dark, neat woman get off before him. She looked up at him, puzzled. She wasn't getting off after all.

He walked out of the station, along the road past Worcester College, past the Ashmolean Museum, then turned back towards the centre of the city and went into the Randolph Hotel, using the side entrance. Two minutes later he left, again by the side entrance, figuring that anybody following him would bet on his leaving from the front.

He disappeared into back streets, emerging in Westgate, by the library. He plodded through the shadows towards Carfax. Few people were about. February was not a month for tourists. They liked to come when the college lawns were green, the flower-beds bright and summery. February for under-graduates was a month for work, although near the covered market a string quartet of students busked in the light of the sodium lamps: only in Oxford, he told himself, would you see this.

He passed Lincoln College and came to a door which had on it a handprinted poster: BAKED BEANS AND THE ARROW OF TIME, and the snappy teaser *Sure-fire Ways to Win the National Lottery*. He went in. A student gave him a ticket and said there was no charge, it was a free lecture, but could he please go in quietly because it had already started. He went in quietly and found a seat. There were thirty or so undergraduates, a few older people – Open University students, he guessed – and a gaggle of sixth-form girls with their teacher. Just in front of him a boy was stroking his girl's neck while she, a hypnotic look on her face, stared intently at the man on the platform, who was saying:

'So, although the *cosmological* arrow of time may point in one direction, outwards, as the universe expands, this arrow, it is fair to assume, will point inwards when the universe contracts. This will have alarming and contradictory consequences for what for convenience I will call the *second arrow of time*, an arrow which is governed by the second law of thermodynamics, which states that matter must progress from a perfect state to an imperfect state, disorder must always increase, never decrease. In other words, a cup on the table can fall to the floor and be smashed, but bits of broken cup on the floor cannot rise from the floor to reassemble themselves on the table. Your room is a squalid mess, yet unfortunately, because of the second law of thermodynamics, you cannot go out to the pub for an hour and get back to find the fag ash reconstituted into a ciggy, and the dishes that you left dirty in the sink, encrusted with dried baked beans, removed from the sink by supernatural forces and stacked clean and sparkling in the cupboard.'

A polite ripple of laughter. Everyone knew it had been years since the lecturer had eaten baked beans in North Oxford digs, and if he smoked cigarettes nobody thought he called them ciggies.

'So we have two arrows of time. The direction of the first is outwards because the universe is moving outwards, but it does not *have* to point outwards. The second arrow, governed by the second law of thermodynamics, and known as the law of increasing entropy, is also pointing outwards, and in fact *must* point outwards, *must* point towards the future, because life depends on decay, on the energy of change and of deconstruction. In a world where the second law of thermodynamics ceased to apply, we would all be dead. The baked beans would not only remove themselves from the dirty plate in the sink, they would reconstitute themselves from your stomach. The fat of your body would be busy extracting itself, turning itself back into the cream cakes and pints of beer from whence it came.'

This was a fun lecture, Richard recalled. A lecture in the series 'Physics for Fun'.

'But what will happen if the universe begins to contract, causing the first arrow of time to go into reverse, and to contradict the second arrow of time? You have already heard in this series of lectures about the seeming paradox contained in the fact that the laws of physics, or such of them as we understand, appear to be reversible in time, whereas we are constantly confronted with large-scale phenomena that are manifestly not reversible. Human existence depends on time's arrow pointing forwards. But the laws of physics allow time to point in any direction. The laws of physics, it seems, are not concerned with the survival or otherwise of the human race.

'But there is the third and final arrow of time. Can that save us? The third arrow of time is the arrow that affects humans and some higher animals, though not,

I am reliably informed, turkeys. It is the psychological arrow. We can remember what happened yesterday – unless hopelessly inebriated, of course . . .'

A ruffle of polite laughter.

'But we cannot remember what happens tomorrow. The third arrow of time, therefore, also points outwards, to the future, and cannot possible turn itself round and start to move back into the past. Again, it is an arrow, a law, that is manifestly not reversible. But again, let me remind you, as far as *physics* is concerned, all arrows of time can point in any direction, and no law of the universe is violated.

'To summarize, the laws of physics do not distinguish between past and future, but the existence of mankind does.'

He paused. He said, 'I want now to consider the concept of imaginary time.'

Richard's arm was hurting. So was his head. A voice behind him whispered, 'Did he say turkeys could remember the future?'

Another whisper, 'No, dumbo, he said they couldn't remember the past.'

'Oh, good. All those turkeys remembering Christmas.'

The lecturer had dropped his populist banter. He was speaking crisply. 'Two times two equals four. OK? But minus two times minus two also equals four. In order to overcome this, we have special numbers, known as imaginary numbers, that give negative numbers when multiplied by themselves.'

He wrote on a blackboard:

$$2i \times 2i = -4$$

'What we suddenly find, using special numbers, is that there is no difference between directions in time and in space. So why should we regard one well-defined mathematical concept, real time, as being in any way more valid than another well-defined concept, imaginary time? Hawking, you are well aware, has said that it is meaningless to ask which is "real" or which is "imaginary", it is simply a question of which is the more useful description . . .'

Richard was lost. He had not enough beacons of knowledge to guide him, not enough reference points; it was humiliating, not being able to keep up with a fun lecture. Near him, the sixth-formers were sitting alert, keen-eyed with intelligence, some of them scribbling in notebooks inscribed 'Stratford-upon-Avon Grammar School for Girls'. The boy who had been fondling the girl's neck was kissing her. The lecture room was warm, discreetly lit by creamy lights recessed into Victorian mahogany; presumably the free entry to the lecture had made it a better option than the movies. The girl, although being kissed, had her eyes open, and on the lecturer. He was a bit of a heart-throb, Richard guessed, to first-year female undergraduates.

He fell into a doze. When he woke the lecturer was writing again on the blackboard:

$$ds \geq o$$

'So the second law of thermodynamics, the law which says that baked beans spilled out of their tin cannot put themselves back into it, essentially is saying that if you start in a very small region of *phase space* – and phase space you recall is *imaginary space with a large number of dimensions* – then you will soon find yourself in a larger region. Remember, entropy is denoted by the letter S . . .'

Despite himself, Richard dozed again. When he awoke the lecturer was saying: 'OK, it's a bit wild, a bit off the wall, but we've five minutes left, so let's just follow it for a moment, see where it takes us.'

The lovers, who had also been asleep, were stirring.

'Let's say a point is reached, perhaps only half-way through its history, when maximum entropy is attained, when the universe starts to contract. The first arrow of time is turned – remember, Hawking did not believe that this would happen, but his own students at Cambridge have proved that this would, in fact, be the case. The arrow is turned but there is no chaos because the second and third arrows *turn with it*. They do not just go into reverse, they *turn*, the way a car might turn at the end of a cul-de-sac. As far as the people in the car are concerned they are still going forward, but – to move back from cars to the universe – the first arrow of time has determined a new direction, a direction opposite to the original direction, a direction that is taking our descendants forward into *our past*.'

He stopped and looked round. The Stratford-upon-Avon sixth-formers, the clever kids, were up there with him; it was simple stuff, this, their looks implied.

'Is there anything to stop us leaving them a message? Launching a space probe, a dozen space probes, for these *contraction* people to find when they come back this way? Probes containing details of what is *our past* but what would be *their future*?

'Or are we, in fact, contraction people ourselves? Has the universe already started to collapse? Are we on our way back to Big Bang? Are we at some point going to find a container floating in space that tells us our future, a future that is really somebody else's past? A message in a bottle, containing the numbers, perhaps, for a future week's National Lottery?'

Generous clapping; an atmosphere of relaxation, of relief. It might be 'Physics for Fun' but it was as much as most undergraduate physicists could do to keep up with it. Students were moving with speed before the pubs closed.

Outside the rain had turned to sleet.

'Here you are. They're all on ten-day loan,' said Vronwy, 'plus three weeks unless recalled.'

He had a temperature, his arm was inflamed. At University College Hospital they had given him a different kind of antibiotic and told him to stay in bed for a few days. 'What is time?' he mused lying there, looking at the tomes, the dissertations and research papers in their chunky red British Library bindings.

'Nearly twelve o'clock,' said Vronwy.

'What is time, what is time, not what is *the* time, idiot.'

'Ah, time,' said Vronwy, making coffee. 'Time is what stops everything from happening at once.'

He pondered on it.

'Do you want any food brought in? Oh, here, I found this on the mat.'

It was a New Year letter from Melanie. Enclosed was another photo of her two boys by husband number two; healthy, white-toothed Vermont kids with freckled noses.

'You really made a pig's ear of that relationship,'

said Vronwy, who had seen a photograph of Whispering Pines. 'You could have been Mine Host, the innkeeper, happy till the end of your days.'

'Can you get me some of those boil-in-the-bag kipper fillets?'

She looked at him.

'And some of Mr Kipling's Bramley apple pies.'

'Oh, God,' she said. 'You'll make me cry.'

He hadn't asked her to come; he hadn't told her that he was ill. She had been told by a librarian in the Institute of Archaeology and had volunteered to bring him the books he had ordered.

She said, awkwardly, looking at all the books, 'Don't get obsessed, OK?'

'Pardon?'

'You know . . . all this time stuff.'

'It's not "time stuff", it's physics.'

'It's a bit unreal.'

'There's a woman dead. I find that gives it a distinct edge of reality.'

She gave him an irritated look. He said, 'Have you heard from your friend at St Mary's?'

She shook her head. She poured water on coffee granules. She sat by the flickering gas fire, eating toast and not mentioning Maurice.

For three days he lay in bed and read the books. February rain beat against the window. His room acquired a deep odour of smoked herring. His gas-fire hissed companionably. He put a large towel against the door to keep out the draught. The tenant of the flat under his was learning the alto sax, and played tunes from *Miss Saigon*, getting better by the day. Occasionally, when he got up to eat, or make coffee, or have a pee, he stood and looked out over the rooftops of Islington. From his little window he could see only dreary warehouses and offices with small-paned dusty windows, yards that in summer were clothed in thick weeds and purple rosebay willow herb, but where in winter the plastic bottles and tin cans and rusting prams were bleakly exposed. Beneath this depressing inner-city decay, he knew, was the Roman-built masonry of London Wall, the buried foundations of medieval Clerkenwell.

When he went out on to the landing and looked out of the front window, he could see a parked car with a man inside it, the car having a discreet but long aerial.

Perhaps a Cabinet minister had taken the top flat for his mistress and was being staked out by the tabloids.

In the afternoon the car was gone but there was a van with 'Richmond ACE Windscreen Repairs' on its side. The van got a ticket from a traffic warden – they were nothing if not sticklers for detail.

Next day there was nothing; they must have moved inside, hired a room, perhaps taken a flat.

That night he slept badly, waking from nightmares drenched in sweat. When he padded over to his window there was a discreet light in the warehouse, the office window directly opposite his flat. Burglars? A security guard? After a few moments the light went out. Would somebody over there speak softly into a little machine, recording the time when he switched on his light, made a drink and went back to his books?

He had written down everything he could remember that Elizabeth had told him at Siwa; he had written it down even though he had not understood it. He was having to start at the beginning.

He already knew that it was easy to travel forward in space. Three-dimensional space combined with time to form *space-time*. Spatial points existed in space as we knew it, and *spatio-temporal* points existed in the fourth dimension. Einstein's special theory of relativity had shown that a space traveller moving through the solar system at a speed approaching the speed of light would be using up time far slower than an earth-bound being. The space traveller would return to earth, after a voyage of several years, noticeably younger than the twin brother he had left behind him. *He would, in other words, have jumped forward in earth time.*

Had Elmer been on a long space voyage? Were his regimental markings not the brotherhood signs of the Kap but his rank as a captain in the Pharaonic Space Fleet? Had he returned back from an ambassadorial visit to Andromeda (How far did you have to travel, and at what speed, to jump forward in earth time by 3,300 years?) only to die of shock in a mortar attack on Egyptian tanks in the Wadi el-Garf in 1973?

It was an explanation based on the accepted, known laws of physics; unfortunately, it was also an explanation that took him back to the pyramids as space beacons.

It was a question of keeping control, of keeping a sense of proportion.

He went back to Einstein.

To the people who had followed Einstein.

To the things Elizabeth had told him at Siwa, when he had said to her, 'Tell me the physics part in all this.'

Life was a worm. Its tail was your birth, its head was your death. You crawled or perhaps you writhed (at times of foolishness and misery, like marriage and divorce) through space-time, through the spatial points as we knew them, through the spatio-temporal points in the fourth dimension.

This line, this line that your life described, that your worm followed, was called your *worldline*.

At the point of your birth a ray of light had shot out at an angle and formed a cone, and because Einstein firmly insisted (though nowadays there were those who would contradict him) that you could not travel faster than light, your worldline had always to remain within this cone.

Your worldline was called *timelike* because it remained within its cone, conforming to Einstein's requirement, his law. Time, *real time*, the time as measured between breakfast and dinner, tick-tocked along within Einstein's cone.

At four o'clock on the afternoon of the fourth day he worked out how, in theory, to travel into the past.

He wrote:

i. The special theory of relativity says that the worldlines of physical objects, including people, *must* be timelike.

ii. Equations of the general theory of relativity indicate that massive bodies like planets and stars can bend worldlines.

iii. A bent worldline, distorted in space-time, might bend over so far that it formed an actual loop.

iv. This loop could be used, in theory and ultimately perhaps in practice, to travel through time.

iv. This loop is called, by physicists and mathematicians, A CLOSED TIMELIKE CURVE or a CTC.

A tear in the fabric of space itself.
A time machine that would carry you into the past.

17
Greenwich

He got up from his bed but stayed in his flat. Books and magazines were biked to him from the London Library, pizzas from Pizza Heaven. One morning Vronwy turned up, ruddy-cheeked and glowing with cold, carrying groceries. 'Worboys is hiding from the Trustees. A New Haven expedition to Tell el-Amarna has been told it's now too dangerous to go to Egypt. The Minya region's where all the trouble is, of course, down round Luxor, but Worboys is terrified that we'll be stopped from going to Sinai. I've brought you some salad stuff. Do you eat any salad stuff?'

Not if he could help it.

'How's the cold?'

'Better.'

'The arm? The hands?'

'They're fine.'

'Let me have a look.'

She looked at his hands, his soft new skin. She looked on his arm at the small, well-knitted rose of pink flesh that covered the hole where the bullet had entered. She said, 'Pow. Zap. When are you going to get up and get some exercise?'

'I don't need exercise. Listen to this. The earth thundering round the sun bends space-time. Gravity is an illusion to our preconditioned vantage point. Curvature of space-time manifests as gravity because of our assumption that space-time is flat, which locally it is.'

Vronwy said, 'Where's your kettle?'

'It's broken.'

'What's the matter with it?'

'How would I know? It refuses to boil water. Use a saucepan.'

'You'd think with all this science stuff you'd be fractionally less useless about kettles.'

'Black holes,' said Richard, 'can exert pressures that would tear the fabric of time, and in so doing form a CTC, a Closed Timelike Curve. OK. Right. But why – this is the question – why should a black hole on the other side of some supernova on the other side of the galaxy want to start fixing up time-trips in North Africa. And how could it actually accomplish this, even assuming it had the inclination?'

'I have no idea,' said Vronwy, honestly.

Richard said, 'Would you be interested to hear the philosophical argument against time travel?'

'I'd be interested in you getting out and about and blowing the cobwebs away. You've not left this hole in a week. Carry on like this and you'll go totally insane.'

Today, this morning, he had seen the neat, dark woman again, the woman from the Oxford train. She had been going into the warehouse offices at the back of his flat, through the builder's yard, the old milk bottles and rusting prams. When he went down to collect the mail, he found that his name had been removed from the mailbox in the hall and from the little plastic pocket next to his doorbell.

'OK,' he said. 'Let's go get some fresh air.'

They took a cab to the Embankment, then a river-boat to Greenwich, the home of mean time. They walked by the river. She talked departmental politics. He grunted occasionally, trying to show an interest. She sighed, and said, 'OK, so what are the philosophical arguments against time travel?'

Richard said, 'Henrietta travels back in a time machine. She meets her grandmother – at a time prior to the conception of her mother – and kills her. So, where does Henrietta come from? We have a paradox. Classical physics argues that Henrietta cannot kill her grandmother, that it would not be allowed to happen, that *something* would get in the way. But what? Some form of divine intervention? Would some unseen force, monitoring the application of the classical laws of physics, stop the knife falling, the cyanide pill dissolving, the rope tightening round poor grandma's throat?'

They went into the lounge bar of the Lord Nelson pub and ordered pints of stout and a pile of toasted sandwiches.

'Well, go on,' said Vronwy. 'Don't keep me in suspense.'

'The classical physicists say, yes, something like this would have to happen. Some force would have to intervene to stop Henrietta doing the dark deed. But, *at the same time* they say that nothing could intervene, because if some force did stop Henrietta killing her grandmother it would violate the *autonomy principle*, which states that we can do whatever we like locally without worrying about what the rest of the universe is doing. You with me?'

'Some of the way,' said Vronwy. There was a blazing

log fire in the pub and a dog stretched out in front of it, a Staffordshire bull terrier, drinking up the warmth just as she was drinking up her stout.

'We don't have to take into account the configuration of the planets before striking a match. No great law of the universe tells us when we can or can't turn on an electric light. The autonomy principle is the basic law of physics that allows us to function. It is the basis of *free will* and organized religion.'

'Why organized religion?'

'What?'

'I just wondered,' she said, 'if there was any other sort.'

'Despite this,' he went on, ignoring her, 'classical physics demands that, one way or another, Henrietta is not allowed to kill her grandmother. However hard she might try, she cannot be allowed to succeed. Classical physics demands that for time travel to happen the autonomy principle must fail, and as the autonomy principle clearly cannot be allowed to fail, classical physics – arguing from a philosophical rather than a scientific standpoint – insists that travel into the past is an impossibility.'

The barman rang the bell. This was not a pub that believed in all-day drinking. They would have to go out into the cold.

'Well,' said Vronwy, 'there we are then.'

'I've not finished.'

'Ah. Right.'

'Classical physicists have a second argument against backward time travel, which is called the *knowledge paradox*. A time traveller goes back to late-nineteenth-century France and finds the young artist

Matisse dabbling away on the Left Bank. Matisse, to be honest, is a pretty rotten artist, the runt of the artistic litter, sneered at by his contemporaries in art school, not the sort of guy the models go to bed with. Our time traveller, however, has taken back with him a coffee-table book of Matisse's great masterpieces. He gives the book to young Matisse. Then he returns home in his time machine. Matisse gets to work. He copies his own great works of art, but because he *is* Matisse, of course, they are not really copies, they are in reality the great paintings which will be later photographed and reproduced and in due course sent back to him through the agency of the time traveller. In no time at all he's got fame, the fawning admiration of his contemporaries, and a different model jumping into his bed every night—'

'Yes, all right,' said Vronwy. 'Never mind the models. I understand it without the models.'

'But these works of art, these masterpieces by Matisse, *have no provenance*. They were never originally conceived. They have come from nowhere and this violates the scientific principle that knowledge can only result from the problem-solving process. The skill needed to invent things, or paint pictures, cannot be allowed to be supplied by the inventions or pictures themselves.'

Vronwy said, 'Put your coat on. It's cold and it's raining. You do realize I won't be able to see you again for a bit?'

'Ah,' he said, then, 'It's OK. I understand.'

She looked at him. 'No, not Maurice,' she said. 'You've forgotten. I'm flying to Tel Aviv.'

'When?'

'Tomorrow. That's why I brought the groceries and

283

stuff. Didn't you wonder why I was bringing you things?'

They went outside.

'The fact is that according to classical physics time travel can't work,' said Richard. 'Hawking himself said that the best argument against time travel is that we are not constantly tripping over tourists from another age.'

The rain sheeted down. They ran to the boat. They sat and shivered as it chugged its way back up the river. 'On our right as we pass the Tower of London,' said the guide, 'you will see Traitors' Gate, the portal through which so many of the enemies of the state were brought to their final imprisonment and death.' Richard looked out of the glass side at the grim, wet stones of the Tower, stones that had a tale to tell.

'Hawking's argument against time travel seems pretty sound, actually,' said Vronwy, trying to be nice and not to hurt his feelings.

'No,' said Richard. 'Hawking has been shown to be in error. There are no tourists from the future because a CTC, a time machine, cannot transport people back to a point *further back than the time that it was created*. In other words a CTC which is built now can bring back people from the future only to this point, to this very point in time. And there are no travellers from the past, no ancient Britons wandering around Piccadilly Circus, because ancient Brits were having too much trouble inventing the wheel to devote research funding to cold-fusion interstellar spaceships. An interesting thing about CTCs, by the way, is that whoever comes back into the past, along a CTC, will find here everyone who has ever, or will

284

ever, come back along that particular CTC. You follow me?'

'No.'

'You're very hopeless.'

'I'm very wet.'

'Well, let's imagine a hypothetical Closed Time-like Curve was created in the Sinai Desert in 1300 BC—'

'Hang on. What do you mean, a *hypothetical* Closed Timelike Curve? What other sort is there?'

'Who knows? The point is, people who travelled, accidentally or otherwise, back down that CTC – a Roman soldier, a Byzantine camel train, a wandering Saracen, a Second World War desert patrol – would all find themselves together in the same place in 1300 BC.'

'How do you know?'

'The maths have been done. This might be theory, but it's not in dispute.'

'What's to stop the Roman soldier wandering off somewhere, looking for a brothel or something? What's to stop the Byzantine camel train going over into the next valley? Who said they had to stay put waiting for the next time traveller to pop out?'

Richard paused. He said, 'Of course they could *wander off*. The autonomy principle insists that they could wander off. But before they did that, they'd all have to have arrived, back in 1300 BC, in the same place and at the same time.'

'What, on top of each other?'

'I sometimes wonder,' he said after a moment's reflection, 'if you're taking any of this seriously.'

'Oh, Richard!'

They got off the boat at Westminster. The rain had

stopped. It had been a shower, a February shower. The wind was cold and damp, coming from the north, sweeping down the Thames. Traffic roared over the bridge. It was getting dark.

'You'll have to look after yourself. Can you look after yourself, Richard?'

She kissed him. He had his arms round her, round her duffle coat.

She said, 'I wonder if that was what happened to Archimedes in the bath? Perhaps he didn't shout "Eureka!" Perhaps he just shouted "Eek!" because a time traveller was standing by him telling him things.'

She spluttered. He cuddled her, or rather cuddled her damp duffle coat and the thick woolly sweater inside it, which was more like cuddling a large teddy bear than a woman. After some time she said, muffled, 'Cheerio, then.'

'Cheerio.'

'You're sure you'll be all right?'

'You're not responsible for me. You're going to Sinai.'

'That's right.'

She pulled away, a tough teddy bear.

'See you in six weeks.'

'Yes.'

She hailed a taxi coming from south of the river. She said, 'Oh, I nearly forgot. My friend from St Mary's phoned. He said DDT.'

'DDT?'

'Look for traces of it. Even the poor old Eskimos have DDT in their liver. There's not a human on this earth who hasn't got DDT poison lodged in their liver.'

She jumped into the taxi. Off it went, round Parliament Square.

He stood on the Embankment and looked down into the black running water. *And Thames which knows the mood of Kings, and Priests and Lords and suchlike things, rolls sweet and gentle as she brings—*

'Her message down from Runnymede.' He spoke loudly, but the man nearby, the man who had been tailing them all afternoon and who was also staring down into the black waters, did not seem to hear.

Richard walked to the Underground. The man followed him at a distance. He was about thirty years old; a wet, unhappy-looking young man, who followed him on to the train, but did not get off at the Angel.

Richard padded home alone. His name tag, which he had replaced next to his doorbell and on his mailbox, had disappeared again.

'Classical physics says that such time travel is not possible,' he said aloud next day, pacing his flat, 'because it cannot be done without violating the autonomy principle. OK? Right? We're quite clear on that one, are we?'

His geranium conformed to the biological laws of the universe and did not reply.

'Good.' (The man in the warehouse office opposite cautiously moved to the window and peered out though binoculars, wondering who Richard was talking to.) 'But we must remember that classical physics itself is false, unreliable, not to be trusted – so say many modern physicists.'

Richard sat at his desk and pondered. Then he went out to meet a friend of a friend, a young, very modern physicist from Imperial College.

'I accept that the laws of physics do not forbid time travel into the past,' the young physicist said cautiously, politely, drinking a pint of bitter and trying to pretend that he found Richard's questions sane and reasonable. 'And the philosophical arguments, the arguments of the classical physicists, can be met in various ways. You've heard all about parallel-universe theories? Most people think they're just something dreamed up by science-fiction writers.'

'They're not?'

'Well, let's say the scientific theories supporting them are more respectable than some might imagine, and these theories have been boosted by our understanding of quantum mechanics.'

'Can you explain that to me?'

'Well, first you must understand quantum theory. Do you know what a quantum is? Up until the dawn of the twentieth century we believed that a hot body would give off electromagnetic waves equally at all frequencies. Then Max Planck put forward the theory that the energy of electromagnetic waves is not continuous but is composed of discrete packets, in other words energy is quantized. He further proposed that each quantum would have a certain amount of energy, and that energy would be greater the higher the frequency of the waves. OK?'

'Just about,' said Richard, his heart sinking.

'That was in 1900. In 1926 Hesenberg formulated his famous uncertainty principle, which we can summarize as follows: the more accurately you try to measure the position of a particle, the less accurately you can measure its speed. Are you still with me?'

'In a superficial sense, but I don't understand the significance of what you're saying.'

'Look,' said the young physicist, 'write this down on a bit of paper: *Uncertainty in the position of the particle, times the uncertainty in its velocity, times the mass of the particle can never be smaller than a certain quantity.* This is known as Planck's constant, and it is this that has been revised into what we call quantum mechanics.'

'Can you possibly,' said Richard, 'summarize without explaining? Can you tell me the significance of quantum mechanics, what importance it has, without trying to make me understand how it works?'

'Basically,' said the physicist, 'quantum mechanics does not predict a single, definite result for an observation. Instead, it predicts a number of different possible outcomes, and tells us the odds on each eventuality.'

'Are we getting close to parallel universes?'

'Listen. If you and I sit here and watch a neutron decay into a proton, the average time we might expect to wait is twenty minutes or so. But in the event, it might go pop in a second or it might take a year. The parallel universe theory states that there would be a separate universe for every instant – not every second, every *instant* – that that neutron might decay. In other words, *if it is possible for something to happen, there is a universe in which it actually will happen, and happen instantly.*

'Now, consider how similar this theory is to the basis of quantum mechanics. Quantum mechanics has as its basic tenet the belief that instead of a single definite result of an observation there are a number of different possible outcomes. Quantum mechanics says that there is not just one thing that will happen. There are different things that might happen, and *all these things are valid*. This is a bizarre theory. It defies rationality as we know it. Imagine you see a man ski towards a tree through the snow. Then you see him ski away from the other side of the tree. You walk over, and find that his ski tracks go round *both sides of the tree*. This uncertainty is crazy and Einstein hated it – "God does not play dice," remember? – but it is the basis of modern chemistry and modern biology. Transistors and integrated circuits are all based on acceptance of it. It is mad, it is irrational to the world as we understand it, but it *works*. It is the basis of all modern physics.'

Parallel-universe theory would deal with philosophical objections to time travel. Henrietta could go back in time through a Closed Timelike Curve and kill her grandmother before her mother has been conceived – but in a universe that was different from the universe in which she, Henrietta, was eventually born. The art dealer could go back to Paris with a folder of Matisse's great works and show them to the young Matisse, but it would be in a universe different from the one in which he, Matisse, originally conceived his masterpieces.

'But for Christ's sake,' Richard said to his young, modern physicist, 'it would mean billions and billions of universes. Where the hell are they all?'

'They probably all form part of a multiverse, all in the same place.'

Probably? *Probably*?

'Mind you, there are those who say that using the theory of parallel universes to overcome the philosophical objections to time travel is relying on something over-complex and inherently unlikely. There are those who say,' he added, 'that it's a bit like building a Boeing 747 to cross the road.'

But could a CTC, a Closed Timelike Curve, actually form itself? Never mind about the celluloid world of Hollywood, the world of eccentric mad professors with home-made time machines. Could it happen in the real world?

'Actually, yes,' said the physicist, and added, rash and expansive after his third lunchtime pint, 'You could say that it's already happening. You could say that the very basis of modern physics relies on the existence of these things. You could say that time travel is going on all around us.'

Not great big CTCs. Not black holes spinning round each other in space, swallowing up stars and galaxies, bending worldlines and distorting space-time. Small, submicroscopic CTCs.

'Space-time' said the physicist, 'may appear smooth on a large scale, but many think it has a foam-like microscopic structure – and this structure contains CTCs reaching about ten to the power of minus forty-two seconds into the past. OK?'

He wrote '10^{-42} seconds' on a Boddington's beermat.

'This submicroscopic world has other peculiarities, as well as time machines. For example, it's got rather more dimensions than we're used to.'

'Could people travel down one of these CTCs?'

'Only if they found a bottle saying "Drink me",' said the physicist, looking at his watch, getting up to go, 'just like Alice did.'

* * *

That night Richard went through the notes he had made of what Elizabeth had told him at Siwa. He had not understood her and his memories were confused. But he remembered her lying in the olive grove, running the pale grey-green leaves through her fingers, chanting softly, 'One dimension, two dimension, three dimension, four . . .'

His mind fogged up. But he felt that he was getting somewhere at last. It was only eight o'clock in the evening, but he lay down and went to sleep. Later he woke. It was almost eleven o'clock. He put a pan of water on the stove, wanting coffee. He suddenly remembered clearly what Elizabeth had said – what she had said about the foam-like structure of space-time, about the submicroscopic world.

He held his head in his hands. He said out loud, 'Electromagnetic waves. Electromagnetic waves in a foam-like, microscopic structure!'

The acoustic listening device across the road clicked to life. A female listener stirred from her torpor, played again through Richard's words, consulted her notes, then put in a call to a number she had been given. A male listener, who was also making coffee said, 'Important, that, was it?' and when she nodded, he stirred in the sugar and looked wise. She marked the time as being 22.57, and it was as she put down her pen that a call came on a CID mobile, from the watcher at the front of the terrace of flats where Richard lived: 'Three men in Ford Sierra, Mike Nine One Zero Lima Tango Hotel. Two of them breaking in. I think they've got submachine-guns. Repeat, they appear to have—' and the two listeners in the warehouse office looked at each other in shock, then the woman grabbed the phone.

18
Islington

'Bravo Nine Zero to Mike Papa Five,' the woman was saying. 'Armed attack on objective. Request ARV—' but the man, DS Halshaw, knew that no Armed Response Vehicle could get to them in time. The nearest was at Love Lane, strategically positioned to cover the Central Criminal Court and the Bank of England.

'Acknowledged, Bravo Nine Zero.'

What strategic hot-spots were there north of Aldersgate? What prestige targets for terrorists north of the Angel, Islington? How many politicians or minor royals did you find being kidnapped in Asda superstores in Haggerston?

'Two armed intruders, suspected submachine-guns—' She was a funny one, this girl. Perhaps twenty-five-years-old, a WDC from Bristol with a degree in physics from Cambridge. 'Objective not covered, repeat objective—'

Objective actually on the phone now, checking notes on high-frequency radiation of electromagnetic waves, e-mailed to him that morning, as the stake-out team knew, from the California Institute of Technology. He was chatting to California and sipping coffee while the gunmen were heading up the stairs towards him, and if the gunmen knew his address, they might well know which flat he was in, even though his name had been removed from the list of occupants; they might well be fifteen seconds away from blasting his door down.

Halshaw took his gun from its holster.

'They say six minutes,' said the girl.

The objective could be dead in three.

'Get me Trevor.'

The other phone, the CID mobile.

'Yes?' said a voice.

'Anything?'

'Nothing. They're still in there.'

Two men, three flights of stairs.

'You're sure about the guns?'

'Yes.'

'Go in after them.'

'With a hand-gun?'

'Make a diversion. Challenge them.'

He crouched, steadied his revolver on the window-ledge. His authority was to fire in defence of himself or of the objective. But he was not part of an Armed Response Unit, he was not part of the Royal Military Police Close Protection Squad, he was routine Special Branch; it wasn't an every day of the week event, this sort of thing.

The girl holding the phone looked at him, startled, and said, 'What are you going to do?'

'Fuck knows.'

Surveillance round the clock was his line. Most Special Branch officers found it boring, but not him. Master criminals, drug dealers. Tory backbenchers with funny sex lives or their greedy fingers in the till, it was all part of the rich tapestry of life. It wasn't, of course, like the old days, when you had Labour MPs and *Guardian* reporters trotting off to sunny Cuba (where did the bastards go for their holidays these days?) or IRA killers in Kilburn pubs, but there were plenty of dodgy buggers who needed watching when MI5 tipped you the wink, and he was happy to spend his days noting the phone calls the dodgy buggers made, the time it took them to go to the lavatory. Most of the time he would be thinking about the fishing, the bream down in Suffolk.

'ARV in London Wall, coming up to the Aldersgate Street junction.'

They'd come up Goswell Road, up past the Angel. No sirens, not yet, and they wouldn't use them unless they had to.

The WDC said, 'Get him on the phone. Get the exchange to break into his call.'

'There isn't time.'

There were eight officers assigned to this job, including this milkmaid from the West Country. It sounded a lot, but you couldn't keep an objective under observation – not without his knowing – with less than twelve officers. Eight officers meant twelve-hour shifts, three officers per shift and two on days off; a killing rota; and then there was the bumph they expected you to read – update assessments on the location of known terrorists, on the shifting allegiances of terrorist organizations. He couldn't keep up with it all.

He crouched down holding the gun. *Offering a low silhouette, this position is well adapted for cover and for a stable firing posture, and ensures that support is being provided by masonry and bones and not just by muscles.*

It wouldn't work. He couldn't get the right angle. He stood up.

'Open the window.'

Her fingers fumbled with the catch. He stood, his feet apart, holding his revolver in both hands. It was a police issue Smith and Wesson 4, model 10. *Do not breathe normally while you are aiming because the rise and fall of your chest will spoil the shot. Breathe in, then release part of the air in your lungs, then stop breathing while you aim and fire – but do not hold your breath for more than ten seconds or you will produce muscular tension and involuntary movement.*

When had he done his weapons training course? It must have been ten years ago – Maggie was still Prime Minister. Since then he'd had refresher sessions once a month at Finsbury, but never in all these years had he fired a shot in anger.

'Mike Papa Five to Bravo Nine Zero—' a voice on the RT phone, from Scotland Yard Information Room, from a man sitting at a computer screen, recording events, his account copied automatically to the central computer at Hendon. 'Update, please.'

The RT radio was multi-channelled and said to be secure against everything except for the press in Wapping and a thousand or so of London's social inadequates who trawled the airwaves from their lonely attics and garden sheds.

'Objective still under observation,' said the girl. Halshaw glanced up for a second and saw that her eyes were fixed intently on his gun. She caught his eyes and looked away, out of the window.

Silence for ten seconds, perhaps fifteen. How long did it take two men, two terrorists, to climb three flights of stairs? Perhaps they'd been waylaid by some old biddy wanting a chat about who'd pinched her milk.

'OK, get the exchange to get him on the phone.'

The Scotland Yard IR operator: 'Mike Papa Five to Bravo Nine Zero.'

The girl: 'Bravo Nine Zero.'

He did not hear the query from control. He heard, instead, the dull, distant sound of a muffled pistol shot. Trevor. Through the window opposite he could see the objective standing up and turning towards the door. There was another distant shot, Trevor again. If he'd followed ground rules, he'd have shouted a verbal challenge, from the safest place he could find covering the stairs, and have opened fire only if personally threatened. The objective was backing away from the table, reaching for something.

Halshaw raised his Smith and Wesson.

Trigger control is the single most important aspect of marksmanship. Your finger should touch the trigger somewhere between the tip and the second joint.

The door into the objective's flat burst open.

The girl: 'Bravo Nine Zero to Mike Papa Five—'

A man with a submachine-gun, raising it into the classic firing position.

Halshaw moved the revolver marginally. *Concentrate not on keeping your weapon perfectly still but instead on getting perfect coordination between hand and eye.*

He fired. Glass shattered in the window opposite, a spider's web of cracks with a neat hole in its centre. Again he fired, still holding the revolver stiffly in both hands, the crack of the gun loud in the small, bleak office.

The objective had disappeared. The gunman was

in the far shadows. He was leaning against the wall, his hands over his face.

Halshaw could hear the girl, behind him, talking to Scotland Yard. 'One alleged intruder has been hit—'

Alleged? Alleged? Jesus, you're not in the West Country now.

He couldn't see the submachine-gun. Had it fallen to the floor? He thought he could make out a second figure grabbing at the first from behind.

His arms came up. Again he fired.

The intruders, the *alleged intruders*, who might yet turn out to be a couple of the objective's chums coming round with their violins for an evening of Mozart, disappeared below the level of the window.

He was tempted to fire again, aiming at the shadowy doorway on the far side of the flat, keeping the bastards pinned down, but remembered the conditions relating to 'visibility of target' and 'safety of general public' printed on the Home Office pink card in his jacket pocket.

Christ only knew what they'd do to him if he'd killed the objective.

Distant sirens. From behind him the girl said, 'Yes, sir', then, calling out to him, 'SO19 arriving any moment now.'

There was no sign of movement opposite. Twenty seconds passed, thirty. He remained standing with his feet apart, his gun raised, aiming at the far wall of the flat.

A voice, this time on the mobile. The girl said, 'They're going up the second flight.'

A black shape opposite, in the doorway of the flat.

'OK, let's go.'

They ran down the stairs. They crossed into the

builder's yard, ran through the gate into the narrow back alley, then down it towards the main street. Kids were standing in the dark doorway of a video hire shop. A Late-Nite foodstore owner was peering through his window, but his door was shut and the blind was down. They turned into Harrison Street. It was starting to rain, a sleety rain. Sirens screaming close, others sounding like answering echoes from the far distance. Doors were open, people peering out. A boy of about fifteen came running out into the street, a voice behind him screamed in sudden panic, 'Clive! Clive, come back here!'

The WDC, running behind Halshaw, shouted, 'Did you kill him?'

He did not reply. He remembered something, though, about this particular WDC; some story about her fiancé having been in the police, in one of the provincial forces, West Midlands or Greater Manchester, and having been killed by a boy with a gun during a drugs raid.

The gunmen's car had gone, scarpered. He could see SO19's armour-plated van, dark and squat, officers standing with their backs against the wall, facing outwards, covering the street with their sniper rifles. A gun barrel swung towards him as he ran up the pavement, over the broken glass. He held out his ID card, shouted who he was, and pushed past them into the hall. There was an inner door with a large cardboard notice in angry red felt-tip: *Please be considerate enough not to bang this door late at night. Signed Ground Floor Flat.* SO19 men were everywhere – huge and beefy in their bullet-proof vests (special issue – ARV officers didn't have to buy second-hand vests from US police departments, the way most of the boys in the Met did). They were telling people to stay in their flats. A man in his twenties, sweater over his pyjamas, was standing in the doorway of the ground-floor flat: 'I'll come out if I want to. Listen, don't tell me what to do, chum—' 'OK, sir. Get fucking shot!' 'I beg your pardon! *I beg your pardon!*'

The voice of a woman: 'Gordon, come inside!' 'That man, *that man* –' pointing at Trevor, who was coming down the stairs – 'came into the hall and fired a gun with no warning, no caution. Jesus, somebody could have been killed. You're not getting away with this—'

An SO19 officer came down the stairs behind Trevor, calling, 'One man badly injured in the face.'

'Paramedics, where are the paramedics?' another voice boomed from up above, loud and stressed, and Halshaw realized that there had been another noise, all this time, a high wailing: the intruder, presumably, the one with his face injured.

Trevor said, 'Afghanis, two of them.'

Afghanis were Muslim fundamentalist gunmen, any Muslim fundamentalist gunmen. The name had been given to them by Paris police in the Cité 4000 housing estates.

'How is he?'

The objective, he meant, not the gunmen.

'He's fine.'

The hallway was crowded. SO19 officers clumping down the stairs, banging the inner door again and again. Halshaw and Trevor went outside.

'The car was the trouble,' said Trevor. 'I was shit scared the driver would come in after me, catch me between two fires, but he scarpered at the first shot.'

'What happened to the second gunman?'

The second gunman – *alleged intruder* – had smashed out through a first-floor window seconds before SO19 arrived. Transport Police were being alerted at the Angel and St Pancras Underground stations, taxi firms were being warned, the man still had a sub-machine-gun unless he'd dumped it in the Grand Union Canal.

A voice from an SO19 car: 'Anybody from Special Branch?'

Trevor said, 'That's the gov'nor.'

'Go and talk to him.'

There were dozens of lights on in the flats opposite. Sirens, still more sirens. The uniformed branch were rolling up, the buttons mob, patrol cars with their lights pulsing. A uniformed inspector from the local nick came hurrying over from his Panda, looking tense and self-important and frightened he was going to be ignored; behind him came a police photographer with a video camera; a woman in her forties from Scotland Yard press office.

The sleet was turning to snow. There was already a coating of slush over the broken glass on the pavement. Uniformed police were putting up a cordon of plastic tape, blue and white, metropolitan police printed all along it.

He turned back inside. The WDC from Somerset and Avon was talking to a bloke from SO19. From the top of the house the wailing was replaced by a sudden scream of pain.

'Anybody here from Special Branch?' said a voice from above. 'Anybody here from the stake-out?'

'Yes, sir,' called the WDC, going up the stairs.

The woman from the Yard, the press officer, was taking out a pad. 'OK, what happened?'

An SO19 officer: 'One armed intruder wounded. But don't look at us, love, this is a Special Branch job. This is the bloke you want to talk to.'

A voice, triumphant, from above, from the top of the house: 'He's FIS, this one. I've seen his mug-shot.'

The young man from the ground-floor flat was popping his head out again, the female behind him calling out in high-pitched irritation, 'All right, Gordon, you bloody go out there!'

'Is anybody at any point going to tell me what is going on?' the young man shouted, and, yes, he had cause to be upset. The door was being banged all the time; nobody was showing any consideration at all.

'Just go back inside your flat, sir.'

'No, I will not go back inside my flat!'

Now paramedics were tumbling into the house, self-important, thick bastards, forever knocking things over with their stretchers. 'Top landing,' said a beefy SO19 officer, his M40 sniper rifle swinging about in its sling.

The inner door banged. The man from the ground-floor flat said, 'I'm going to ring the press. You can't seriously believe you can come barging in, shooting—'

'Get inside or I'll do you for obstruction, OK?'

The young man looked outraged, then shook his head in laughing, scornful disbelief and turned on his heels. His door slammed.

A senior officer from SO19: 'OK, what happened?'

He told him.

Another SO19 officer came down the stairs.

'You the one who fired?'

'Yes.'

It seemed that he hadn't hit the gunman, but a

splinter of wood from the doorpost had gone into the man's eye.

The woman press officer said loudly, 'Statements only issued through the Scotland Yard press office, all right? Everybody understand? You're clear about that, sir?' – this to the uniformed inspector from the local nick.

The WDC said quietly, 'Is it OK for me to go up? I need to talk to Dr Corrigan.'

Corrigan. The stake-out was over. The objective now had a name.

Richard offered his tablecloth to staunch the blood pouring down the gunman's face. The policeman said, 'It's OK. Leave it to the paramedics, sir. Anyway, you'd never get the blood out, it's terrible stuff blood. You took his weapon off him?'

'Yes.'

Richard had been holding it, the stubby barrel aimed towards the stairs, the safety catch off, when the first policeman had appeared.

Paramedics tried to fix a thick white pad over the gunman's injured eye, winding bandages to keep it in place. The man was moaning, a constant long-drawn-out howl of distress.

'Dr Corrigan?'

A woman was standing in the shattered, splintered doorway. Where had he seen her before? Ah, yes, sitting in the Oxford lecture theatre, with a boy stroking her neck.

He said, 'Hi.'

The fax machine was lying on its side bleeping angrily, perplexed by its ill-treatment. He lifted it up, put it back on the table. It instantly spewed out a list of documents it had sent or received in the last twenty-four hours. The woman started to pick books up from the floor. She held a PhD thesis from a bright postgraduate in Seattle and looked at it for a moment. 'I have to say I'm not totally convinced myself,' she said, giving him a little friendly smile, 'of the cosmic censorship hypothesis.'

The gunman screamed as a needle went into his arm. A paramedic said, 'You'll be OK in a minute, mate. Just lie quietly.'

'Fifteen seconds,' said the second paramedic.

The seconds passed. The man's groans grew quieter. Above the bloodstained eyepad was a mop of curly black hair. How old was he? Twenty-two, twenty-three?

'It seems to me,' said the woman, 'all very well for Hawking to say that the event horizon is the path in space-time of light that is trying to escape from the black hole, and nothing can travel faster than light—'

'You with the stake-out?' A police sergeant, uniformed.

'Yes. The boss is downstairs.'

The man turned to Richard. 'Sorry about all this, sir.'

'That's all right.'

A stupid reply to a stupid remark. The man went.

'But as we both know,' the woman went on, 'the latest quantum mechanics research seems to show that in subatomic particles things do travel faster than light, or at least the plasma web woven by the subatomic particles' electric lines of force resonates at a speed faster than light. Do you want some tea?'

'Yes, I do.'

'Shall I?'

'No, it's OK.' He filled the pan at the sink. She got two mugs out of his cupboard, knowing exactly where to look.

The boy was quiet now. The paramedics were lifting the stretcher. 'Easy,' they were saying. 'Easy does it.' They carried him out and down the stairs.

Richard found his teabags and his brown teapot, got a bottle of milk out of the fridge. He said, 'You're a physicist?'

'I'm a police officer.'

'Some police officer.'

She smiled briefly. Smudgy eyes, a white, strained face. Not pretty, not glamorous, but attractive. Straightforward-looking. Not devious-looking, and that was a change.

'I was very interested,' she said, 'when you moved on to subatomic particles and to electromagnetic waves in a foam-like, microscopic structure. It's always seemed to me—'

'Listen, are we having a seminar here, a tutorial on quantum mechanics? I'm grateful but I'm not at my best.'

'Sorry.'

He poured water into the teapot. 'Was it you who fired in through the window?'

'My boss. Detective Sergeant Halshaw.'

'I'd like to thank him.'

'He's about somewhere. He's a modest bloke. He likes fishing.'

'And the shots from downstairs?'

'That was Trevor. I don't know what he likes.'

'And you are?'

'WDC Henry.'

'Hi, Henry.'

'My Christian name's Val. Henry's my surname.'

They sat in silence. He sipped his tea, gratefully.

Footsteps on the stairs. Two men in the doorway. One of them a pale young man in his mid-twenties wearing a suit, a tie, looking meaningfully at WDC Henry.

'Actually, when you've had your tea, sir,' she said to Richard, 'we'd like you to move to somewhere a bit more secure. And there are some people who want to talk to you if you don't mind.'

As he got into the car a police officer came over and said, 'It's been confirmed. The injured man is FIS.'

'FIS, the Islamic Salvation Front,' said the young man as they moved off. 'The French hate them but we've been quite sympathetic. Our Foreign Office types are said to admire the asceticism of Islam, or, to look at it from the French point of view, our Foreign Office types are a gang of cold English homosexuals reading *Pillars of Wisdom* while they sip their sherbet.'

The car sped along the Marylebone Road, past Madame Tussaud's and the corner of Baker Street.

'Did the press get on to it?'

'Yes, sir,' said the woman, WDC Henry, who had been talking quietly on the car's phone. '*The Times* and *Sun* are there now.'

'Did they get on to Dr Corrigan?'

'We don't think so.'

'OK,' said Richard, 'so why were Arab fundamentalist gunmen trying to kill me?'

'I think we're hoping you can tell us the answer to that.'

'Why were you watching me?'

'We have to watch a lot of people. It's an unquiet world.'

They were heading west, out of London.

'Look at Iran. They've got two thousand per cent inflation and food riots in Mashhad. The Muslim World Revolution can't go into the next generation without free American powdered baby milk, but they've still got an Al Qud team of gunmen in every one of their embassies in Europe.'

'Are you telling me the Iranians tried to kill me?'

'It doesn't make a lot of difference who it was. I don't know why we spend so much time puzzling out which organization is responsible for this, what department is funding that. Hizb, Gama'a, Unity, Algerian GIA, Brotherhood, PLO, FIS, they're all the fucking same.'

A young Englishman of the old school, though not, apparently, a sherbet-sucker.

The car swung on to the M25, heading south. An aircraft passed low overhead, taking off from Heathrow.

'Mind you, Libya's spent,' he said, sounding genuinely regretful, 'whoever's behind it all, it certainly isn't Libya. You should have seen the last photos I saw of Gaddafi. He was two years in that bedouin tent in the Western Desert, telling his guards that Shakespeare was really Sheik Zubayr, a playwright of African origin, that America was named after the noted Libyan Emir Ka. How did you get on with the CIA?'

'They were not interested.'

'No?' He sounded politely sympathetic.

He leant forward. 'You know to take the next exit?'

'Sir.'

Surrey. Trees tossing fantastically in the storm, the dead leaves of last autumn whirling across a lane. It was almost one o'clock in the morning. A local police patrol was in a lay-by. It moved smoothly out behind them.

'Almost there,' said WDC Henry. She sounded bright and clear-headed. Her white shirt, he knew, though it was too dark to see, would be as neat and crisp as when she had put it on over her crisp white bra. He felt grubby. He thought about Vronwy: thank Christ she didn't know about this, thank Christ he wouldn't have to explain this one.

'That police car following us,' he said, 'it's OK, I suppose?'

'OK?'

'You don't think it's the Iranians or the FIS?'

Dearie me no, they laughed.

'Wicked,' said WDC Henry.

A grand mansion in extensive grounds. Vending-machine coffee and bacon sandwiches in a bleak interview room, overheated, the way these places were always overheated. He would stay the night – what was left of it – in police officers' quarters. The young man with views on Arabs had gone. The duty sergeant, middle-aged and jowly, asked him if he had any pyjamas. 'They didn't even let you pack a pair of pyjamas?' he cried, shocked.

'We were ten seconds ahead of the *Sun*,' said WDC Henry, defensively.

A man came through the swing doors. He was in his late thirties, wearing a sports jacket and cord trousers and shoes that the English, and perhaps everybody else, called brogues. He looked as though he were police or military, and Richard did not think he was police. He said, 'Dr Corrigan? Sorry to keep you. Can you come through to the secure room? I think we're just about ready.'

19
Surrey

There was a middle-aged woman who looked as though she'd not long ago been got out of bed, which was probably the case. There was a small, gnome-like man in his fifties. There was the military guy in the Daks sports jacket. There was a young man with a thin, white face, blue jeans, Reebok trainers and a look of suppressed excitement on his face.

WDC Henry followed him into the room and closed the door.

'Are we ready?' The woman looked round, inquiringly. WDC Henry sat on an upright chair by the door, her legs crossed, ready to zap any terrorists who burst in.

'Two gunmen, members of FIS, believed to be from France, tonight tried to kill Dr Corrigan, who was under protective observation following an earlier warning from Cairo and a request from the CIA. Now I don't want to be less open and frank than I need to be. This is Nicholas Bluglass, a physicist from Wolfson College, Oxford' – the thin young man in the Reeboks. 'This is Geoffrey Huddleston, who represents the Security Services' – the man in his fifties, who gave Richard a brief, cold glance. 'And this is John Biggin, who represents JIC.'

'JIC?'

'The Joint Intelligence Committee, which coordinates the field and research work of Britain's main security services, and reports directly to the Permanent Secretaries Committee, which reports directly to the Cabinet.'

She gave him an apologetic sort of smile, sorry if she had said something that was not open and frank.

'I'm Lisa Cook and I'm here to chair this meeting. What we want to know is why an American physics postgraduate's research project into paranormal incidents in the Sinai should have led to her death, and to two Muslim fundamentalist gunmen trying to kill Dr Corrigan at his flat in north London.'

Silence.

He closed his eyes. Deep silence. Not a clock ticking. A thick, palpable silence, pressing in on his ears. This, then, was a secure room, padded and protected against sound, sound flowing in or flowing out.

He opened his eyes. They were looking at him. He said, 'Elizabeth thought there was a CTC in Sinai.'

'A CTC?' The woman looked at him questioningly.

Bluglass, the physicist, said, 'A Closed Timelike Curve.'

'A tear,' said Richard, 'in the fabric of time.'

Bluglass smiled faintly.

Huddleston: 'Can there be such a thing? Can she be right?'

Bluglass said, 'No, not really.'

'Not really?'

'No, definitely.'

Silence again. Perhaps they could all go home.

Huddleston: 'All right, about this CTC. If that's

what she thought it was. Can somebody explain to me a CTC?'

Richard closed his eyes again. He heard Bluglass say, 'I'll have to simplify a great deal', and Huddleston say coldly, 'We appreciate that.' He wondered if they would just carry on, among themselves, if he went to sleep.

'Equations of the general theory of relativity indicate that huge bodies bend worldlines—'

'Define a worldline.'

A pause. Richard opened his eyes, interested despite himself.

'We live in three dimensions. We occupy three dimensions. We also occupy space in the fourth dimension, which is time. The space we occupy, as we move around physically in three dimensions and also progress through the fourth dimension, forms a line – not a straight line but a line that moves, squiggles about – that is our worldline. Every person, every living thing, every *object* even, has a worldline, from its creation to its destruction. Every electron, every particle—'

'Yes, all right. I've got it.'

WDC Henry gave Richard another encouraging little smile. He had got it a long time ago, her look implied.

Bluglass said, 'The worldlines of massive bodies, spinning in space, can have certain effects. It is the earth's worldline, for example, spiralling round the sun, that gives rise to gravity. If space-time becomes sufficiently distorted by this bending process, it is theoretically possible that it could form a sort of loop.'

He stopped and waited for them to gasp in amazement.

313

Huddleston said, 'And?'

Bluglass said, 'A Closed Timelike Curve. Because it's timelike all the way round, it would conform to the physical laws as we know them and would, in effect, be a corridor into the past. If you were able to follow your own worldline round such a loop, you'd bump into yourself as you were a week last Wednesday, or when you were five, or whenever.'

'Depending on the size of the loop?'

'Yes. If the loop were large enough you could go back in time and visit your ancestors.'

'Could a time machine be built capable of using one of these CTCs?'

'You wouldn't need a special time machine. An ordinary spacecraft could use a CTC. It's a corridor, a timelike corridor, as I said.'

'So spaceships could zip backwards and forwards?'

'No, they could only go one way, and they'd have to be careful not to zip too often. A CTC isn't a spatial route. Its tube can only be used a certain number of times. It can only accommodate a certain number of worldlines.'

A pause. Lisa Cook said, 'We seem to know a great deal about something that you say doesn't exist.'

'I only said that I did not believe one existed in the Sinai Desert. A lot of work has been done on the theory.'

'So two planets or stars or whatever,' said Huddleston, 'could make one of these Closed Timelike Curves?'

'Yes,' said Bluglass. 'Planets, stars or black holes.'

'But there are no planets or stars or black holes in the Sinai?'

'No.'

'Not pretending to be something else? Not lurking behind camels, or hiding away in the hills?'

'No.'

'So we rule out CTCs in the Sinai.'

Bluglass said, 'Not necessarily.'

Huddleston stared at him bleakly.

'If we're speculating, there are other ways, perhaps, in which CTCs could be formed, ways that would not need the rapid movements of vast heavenly bodies. Kip Thorne of the California Institute of Technology has put forward the theoretical possibility that two ends of a wormhole could be moved to form a CTC.'

'A wormhole,' said Huddleston, 'is something that joins two universes? A sort of shortcut?'

Bluglass said, 'Well, loosely speaking—'

'The sort of thing they use in science-fiction paperbacks?'

'All the time.'

Lisa Cook said, 'But nevertheless based on genuine physics, on existing, reputable, scientific theories?'

'Very much so.'

'OK, can a CTC,' said Huddleston, 'be created in a laboratory?'

'You are looking a long way ahead.'

'But in theory, even looking a long way ahead?'

'No, I don't believe so.'

Biggin, the man from JIC, said, 'Ten years ago everybody thought a quantum computer that used the theory of parallel universes to solve problems was science fiction. It's no longer science fiction. It's been built. It's been built, and it's been stolen.'

Huddleston said, 'Is there anybody, anybody of *reputation*, who does believe that it could happen?'

'Not to my knowledge. But it really does depend on

how far ahead you are looking. If something is possible in theory, if the laws of physics permit it, then who can say what might or might not be possible in practice in a hundred or five hundred years?'

'You're looking that far ahead?'

'Let's say our technology is as close to building CTCs as Bronze Age culture was to building television sets.'

There was a faint relaxation round the table.

'At any rate,' said Huddleston, 'a wormhole is not something your government physicist could requisition from war-department stocks? He couldn't send in a chitty for two wormholes, one Bunsen burner, that sort of thing?'

'No, of course not.'

Biggin said, 'Are there any other ways in which a CTC might be created?'

Bluglass looked politely at Richard.

Richard shook his head. In her corner, WDC Henry looked at him reproachfully. He could do better than this, her look implied. He sighed and said, 'In my research I got as far as cosmic string theory.'

Bluglass said, 'Well, yes. Research at Princeton indicates it may be possible that a cosmic string passing rapidly by another cosmic string would generate a CTC.'

'But this is all theoretical?'

'Highly theoretical,' said Bluglass.

'No black holes in Sinai,' Huddleston said. 'No wormholes being manipulated, no cosmic strings being swung about. So what reason did Miss St George, or Miss Ford, have to think that a Closed Timelike Curve could occur, a CTC that would allow a body from 1300 BC to come forward in time? And didn't you just say that CTCs cannot, in any case, bring things forward in time?'

'It doesn't need to. The laws of physics that allow travel forward in time are well known.'

'In practice?'

'Well, no, not yet, but once spaceships are developed that can move at something approaching the speed of light, there are going to be some interesting social problems – young astronauts coming back from what appeared to them to be a short voyage and finding their sweethearts are seventy or eighty, that sort of thing—'

'I want us to move on,' said Biggin. 'This is very interesting, it's fascinating, but there are things we have to do.'

'I want to know what reason Miss Ford had,' said Huddleston, 'to think that a CTC existed in Sinai that could bring a body from 1300 BC forward in time and carry a tank and its crew back to 1300 BC. We all know it didn't happen, we all know it's impossible that it should happen, but what made an intelligent, articulate physics graduate from Drextel and Harvard believe it and spend two years trying to prove it?'

They were looking at Richard again. They were seemingly civilized and relaxed, particularly the woman, but they had sharp, intelligent eyes. Huddleston knew most of the answers before he asked them. He had known all about CTCs even though he had played dumb. Biggin was army. Lisa Cook was MI5, British internal security.

He wondered why Bluglass hadn't mentioned the other way in which CTCs could be formed. The other way in which they existed.

317

A clock sounded somewhere outside, far away beyond the broad acres surrounding Surrey Police Headquarters, in distant Guildford, perhaps. A church clock striking the half-hour in the dark, misty English morning. Time passing. *Time flowing*, Elizabeth had said in the olive grove, and he could hear her even now, and he could hear the distant cry from the mosque, and see the slim tower white against the dark royal-blue sky: 'Come and pray, come and pray, brothers in God, brothers in Allah, packers of dates, of the sweet dates of Allah.' Elizabeth lying in the deep shadows of the olive bushes: '*CTCs are postulated as resulting from the interaction of huge cosmic bodies – black holes, stars, planets. They are also postulated as resulting from the interaction of very small bodies. Space-time is smooth when you look at it from a distance, but close up it is a foam-like structure with lots of wormholes or connecting passages and it is ten-dimensional.*'

'*Ten-dimensional? There are only four dimensions, Elizabeth, even I know that there are only four—*'

'*If string theory is correct, there are ten dimensions or there are twenty-six. But of course there are more than four! How do starships move between galaxies in only four dimensions?*'

'*Starships are fiction, Elizabeth.*'

'*A joke, Rich.*'

'*Well, I'm glad about that.*'

'*Listen and believe. There are six extra dimensions – apart from those four dimensions that we are used to – and those six dimensions are curved and curled into an elementary particle that is approximately – I am speaking very approximately you understand – a million*

318

million
million
million
millionth of an inch in cubic diameter.'

She had dropped an olive, hard and green, into the palm of his hand for every million, confident, though only just, that he could at least count up to five.

'And inside these curly little balls, these little magic balls, there are wormholes that will take you into another universe, Rich, a universe a million million light years away from Planet Earth; and CTCs that will take you back in time to Valley Forge and Gettysburg, to Agincourt and Actium, to the first performance of Hamlet *and the first playing of Beethoven symphonies, to Rameses the Second's war with the Hittites – or to Mount Sinai, to watch Moses and the Israelites as God came down in a cloud of fire—'*

'Dr Corrigan?' said Huddleston.

He looked at them.

'Elizabeth Ford didn't say anything to you, give you any indication, of why she had reached such extraordinary conclusions?'

Richard said, 'Elizabeth spent two years, an entire research grant and all her own money trying to collate evidence that a naturally occurring CTC existed in the Sinai. It was her Holy Grail.'

'But what was this evidence—'

'She had high courage, Elizabeth,' he said loudly, interrupting. 'You know what I'm talking about?' He stared round. They stared back, Biggin, the army man, interested, Huddleston bleak, Bluglass nodding his head, trying to be friendly. 'She was a brave heart. She didn't take no from anybody. She didn't take no from me, from Drextel, or from the American

Universities Science Research Fund. She didn't know what she was heading into, but she didn't care. It was a voyage of adventure. The unification of physics – it had to come by the end of the century, that's right? That's what everybody has been predicting, the unification of physics, the ultimate theory of the universe? She wanted to be there when it happened, when the last equation fell into place, when the handiwork of God was finally revealed. Was she mad? Is anyone here saying she was mad?'

Nobody was saying it. Everyone was thinking it.

'Yes, well, OK. She was crazy to go into Egypt, exposing the secrets of the Mukhabarat, crashing into high-security morgues and dissecting corpses, sneaking into military security areas – that was madness, sure enough – but you know all this. You know it because you were there, all the time. Mac was a British agent. Elizabeth thought she was being funded by the CIA. She was amused – no, she was *excited* – to think that the CIA was interested in her research. She was over the moon when she suddenly got the funds for her last visit to Cairo, the airline credits – British Airways? Not very clever of you – the cash in her account in New York, the contact names in the Egyptian Interior Ministry, the petty clerks who could let her into places. She thought it was the CIA feeding her money and information, but it wasn't, it was the British. And it wasn't the French who wanted me put under *protective observation*, it was you, because Mac was dead and Elizabeth was dead and you didn't have much to show for your investment. You could have said to me, "Hey, there's some Muslim gunmen after you, we're putting you under protection", but you didn't because you wanted to know what I was doing.

You wanted to listen to every phone call I made. You were the bastards, the murderous fuckers, who sent Elizabeth back to Egypt knowing, *knowing* the appalling danger she was going into.'

Silence.

He could see snow beating soundlessly against the thick-glazed window.

He stood up. 'I'm going to bed, OK?'

WDC Henry stood up.

Huddleston said crisply, 'Nobody from this country, nobody in government or the security services, asked you to go to Egypt with Elizabeth Ford. It was only the considerable diplomatic efforts of Britain and America that secured your release from the prison at Siwa—'

'They released us so that they could kill us!'

'It was our influence – in fact our physical intervention – that got you out of Egypt. It was only because we kept you under protective observation that you are alive tonight. The CIA know what is going on. They are fully briefed. You must appreciate the importance of our discovering why a major Muslim terrorist organization – which has enough on its hands – should think you important enough to kill. It is, I would have thought, of importance to yourself as well as to us. Electromagnetic waves, Dr Bluglass. The uncertainty principle and the revised theory of quantum mechanics as applied to electromagnetic waves somehow allow the theory of small-scale CTCs. Right?'

Yes, he'd known all along. He'd known about CTCs, about wormholes. He probably had a better physics degree than Bluglass.

'It's difficult to summarize—'

'It also governs the behaviour of every electronic aspect of our lives. Transistors, integrated circuits. You agree?'

'Not only electronic. It forms the basis of modern chemistry and biology.'

'Transistors,' repeated Huddleston, 'integrated circuits, weapons systems. Why did the heat-seeking scanners of the UN helicopter searching for Herr Gabriel go down on the night of 19 December on the Jebel Samghi ridge? Why did the entire computer-guidance system of an American Sabre go down twelve hours ago — twelve hours ago, Dr Corrigan — 25,000 feet over the El-Tîh plateau? The Sabre is the very latest reconnaissance aircraft. It should not be possible to jam its equipment. It certainly ought not to be possible for anyone in Sinai to jam it. Elizabeth Ford has stumbled into the debris of some very advanced weapons research.'

'Listen stupid, let me try one more time,' Elizabeth had said, as they had walked back to the café, holding his arm and leaning on him companionably. *'The CIA are funding me because they think the FIS is involved in weapons research into electromagnetic waves, and it might well be true, but if it is, it only means that the El-Garf Research programme is activating a naturally formed CTC that has existed for the last two thousand or maybe two million years, just as the electromagnetic sound surveillance systems along the canal activated the same CTC in 1973. Why are there no records of paranormal occurrences before the seventies? Dear God, Rich, they're even asking stupid dumb questions like that. For God's sake, who was there to note down the time travelling of prehistoric larvae, the voyaging through space-time of sand lizards a million years*

ago? Who's ever been around to write up the story when a few bedouin vanished, a few ibex, a fox travelling through the night. Oh, listen, please . . . ' Her hand, warm, on his arm. *'Science tells us that CTCs can be formed by huge bodies in space bending space-time. You remember what space-time is, Rich?'*

'It's the combination of three-dimensional space and the fourth dimension of time.'

'Yes, the manifold through which our worldlines flow. But science also tells us, slightly more controversially, that CTCs can be formed in the microscopic foam-like substance of space-time – tiny, baby CTCs. OK, so big CTCs and small CTCs, all out there, all existing naturally in the universe – what's so special, Rich, what's so remarkable, what's so fucking goddam unbelievable about a CTC the right size to bring a human being from 1300 BC to the present day? What is so remarkable, Rich, what is so difficult to accept in the theory that research into electromagnetic waves or electromagnetic sound surveillance in 1973 somehow changed the structure of a baby CTC and made it bigger, and that scientists at El-Garf are doing it again right now? But how do we get there? How do we get there?'

'Some very advanced weapons research . . .' Huddleston was repeating. 'Except in so far as it has a bearing on this research, we have no interest in her theories of time transference, fascinating though they are.'

'And the body,' said Richard. 'The body in the morgue?'

'What about it?'

'An Egyptian boy soldier of 1300 BC, with the mark of the Kap on its forearm, found in Sinai in 1973? A sample of flesh, nail and bone was sent to an American laboratory. You telling me you know nothing of that? Christ, Mac was your agent—'

'According to the Americans all tests are completely normal, lead, iodine, atomic radiation. Whatever that corpse might be, whatever place it occupies in the fantasy world Elizabeth Ford was creating, it is undoubtedly the body of a late-twentieth-century young male.'

'Can I see those results?'

'We'll have them sent to you when we get them ourselves from America.'

A gleam of satisfaction, a question anticipated.

Biggin said, 'We've got to move on. We haven't time for this. We simply haven't got the time.'

Now there were only Huddleston and Biggin, but on a screen there was a map, a hugely detailed satellite photo-map, a map big enough to show St Catherine's monastery, the hotel and the airstrip, and the pilgrim path up the Jebel Musa; to show every curve of the Wadi el-Sheikh, the place where, as a teenager, he had first picked the gummy, saccharine manna from the tamarisk tree (the manna that fell only, said his bedouin friend and guide, in the season of the apricot); a map that allowed him to trace the length of his first journey in Sinai, as a student, by horseback along the Wadi Feiran; to identify the very oasis of palms where his bedouin friend had shown him the red berries of the *gharkad*, a bush that bedouin tradition said was the 'tree' used by Moses to sweeten the waters at Marah – and he remembered his satisfaction when he discovered that in the local bedouin dialect the word tree, *shejer*, was synonymous with the word for a drug or medicament of any kind.

The wandering tribes of Israel . . . no wonder they *wandered*, high as kites on Bronze Age cannabis.

'This is the so-called Science Nature Park that was closed off two years ago.'

Green lines superimposed themselves over the screen. Biggin said, 'No tourists are allowed, not that there were ever many.'

No. Not on El-Tîh, not on the dry, harsh plateau. Not north of the Coloured Canyon.

'No UN Peacekeepers, either on ground patrol or overflying. No civilian overflying. Three months ago it was closed to civilian traffic entirely. It's described as a Science Nature Park, by which they appear to mean a site of scientific interest. There's a water meadow not far from my place in Henley that's an SSI – you can do bugger all in the way of building, the farmer gets paid a fortune to agree that he won't plough it up. I don't suppose they're giving the bedouin any hand-outs, but at El-Tîh they claim they're trying to reintroduce certain types of ibex, reintroduce the wolf, give breeding space to the eagle – they actually got a grant from the European Union for that. It was supposedly in order to protect the golden eagle that they first banned overflying by helicopter but it's now extended to a general ban on flying under 30,000 feet, and not many eagles fly at 30,000 feet that I've noticed.'

The green line ran from the head of the Wadi el-Arish, some twenty kilometres south of Nakhi, and followed the bedouin track across the plateau to the point where it joined the Taba road at El-Thamad. To the south it took in the edge of El-Tîh and extended east beyond the Wadi Biyar to the very ridge of the

Jebel Samghi – less than two kilometres, Richard guessed, from the hills behind the Desert Oasis motel; in fact it excluded only a narrow coastal strip alongside the Gulf of Aqaba. On the west it ran to the Wadi el-Garf, and stopped just south of Sarabit el-Khâdem. It was a roughly drawn circle round the emptiest, most desolate landscape of central Sinai.

'It's organized like Ras Muhammad National Park. Army roadblocks, army patrols, helicopters, seismic intrusion detectors. And here, down here,' said Biggin, pointing with his ruler at a black smudge on the ridge north of Sarabit el-Khâdem, 'we have the climatology research station. You will also notice,' he went on, but Richard had already noticed, 'what happens to be on the plain south-east of Nakhi, on the very edge of the exclusion zone.'

A red circle marked the spot.

El-Misheili.

'A series of Bronze Age tombs,' said Biggin. 'The archaeologist is Dr Keith Worboys. He's a friend of yours, I think?'

It was two-thirty a.m. He lay in his bed in his borrowed pyjamas. The night-duty police sergeant had said, 'If you go for a walk round the grounds in the morning, don't go out of the gates, will you, not without telling us? There's breakfast in the canteen from six-thirty.' The room was functional and shabby, but warm. It smelled of institutional furniture polish. As he tried to sleep, he remembered something else Elizabeth had said as they waited in the square at Siwa, sitting in the dirt, their heads resting against the mud wall of the hotel.

'They're so arrogant, and yet they know so little.

*Forty days and forty nights, Rich, Christ fasted in the
desert, that desert. There have been more miracles in
Sinai than you've had chicken dinners—'*

'Don't talk about chicken dinners.'

*'Listen, when we get out of here, I'll buy you dinner
at Angelo's, the best restaurant in Cairo. Chicken with
forty cloves of garlic. Have you been in Cairo in the
garlic season? You should see the carts coming over
the 6 October Bridge, loaded with fat white bulbs, that
glorious rich smell wafting over the Nile, the one time
of the year when the air's fresh and clean. . . . '*

He remembered her last words, spoken in the
Interior Ministry car as they crawled in the convoy
across the sand dunes through the thick night – not
the murmured, 'You don't suppose those boys in the
truck have any cans of Coke? I'd kill for a can of
warm Coke. . . .' but the words, spoken a few moments
before:

*'I'm going to find Mac and go to El-Garf. To the Tîh
plateau and to El-Khâdem. That's where it's all been
happening. That's why it's suddenly become a national
park, a military no-go area. How are we going to get
to El-Garf, Rich?'*

He could not sleep. It was past three o'clock but he
could not sleep. The heat in the room, the coffee
he had consumed – his head buzzed, his skin itched.
He got up and tried, without success, to open the
window. He lay down again and dozed fretfully. He
wondered when they had first known that he planned
to return to Sinai. Had they had psychologists listening in on his dreams? He wondered when they had
first marked him out as a latter-day Palmer. Old
habits die hard, and it was the old way, after all, the

old British way of doing things. If you don't have a Lord Almoner's Reader in Arabic from St John's, Cambridge, handy, how about a research fellow in Egyptology from UCL?

He suddenly laughed out loud, wondering if they'd give him 20,000 guineas.

At six-fifteen he got up and drank tepid water from the wash basin, and went for a bacon sandwich and a mug of thick tea in the canteen, where the woman behind the counter said, 'Have you seen the weather this morning? Snow in March! Pity poor sailors. That's one pound forty. Didn't they give you a breakfast chitty?'

He put on his coat and walked out into the grounds. He could see yellow lights on a road; early risers heading into Guildford, commuters grimly making towards London. A robin, its breast dark and bedraggled, sat on a sign that read: 'Civil Defence Incident Room'. It watched him beadily. The snow had not quite covered the gravel path. He walked past swathes of green daffodil shoots. He gratefully breathed in the damp raw air and plodded along the drive, following tyre marks in the slush, towards the main gate, thinking what a picture the daffodils would make in another month or so.

In her room, WDC Henry was awakened by the phone and groaned softly. She was only twenty-five and had had four hours sleep when her body craved eight.

'Yes?'

'Your friend, Dr Corrigan, heading towards the main exit.'

She leant back against the pillow and sighed.

'Hello?'

'I'm thinking.'

'Don't think too long, love.'

A pause.

'Hello?'

'Yes, all right. I don't suppose you've a car handy?'

'Well, now –' coy and jocular – 'I wouldn't say it was entirely out of the question.'

'If he goes out of the gate, go after him, will you?'

'You want us to bring him back?'

'Either that or give him a lift to the station.'

In the canteen, at a corner table, looking out over the snowy rhododendrons, Huddleston sat over a full cooked breakfast, a policeman's breakfast.

'Morning, sir.' WDC Henry sat down with her toast and tea on a tray. He nodded. She didn't like him. She didn't like the way he carefully dissected his fried egg, sliced his pink sausage.

'I understand Corrigan's gone.'

'Yes, sir.'

'Do we know where?'

'He caught a train to London.'

'You spoke to him this morning?'

'No, sir.'

'Why not?'

'I was in bed.'

A pause. Perhaps he was thinking about her being in bed. She suspected that he was.

'He knows,' said Huddleston, 'that he must not go back to his flat until he gets the all clear?'

'Yes, sir. I sent a message via the patrol car and he sent a message back saying he understood. We know where he's staying. It's the flat of a friend. In Belsize Park.'

Huddleston ate his breakfast. 'It's not the terrorists,' he said, 'so much as the tabloids.'

'Yes, sir.' She had listened to the radio news: 'Mystery this morning surrounds the intended victim of an Islington terrorist attack'. She had seen the *Sun*'s KILLERS OF ISLAM and the *Guardian*'s interview with the man from the ground-floor flat whose door had been banged, and banged, and who wanted the world to know that Britain was a fascist police state, no question.

'Do you think there's anything in it?'

'Sir?'

'This time-transference stuff.'

She pulled her brain together. 'As Dr Bluglass said, there are some very respectable people who believe in the possibility that CTCs either exist naturally or could be made—'

'Capable of transmitting human bodies through time?'

'In theory—'

'Bugger the theory, the practical possibility.'

'No.' She ate her toast.

'Why not?'

'Whatever the physicists say about the laws of physics not disproving backward time travel, I believe myself that the anthropic principle would come into play perhaps in a way that we do not yet understand.'

'The anthropic principle?'

'Which states that mankind can only exist, only function, in three practical dimensions, plus the dimension of time as it currently operates.'

'Sounds fair enough.'

He moved to toast and marmalade. 'If I were to go back in time twenty-four hours, now, there'd be somebody else occupying this chair. Right? I'd find myself sharing the space with some hairy traffic sergeant. Right? Couldn't guarantee finding myself inside the knickers of some blonde lovely such as yourself. Right?'

'No, sir.'

'No, I'd be sharing the underpants of a hairy sergeant.'

'I expect so.'

This was not, she decided, the place to consider two-dimensional time, a state which might allow the events of any particular moment of time to be subdivided into dissimilar temporal parts; which might indeed allow him the share of the same chair at the same time with a traffic sergeant, hairy or otherwise, without either intruding on the other's personal privacy.

He said, 'You know we want him to go out there?'

'Pardon, sir?'

'To Sinai. Corrigan to Sinai.' Impatient, irritable.

'No, I didn't know that.'

'The exclusion zone. Under cover of some archaeological dig.'

'So we think there really is a CTC—'

'No, of course not.'

A pause. 'We originally planned to send in the SAS. You'd be surprised how many SAS officers have degrees in physics. The thing is, nobody's quite sure what's going on, if anything at all. We'd look bloody stupid if the SAS were caught breaking into a genuine Arab nature reserve, or shooting up a genuine climatology research station. Anyway the plan was vetoed by the Foreign Office. The thought of a trade ban by the Saudis gave them hysterics, quite apart from the effect a cock-up would have on the Egyptian power struggle. A compromise has been reached. Corrigan is going in through our good offices, so you're to look after him.'

'Me go to Egypt?' Startled, dropping her toast.

'No, of course not. Help him pack his bag and that sort of thing.'

'Yes, sir.'

'Make sure he has enough hankies.'

'Yes, sir.'

For a moment she fantasized about rubbing his nose in the egg congealing on his plate.

'You look pensive,' he said with heavy humour. 'What are your thoughts, I wonder, WDC Henry?'

Once again Richard was at Heathrow. A great number of people in Terminal Four were wearing ski clothes; pink and blue, the colours of this season. American Airlines – *It's American All the Way* – was announcing flights to Albuquerque and to Reno, Nevada, to Steamboat Springs and to Jackson Hole, Wyoming. He wished he were on a flight to Wyoming. He wished he were taking Vronwy to the crisp, sparkling, champagne air of the West. The air in Terminal Four was perfumed and warm, recycled, refiltered. Outside the huge windows, slush and snow were driving against the aluminium mammoths that taxied back and forth in the dirty afternoon. Suddenly through the driving slush came the vivid green and orange livery of a South American airliner, a peacock of a plane that spoke of sun and blue skies and carnival time in Rio. He wandered past the Caviare House and was not tempted by a small tin of best Beluga at twenty pounds sterling. In the Pringle knitwear shop were tartan scarves, in the food hall were displays of short-bread fingers in tartan wrappers, and he wondered, not for the first time, why, after over a thousand years of colourful and romantic English history, the two supreme examples of English national identity should be Scottish knitwear and Scottish biscuits. In W H Smith's he bought a *Daily Telegraph* and a *Wall Street Journal*. A US Army Sabre attached to the UN Peace-keeping Force was reported as having made an emergency landing in the Negev Desert. Sinai was not mentioned. The *Telegraph* had a story, 'Egypt on the Brink', and Richard bought himself a coffee and sat down to read it, but it was only a colour piece from the Cairo district of Imbaba, the place where funda-mentalism and poverty went hand-in-hand, and the radical mosques had been running the medical clinics for a decade. The West was trying to destroy Islam by inflicting homosexuality, abortion and sexual promiscuity on the Muslim world, cried out the aya-tollahs. The Pope was plotting to sterilize Muslim women through the American-funded Third World contraception programme. What will these Jesuits think of next? thought Richard, grimly amused – but he was sick at heart, because the *hapiru* of the nine-teenth dynasty had fled Egypt fearing that their first-born males would be slaughtered by the king, and nothing, in over 3,000 years, seemed to have changed.

He looked for a story about himself, for he was the *mystery target* of the Islington Outrage, but a week had passed, and the world had moved on.

He wandered aimlessly through the terminal. WDC Henry found him in the Harrods tax-free shop, look-ing at travel bags. They went to the bar and he bought her a half of bitter.

She said, 'We've cancelled your papers and milk. I'll bet you'd forgotten.'

'Yes.'

'Your door's been mended. No letters, no faxes, your fax machine was hit by a bullet, that's why it was making that awful noise, but the answerphone works and there are a couple of messages.'

She handed them over. She said, 'You didn't mind not going back to your flat?'

'Modern man needs a plastic card, and I'd got mine.'

'You sound like an advert. Oh, my God, where are the cameras?' She peered round humorously, pretending she didn't know who was footing the bill, who had bought the plane ticket. She passed a document out of her bag. 'If you'll sign here, and here—' she had already marked the places with neat pencil crosses.

'What is it?'

'Your insurance claim. For the door. You don't have to worry. I checked your policy and they'll pay up. It doesn't classify as civil disorder or riot.'

'I feel well looked after.'

'You can rely on the Met.'

'You are not the Met. You are the Somerset and Avon Constabulary.'

'That's right.'

'So deep,' he sighed sadly, 'so deceitful, and yet such an open face.'

She blushed faintly.

He said, 'I had a geranium.'

'Yes. I saw it.'

'It is not a geranium that has been nurtured.'

'It's bad to over-water them in the winter.'

'You become callous, I suppose, in the police force. Listen, there's one thing that's been worrying me.'

'Oh?' She looked alarmed.

'How do you account for cathedrals?'

'What?'

'You were at the lecture in Oxford. Was that your boyfriend, by the way? With his arm round you, kissing you?'

'No – not at all.'

She looked unhappy, distressed for a moment. She said, 'What about cathedrals?'

'How do you reconcile them with the arrow of time which states that everything must dissolve into chaos, everything must collapse into corruption, a cigarette can turn from being an ordered white tube into a pile of ash but not from a pile of ash into an ordered white tube—'

'Entropy.'

'Yeah, entropy. How do those disordered chunks of stone scattered about the place get turned into a lovely, ordered, *designed* thing like a cathedral? How did Chartres ever come into existence? How was Salisbury possible?'

'Well, in principle the building of something goes against nature. The creation of a human opinion, a human attachment for that matter, goes against nature.'

'A human attachment?'

'The chemical process involved in the formation of perceptions, of memories, of love if you like—'

'Love?'

'Requires a chemical process. Falling in love is a process that represents an abatement of chaos. As such, it flies in the face of science.'

She finished her beer. She sat and looked at the empty glass.

'OK. So why then does science allow cathedrals to be built, allow human relationships, falling in love? How come science plays Cupid when it shouldn't?'

'Physicists believe that local abatement of chaos is allowed – building something, creating something, *thinking* something – if the overall effect is to increase universal entropy. For example, if you use an engine – or a gang of men if you like – to cut the stone blocks and raise them into place, then entropy has been increased enough to overcome the loss of chaos caused locally by creation of the cathedral.'

'And human attachments? Human thoughts? How are they compensated for?'

'I think that falling in love causes enough chaos, don't you?'

She was still staring down into her glass.

'Yes,' he said, thinking of Kirsty, and of Melanie. 'Yes, I do see what you mean.'

'My bloke was shot. He was in the police. He was killed.'

He said, 'I'm sorry.'

After a moment she said, in a neutral voice, 'It's a few years ago now. Remember that universal entropy is increased by the flow of energy from hot to cold.' She looked up at him. 'And I've become terribly cold.'

'I'm very sorry.'

His flight was boarding; the departure-board light flicking on and off.

At the gate she showed a pass and followed him down the rubber-matted tube. A brisk wind blew through the cracks in the plastic. An air hostess stood shivering, rubbing her hands together. He turned and said to WDC Henry, 'Well, goodbye.'

She said, 'Goodbye', and smiled, but followed him on to the plane.

He found his seat. WDC Henry stood next to a steward, watching other passengers as they came aboard. After a while she brought him a copy of *The Tatler* from first class and said quietly, 'It all looks OK. If I were you I'd have the fillet steak from the low-salt menu.'

'Yes?' he said.

'I've just seen it. It looks very nice. Oh. There was this, for you.'

A note, typed on a word processor. 'Analysis of the bone sample and red blood cells of the surrounding tissue show biochemical changes in blood and reduced haemoglobin synthesis concomitant with normal levels of lead contamination in the bone.'

'From the Americans,' she said, 'from the University of Pennsylvania Medical Center. The average lead contamination you'd expect from a boy raised in Cairo.'

'Did they check for DDT?'

'They couldn't, not without a bit of liver. If she'd sent back a bit of liver they could have checked for DDT.'

'I expect,' he said, feeling the need to apologize for Elizabeth, 'there really wasn't time to start cutting Elmer open.'

'No.'

'And the lead contamination seems conclusive.'

'I would say it is.'

If the report was true, that was. If it hadn't been written just for his benefit.

'Well,' he said, 'I'll say goodbye again.'

She leant over him. 'The man two rows back, in

337

the aisle seat, he's El-Al security. He might well be wondering who you are, I don't suppose he'll bother you. You've got the contact in Jerusalem?'

He nodded. The Palestine Exploration Society, digging out the tells, the graves of the Jordan Valley, worrying over the bones, dabbling in espionage, as it had since the middle of the nineteenth century.

'Take care of yourself, Dr Corrigan.'

'And you, WDC Henry.'

She went.

Music played. The captain told them that they had been given a time for take-off, allocated a place in the queue. This flight deck was not as chatty as a British Airways flight deck – no other flight decks, thank God, were ever as chatty as British Airways – and he drank his jaffa orange juice, freshly pressed that very morning, and listened to the sound of pretend Israeli folk-music. 'Doors to automatic,' said a voice quietly on the Tannoy. Five minutes later the plane rose into the sodden cloud. Below, there was a momentary glimpse of traffic racing along the M25, headlights making a ribbon of lights in the murky late afternoon, then the grey curtains swept in.

The Airbus climbed into the sun, then turned somewhere over Surrey, circled to the east and headed into the darkness.

Part Three

20
The Army of Israel

There was to be an army. An army of Israel. Every free man, every bondsman, would be a soldier. The Levites would be soldiers, and Aaron the priest would become Aaron the warrior. 'A priest among priests,' his acolytes cried, riding from camp to camp on the mules they had conscripted, 'a warrior among warriors!'

Many remembered the time, not so very long ago, when the Levites had fled barefoot from their temples, and begged their bread as they scuttled along the road to Succoth and the salt marshes. They had been humble and mouse-like in those days, frantic to reach the Wilderness, where the terrible priests of Amun could not find them.

In the Wilderness, it was said, the Levites had *flowered*.

The Soldier was to be captain general of the army, the chief and commander of the host. He came to speak to the men of Simeon, Reuben, Asher and Gershon. They were gathered against the cliff where the Valley of Laha narrowed into a defile as it climbed eastward towards Ti.

'I say to you that we will become an army that is good enough to defeat the Dinkas,' he shouted, his voice loud among the rocks. 'An army good enough to stand up to Egyptian regulars. An army that will send the Sherden running back to their boats. I'm talking about an army that will be feared from Hebron to the land of the Hittites.'

Around the base of the cliff, on the sour, arid sands, were peaceable herdsmen and shepherds from Goshen. Barley farmers and fruit growers from the black-soiled gardens of the Nile. Jewellers, and scribes, and money-lenders from Migdol. Brick-makers and stone masons from Pi-Ramese.

'We will make this army here,' the Soldier shouted, his face glowing orange in the sun, 'here in the Wilderness. Perhaps that is why God has brought us to the Wilderness. Perhaps that is why God did not send us to Canaan along the Way of the Philistines, or along the Way of the Hajji. Because we need *time* in the Wilderness. Time to make an army. Listen to me, my friends, if you won't listen to the priests.'

A few men laughed.

'The land of Canaan might overflow with milk and honey,' the Soldier shouted. 'I'm not arguing with Aaron and the Levites. But I tell you this – we'll have a bloody fight to get any of it!'

The men laughed again. Ahiezer, the master brewer of Gershon (permanently drunk, it was said, from breathing his own fermentations), guffawed loudly.

'There are no handmaidens waiting with flagons of new milk and honey beer, saying, "Welcome home, O soldiers of Israel", not in Canaan, my friends, not anywhere!'

A few cried in mockery, 'Shame! Shame!'

In the rocks, watching, Ruth, Esther and Rebecca sniggered.

'There, over there,' whispered Rebecca, 'is a son of Abidan who likes me.'

'A boy of Abidan?' said Ester, shocked. 'What about the boy of Dan? What about Shimi? What about the Wolf?'

'Be quiet,' said Ruth.

They were watching Giliad, who was assembled with the men. They were watching him intently, fascinated and amazed to see him cry 'Shame!' when the Soldier said there would be no handmaidens or honey beer. He had a sword – a short falchion of iron presented to him, with much ceremony, by the chief elder of the house of Gershon.

The Soldier raised his arm. His Egyptian cloak flashed bright blue in the light of the setting sun. He pointed to Ti, to the dark rim of the world, visible over the top of the defile. 'There are Amalekite tribes waiting over there, on the other side of Ti, and they won't strew garlands at our feet. There are Jebusites, and they're filthy fighters, by God – I saw them, and the bedouin, when I was with the First Division. And after the Amalekites and the Jebusites there are the Canaanite farmers, who won't be in any hurry to surrender their pasture lands by the Great Sea, not without a fight. There's an Egyptian construction corps building forts along the coast of Canaan, we know that much from the regimental supply office at Etham – Deu-el the scribe has told us that much. The King's army is on the move, and it's heading eastwards towards Hatti and maybe Assyria, and it has no time to think about a few wandering tribes of Amorites, about the Children of Israel, but it might trample over us, all the same, *squash us* without noticing.' He paused. 'And perhaps there's the Anaks.

343

Perhaps the Anaks do exist, who knows?'

Esther shivered. The Anaks were giants. Giants that grazed in herds. Giants bigger than the funeral pyramid of King Cheops. Human people were all the size of grasshoppers to an Anak. The very soil grazed by the Anaks, it was said, *ate* people who were not Anak. The soil opened – said the legend told to generations of Egyptian children – and ate civilized people, Egyptian people – just like grasshoppers swept away in Nile mud.

There was silence at the foot of the cliff. Ruth could hear the trickle of water that fell over the stones as it came down the stream that was the Laha. The water was less with each passing day. The cold season was almost over.

'And before we get near the Hittites, and the Amalekites and the Anaks, before we get within a four-week march of the *Promised Land*, we're likely to meet Egyptian garrison troops again, the Dinkas perhaps. Yes, we might meet again with the Dinkas. But I'll tell you this. We won't be slaughtered the next time. It's the Dinkas who'll be fucking slaughtered next time.'

'Hurray!' shouted Rebecca strongly.

'Be quiet!' hissed Ruth and Esther.

Rebecca collapsed on the ground, trembling.

The Soldier said, 'This is how we are going to do it.'

He told them that they would fight in phalanxes. A man standing alone might find his courage tested, might find his heart fail – they had seen it when the Dinkas attacked them, it was nothing to be ashamed of – but when a man was eight ranks deep behind a wall of shields and spears, he would be strong enough.

Even a frightened man could do service when he had his comrades around him.

'Frightened? Who's frightened?' cried the master brewer of Gershon, and the thin-faced young scribes and clerks from the counting house in Migdol looked stern and unafraid.

They would need archers, said the Soldier. A good archer could shoot twenty arrows a distance of eighty paces in one minute. It was difficult to train an archer, but once trained he was cheaper to equip than an infantryman – and arrowheads of flint would penetrate all but the finest of Egyptian shields.

The men of Gershon and Asher would be given javelins. The javelin had a shorter range than an arrow, and could be thrown only twenty paces, but it was easier to teach a man to throw a javelin than to shoot an arrow, and the men of Gershon and Asher (said the Soldier, raising a laugh) had never been easy to teach anything.

He told them that Bezaleel, the son of Uri, who once did fine work in gold and silver in his own shop in Pi-Ramese, would be making spears and javelins. Aholiab, his assistant, would make bronze arrowheads. Others, with older skills, were already fashioning arrowheads of flint.

'Yes, we will make an army,' said the Soldier. The army of Israel will be formed here in the valley of Soh, by the banks of the Laha.'

It would be an army made out of gypsies, of *hapiru*, of heretics. An army created from Amorite tribesmen who were believed, in the King's foreign office, to be wandering, lost, with their thin, starving animals, in the badlands south of Shur.

Its training would be watched, perhaps, with

amusement by men on the King's great lateen-rigged sailing boats as they plied the Yam Suf.

The sun fell. Darkness came swiftly. The men returned to their camps. Ruth and the two girls climbed down from the rocks and turned back towards the tent of Zuri. There was the smell of mountain thyme on the air, borne by the cool, drifting scent of water. The voice of Wolf called, 'Mouse, Mouse', out of the gloom, and Rebecca said, 'Who is that? Who is that?' and Esther cried, 'No hand-maidens with honey beer. Oh, shame!' to Giliad when he joined them.

Before she climbed down from the rocks, Ruth saw the silhouettes of two bedouin watching from the other side of the defile, two black figures against the deep rose of the western sky.

That night, and for many nights after, the fire from Bezaleel's workshop shone over the Soh Valley. The Soldier was having a banner made by Miriam and her dancing girls – a moon banner of black and gold. Shelumiel said to Ruth, 'You must make a banner for the house of Simeon.' Each day he practised at archery, teaching the shepherds and the herds-men to draw the composite bow, its springy wood stiffened with glue from ox bones. In the evenings he was exhausted and lay on the skins and groaned, and called out for Nubian girls to pour water down his back, just as though he were still in Egypt.

'There are no Nubian girls to fetch you water here!' said Ruth bitterly – daring, for she was sure he would beat her when Zuri was dead, and make her his concubine, and deny her the money from her marriage contract.

Shelumiel lay and groaned. 'Ohh, ohh! Dear God, I'm tired!'

She poured him wine. She said, 'My mother had a Nubian girl who was brought to Egypt by a merchant. She wept every day for the mountains of the south. Some say, Shelumiel,' she said, stirring trouble, 'some say we should not own people in bondage, as we left Egypt because the king wanted to force our people to the corvée, which would have made us little better than slaves ourselves.'

Shelumiel lay on the sand with his eyes closed, the sweat still running down his back.

'The Benjaminites say it is now wrong to own slaves,' persisted Ruth, 'just as it is forbidden to eat the camel.'

'The Benjaminites say that,' said Shelumiel, 'because all their slaves have been taken by the priests.'

Zuri, mumbling over his ash cake, said, 'The Levites are taking everything. But what does it matter? What does it matter?'

He rocked backwards and forwards, spilling his wine.

Shelumiel said, 'The God Yahweh has ordered the Levites to build a temple.'

'What?' cried Zuri. 'A temple like the temple of the people in the slave village at Pi-Ramese?'

'A tabernacle of cedarwood, of the cedars of Lebanon, and do you know what is to cover this tabernacle? A hundred cubits' length of fine linen, and it must have twenty pillars of cedarwood, and twenty sockets of brass, and the hooks of the pillars must be of silver, and the tabernacle must be hung with blue and purple and scarlet cloth that is wrought with needlework.'

Zuri sat stunned.

'It is a temple,' he said finally, 'to placate the God of the Levites.'

Shelumiel said, 'The pasture is exhausted. Tomorrow we must start south again. We must start before the Asherites, we must start early and get the best pasture along the road.'

Many of the cattle were dying. They had been bred in the Delta and they were dying in the Wilderness. Half the cattle of the family of Reuben were dead; each day the Reubenites ate their stew of bones and skin.

The priests said they were going to Elim. They said it would be a four-day march. The army would train in the desert while the women and children drove the flocks and herds south. In four days they would be in Elim, where the red date palms stooped over the running waters, and the acacia bloomed, and there was thick juicy pasture for the sheep and for the cattle.

They were going to Elim, which had a river and twelve springs.

They travelled south for five days. Each day, on the march, Ruth felt the sun burn into her back. They were still in the cold season. What would happen to them when the hot season came? The consul at Migdol might send soldiers to kill them, she thought, sorry for herself – but Najim's soldiers would have a wasted journey, because they would be already dead!

Each day, by her side, Esther carried the pot of living fire. Everyone admired her magic. Even dead embers flamed when she breathed on the pot of fire. But she was tired, and one day she stumbled and the coals fell in the sand and were dead and cold. She sat and wept.

Get up! Get up! Ruth told her. They would soon be in Elim! Spies had already been there! They said the dates were turning red, and would soon be plump and sticky and sweet. Get up! Get up! said Giliad, helping to collect up the dead coals.

Rebecca, as always, wandered ahead, alone, a thin little wand in the vast desert.

The cattle began to die. The lambs that had started to be born at Marah were too weak to be driven and were carried by the shepherds. The ewes were skeletons, and had not milk to feed their young.

On the sixth day they reached a small oasis, a thin trickle of water through the shale. There were a few stunted palms, their trunks hacked by Dinkas' knives, sand sticky with Dinka excrement. Zuri recited a spell that would save him eating excrement in the next world. The tribes set up camp, turning out their cattle and their sheep on to the thin herbage.

The ravens wheeled overhead. Every so often they swooped down.

The men of Korah rose in revolt.

They marched on the camp of the Levites, calling for Moses, for the *Lawgiver*, demanding to know if this was Elim. Where were the sticky dates? Where were the fields of corn? Where were the rich pastures?

Again the men of Korah cried, 'Were there no

graves in Egypt, that you brought us to the Wilderness to die, to be cut down by Dinkas or to starve?'

Guards, men with javelins sent by the soldier, stood in front of the Levites' tent and kept the men of Korah back, and stopped them throwing stones.

Then shepherds came, shepherds of Gad. They had heard of a path through the mountains called the path of Shawi. A path that followed a valley up into the tree-covered hills. They wanted to turn up into the mountains, to get away from the gritty Wilderness that stretched between the hills and the Yam Suf.

Moses came out of his tent. He said, 'Do not go on the path of Shawi. Even the bedouin do not take cattle along the path of Shawi.'

The men of Korah shouted him down.

Moses said, 'Wait, wait, and I will speak with God.'

The priests, the Levites, all said, 'Wait, and Moses will speak with God.'

That night Moses went into the hills. Aaron followed behind with soldiers to protect him from leopard and wild bear. In the mountains, the Levites said, Moses would speak to God and only Aaron would be with him. A cloud would come down, and cover Moses and Aaron. People watched for the cloud until it went dark. In the morning the people waited anxiously. The sheep and cattle had eaten all the herbage, and there was only mud to drink.

Moses came down from the hills. Waiting for him was a vast gathering, men and women and children from all the tribes.

Moses said, 'God has spoken to me. He will go before us to lead us in a pillar of dust, and at night in a pillar of light. Has nobody seen him in the dust of the day, or in darkness in a pillar of light?'

'Yes, yes,' howled the Benjaminites. 'Yes, we have seen God at night, we have seen God in a pillar of light!'

But nobody else had seen this God; nobody else had seen this Yahweh.

Moses said, 'God will protect us, if we trust in him.'

'God will protect us!' cried Rebecca.

'Be quiet!' hissed Ruth and Esther.

Rebecca sat down, trembling.

An elder of Judah started to speak. He was a puzzled, despairing man, mumbling so that only those close to the front could hear him. He said that the men of Judah were barley farmers. They had few sheep, few cattle, and their oxen had pulled their wooden ploughs across the dry, hard desert. Now their ploughs had fallen to pieces, and they had no fodder for their animals.

A Benjaminite (the Benjaminites were always the boys for a bargain) asked if they wanted to sell their oxen and for how much.

Moses said, 'Listen! Listen! We must go south to Elim. We must put our trust in the Lord God!' He came forward, hesitantly, then held his arms out in a gesture of appeal. 'How can I keep you together? If I do not keep you together we will surely die, or be captured by the King's soldiers. How can I keep you together?'

Rebecca, on the ground, said, 'How can he keep us together?'

Miriam stood up. She said, 'Listen! Listen! We have come this far. Could anybody else here have brought us this far?'

'Not with a good conscience,' called a wag.

'Listen!' said Miriam. 'We have left ten thousand of

our families dead in Egypt. We have left our brothers and sisters dead. We have left our children dead. Would you be a bondsman building the grain stores of Kantarah? Can't you see, *shitbag*, that this is the one man who can save us?'

Moses said, 'No.' He shook his head (he was always, said Ruth in later life, a meek and modest man) and said, 'No, it is not me. It is God. We must trust in God, but we must also move faster through the desert. We must abandon our *belongings*.'

There was a stunned silence.

Then there was a howl of rage and despair.

Zuri sat on a stone, his shawl round his shoulders. He no longer howled, but moaned softly. He moaned for his chair, inlaid with ebony and ivory, that he had possessed for a hundred of his two hundred years, and for his cedar pot-stand, and for his painted lamp-stand fancifully shaped to imitate a column of papyrus. He cried, 'What of my bed? What of my bed?'

Ruth ignored him. She was stewing up bones. Bones and skin, just like the Reubenites. The old Ethiopians sat nearby on stones, whimpering softly to each other. They were ill with dysentery. In Egypt they had never tasted meat. Now they had nothing to eat but bones and skin, and nobody would give them barley-cake.

Zuri moaned loudly. Ruth said, 'Be quiet, old man!' then looked round furtively, afraid that Shelumiel might have heard her. But Shelumiel was away with his archers. Instead there came a waft of spice on the night air, a waft of incense, of myrrh, of orange flowers. There was a silvery tinkle of bells. Then Miriam – dark Miriam, with the dark red lips – was leaning over Giliad, who nearly fainted from her perfume, and kissing Zuri on the cheek. Esther, who thought it daring to rub noses and was shocked even to think of the Egyptian high-society fashion of kissing with lips, sat in the firelight, wide-eyed.

Zuri, pleased, said, 'So Akhenaten is Yahweh the Thunderer!'

Miriam said, 'It is necessary.'

'And we must abandon our possessions!'

'Our animals are dying. The oxen are being used to cart tables and chairs and lamp-stands and birthing beds. Can we eat tables and chairs?'

'I do not trust the Levites. I do not trust Aaron.'

'No,' said Miriam, 'you must not trust Aaron.'

'The men of Korah do not trust him – or your Moses.'

'The men of Korah are happy tonight. God has spoken to Moses. In Canaan there shall be six days of labour, and on the seventh day there shall be rest.'

Zuri said confidently, 'No, no. There shall be ten days of labour and on the eleventh day there shall be rest.'

'Not now.'

'In Egypt the law says—'

'We are not in Egypt.'

'This God,' said Zuri, amazed, 'will give brickmakers and bondsmen a day of rest every seven days?'

'It is being written in clay.'

'I wish I had stayed in Egypt!'

'You would have died in Egypt.'

'So now I will die in the Wilderness.'

'You have to die somewhere.'

Zuri stared into the fire.

Miriam said, 'But not yet.'

'Perhaps,' said Zuri, looking at her slyly with his yellow eyes, 'you will send one of your sisters to cheer me. One who can play the flute.'

'Ah! One who can play the flute' – mocking.

'One who can sing,' said Zuri, his voice suddenly pathetic, 'the songs of old Egypt.'

'You must forget about old Egypt.'

Zuri stared into the flames. Miriam sighed. She said gently, 'I will come to you, and play the lyre, and sing you songs.'

She went. Esther's eyes in the firelight were huge. Ruth said coldly, 'Husband. Old man. Shall I sing you songs?'

Zuri said: *Your love is in me, your love holds me, like the reed in the arms of the wind.* He was crying.

'Ah, me,' sighed Esther, who longed to be betrothed.

'Ah, for the night wind across the Nile! Across the reedbeds of the mighty Nile!' quavered Zuri. 'Ah, for the little lapping of water around our home!'

Later that night, when they had eaten the skin and sucked the bones, a Levite priest wearing the black cloak of a spy came to the tent and sat by the fire and spoke to Zuri. 'You heard Moses and the lord Aaron. We cannot carry dross through the desert. We cannot carry chairs and tables across the Mountains of Ti. You are an elder of Simeon. I ask you to give up the *belongings* that were brought out of Egypt.'

Zuri said, 'I had a house in Goshen that has been burned down. Even now Renenutet looks for me among the vines that are full of fruit and that strangers will harvest. The *belongings* I brought from Egypt are all I have to take me to the Land of Osiris.'

The priest said, 'You have no need of Osiris or of

serpent gods. Yahweh is our God.'

'I have no penny for the ferryman. I have no fee for the Dog God to let my ka go free. I have nothing for my ka to live in when I am dead. I say spells against the eating of excrement, but how do I know that they will work?'

'Yahweh is our God. Remember before you speak that Yahweh is a jealous God.'

Zuri said nothing. Ruth knew that he was thinking of the Lord Akhenaten, who was now Yahweh; how he had seen him when he walked the earth, which was more than Moses the scribe had ever done.

'So Yahweh is a jealous God!' said Zuri. 'At the Levites' command we fled the mortuary priests of Thebes, the terrible priests of Amun. And now there is a *jealous God* that rules over us!'

'You do not understand.'

'No, I do not understand.'

Already, he knew, the Danites were being forced to deny their Serpent God, Nehushtan. Would they make him deny Renenutet, who lay coiled even now on his bed in Goshen, waiting for him to come home, watching the door with sad serpent eyes?

The Levite asked after Rebecca. He was a *hawi*, a physician of sorts, though he did no magic with snakes. He said to Rebecca, 'God be with you', then went from the fireside, his black cloak hiding him in the black night. Shelumiel returned. He had been round the flock after training with the army. To Ruth he seemed taller these days. He was titled a Lord of the Tribes, though when they lived in Goshen he had been a farmer, a manager of his father's vineyards. 'He has become a lord in the Wilderness,' thought Ruth. 'He has become a prince of the house of Simeon.'

Zuri said, 'The Levites are giving one day in seven to be a holiday.'

'It is to buy the men of Korah.'

'They want our *belongings*.'

Shelumiel said, 'An army has no need of *belongings*, but only the *belongings* that will help us to fight, or to feed our soldiers, or keep our soldiers warm.'

Zuri said, 'I wish, oh, I wish I were in Egypt.'

Later, sitting round the fire, her eyes stinging (there was a wind from the mountains that twisted and tossed the smoke from the flaring desert broom), Ruth said, 'Shall I sing for you, then, husband?'

She looked, as she spoke, at Shelumiel.

'Yes, sing for me,' said Zuri, mournful but pleased. Ruth sang a love song of Thebes.

Oh, my lover torments my heart with his voice.
He makes sickness take hold of me.
He is neighbour to my mother's house, and I cannot go to him!
Lover! I am promised to you by the God of Women,
Come to me, that I might see your beauty.

She stopped. Shelumiel was staring into the fire; he had not been listening. Esther said, 'The women of Thebes are so shocking.' She was thirteen, like Giliad, and worried that she had only a year to go before she ought to marry, and there was only Eli, of the tribe of Dan, interested in her, and he already had two wives. She had a toy, a wooden hippopotamus with a jaw that opened and closed when she pulled the cord. She had had it since she was born. She was holding it now. Ruth said, 'You will never be a married woman while you have a toy hippopotamus.'

A new law of property was issued by the Levites. Henceforth people could carry only what could be burned on the fires, or eaten, or drunk, or what served to keep them warm at night.

Soldier priests went from camp to camp, from tent to tent. There was a list of goods that could be kept, and of goods that were to be handed to the Levites or abandoned. The birthing bed of the Benjaminites was taken. The last remaining slaves of the Benjaminites, who were hiding in the herd of hyena to avoid the conscript, were taken away. The slaves moaned when they were taken. They did not want to serve the priest-soldiers, to carry the tabernacle of Yahweh across the vastness of Ti.

From Zuri were taken twelve amphorae of wine worth forty silver shekels, and one talent of copper worth fifteen silver shekels, and the wine bowl that weighed 200 shekels and was valued at sixty shekels of gold by the venal Vizier of El-Yahudiyeh after it had been given to Zuri by the man who was frightened of frogs; and one talent of woven wool that was worth two silver shekels, and one talent of lapis lazuli that, Zuri cried, was beyond price (although the Levite marked it on his tablet at five and a half shekels), and one robe of Tyrian blue cloth, and the scarlet and gold garment that cost eight shekels of silver in the bazaar (or was given to Zuri by the corrupt Vizier himself) and was never part of the *belongings* given to the Children of Israel for their journey to Canaan.

They were taken by the priests, and the scribe Gsarshon wrote them down in wax and clay.

As an elder of Simeon, Zuri kept his bed, and the furniture of his chamber, and the pot of balm.

Giliad was in the new militia. He stood to attention, under orders, as the priest-soldiers went through Zuri's goods. A soldier, a new recruit from the brick-makers of Pi-Ramese, marvelled at the number of the *belongings* brought by Zuri out of Egypt. 'The lord Moses said, Let my people go,' said the soldier. 'He didn't say we had to steal everything that fucking moved.'

Now they were travelling again. The word had gone round in the night, and as the sun rose over Ti the tribes left the stunted trees and fouled spring and moved south in the dawn.

Looking back, Ruth saw bedouin come out from the dunes of sand, and approach the piles of furniture and household goods rejected by the soldier-priests.

She looked for her *bedu*, for Jaha, but could not see him.

Zuri was carried in his litter by the four old Ethiopians. His statue of Bes had been seized by the soldier-priests as an image of a *false god*. He had hidden the silver statue of Ka-nefer in his bedroll.

Ruth looked at him; he stared back at her miserably. He was thin enough now, but the old Ethiopians still staggered under his weight.

She turned and plodded on. Esther was in front of her; Giliad, his back bent, the stone quern over his shoulder.

Rebecca, pale and thin.

The sun was white at midday, white hot.
They were moving slowly now, so very slowly.

In two days, said the Spies, they would come to Elim.

21
Soubeita, Israel

High in the deep-blue heavens there was a tiny flash of silver, a small exhaust trail of what appeared to be smoke circles – then the US spy plane's turbo burners fired and she was gone, into the upper ether, out beyond the Lockheed Blackbird's limit of nineteen miles, flying on the very edge of space; while below her the earth's rim curved, and the Negev and Sinai were reduced to a small triangle of land between the Red Sea, the Gulf of Aqaba and the Mediterranean. Ten seconds more and her engines cut back. She was cruising, now, still moving outwards from the earth, but then, after five seconds, stabilizing. Fifteen seconds later her high-powered cameras and cloud-penetrating infra-red radar were fully operational, and her X-band transponder antenna and sensor packs were relaying information earthwards in a dense stream. The high skies were her dominion, and hers alone. Pilotless drones could reach higher, but there was no other manned craft, friend or foe, between the spy plane and NASA's KH-11 space-shuttle satellite which was orbiting at 200 miles. Black-painted, matt black, as big as Concorde, the result of some eight billion dollars spent at Lockheed's top-secret military factory in California, powered by the world's most advanced pulser engines, guarded night and day by US Seals when she was at her remote Scottish base of Machrihanish, she was the fabulous Aurora; the spy plane that could fly at six times the speed of sound.

One minute twenty seconds. The F-111 fighter bombers that had escorted her upwards on her first 40,000 feet were returning to base, curling down across the western limestone escarpment, down over the desert road that ran some five kilometres from the airfield, their exhausts leaving shimmering bars of heat as they came down on the desert runway.

'Bang bang bang,' said the bedouin Magdi, taking his hands for a long moment from the wheel and holding them over his ears in pretend pain, though the pain could perhaps have been real and caused by the music blasting out from the stereo. 'Noise everywhere,' he said. Richard nodded absently, peering ahead through the windscreen of Magdi's battered car, one of the original Peugeots given to the Negev bedouin by the Israelis, back in the sixties, to replace their camels.

He had left Jerusalem an hour before dawn, travelling in a powerful hired Mercedes down empty roads through Hebron and Az Zahiriyah, out into the eastern Negev, past huge squares of irrigated land where the tips of green wheat were just showing. He had stopped for breakfast at Beersheba, a place he had last visited in the late seventies. In those days it had been a Wild West sort of town that boasted more fast-food cafés and more prostitutes than anywhere else in Israel. It seemed quieter now, but then all

Israel seemed quiet – subdued, people staying close to their television sets, waiting for the scream of jet turbos, waiting for the bombs. There was a tiredness, a grim disbelief that it might all be going to happen again.

He had parked the car, given the keys in at the Avis office, and wandered down back-streets until he found Magdi, asleep, curled up on the back seat of his Peugeot. He had woken him, not without effort and a certain necessary brutality, and negotiated a price to the frontier.

Now they were out in the Negev proper. Ahead, some-where, was the Sinai; the state of Egypt. On either side could be seen tracks leading off to military camps, most of them empty for the past decade, now quietly filling as Israel's Seventh Armoured Brigade came back to its old stamping ground; the Second Infantry Division slotted back into its customary place.

A group of young soldiers sat by a bus stop where they had been dropped, waiting for army transport. Each had his regulation-size suitcase, his shiny sports bag, his plastic carrier bag with food and bottled water.

'Israeli kids,' said Magdi contemptuously, shaking his head.

'You don't like the Israelis?' A mechanical question, being polite.

Magdi made a sound like a camel snickering.

'They gave you your Peugeot,' said Richard.

Magdi thought about it for five kilometres. He said, 'Yeah, OK, OK. Life is dynamic these days. The camel is not dynamic.'

No, thought Richard, the camel was many things, dynamic it was not.

'We move with the times,' said Magdi toughly.

The highway stretched ahead. The Rolling Stones tape popped out and the radio cut in, Kaka wailing a song of great beauty. Her lover was the flower of a tamarisk, her lover was a desert rose. 'Aaaaa-aa,' wailed Magdi, catching the refrain. Kaka's lover had a sword of chased silver, a saddle with a pommel of gold. 'Aaaa-oooo,' wailed Magdi, bristly and unwashed, lighting a Marlboro, seeing himself as Kaka's sheikh. Over to their right an American M-151 jeep was keeping pace with them. They were well clear of the Soubeita military airfield – they had never been closer than five kilometres – but it wasn't taking any chances. Richard watched it bounce over the dunes at seventy kilometres an hour. Its occupants had let two-thirds of the air out of its tyres, converting it into a powerful dune buggy.

A sign by the desert road, advertising Orangina. There was a warning, red on white, of the Egyptian border. A military police checkpoint, manned by grim, unsmiling Israeli soldiers. Another advert, this time for the Taba Ramada hotel. A few minutes later there was a track to the left, and a sign BEDOUIN HERITAGE CENTER. Magdi swung the wheel. They rattled across empty desert. Ahead, now, was a long dark escarpment, the mountains of the Negev. Soon, on the distant desert floor, there appeared a cluster of grey brick buildings round a mud mosque, a tiny toy-town against the mountains. Turning to look back, Richard saw that the dune buggy was stationary on a slight rise. Somebody was standing to watch them through binoculars, or to record them on video.

The girls were sitting on a mud wall. Next to them were several large boxes of groceries.

'Did you bring Worboys's *Archaeological Review?*' called Di.

'Yes, I got his message,' said Richard. 'Where's Vronwy?'

'Beersheba, picking up some parts for a new CAT-scan from the airport. Did you know we had a proto-type portable CAT-scan? We tried to call you so you could meet her there, but we didn't have your hotel.'

'No, I was in Jerusalem. How's the dig going?'

He was looking, from old habit, through the brown paper bags of groceries. Morale in the desert depended on the quality of the food, a point that so many archaeologists had made, so many times, to their unfeeling and callous sponsors. Here he found Uncle Ben's rice, tinned mackerel, and tinned mince that came, improbably, from Newcastle upon Tyne. An entire box was filled with cans of 'Beefy'-brand beef, an old desert stand-by that Richard recalled, with horror, as being Worboys's favourite delicacy. There was dried pasta and a dozen packs of Time cigarettes. There were Pepsi-Colas bottled in Haifa, tinned peaches, fresh figs and several dozen wizened green-tinged oranges, for although there might well have been several million big juicy oranges in Israel, the bedouin village culturally looked north to Gaza rather than to the Jewish settlements of the east.

'I hope you're not going to complain,' said Jo, the severe one. 'Do you know how much money Worboys gave us?'

'No, it's all right,' he said, ashamed to pry into the paucity of Worboys's means.

'He's very excited,' said Di. 'We've turned up a

365

necklace of green-glazed scarabs in a grave on the lower tell, Egyptian, eighteenth dynasty. He thinks he might be able to get the Rijksmuseum van Oudheden to come in as a co-partner. He says it's a far more important site than anybody realizes, and he wants to know how you found out.'

Richard paid Magdi, who was hanging about, interested in the girls, interested in dynamic living. 'This OK?' he said, giving a ten-dollar tip.

'Yeah, OK, OK,' said Magdi, carelessly, stuffing the money into a pocket, showing off.

Richard sat down on the sand between Di and Jo, leaning his head back against the wall, one pair of bronzed legs dangling down on either side of his head. Magdi looked at him jealously, then sat down too, on the sand in front of them. He said, 'Well, hi, girls.'

'Well, hi,' said Di, politely. Jo, snooty, a girl from Double Bay, Sydney, took no notice of him.

Magdi said, 'My name is Magdi. I'm an entrepreneurial guy.'

'You are?'

He nodded. 'This car is mine.'

'It is?' Di looked impressed.

'You need a car and driver? You want to go to Beersheba?'

'Not right now.'

'You want a job in Beersheba?'

'No, thanks,' said Di, not unconscious of the compliment.

'Big money.'

'I'll bet.

'How about you, honey?' he said enticingly to Jo. She looked at him as though he were a patch of lichen.

Richard said, 'Well, cheerio then.'

'*Cheerio*' parroted Magdi, trying to be funny.

Diane said soothingly, 'I think you ought to piss off now, OK?'

They all gave little waves to Magdi, sitting in front of them. Magdi did not want to go. 'In the old days,' he said, 'my tribe had three hundred camels and five thousand sheep and my father had twenty-nine wives.'

They all looked at the battered Peugeot.

'You are the son of a sheikh?' said Di.

'The son of a sheikh of sheikhs,' said Magdi passionately, 'A sheikh of sheikhs of El-Arish!'

It might have been true. A sheikh of sheikhs of El-arish would not, in the old days, have sent his son taxi-driving in Beersheba; but the old days, like the camels, the sheep and the twenty-nine wives, were gone.

'Perhaps you ought to be getting back to Beersheba, Magdi,' said Di.

'That's OK.' A man whose time was his own.

They decided, by unspoken consent, to ignore him. The sun was high, but at this time of year the heat was not oppressive. Only three weeks ago there had been snow in Jerusalem. Richard felt the sun's warmth seep into his bones. He leant back and breathed in the desert air, clean and sharp.

'You with us for long, Richard?' asked Di.

'A month, perhaps. I've some places I want to look at. What time are you expecting Vronwy?'

'It depends how long it takes to get these CAT-scan parts through customs.'

'We still can't think,' said Di, 'how Worboys talked himself into the only portable CAT-scan in the known universe.'

'The world,' said Richard, 'the universe even, has always underestimated Worboys.'

Jo began to sing quietly, a song of the Outback:

> *Now father's got a four-year stretch,*
> *As everybody knows,*
> *And now he lies in Maitland Gaol,*
> *Broad arrows on his clothes . . .*

Several dogs and a small, black, Vietnamese pig shuffled past. Richard looked at the pig and thought what a strange animal it was to be found in a part of the world traditionally prejudiced against the consumption of pork. Magdi tried to join in the song, warbling with pretend enjoyment, betraying his true love, Kaka, the nightingale of the Muslim world. Jo stopped singing. Israeli children came out of the Heritage Center and climbed into a coach. Richard asked what the Heritage Museum was like, and Jo told him it had photographs of old-time bedouin in black tents and bugger-all else.

Di said, 'Want to take a look?'

They went across the square. In the village café two old men were playing dominoes, the pinpricks of light from their hookahs glowing in the gloom. They strolled past grey-brick houses, each one built with a quarter of an acre of private desert. Next to some of the houses were bedouin tents, open-sided with woven grass mats and decorated blankets – a few of them with cheap brassware and pottery on display to tempt Israelis visiting the Heritage Center, but somehow shabby, because the Israelis were cautious spenders, day-trippers calling in after a desert barbecue, schoolchildren on culture tours. No Americans or

Europeans, not out here. No Japanese.

They paid the woman at the door and went in. There was a big photo-display of Ein Gedeirat oasis, where Jarvis had reconstructed ancient Byzantine waterworks and planted 300 acres of olive trees and vines. Jarvis had been governor of the Negev for thirteen years after the British had smashed the power of the Turks. Richard looked at a blown-up photograph: a man in a black dinner jacket, sitting on a camp stool, a sheikh at either hand. Below the photo was an enlarged quotation from Jarvis's book *Desert and Delta*:

> It may be argued that the wearing of a black tie at night is a queer and petty method of fighting against this Bedouin bewitchment, but it is a gesture, a definite stand in fact, against the very natural desire to let all detail and routine go by the board . . . if master goes slack, it is a most excellent excuse for his slackness extending to the kitchen.

'Who is on cooking duty tonight?'

'Vronwy,' said Di.

'Ah. There's no slackness in the kitchen with Vronwy.'

It was a shock, going round a corner, to come face to face with a huge picture of Palmer, smoking a pipe and wearing a fez. Palmer was not, a notice said, a friend of the bedouin. He had called them 'a terrible scourge' and accused them of spreading 'ruin, violence and neglect'. He had declared that, 'If the military authorities were to make systematic expeditions against these tribes and take away from them every camel and sheep which they possess, they would no longer be able to roam over the deserts, but would be compelled to settle down to agricultural pursuits or starve.'

'Who he?' said Di, wandering over, putting her arm through his and leaning against him affectionately. Who he, indeed? Palmer the explorer, whose bones perhaps lay deep in the vault of St Paul's? Palmer the pious man of religion, the professor of Arabic? Palmer the Victorian super-spy, the Sherlock Holmes of the British Foreign Office?

'Public enemy number one,' he said. 'An Englishman.'

' "The English," ' recited Di in a funny deep voice, ' "have a love of desolate places." Did you ever see Peter O'Toole as Lawrence of Arabia?'

'It was King Feisal who said that,' said Richard, 'it wasn't Lawrence.'

'Come and look at my sheikh of Araby on a dashing white charger,' said Di. 'Come and look at this.'

She led him to look at the last sheikh of sheikhs to have lived in the Negev. A slim young warrior with guns sticking out of his belt, standing outside his magnificent arabesque villa, surrounded by some dozen of his thirty wives, photographed just before the Second World War. He looked like the lover of Kaka's dreams; possibly, it seemed, of Di's dreams.

They went outside. The Vietnamese pig was trotting back and forth with its cortège of dogs. Bedouin children played in the dirt round their squatting, black-robed, black-veiled mothers. Against the mud wall Magdi was whispering to Jo, and Jo was saying loudly, 'No fucky-fucky, but *you* fuck off.' A truck was slowly coming in from the desert, over the dunes.

Soon he could see Vronwy, standing in the back and waving. He waved back, filled for a moment with a feeling of release. Now at least things would be simpler, the desert would make things simpler, the well-remembered routines and companionship would restore his sanity.

'Richard!' shouted Vronwy, holding on to the cab with one hand.

He waved and laughed.

Above him, above them all, some sixteen miles above them all, in atmosphere so thin it scarcely existed, in cold so intense it would kill in a hundredth of a second, the US spy plane Aurora swung gently in geosynchronous orbit. It was a terrible waste of the capabilities of such a craft, to hover like this, swaying on the edge of space like an eagle over El-Tîh, but not a voice in the Pentagon had been raised to object. As a potential world troublespot, the Negev and Sinai were acquiring treble-A status.

22
The River of Egypt

'The border will be closed at thirteen hundred hours, once a convoy of Egyptian trucks has crossed,' the woman in Jerusalem had told him, but the intelligence was faulty. The trucks had driven west from Tel Aviv at dawn and were already in Sinai, and at noon, when UCL's Toyota Land Cruiser – an older, more battered Land Cruiser than the metallic-gold jobs favoured by the Egyptian Security Police – reached the Egyptian border the guards had already wound barbed wire along the padlocked steel barrier, and a tracked APC with a stubby machine-gun was ready to deal with anyone who might argue.

Vronwy swore and grabbed their papers, and went to the customs post. Jo and Di went outside and sat under a dusty palm and traded insults with waiting truck drivers, who called them pretty whores and offered them five Egyptian pounds for a quickie in the bedouin love tent. 'Go home to your wives,' they called, 'oh poor, poor husbands.'

'*El benat battaleh*' – girls are good for nothing! – the truck drivers cried out, shaking their heads.

'When will the border open? When are we going to move?'

'*Inshallah*' – it's in God's hands! – they said; if one

373

thing doesn't happen then something else surely will. *Inshallah....*

The sun became hotter. The cool rising air shimmered and formed itself into mirages that rose and fell out in the Negev. Blue lakes appeared, and red palms, and shining airstrips that were not mirages at all; and perhaps they themselves were being seen as a mirage by people out there in the desert, by the Egyptian tank commanders and signallers beyond the dunes.

A bedouin boy sat on the concrete brewing coffee. Richard got out of the Land Cruiser and bought a cup. It was thick with sugar, served boiling from a copper ladle. The scent of coffee mingled with the smell of every desert way-station from Morocco to the Afghan border: diesel oil, hot sand, a whiff of decaying fruit, of animal and human excrement, then, with a slight shift in the air, the scent of acacia and desert palm.

The frontier was a small crossing south of Qezi'ot. There were a few breeze-block buildings, a barrier, a white flagstaff. There were the remains of the old British police post and barracks, now demilitarized, the border troops being eight kilometres back down the road in underground dug-outs. Nearby was a small bedouin encampment, a mosque, a water tower, a few camels and mules.

Only the dry mud mound of a Bronze Age tell indicated that travellers had been passing this way, resting at this small oasis, since the dawn of history.

Richard walked over to it. On a sign he read: 'Captured by Israel Defence Forces in December 1948. Archaeological excavations in 1979 revealed artefacts of first-century-CE Roman origin.'

But the tell, he knew, went further back than the first century. There would have been buildings here, old buildings even, when Joseph brought Mary and the boy child along the desert track from Nazareth. Shading his eyes, he looked out across the desert, seeking the line of the road that had once brought the camel trains of Ophir, laden with gold and ivory, north from Elath to the Jerusalem Temple. Over this desert, over these shifting dunes, the Phoenicians had hauled their disassembled ships of Lebanese cedar, south down the back of the Sinai, to make King Solomon's fabulous Red Sea fleet.

Nothing remained. The lone and level sands stretched away. All he could see were the rusting posts that marked out a fifties minefield; the wreck of an Israeli army truck. In the distance two burntout tanks were half buried in sand.

Vronwy was sitting outside the police post, a small figure on the wooden steps. He had not yet told her how he had borrowed her flat in London, slept in her sheets, eaten her tinned olives, drunk her Australian chardonnay, held meetings in her little sitting room with the British Secret Service.

Sitting on her sofa, Biggin had said, 'The Finance Ministry is still pro-Western, and the Culture Ministry. We have friends, but not in many of the places that count, and those friends we have are very frightened. Don't cry for help unless you have to.'

But Biggin had also said, 'If you're going to be of any use, you have to get in there fast. The RV's fixed for twenty-one hundred hours on Wednesday.'

It was Monday afternoon, and he was still in Israel.

He wandered round the tell. He took out of his pocket the mobile he had been given in Jerusalem:

an ordinary, grey mobile, slightly larger and heavier
perhaps than usual, a longer aerial. He punched in a
code, his eyes wandering up to the sky, pale milky
blue, a springtime sky. Up there, somewhere, the US
military communications satellite was sending its
little messages back and forth. An American voice.
He spoke briefly, the voice said, 'OK I'll pass it on',
and the line went dead.

'There you are,' said Di, popping up from nowhere.
'We wondered where you'd wandered off to.'

She sat down next to him.

He said, 'You see those tanks? This is where General Sharon broke through the Egyptian line in '67.
His armour crashed through Egypt's Second Tank
Division while a dismounted infantry brigade – that
he'd sent through the sand dunes during the night –
destroyed Egyptian positions from the north. By the
time the Egyptian army was properly awake, Sharon
had pounded his way south to Nakhi, Yoffe had swung
round from the north to capture the passes at Mitla
and Jiddi, and the Egyptian army was cut off. It must
have been the biggest shock to the Egyptian High
Command since the Semites came thundering out of
Canaan in horse-drawn chariots.'

'Poor old Egyptians,' said Di. 'They never liked
fighting, did they? They enjoyed life too much.'

They walked back to the Land Cruiser. The line of
waiting cars and trucks now snaked way back down
the road towards Beersheba. There was a helicopter
overhead, lazily viewing the scene. Jo was eating an
orange, being careful not to let the truck drivers see
what she was up to. She said, 'Vronwy's wasting her
time. They won't do anything during the day, not in
Ramadan. They'll put her off till after the sun's gone

down, and then they'll put her off while they stuff themselves, then they'll all fall asleep. We'll be lucky if we get out of here by midnight.'

'Poor Worboys,' said Di.

'Hey up,' said Paul, their driver.

Vronwy was running out from the police post, waving her arms. 'Go!' she shouted, 'Go, go!' The truck drivers lying in the shade whistled and shouted the timeless insults of Islam for the foreigner. Vronwy clambered aboard. Paul slammed into gear and let out the clutch.

Jo said, 'Why are they letting us through?'

'The bloke in charge got a call from Cairo, from the Ministry of Culture. Worboys must have been on to them. The bloke didn't like it – he said the Sinai was a dangerous place now, and I should telephone and speak to my father or brothers. He said it was a great scandal them letting me wander around like this.'

They rocked round the end of the barrier, past soldiers who waved their Maddi AK47s with frenzied energy. An official ran out and shouted after them, asking if they wanted him to send two soldiers with them to Isma'ilia. They shouted back that they were OK.

Suddenly the Sinai lay before them. They gave a great cheer. Around them the scenery changed. It shouldn't have been possible for a line drawn by a British Army cartographer to influence nature, but the Sinai always seemed more noble in its desolation than the Negev, its dunes more sweeping and majestic.

'Why did he want to send soldiers with us?' shouted Jo.

'There's some story about tourists being kidnapped,'

said Vronwy. 'A coach of tourists somewhere in the south.'

Once they were clear of the border they stopped to eat. The road was empty. Richard walked a little way from the truck and peed behind a stunted acacia. To the west lay mountains, rust red. He could see the peak of Jebel Halal, regarded by some as being a possible Mount Sinai. This was the Cairo-Tel Aviv Highway, but once it had been the Way of Shur, and all the world must have passed this way in the time of Rameses the Great – the pack caravans of the Babylonians and the Moabites, the travelling doctors, the bronzesmiths. Had the Children of Israel come along this road, this ancient trading route? Had they also, perhaps, peed behind the ancestral seed of this acacia bush?

Remember then that also we in a Moon's course are history.

Vronwy was eating pitta bread spread with jam. The girls were sitting, rocking from side to side and crying strangely, 'Yo, heave ho! Yo, heave ho!' and saying to Paul, 'Why are we sailors, Paul? Come on, let's play I guess with my little brain', and Paul was saying, 'You're both bonkers. I wish I'd stayed in Pelusium.' After a moment Richard spotted a dozen ships of the desert wandering untethered by a sand dune. They looked like strays, but there would be bedouin about somewhere; there was no such thing as a wild camel. He took a sandwich and a mug of tea and started fiddling with the television, adjusting the aerial and satellite dishes on the roof of the truck. 'Worboys begrudged us that telly,' said Jo. 'We had to stand very firm to get that telly. We told him, the days when students sang campfire songs every night

378

or slipped away for sex behind the rocks were over.'

'Yeah,' said Di, stretching her brown legs, 'We said, "Listen, Worboys, there's only you and Paul, and Paul has a fiancée in Leeds."'

Richard found an English-language news bulletin from Tel Aviv. In Alexandria the Coptic Pope had appealed for a return to the religious tolerance that had been the pride of Egyptian life for centuries. An Israeli government spokesman talked of the loss of trade. There was speculation about an American-brokered summit at Camp David. The American tourist bus that had failed to arrive at Sharm el-Sheikh after a visit to St Catherine's Monastery was still missing.

Vronwy came round the back of the truck. She said, 'Can we get a move on? I'm worried about the time. It's at least two hours to Nakhi, and after that the road to El-Misheili is terrible.'

They got back in the truck and moved off. Paul said, 'How about a sing-song then?'

Jo said, 'Oh Christ, no.'

'We're going to the zoo, zoo, zoo,' sang Paul loudly.

'You can come too, too, too,' sang the girls.

It was like being in a remake of *The Sound of Music*, thought Richard, except that the El-Tîh plateau was not the Alps, and Paul was not Julie Andrews.

At the Wadi el-Itheili they swung off the metalled road and drove south through Bir Hasana. The road turned into desert track. Vronwy slept, her head on Richard's shoulder. 'I feel so broke up,' Paul and the girls were singing, but quietly now, the desert outside an unending pancake of grit, the sun starting to fall over the western mountains, 'I wanna go home.'

Richard tensed his weary muscles in an attempt to protect Vronwy from the bumps as they lurched from one pot-hole to the next. He tried to remember if Celia was still in Sinai. He tried to remember what she had written in her letter. His mind went back to the time he had read it, in the Thames Valley Turbo. He remembered the flooded fields near Pangbourne, and the lecture room behind Lincoln College, and the lecturer saying: *'All arrows of time can point in any direction, and no law of the universe is violated. The laws of physics do not distinguish between past and future.'*

And he remembered Elizabeth: *'Time travel is going on constantly in the subatomic-particle world. In the electromagnetic sphere. In the microscopic structure of space-time.'*

Celia wasn't the type to disappear in a Closed Time-like Curve. Big-boned Lancashire girls didn't get swept off in CTCs. She must be back in the UK by now. Or cooking up beef bourgignon in some Swiss ski chalet.

It was past four o'clock when they entered Nakhi.

'I hope we can get a fried egg,' said Di, the hungry one.

They pulled up in the square, next to a flock of goats and two army trucks. Jo said, 'Hiya, kid,' to the goat boy, who grinned. They trooped into the Nakhi eating house. Di tried to order food. The waiter shook his head, frightened, indicating the huddle of black-bearded mullahs sitting in the corner. A few soldiers smoked and played cards. *'A few miserable soldiers are maintained by the Egyptian Government for the protection of the caravan of pilgrims,'* Palmer had written of Nakhi. *'They were as scoundrelly a set as one could well conceive.'*

'Nothing changes,' Richard said.

'Have you been here before?' said Paul.

'I've read about it in the *World's Greatest Food Guide*.'

Paul laughed, enjoying a good joke.

A bedouin tried to sell them a headdress. A soldier, overwhelmed by Jo's cool sexuality, offered her a cigarette. They drank Egyptian-bottled cola. They went outside and settled back into the truck, the girls next to Richard, who was now driving.

They headed south towards Bir Umm Sa'id, round to the south of the Wadi el-Arish. They passed a square of cultivated land where bedouin were trying to grow grapes and watermelons. A sign, decorated with the European Union flag, said 'Sinai Irrigation Scheme'. They topped a small rise, rounded a bend, and found the road blocked by oil drums and soldiers.

Vronwy tried to negotiate. Richard sat in the back of the vehicle, fiddling with the television, seeking out news bulletins. Vronwy came striding back, angry, almost in tears. 'You speak Arabic. For Christ's sake, Richard, you might *help me*.'

The girls, and Paul, looked away, embarrassed. Richard said, 'No. Turn the car round. Let's go back.'

'We can't go back!'

'Do it, Vronwy.'

'Go back where? There's no other road!'

'Just get in, OK. Paul?'

Paul hesitated. Vronwy got into the vehicle, furious. Paul did a difficult three-point turn. The soldiers at the roadblock watched impassively. It was moments like this, presumably, that really made their day.

Richard rummaged in his new rucksack and took out

381

a map. They spread it on the bonnet.

'Look.'

He pointed to the copperplate annotation: 'Cala'at Nakhl, camp January 17 to 20th.' His finger traced a red line south-east to a ridge called Fersh el-Khadid. At the ridge were the words 'small pass descent of 150ft'.

Vronwy said, 'There's no road there now. How old is this map?'

'Things don't change. We can take the road to Taba, then branch south.'

'We'll have to go back to Nakhi.'

'OK, let's get moving.'

There were dark clouds on the northern horizon, over the hills. They had an hour of daylight, perhaps less.

In Nakhi they swung round the square. Jo waved again at her shepherd boy, who looked startled. An Egyptian army jeep stood outside the café. Two officers looked at them, puzzled. Richard saw one of them talking into a radio telephone as they took the road to Taba. After a mile he said, 'Pull up.'

'Here?'

'Yes.'

Paul stopped the Land Cruiser.

'But there isn't anything,' said Vronwy. 'There isn't even a track.'

A faint wind was blowing over the wastes, the badlands. Vronwy said, 'You're sure this is all right, Richard?'

Richard said, 'It's the road south to El-Khâdem. It's been all right since the early Bronze Age.'

They turned off the road and headed slowly south

across the desert. After half a kilometre they passed a rusting sign, blown down by the winds, or leant against by camels, lying in the sand. Paul stopped the vehicle. The sign said, in English, Hebrew and Arabic: FOUR-WHEEL-DRIVE VEHICLES ONLY. Beyond it a bedouin track was clearly visible, a straight line into the desert to El-Tîh, marked out by stones.

Richard glanced behind them, making sure they had not been spotted by traffic on the Nakhi-Taba road, checking to see if they had been followed by an army patrol.

Soon the highway behind them was lost to sight.

'This is eerie,' said Di.

There was a wind rising, blowing over the gritty desert. The storm clouds were massed to the north, behind them, but the western sky was bright yellow.

'This,' said Di, ten minutes later, 'is weird.'

They were driving through new daisies that stretched as far as the eye could see.

They were up on the high plateau, going slowly in bottom gear. Once they hit a long strip of green flint, and the Land Cruiser fairly raced along; then they were back on the stony ground, making no more than fifteen kilometres an hour. There must have been rain in the last few days, because they came across pools in the rocks.

Still the badlands, the rock-strewn desert. It was a moonscape, thought Richard, the truck lurching, his arm throbbing as it had not throbbed since he left London. They were all on the moon, for Sin was the Moon God of Babylon and this was Sinai, the land of the Moon God since the Old Kingdom.

There was a wadi, a trickle of water, and a rock

face ahead. Acacia spikes spearing upwards from the bare rocks. It was almost dark, the yellow had gone from the sky, there was a streak of red in the west, dark as blood, the day-gate of the bedouin.

'OK, let's stop and look at the map.'

They stopped, got out, stretched their legs.

They were high on the pale limestone plateau. Behind them were the Mountains of Judah, to the east the 'Arabah depression. Across this wasteland, along this ancient road by the Wadi el-Arish, had come Jacob on his journey to Egypt; had come Mary and Joseph with the boy child, taking the same road that they were taking now, travelling by night, as all travellers across this sun-scorched desert travelled, walking the white moonscape with their donkey, under the stars.

They were in the heart of Tîh.

The Great and Terrible Wilderness.

Jo and Di went to look at some piles of stones a little beyond the wadi. Bedouin graves. It was normal to find bedouin graves near water – the bodies of dead bedouin had to be washed and purified, then buried as deep as a man could stand. This would have been a burial ground of a tribe of El-Tîh, a family of the Kadeirat, the ancient peoples of central Sinai.

'The trouble is,' said Paul, poring over the map, a note of frustration in his voice, 'the wadi and the mountains all have different names on this map compared to ours. For God's sake, this bloke Palmer has the Wadi el-Arish going round the west of Jebel Halal.'

'That was because everybody lied to him,' said Richard.

'El kizb milh el insan!' Palmer had reported back

384

to the Foreign Office in London. *'Lying is the salt of a man! How, with such a people to deal with, could we rely upon the truth of anything they might tell us? The reason is simple enough; an Arab is a bad actor, and with but a very little practice you may infallibly detect him in a lie; when directly accused of it, he is astonished at your, to him, incomprehensible sagacity, and at once gives up the game.'*

Not always. Not often perhaps, for the Arab was in the end a better actor than Palmer, whose throat was finally slit in the sands of El-Tur, his 20,000 pieces of gold traded for carpets and dancing girls in the market at Nakhi.

'I don't like this,' said Vronwy. 'I think we ought to go back.'

Nobody spoke. Nobody wanted to go back.

'Look, if we point in the right direction we can hardly go wrong,' said Di, a girl who had never in her life had anything go really wrong.

Paul said, 'We've plenty of grub, but it's a bloody stupid game. I'd give a lot for a GPS compass or even a satellite phone.'

Richard, who had both, and to a higher specification than Paul could dream of, said nothing.

'Well,' said Vronwy, looking at him, 'do we keep going?'

They were in a sea of churning sand, the engine racing, the vehicle in four-wheel drive, fuel being used up, everybody edgy.

'We can't go on like this,' shouted Paul. In the last hour they had covered five kilometres.

Richard took the wheel. The others got out and plodded by the vehicle through a dead world. Ghostly paths that shone white but were not paths at all, but ribs of the limestone escarpment. To the south, out beyond the long ridge of the Jebel el-Ejmeh, they could see a mass of low sandstone mountains, and far away the Jebel Ferani, the Jebel Umm Alawi, and the distant peaks of Mount Catherina. To the south-west were Tarbush and Serbal.

Eventually the track – if, indeed, they were still on a track – led them to a stretch of firmer ground, black flint, swept clean of sand by the wind. Richard stopped the Land Cruiser and turned off the engine.

It was nine o'clock.

'OK,' said Vronwy wearily. 'Let's set up camp. It's at least another four hours to El-Misheili. Let's do it in daylight.'

Paul said, 'Do you want to put up a tent?'

Di said, 'When you sleep in a house your thoughts are as high as the ceiling. When you sleep in the open, they are as high as the stars.'

Paul said earnestly, 'That's good. That's really good', and Di smirked as though she'd made it up herself. Jo saw what looked like prehistoric stone beehive-like buildings on the ridge, and wanted to go and examine them. Off she went, with Paul and Di.

'They've so much energy,' said Vronwy.

'They're so young,' said Richard.

'Oh, well, thanks,' she said.

They collected stones to make a hearth and desert broom for a fire. There was a plant with fleshy leaves growing in the broken rocks. Richard said it was called *gataf* and the bedouin ate it when very hungry. They tasted it; the leaves were acrid but not unpleasant. They laid out their sleeping bags on foam mattresses.

Richard said, 'Do you have a kettle?'

They had a kettle. He filled it from a plastic container, threw a handful of tea leaves into it, and hung it over the flames, boiling it up in the Arab way. Tea with sugar, milkless, smoky with the flavour of desert broom; it was tea the way he liked it, even down to the sand in the bottom of the tin mug.

Vronwy said, 'Why do I keep thinking of the Exodus?'

'Because Di and Jo keep going on about Worboys finding the Ark of the Covenant?'

She shook her head.

Richard said, 'Eh-Tîh has been called Badiet el-Tîh, the Desert of the Wanderings. Ejmeh has been suggested as the true Mount Sinai, the scene of the Revelation of the Law.'

'Might it have been?'

'Palmer thought not. He didn't like it because it's really just a cliff along the El-Tîh plateau, not a proper mountain. He thought the ground beneath it too irregular for the army of Israel to camp on. But who can say? The Israelites must have crossed El-Tîh by hundreds of paths.'

The fire burned with sudden brightness, consuming the dry branches of broom.

Vronwy said, 'OK, Richard, so why are you here?'

After a moment he stirred himself. He said, 'I want to see the place where the body in the Cairo morgue was found. It's a small bedouin pass north of Sarabit el-Khâdem, somewhere under the cliff of El-Tîh. It's also the place where Sayed el-Prince saw phantoms, ghosts. It's a remote place. Bedouin might pass by once in a moon, otherwise no one. Except,' he added, after a moment, 'during the Yom Kippur War, and

387

perhaps during another war, a very distant war. I just want to go there.'

She said in a tight voice, 'And what do you expect to see?'

Barren rocks. A pass of some kind, a way up to El-Tîh. A watering place if he was lucky, some evidence of Pharaonic occupation. Burnt-out Russian tanks, perhaps, bits of blackened metal amid the bleached camel bones.

'I don't know.'

They stared into the fire. The smoke of the broom stung their eyes.

'Elizabeth St George,' said Vronwy, 'thought there was a paranormal psychic recurrence, right? A physical instability in the desert that was distorting time?'

'A CTC. A Closed Timelike Curve.'

'Yes. I remember you saying. A Closed Timelike Curve.'

She drank from her mug. She said, 'Did you get any word about DDT build-up in the body, in the corpse?'

'Nothing on DDT, but lead levels were normal late twentieth century. At least, that's what they told me. I think they might have been lying.'

Again in a tight voice, 'Yes. Right.'

'There's something else,' said Richard. 'Something I haven't told you.'

'Oh, Christ, Richard. Ancient Egyptian corpses. Closed Timelike Curves. I don't think I could take anything else.'

There was a moving light on the ridge, a pixie light, a will-o'-the-wisp. Paul and the girls were coming down, their voices calling out to each other so that they did not get lost. On the ridge they had found two *nawamis*, prehistoric chambers, each about two metres high. Di had found a flint arrowhead and a handful of small shells.

Richard used the spirit stove to heat up baked beans and they ate the remains of the pitta bread.

They did not sit long round the fire. Jo said, 'I'm wacked. I'm turning in.' Di and Paul also crawled into their sleeping bags. Richard had put his bag next to Vronwy's, but everybody pretended not to have noticed.

'Night everybody.'

Zips were zipped tight, for the night would be cold.

Richard lay next to Vronwy and looked up at the heavens.

He was in a tent lit by tallow candles that a boy slave, a boy with smooth oiled skin, trimmed endlessly, while an Egyptian army officer wearing a dirty white uniform, and a second boy wearing a red fez, sat at a desk with pen and ink, and a cockerel without a tail strutted back and forth in front of four bedouin sitting cross-legged on the carpet – except that one of the bedouin, he now saw, was Palmer and another was his travelling companion, Tyrwhitt-Drake.

Palmer sat cross-legged, smoking a hookah. Tyrwhitt-Drake, the Cambridge naturalist, sat watching the boy slave trim the lamps. The bedouin were arguing terms for camel hire in the lands of the Teyahah. 'A contract has been entered upon between the Khawajat Palmer and Dirrek,' the Egyptian soldier, the Governor of Nakhi, said, 'and Mislih chief of the Sagairat Arabs, the said sheikh, engaging to provide five camels—'

'Hear him, how he would eat up the poor bedawin!'

cried the sheikh Mislih, and the tailless cockerel leapt on to the table in a flutter of bronze. 'Six camels, by your father's head!'

'Allah set you right!' cried Palmer, taking the pipe from his mouth. 'Five camels was the number agreed upon, and even that is a manifest injustice, for we want but four.'

The Governor of Nakhi banged on the table. The tailless cockerel jumped. A sheikh of the Towarah, whose camel had been impounded that morning, shouted, 'The Egyptian army is an army of dirt!' and Tyrwhitt-Drake smiled a placatory smile at the slave-boy, and prepared to write to his wife: *You will perhaps be interested in the evening we spent with the Egyptian Government's governor in Nakhl. . . .*

'Write five camels,' said the Governor, 'and write moreover five camels well equipped and strong.'

'Hear the tyrant and despoiler of the poor!' cried the sheikh Mislih. 'The strength of a camel is Allah's affair!' And his voice was filled with indignation, and a chorus of classical physicists in Oxford cried out in agreement that what would be would be, and could not be altered, and Palmer said, 'Write "well equipped and strong", and write that should one fall sick, the sheikh shall supply a substitute.' And the boy at the table, the second boy slave, dipped his pen in the ink and wrote by the light of the flickering tallow 'well equipped and strong', and the sheikh Mislih moaned, 'Ah, these pitiless oppressors! Whence can I bring a substitute from the desert? I seek refuge in Allah from Satan the accursed.'

'The Egyptian army,' said the sheikh of the Towarah, 'is an army of curs.'

And the Governor said loudly, 'Write. . . .'

23
El-Misheili

'I hope you won't be disappointed,' said Worboys anxiously. 'I know that some expeditions go in for luxurious living, but we are no Chicago House or University of Delaware. We have no refrigerated lobster claws or American rump steaks!'

Richard said, 'Don't worry about me.'

'A tin of "Beefy" beef, that's our dinner,' cried Worboys, getting worked up, 'and perhaps some cocoabutter cookies for afters.'

'It's all right. It's what he's used to. He's nothing special,' said Vronwy.

'We live the lives of simple men,' said Worboys, looking round him for confirmation, 'like simple men of the desert.'

Jo and Di nodded gravely, standing there in their short shorts, with their long brown legs; yes, they lived like simple men.

Outside the large communal tent a beaten path led to the excavation site: broken rocks, the slight, smooth curve of an ancient mound against the side of a hill, the crumbled debris left by generations of human inhabitants from the Stone Age to the Romans and beyond, a tell that might have gone unregarded for another 2,000 years had not an Egyptian army earth-mover come this way. It was a small, quiet expedition that had merited only a few lines in the *Egyptian Archaeology* Digging Diary:

> Dr Keith Worboys (British Museum) and a University College-sponsored team leave in March to begin a short season of work at a series of late Bronze Age graves on the southern edge of the Jebel el-Ejmeh, Sinai.

Richard and Worboys walked up to the mound. They looked down at the three graves broken into by the earth-moving machine. Two graves had been shattered open, the third barely touched. 'There are bones and pottery shards in the debris,' said Worboys, 'but it's impossible to say which bones were from which grave. E4 is virtually intact, as you see. The body was laid on bricks at the head and hips and feet, which tells us a little.'

'Roman?'

'Late Roman at a guess – there are late Roman amphora shards in the fill. The graves have been robbed. In E2 the body was pulled part of the way out, the head is missing and the clavicle was nothing more than a decomposed trace in the sand. No, what excited old Ashraf was the fourth grave.'

They walked up, over the broken land.

'You see how the earth-mover had gouged its way into one end of the tell? Well, the mound itself stretches back towards the side of the hill, as you see, and the earth-mover hit it again up here. The Egyptians hadn't even noticed when their machine smashed the first three graves, but their machine pulled away the top of this grave, rather neatly – '

There was a protective blue and white plastic shade over the excavation.

'It exposed two urns that are definitely late Bronze Age, and skeletal remains of a juvenile. I'll show you the photographs in a moment. The Egyptians stopped their road-building, thank the Lord, and called in the EAO. The exciting thing, the most exciting thing, of course, is that this grave had not been robbed. True, it did not contain anything of value, but who knows what we might not come across as we probe deeper.'

Deeper into the tell, deeper into the layers of time: graves where bodies lay in peace, in the darkness and solitude of 3,000 years; bony fingers still clutching amulets, perhaps; pots still containing barley grain harvested on this plateau; honey made by Bronze Age bees from clover that flowered in the days of Rameses the Great.

Richard looked out over the plateau. To the south was the cliff that dropped down to El-Biyar. To the west, somewhere, was the Exclusion Zone, the new Science Nature Park.

It had not always been dry and desolate like this. The rocks might give no indication of former fertility, and there were few signs of habitation within a historic period – which was what made Worboys's tell so interesting – but there were countless cairns and stone circles on El-Tîh, the marks of early man.

He said, 'What were they doing up here?'

Worboys said, 'Doing? Doing? What should they be doing? There's very little skeletal remains can do, apart from wait a thousand years to be robbed, and another two thousand years to be tossed in the air by earth-moving machinery.'

'The army?' said Richard. 'What was the Egyptian army doing here?'

Worboys was chuckling at his own joke. 'There's some sort of research station on the hill behind Wadi Suwig, near Sarabit el-Khâdem. You can't get near it, it's inside this new Science Nature Park. They are making a road to connect it to the interior.'

'What for?' asked Richard.

'I have absolutely no idea,' said Worboys, who neither knew nor cared. The Egyptian army supplied him with water every two days, they offered to send their earth-moving equipment to open the mound and expose all the graves in five minutes (a great joke this; their officer and Worboys laughed and laughed every time the offer was made), and they mooned about watching Jo and Di go tap-tap-tap with their little hammers and chisels.

Richard said, 'Where exactly does the Science Nature Park begin?'

'It runs north along the Abu el-Gain. But you can't go more than a kilometre towards it without a helicopter coming to take a look, and there are army roadblocks on all the passes. They're reintroducing wolves, according to the officer who brings our water.'

They went back down to the camp. At noon Jo banged a tin plate with a stick, calling them to eat. There were mashed fava beans with tahina and lemon, followed by tinned hot-dog sausages, the tins jumping around in boiling water on the stove. Worboys said heavily, anxious that Richard's expectations might not even now be raised to impossible heights, 'A feast in your honour.'

'I'm very honoured indeed, Worboys.'

Paul came, sat down and said, 'It says on the news

that the border's closed at Taba. That's the last land-link with Israel. Are we going to be OK, Ashraf?'

Ashraf was the official liaison officer from the Egyptian government's Department of Archaeology. He shrugged and said, 'No problem', just like a Cairo taxi driver.

'This childish fist-waving is getting beyond a joke,' said Worboys. 'Ashraf had trouble getting us through, didn't you, Ashraf? And that was two weeks ago, and we've got written authority from the Ministry of Culture. He had to cross a few palms with silver, didn't you, Ashraf? I thought at one point we were going to have to slip through the border south of Har Hamran.'

Richard remembered the huge illuminated satellite map on the screen in the secure room at Guildford. 'It's as well you didn't. It's mined.'

'Oh, no. The Poles cleared it.'

'Not fully.'

'My dear chap, the bedouin have been using it as a cannabis trail for the past twelve months.'

Worboys looked different out here from how he looked in London. In his shorts and shirt, he had a buccaneering air about him. 'Mind you, I'll admit that Ashraf wasn't too keen. He said all our vehicles would be impounded by the Egyptian Frontier Police. Where do the Egyptians get this taste for bureaucracy? Mind you,' he grinned chummily at Ashraf, a man he had to cultivate, 'the bureaucrats are everywhere these days. They rule all our lives.' At the end of the dig the two of them would share out the spoils – an artefact for the British Museum, an artefact for Cairo, one for you and one for me – each trying to get the best of the bargain, except that to Worboys it mattered, whereas to Ashraf, flattered and moderately bribed, it was just another job.

Richard went to his tent and lay down on his sleeping bag, breathing in the familiar smell of canvas. Outside he could hear the gentle tinkle of a dental hammer carefully striking ancient, encrusted earth, the creak of the bedouins' wheelbarrow.

Something had gone wrong. He had seventy-two hours, that was what they had said in London, and the minutes were ticking away.

He pulled a small, black plastic case out of his rucksack. On it was a large sticker bearing the message: IDV COMPUTERS OHIO SUPPORT ARCHAEOLOGICAL RESEARCH. Two further stickers stated boldly, 'University College London Sinai Expedition', so that no customs official or prying soldier should get the wrong idea and think for one second that the case contained anything other than the gadgetry of modern archaeological exploration. He clicked the case open. Most of the interior was black plastic foam. Nestling next to a battery powerpack were two slim handsets. He lifted one out.

A voice outside the tent, Vronwy's, said, 'Richard?'

He hesitated, then leant forward and pulled apart the Velcro flaps. She crawled in. She looked at the case, its contents.

'What,' she said, 'is that?'

'A GPS.'

'It doesn't look like a GPS.'

'It's army.'

'Army?'

'Commercial models only tell you where you are to an accuracy of fifteen metres – all you need, really, if you're a scientist tracking migrating kangaroos in

Australia, or guiding a combine harvester in the Midwest—'

'I do understand,' her voice was tense again, 'what a GPS is for.'

'This version is Navstar, US military. It can tell us where we are to an accuracy of one metre. It uses coded signals. It takes its position from any four of fifteen satellites.'

She picked it up. 'A toy.'

'A toy for grown-ups.'

'I wouldn't,' she said, 'be too sure about that.'

'For grown-ups,' he said again, 'believe me.'

The man who had given it to him, in the room on the fourteenth floor of the Jerusalem Bristol Hotel, had said, 'This handset cost less than one thousand dollars. But five years ago the Libyans tried to buy five hundred of an earlier version through a Paris-based front company and offered five thousand dollars apiece. They tried to bribe a US executive to put the deal through. You know why? Because you can adapt this transceiver, this simple, thousand-dollar transceiver, to feed into a plane's autopilot. Because a guy who can handle simple electronics can fix this to a target drone and get himself an instant Cruise missile.'

The man was from the CIA's Science and Technology directorate. He had flown in from Washington. He said, 'You're British?'

'American.'

He didn't seem reassured.

'This room OK?'

'Fine, thanks,' said Richard, who liked the view towards the Dead Sea, to the distant purple hills of Moab.

The man closed his eyes and sighed gently.

The woman from MI6 said, 'It was only booked this morning. We haven't used it before. We find it's the safest way.'

The man wore a dark-grey suit, striped tie, white shirt that was slightly grubby from its long flight; he looked like an IBM executive. 'Take care and remember you're using open satellite emissions,' he said. 'You can be picked up by anybody. You can even be picked up by a guy mending a TV set. He won't know what you're doing, but he'll know where you're doing it. Am I OK to get a cab to the airport?'

'You'll pick one up outside,' said Richard.

The man again closed his eyes and again sighed for the innocence of the world.

The woman said, 'This isn't Beirut in the eighties, for Heaven's sake.'

The man said, 'Famous last words, honey', and went.

The woman was English, middle-aged and toothy. She ran a donkey sanctuary when not organizing archaeological conferences for the Palestine Exploration Society. She said, thrilled, 'We don't get the *Company* in Jerusalem very often. It's still *ours*, you see.'

Vronwy had picked up the second handset, also with buttons, a LED display window. 'And this?'

'It's part of the Science Research Council's miniature CAT-scan.'

'And that is God's honest truth?'

'God's honest truth is that it is one half of a device which measures electromagnetic waves.'

'Oh, Jesus— '

'Linked to the GPS, ground transmissions of electromagnetic origin can be monitored, with accurate location to a metre, in three dimensions.'

'What happens,' she said, wittily enough, 'if it shows up four dimensions?'

'The fourth dimension, Vronwy, is time.'

'OK, so it disappears a while.'

'Right,' said Richard wearily.

'But why? Why, for God's sake? What's this all about? And where's the other half?'

'Somebody else has got it.'

'Richard, are you telling me you're some sort of spy? That you're an *agent*?'

She was staring at him, incredulous.

He told her about the terrorist attack in Islington, about the Afghanis. He told her about Guildford, the midnight session with the Security Services.

She sat shaking her head. She said, 'I don't believe any of this.'

He told her he had borrowed her flat, drunk her coffee and eaten her olives, held meetings with members of MI6, of the Joint Intelligence Committee, in her sitting room.

She said, 'You're in a fantasy world. You've freaked out.'

He said, 'I thought you'd be pleased.'

She looked at him.

'It's a logical explanation. Weapons research is a logical explanation. Why aren't you pleased?'

'Because you're out of your mind.'

He fitted the leads into the back of the transceiver. He attached it to the small powerpack. He pressed a button. Green lights flickered, numbers changing rapidly on the small screen, then settling, oscillating only fractionally.

'Electromagnetic waves,' he said. 'It manages this bit on its own.'

'This is why Worboys got his miniature CAT-scan, is it? The CAT-scan he'd been pleading for all those months in London? This is why the Archaeology Research Council suddenly relented, why Imperial College turned suddenly generous, why it was suddenly sent out by plane?'

He switched off the powerpack.

'God moves in mysterious ways,' he said, 'His wonders to perform.'

'The bastards,' she said. 'Oh, the bastards. They know there's something hellish going on in that Science Park, they know the Muslim fundamentalists have tried to kill you!'

Her 'they' were not the kindly if sometimes confused members of the Archaeology Research Council. They were the sinister 'they' who influenced everything; the 'they' who dug up roads and caused traffic jams in the holiday season; the 'they' who meant authority, who controlled all our lives.

'But they just don't care, they just need somebody to go in there and you're the only poor bugger with an excuse to get near. What happens when you get caught? Why are you *doing this*?'

'Because I need help to get to El-Garf.'

'You're obsessed, Richard. You're insane, and it's not funny, it's not funny any more.'

She was going to cry.

A voice outside the tent: 'Hello? Are you there, Corrigan?'

'Yes,' he called, covering the black case.

Worboys stuck his head through the tent flaps and said, 'Oh, hello, Vronwy.'

'Hello, Worboys.' Her face was flushed bright red. She was breathing quickly. She looked sinful, ravished, replete. Worboys stared at her reproachfully; she ought not to be canoodling, romancing, shagging, his look implied, while the bedouin chaps were still toiling in the sun.

'This letter, Corrigan. This fax. It asks me to let you have the Land Rover Discovery for a couple of days.'

'Yes. I want to look at some caves south of El-Tîh.'

'You didn't mention this.'

'I'm sorry. I expected you to have had the fax before I got here.'

'The machine had been turned off.'

'I see.'

'Is this why you are here? Is this why you came?'

'Partly. I was talking to Rand about the caves when I was arranging for you to have the CAT-scan.'

'Dr Rand thinks these caves are worth investigating?'

Worboys revered Rand, an eminence on the Archaeology Research Council.

'Yes, and he thought that as they were sending you the CAT-scan, and you did have the Land Cruiser and you didn't really need more than one vehicle—'

'I think I can be the judge of how many vehicles I need, Corrigan.'

'Of course.'

'Well, where are these caves? What period are they?'

'They're on the plateau's edge, west of El-Biyar. There are said to be some hieroglyphs – mainly proto-Sinatic alphabet, New Kingdom at any rate.'

Worboys didn't like it. Things were happening

behind his back. He would have liked to say no. But the Land Rover wasn't his. And he did have the miniature CAT-scan, the three-dimensional X-ray machine, and even this afternoon, when they had lowered it over grave DD19, it had shown something of extraordinary interest.

'Three days?' he said.

Richard nodded.

'Well, all right.'

Vronwy sat staring into the middle distance, her thoughts on another plane entirely.

Worboys implored Richard to be careful. He reminded him of the debt they owed to the Archaeological Research Council, and to the British School of Archaeology. He went.

Vronwy said, 'When do you go?'

'Tomorrow, first light.'

He reached out, but she slapped his arm away and wriggled out of the tent.

At supper Worboys remarked, as he often did, on the perfidy of his one-time friend Saltman. Vronwy said, suddenly and vehemently, 'You never really know people, do you? Not really. You might think you know somebody. You might be friends with them for a year – two years. You might talk to them, spend time with them, sleep with them, but you don't know them, you don't really know *anything* about them at all.'

Di sat paralysed, a fork of food poised half-way up from her plate, her mouth open, her eyes moving from Vronwy to Richard, then back again.

Worboys sighed and said, 'It's true. It's very true.'

Jo wondered how long Richard and Vronwy had been sleeping together.

* * *

At dawn Richard awoke automatically, rolled out of his bag, shivering in the cold, lit his stove for a mug of coffee and quickly packed. Outside, the distant hills were suffused in red light. He ran across to the Land Rover. Vronwy was sitting in the passenger seat.

'Oh, no,' he said, shaking his head. 'Oh, no.'

'Ah, Corrigan.'

Worboys, his face covered in shaving foam, his badger-hair shaving brush dipping in and out of his Elizabeth the Second Jubilee shaving mug, came round the back of the Land Rover. 'I've told Vronwy she can go with you as it's only three days. I'm not an unreasonable man, Corrigan, I'm not a man in whom,' he waved his brush, enjoying himself, 'passion's flame has totally died. But in three days we shall have opened graves DD2 and DD9, and Vronwy really *must* be here because there is no point in bringing an anthropologist all the way to Sinai just so that she can go romancing in the desert.'

Vronwy gave him a tight smile through the window. Richard said, 'Thank you, Keith.'

Worboys, who had been briefed on the situation by Di and Jo, said, 'To be frank, Corrigan, I find you an unlikely sheikh of Araby.'

He tittered, his foam-covered face rosy red from the dawn sky. He followed Richard round the Land Rover. He said, 'I don't know if the Egyptians will let you go down the pass at El-Igma. You might have to go back to El-Thamad and round by the Watir Valley.'

Richard threw his bag, bedroll, tent and cooking gear into the back. It already contained, he saw, a forty-litre water canister and a box of groceries. He got into the driving seat.

'The sheikh of Araby, eh?' said Worboys, poking his pink chin at them and laughing again.

'Goodbye, Worboys,' said Vronwy.

'Goodbye, Vronwy. Goodbye, Richard.'

The turbo diesel shuddered and threw out a cloud of black smoke. They moved away. Worboys raised his hand, waving his badger brush. Behind him the camp was silent and still. They drove slowly east, the sun in their eyes, towards the bedouin track to El-Thamad.

Vronwy said, 'You know you can't drive alone. You know the police would turn you back at the first control point. You know it's illegal to travel without a companion in the desert.'

He said, 'I've seen a woman killed in Egypt. In the desert. If anything happens to you—'

'Nobody wants to kill me.'

'Oh, Christ, Vronwy.'

'Why should anybody want to kill me? And why are you turning north? You said you were going to El-Biyar.'

'We are going to Gharandal.'

'Yeah, right, we're now going to Gharandal.'

'We have to approach El-Garf from the west. There's no cover from the east, the plateau is too exposed.'

He stopped in Nakhi. He left her in the Land Rover, and told her to keep the doors locked. In the store he bought tinned food. In the café he bought a further twenty litres of bottled water. A boy helped him carry the stuff back to the vehicle.

She said, 'How much tinned mackerel can two people eat in three days?'

Richard said, 'It's not two people, it's three people.'

Vronwy said, 'What? What did you say?'

'What do you think I am? Some sort of systems expert? You think I can work advanced electromagnetic surveillance devices?'

'I no longer know what you are, Richard, or what you can do. If you told me you designed *haute-couture* underwear for the Princess of Wales my surprise would be minimal, my belief absolute.'

'I'm taking the road down to Bir Umm Sa'id. It's longer and it's rough, but we won't have to go through as many police points.'

It was twenty-eight kilometres. It took them an hour. They were back following the Wadi el-Arish, the river of Egypt, now winding upwards towards its source. Bir Umm Sa'id was the most desolate, inhospitable place on earth, a bedouin burial ground, the junction of two desert tracks. They turned west again. At Qu'lat el-Jundi there was an army checkpoint, and no way round it. They showed their passports, their *cartes d'autorité* issued by the Egyptian Ministry of Culture, their British Museum passes. They were heading south to Râs el-Sudr, they said, and then to Suez and to Cairo. The soldiers politely but firmly directed them north, back to the main Cairo road; it would be easier for them, they said – a better road, a shorter road. Richard smiled and said thank you, then cursed foully for ten kilometres.

Vronwy said, 'If we went east we could be in Taba in three hours. Drinking tequila sunrises. Eating lamb and okra stew and stuffed baby chickens.'

They travelled ten more kilometres. Richard said, 'Maybe we can go to Taba afterwards.'

'Afterwards? After what? Twenty years' solitary in a penal camp?'

'There's a place at Taba that serves grilled beef

tenderloin and shrimps,' said Richard, 'glazed with Café de Paris butter on a sesame and garlic bun.'

'Dear God,' said Vronwy, shaken.

A desert crossing, the bisection of two ancient camel-routes. They swung back on to the Cairo Highway, Route 33. By late afternoon they were crawling through the Mitla Pass, weaving round the old gun emplacements with their rotting sandbags. As the sun began to fall they came out of the mountains. Below them the hills fell away to a grey desert, a vast plain: the ancient Wilderness of Shur. The falling sun reflected on oil tanks at the Suez refinery. The canal was a ribbon of gold.

Vronwy said, 'What if he isn't there, this guy?'

'I go to El-Garf without him.'

'Right,' she said grimly.

At the Ahmed Hamdi Tunnel they turned south. They avoided the police control point at Uyûn Mûsa by turning off the road and bumping along the shore, through the ancient oasis of Marah, the wells that Moses had made sweet. They joined the road again a kilometre south of the settlement.

At Râs el-Sudr they almost ran into an unlit roadblock by the airfield, skidding to a standstill in a cloud of dust. Soldiers with automatics opened the doors and pulled them out. Richard felt the sweat break out on his skin as a soldier pressed him back against the vehicle – he was back in Cairo, in the taxi on the way to Giza, with the gold Land Cruisers forcing them to a standstill, the Security Police digging their AK47s into his stomach.

Soldiers were rifling through their cooking gear, their rucksacks. Richard saw the black case fall to the ground. He shouted, suddenly, in a rage that was only half assumed. What the hell did they think they were doing? Who the hell did they think they were? A soldier raised his rifle, pointing the barrel into his chest. Richard grabbed it and pushed it away. Vronwy screamed. Everybody turned, startled. There was a moment's silence.

They all stood there in the dusk.

Then the officer suddenly shouted, bad-temperedly, angrily. Nobody was allowed to travel down Route 66 at night! Had they not been told at Cairo? At the Ahmed Hamdi Tunnel?

No, they said, they had come from Nakhi.

Didn't they know the president had declared a state of emergency? Had they no radio? What sort of car was this, without a radio?

Yes, they had a radio. They'd been listening to tapes. They'd been listening to Frank Sinatra, to Gershwin, to Led Zeppelin, the officer could take a look—

All Israeli citizens in Sinai were being arrested! All foreigners without *cartes d'autorité* issued in the last forty-eight hours had been ordered to leave Sinai, to return to Egypt proper, or were restricted to the tourist hotels of Sharm el-Sheikh and Dahab.

Did they not know this? Were they stupid?

Richard said they were going to Sharm, they were going to Sharm now. They would be in Sharm by ten p.m.

The soldiers were looking longingly at the rucksacks, the gas stove, the video camera and the interesting black plastic case. Richard said, 'We are members of an important British Archaeological Expedition, we have United Nations backing, we are sponsored by the Egyptian Ministry of Culture', and pointed to the words UNIVERSITY COLLEGE LONDON

EL-MISHEILI DIG on the side of the Land Rover.

The officer looked deeply unimpressed, which was not what they had hoped for in London. Everybody said the British had adapted to their new, modest place in the world pecking order, but they hadn't, not really, and he, Richard, should have known this. Vronwy said, 'Hey, you guys like tinned mackerel? You want to try some tinned mackerel?' She grabbed tins of fish and handed them round. The soldiers really wanted Marlboro cigarettes, personal CD players, pocket computers, but they took the tinned fish and, with the innate courtesy of the Egyptian, smiled and offered their thanks. Richard gave the officer 100 US dollars – a fine, they agreed, for travelling after dark. The officer told his men to open the barrier and let them through. Before they moved off he leant in at the window and said, 'Listen, friend. There are five more checkpoints between Râs el-Sudr and Sharm el-Sheikh. Five. You understand me?'

What he meant was, How many tins of mackerel, how many dollars did they have?

Richard nodded. They moved off.

Vronwy said, 'I can't go through that again. I can't scream like that again. I'm no actress. Next time you get punched up, right?'

She was holding the Navstar handset. She said, 'OK, this is it.'

Richard slowed to a standstill. He switched off the vehicle's lights. It was totally dark. There was no moon, tonight, no stars. In the silence he could hear the distant sound of an aircraft, somewhere above the clouds.

She said, 'Do you want to check?'

He looked at the Navstar reading, read it off against the map. Then he gently turned the wheel and drove the Land Rover off the metalled road. They swayed across the desert, heading inland. It was easy enough – a surface gritty, like old crumbling cement, here and there a thorn bush. He tried turning his lights off, but the blackness was sudden and intense and Vronwy said, 'For Christ's sake!' – and he turned them on again.

'Will he be waiting for us?'

'Maybe.'

They started to climb. Vronwy looked at the map, holding it under the tiny green navigation light. They were winding their way up the Jebel Fûl. Occasionally they hit soft gravel, and churned along in four-wheel drive, but for the most part the surface was hard. Eventually she said, 'Stop here.'

They got out and walked a little way to a rocky outcrop.

Beneath them was El-Gharandal. Looking down the Gulf of Suez, they could see lights at Abu Rudeis, and in the blackness to the west, the lights of a ship out at sea. To the east of the coastal plain the mountains of central Sinai reared like dinosaurs. Looking inland, they saw that there was a storm over El-Tîh. Snakes of blue lightning coiled down over the distant plateau, split seconds of sheet whiteness that threw the dark rim into silhouette.

The wind was rising, smelling of rain, blowing down from the mountains.

Vronwy shivered. She went back to the Land Rover and pulled a warm jumper out of her rucksack. She got the stove going, filled the kettle with bottled water. Richard put up the tent, laid out their sleeping bags. They cooked a meal. They sat and ate it. He put his arm round her. He said, 'Stupid.'

'Me? *Me* stupid?'

They listened to a news bulletin on the BBC World Service. The Egyptian government was expected to fall within hours. Israel and Jordan were calling urgently for a US peace mission. Syria was mute – too concerned, said a commentator, with its internal problems. There was no mention of the tourist bus missing in Sinai. The world had moved on, there were fifty Hizb ut-Tahrir soldiers of Islam dead on the streets of Gaza.

Vronwy said, 'They've been killing each other since the time of the first Hyksos invasion. Jews, Egyptians – it's been more than four thousand years and they're still killing each other.'

The moon came out from behind the scudding storm clouds. It showed the coastline, a glint of silver that was the Wadi Gharandal, a chalk cliff.

'There's a fort down there,' said Richard, 'on the other side of the wadi. It's mainly Roman, the Sinus Granda, but it goes back beyond the Romans. It's where ships docked in Pharaonic times. It's where the road turned up into the mountains, up to the turquoise mines at Sarabit el-Khâdem.'

'Isn't this where the Parting of the Red Sea was supposed to have happened?'

'Well, some fairly distinguished revisionists have put it on the Mediterranean. But the bedouin tradition puts it here, or further north, near Uyûn Mûsa. That hill you can see, over beyond the wadi, is called Jebel Hammam Pharaon. There's a sulphur spring that was supposedly started by the Pharaoh's last drowning gasp.'

410

There were palms still under Hammam Pharaon. Feathery palms. Green tamarisks. Palmer had once asked his guide how the bedouin could reconcile their belief that Moses crossed the Red Sea at two different places, and the guide had said to him, 'What seems remote to us is near to God Most High.'

The storm was still raging over the distant plateau. Richard said, 'Five hours and there'll be a flash flood in Wadi Gharandal.'

'What?'

'The bedouin call them *seils*. A wall of water will come crashing down from Tîh, round the base of Hammam Pharaon, sweeping everything from its path.'

Out in the Gulf of Suez a yellow flame suddenly rose out of the sea: tongues of fire that shot up into the black sky.

They watched it in silence. Then Vronwy said shakily, 'A pillar of fire? Right? A pillar of fire that guided the Israelites by night, a column of smoke that guided them by day?'

There was a flicker of distant lightning. A man was standing against the rock outcrop.

'Râs Ami oilfield, actually,' said Richard, standing up. 'They're burning off the gas.'

24
The Parting of the Waves

The silver trumpets had sounded. The silver trumpets had sounded in the night. Esther had screamed, and Ruth had jumped to her feet, whimpering, her mind still fogged with sleep. Around her the wind was blowing, and sand was being swept in stinging wraiths across the dunes. Shelumiel was already shouting orders to the old herdsmen and shepherds, telling them to drive the flocks and the cattle out into the desert. The young men were running to answer the summons of the trumpets. Ruth called out, 'Shelumiel! Shelumiel!' and he turned and ran back.

He took both her hands and said, 'Get the old man to safety, get him up into the rocks.'

'What's happening?' she cried. Already the oxen were pulling the sledges, and the flocks were being driven from the pens, and the soldiers of the night guard were running from place to place shouting, 'Go, go!'

'I trust you,' he said. 'I trust you.'

Then he ran off, into the darkness. She shook Rebecca awake, Rebecca who slept as soundly as death, curled up by the hearth.

The silver trumpet sounded again and again.

'Go, go, go!' screamed shepherds of Zebulun, almost

driving their flocks over the tent of Zuri. She grabbed a boy. He told her that in the darkness the sons of Benjamin had stumbled over Egyptian soldiers coming across the river to attack the Israelites. The Egyptians had come from the fort where the King's ships came to collect the copper and turquoise from Khadem. The Benjaminites had saved them all from destruction.

The boy pulled away from her and ran off.

She looked round for the old Ethiopians. It was they who would have to carry Zuri to safety. They had vanished into the night. A Benjaminite materialized out of the darkness. He told her what had happened: that Benjaminite herdsmen had been down by the Yam Suf to steal sheep from the fort, which was on the other side of the Elim river, and had seen Egyptian soldiers creeping in battle order up the stream. The clouds had parted and the moon had shone on the Egyptians' javelins and on their spears. The Benjaminites had seen the moon shine down on the banner of Amarek.

Amarek! The captain general of the Northern Corps of the army of Egypt!

Again the silver trumpets rang out. The Benjaminite ran off, crying his tale through the camp. Ruth said to Esther and Rebecca, 'Get food and run to the rocks! Remember the Dinkas!' Already in her imagination the tribes were being slaughtered, already she could see the fields of the slain, the ground swallowing up the blood, the Dinkas eating the oxen and the sheep. How long would they have to hide themselves in the rocks while the Dinkas ate their fill?

Rebecca said, 'What about Zuri, what about your husband Zuri-shaddai?'

Ruth shot her a quick look of rage. She did not need to be told who her husband was.

She went into the tent. Zuri lay on his bed. He blinked at her and said comfortably, 'I dreamt that I was looking out of the window of my house. It was a good dream, because it means that my God is hearing me when I cry out.'

A small light burned. She looked at his old face, at the tiny rivers of oil that ran down it. Before he slept, she had placed a cone of perfumed grease on his forehead, to melt through the night and cool his blood.

There was a sudden high wind, a wind blowing down from Ti, and the tent's walls stretched and smacked angrily.

He said, 'What is it?' Then, frightened, 'Where is Shelumiel?'

She turned and went outside. It was pitch black. Then the clouds parted and the moon shone down. A camp guard was running towards them, his lamp swaying and flickering. He shouted that the army of Israel had tried to bar the way across the ford and had been beaten back by the Egyptians. Almost everyone had been killed – the Soldier was dead, as was Ahiezer, the captain of the house of Dan, and Elizur, the captain of the house of Reuben.

'And Shelumiel?' Ruth cried. 'Shelumiel of the house of Simeon?'

He said. 'Go! Go!' and ran off. Esther said, 'Giliad is dead.' She and Rebecca began to howl, standing there with the wind blowing out their long hair, their bare arms clutching small sacks of food. Ruth stared out towards the Yam Suf, looking for God, looking for the Pillar of Light.

She saw Him.

He was out there, out on the Yam Suf.

But He was no longer a confident, powerful God. He was a God bewildered and doubtful, a flickering, uneasy God. Some other God was sending this wind, this tempest, sending it to kill the God of Moses, the God of Israel. She looked back at the tent. Zuri could not go. They would have to leave him. If Shelumiel survived he would kill her.

She would blame it on the Ethiopians.

She turned and went back again into the tent. She said, 'Old man, give me the silver statue.'

He was in a far-away world. He said, 'I dreamt my heart was being weighed – not against the divine feather, but against the Goddess of Truth. I dreamt that Anubis was honest, and Amnit was forced to go hungry, and that the Great and Little Enneads, with shepherd's crooks, took me across the river, and that my ka went free.'

The grease from the scent cone had dribbled down his face. His eyes were old yellow, old papyrus, in the lamplight.

'Give me the statue of the priest of Ptah.'

Even saying his name out loud frightened her. But Shelumiel would not marry her, he would make her his concubine, his slave, and her marriage portion would be gone.

'Give me the silver statue!'

Zuri's old eyes widened.

There came a terrible sound, the sound of falling frogs.

She turned and went outside. Rain was sheeting down. It came from the east, from Ti, from the black rim of the world. Rebecca was screaming, dancing, trying to brush the raindrops from her skin. Esther

416

was bending down over the fire, cradling it, crooning to it, imploring it to defy the raindrops that hissed like snakes. Black clouds rolled across the sky, smothering the last rays of moonlight. There was thunder over the sea, over the Yam Suf.

And there was blackness.

Yahweh was no longer with them.

The pillar of fire that for over three weeks, for thirty-six Egyptian days, had comforted them, had gone.

They stood in the rain, paralysed.

The water came down so fast that when they breathed they nearly drowned.

They scrambled into the tent and buried themselves under skins. Zuri called out, puzzled, but they ignored him. In time, his little oil light went out. In the darkness he called, 'Ruth? Ruth?' Then he called, 'Esther?' but Esther did not move.

After a while he called, 'Rebecca?' but these days Rebecca responded only to 'Mouse', and listened only to Wolf.

Water thundered down on the roof of the tent. It dripped through the wool. It pushed its way under the walls and made rivers, and lapped round Zuri's bed, round the gilt serpent feet. He dangled his hand in the water and made little splashing noises in the darkness.

At some point they slept. When Ruth woke she thought she had been under the cold sodden skins for hundreds of hours, but when she crawled out of the tent it was still dark, and the rain was still falling. One of the old Ethiopians was sitting in the wind and rain. She hit him and he cried out. He told her there had been no Egyptians, only the mad Benjaminites who had been stealing the Egyptians' cattle from the harbour, and had run into each other in the darkness. There had been no Egyptian soldiers at the fort of Elim. There had been no Amarek, no captain general of the Northern Corps. There had only been the Benjaminites, stealing sheep that were meant for the camp guards of Khadem, and the sheep had drowned in the river.

She hit him again, and he wailed and shivered.

She told him Shelumiel would beat him till his back ran with blood, which was true, and which indeed came to happen.

It was almost dawn. She could see a lightening of the blackness over Ti. A guard of the house of Asher came through the camps and said, 'It is sheeps' heads floating out to the Yam Suf, not the war horses of the Egyptians.'

She woke up Esther, and Esther fought for her fire, magic against magic, spell against spell. Nobody else would have thought it possible to make fire out of the sodden ash, the rain-blackened twigs.

The river was a torrent. Even from here, from the high ground, they could hear the waters roar. Giliad came back, his thin body shivering and blue with cold. He said great boulders of rock were crashing down the river, huge boulders carried by the raging flood. His company had stood guard by the shore, watching the great rocks come swirling down in the darkness. He said there had certainly been a great Egyptian army destroyed in the river. At one point he had seen war chariots tossing on the black waters like ships, and had heard the screams of the dying horses. His friend Shimi – he who had once been kind to Rebecca – had heard spells against death, shouted

418

desperately against the gurgling flood: *My phallus is Osiris! My feet are Ptah, and Thoth is the protection of all my flesh.* . . .

An hour after dawn the rain stopped. The other three Ethiopians came back from the place where they had been hiding and stood shivering and sodden, waiting, not in vain, to be beaten.

Esther crooned over the fire hearth. Smoke rose in a thin, wispy wand and eventually a yellow flame flickered. Ruth watched out for Shelumiel. When he came back he smiled at her; a weary smile, for the men had driven the flocks a great distance out into the desert and he had taken hours to find them. She said, 'I stayed with my husband. The Ethiopians ran off.'

He again took her hands, which were cold and damp, and warmed them in his own.

A soldier-priest, a Levite, had appeared out of nowhere and stood smoking gently at the fireside, steam rising from his black robe. He waited until all the herdsmen and shepherds and bondsmen and slaves of Simeon were together.

Then he shouted, 'God's nostrils blew and the waters parted!'

Later in the day there came a message from the camp of the Levites.

'The Lord God Yahweh saved Israel from out of the hands of the Egyptians. The Lord God caused the wind to hold back the waters of the River Elim, even as it flows into the Yam Suf, and made the river dry for the Children of Israel. The Lord God looked down on the host of Egypt through a pillar of fire and poured down water over the Egyptians, and over their horsemen, and their chariots. The Lord God Yahweh destroyed Amarek, the captain general of the Northern Corps.'

Written on clay and fired in the kiln were the words:

I *AM* THE LORD YOUR GOD, WHICH BROUGHT YOU OUT OF THE LAND OF EGYPT, TO BE YOUR GOD: I *AM* THE LORD YOUR GOD.

The image of the Wolf God of Benjamin was burned by angry men from the tribe of Zebulun. The people of Judah themselves cast off their yellow Lion God with its womanish head. For three days the Living Goddess of Asher sulked in her tent and no men went near, and her priestesses had to slip furtively through the camps at night to sell their wares, avoiding the Levites, who went round on donkeys, shouting, 'Now the people of Egypt will tremble and fear! Now the people of Palestine will be afraid! Now the Dukes of Edom will be amazed and the *mighty men* of Moab will tremble! The people of Canaan will collapse in fear and dread, and the Land of Canaan will be ours!'

Miriam followed the priests with her dancing women. They played their timbrels and Miriam sang:

> '*Sing ye to the Lord!*
> *Sing ye to the Lord!*
> *He has triumphed gloriously!*'

The sun warmed them, and the desert burst into bloom with red and yellow flowers as far as the eye could see, and flocks of sleek young gazelles came running madcap in the dawn, through the tall dewy flowers, and badgers snuffled in the leafy undergrowth. Everyone drank *shedah*, the wine of the pomegranate. Giliad drank *shedah*, and told the story of the chariots in the flood until he fell over in the sand. 'You're an old soldier now,' said a soldier, a man of Korah, picking him up.

Shelumiel, who was also drunk, said, 'Ruth, Ruth. There were no Egyptian soldiers in the river. There were two dead Egyptian shepherds from the fort, and a number of dead sheep, but there were no Egyptian soldiers.'

'Yes, they were there,' said Ruth, frightened. 'They were there but you did not see them.'

The pillar of fire no longer blazed over the Yam Suf. It was time to go east, said the Levites, time to go up into the mountains, to find the King's Highway.

Next day the first of the tribes left Elim. Two days later the tribe of Simeon followed. They left the seventy date palms by the green river, the twelve springs by the Yam Suf. They went across the desert towards the hills, seeking a path that had not been used by other tribes, a path where there was a chance of greenstuff for the sheep and oxen. They were followed by Miriam and her girls, and by the flockless, herdless Levites.

Giliad carried his quernstone, Esther carried her pot of fire. Zuri lay in his litter, carried by the smarting, bloody-backed Ethiopians.

25
Wadi Gharandal

They had been churning their way through loose sand up the Wadi el-Homur for three hours when Corporal Cartwright said, 'Stop the vehicle. Stop the vehicle now.'

Vronwy braked gently. Cartwright said, 'Turn the engine off.'

Silence.

Richard said, 'What's the matter?'

Cartwright said, 'Over there.'

Vronwy looked for a cobra, a sidewinder viper, a rare and interesting sort of eagle – a café, perhaps, with little shaded tables and cold bottled beer.

'By the small pile of stones, next to the track.'

'Track?' said Vronwy. 'Track?'

It was only nine o'clock, but the sun was baking; the first hot sun of the year. Ahead of them the wadi narrowed into a defile. She could see deep, inviting shade, the coolness of smooth black rocks with the swollen waters tumbling over them.

Cartwright took the binoculars. He got out, closing the Land Rover door quietly. He walked carefully towards the small pile of rocks, stepping like a ballerina, which was funny because you didn't often see men in fatigues and desert boots doing *Swan Lake* in

Sinai. He reached the cairn and scanned the surrounding rocks with the binoculars. He came back to the Land Rover. He climbed in, again closing the door quietly.

'OK, here. Look through these.' He failed to notice Vronwy's outstretched hand and passed the binoculars back to Richard. 'This side of the rocks, by the greenstuff. You'll see a thin metal antenna. There's another one – two hundred half left, by the tree, this side of the track.'

Richard said, 'OK, got them.'

A thin bright wand of metal. A few moments searching, then he saw the other.

Cartwright spoke softly. 'Seismic intrusion detectors. Each one has two tubes in the ground, one for the battery, the other for a VHF radio transmitter and geophone.'

Vronwy said, 'What do they do?'

'Once the geophone senses something, it encodes the vibration in digital format and sends a message back to base. The signal might automatically trigger an acoustic microphone, or it might be left to the listeners to activate it manually. You with me?'

Richard said, 'Yes.'

Vronwy looked again at the thin, shiny wand. They were five kilometres inside the Science Nature Park. She felt ill, sick, but didn't dare say anything.

Cartwright pointed again.

'See further up the track? Focus on the rock overhang, then come down, past that bush growing out of the cliff. There's a tripod. OK? That's DIRID – Directional Infra-red Intrusion Detector. Those two shotgun-barrel tubes aren't actually shotguns at all – "Oh good" indeed, love – but what they do is sense

424

any change between the background temperature and the temperature of an intruder. They have a passive optical device that shows both the presence of the intruder and the direction he's moving. It also shows how big the intruder is, and – yes, love – the number of humps he's got.'

Richard passed the binoculars to Vronwy.

'Mind you,' said Cartwright, 'it's not what you'd call at the cutting edge of surveillance technology. It's old American stuff. You can pick it up in any army surplus sale in the States. The Egyptians have probably had it since Yom Kippur.'

Richard said, 'What happens if we go back?'

'They might hear us. On the other hand, if we wait for the equipment to shut down we might still be sitting here holding our breath when a chopper comes. I reckon we should go back now.'

'If we go back,' said Vronwy hopefully, 'will we go all the way to Nakhi?'

'Very funny,' said Corporal Cartwright heavily.

She started the engine. The noise seemed amazingly loud. She felt sweat break out on her forehead. 'Shit!'

She slowly backed down the wadi.

Cartwright said, 'How many other ways are there?'

Richard said, 'There's the low pass at Silfeh, over to the north, but that will certainly have a guard on it. There's an old bedouin track at Nagb et-Bir that they might not know about – it leads up to the head of the Wadi Gharandal and the Wadi Wutah.'

'Is it the sort of place an archaeological expedition might go? The sort of place you could talk your way out of if things turned awkward?'

There were some fine prehistoric *nawamis* at the

head of the Wadi Gharandal. A cave with bedouin inscriptions that he hadn't seen in years. 'I think I could argue that the footprint of history,' he said, 'is imprinted in the sands of the Gharandal, and of the Wutah.'

'As long as you could play the mad professor, the potty archaeologist,' said Cartwright.

'I suppose somebody's thought to wonder what University College would think of all this?' asked Vronwy, not expecting an answer. 'The Science Research Council? The Trustees of the British Museum?'

At noon they stopped in the shadow of an overhanging rock. They made tea on the spirit stove. Cartwright said, 'OK, now my job's to take a series of readings. I have to take them at certain, set times, and the closer I can get to the so-called research station at El-Khâdem the better. You've got your own agenda as I understand it.'

'Yes,' said Richard.

'Anybody stops us, I leave you to do the talking. I'm just the gopher, the hired hand. You're legit, that's the beauty of it, and it was bloody brilliant bringing the girl.'

Vronwy looked at him unpleasantly.

They ate and slept. Richard awoke to see Vronwy leaning back against one of the wheels of the Land Rover. She had spread a bedouin rug to sit on. In the setting sun her brown hair glowed orange, and her limbs were suffused in an orange light. Her eyes were closed; freckles stood out round her nose. He looked round for Cartwright, then said, surprised, 'Where is he?'

'I don't know.'

She didn't open her eyes.

He sat up and scratched.

'Do we have insect bite cream?'

'In the first-aid box.'

He put cream on his bitten arms. He said, 'I'll go and look for him.'

Cartwright would be crawling about somewhere, upsetting the wildlife.

He climbed the side of the gully. The sun was hanging from the sky. Looking back he saw that Vronwy was totally orange now; even her clothes, even the black bedouin rug had an orange glow; even the Land Rover glowed orange.

He reached a low summit. Beyond it he could see a jumble of ridges dissected by narrow, steep wadis. Range after range of hills, like rumpled cloth, stretched to the south, to the peaks of the Jebel Musa, the Jebel Umm Sjhaumar. Eastward, still high above them, was the long rim of El-Tîh.

He looked again to the south, to the land of ridges and ravines. It had long been argued – he had argued himself – that the Bronze Age Israelites could not have come this way, could never have risked passing so close to the Egyptian army stationed at El-Khâdem. Palmer had believed this to be the case: *they would have passed through a district actually held by a large military force of the very enemies from whom they were fleeing,* he had written. But looking down now, it was clear that a million Israelites could have crept through these gullies, these steep ravines, without a military force at El-Khâdem being any the wiser.

And there hadn't been anything like a million Israelites.

A few thousand, a few hundred perhaps, he thought, looking at the narrow Wadi Gharandal where it broadened out into the Wadi Wutah and formed a small plateau of broken, rocky ground through which ran the small trickling stream of the Gharandal.

Yes, some of them must have passed this way; driven their animals across this open space broken up with sand hills, now covered with the tracks of gazelle and ibex, past those prehistoric stones, those *nawamis* that even in the time of the Exodus were half as old as time itself.

He thought of the torch of light out in the Red Sea. Would Elizabeth have argued this as an example of time transference? Would she have claimed that the Children of Israel were guided by industrial waste from an Egyptian oilfield? He smiled faintly. The pillar of fire could be explained without the aid of the paranormal. There would have been natural fires on the Yam Suf in Pharaonic times, gas escaping from an oilfield that nobody knew existed until the Israelis took Sinai in the Six Day War.

His eyes made out the faint zigzag path leading up to an overhanging gallery he had visited as a student. He climbed slowly along the scree until he reached the shelf. There was graffiti on the gallery wall; the scratchings of bedouin travellers – bored, sheltering from bad weather. The scratchings were impossible to date, although one animal figure, repeated several times, had a passing resemblance to the ibis of Egyptian hieroglyphics.

He went and sat on a rock, at the entrance to the gallery. The full moon was rising palely in the east, but in the west the deep burnt-orange disc of the sun still remained over the Jebel Fûl. He could see, in the far distance to the south, the smudgy ridge of Sarabit el-Khâdem.

He wondered what Cartwright was up to. He wondered about the exact nature of this research at the climatology centre, of the experiments taking place there.

He shouldn't have let Vronwy come. FIS gunmen were on their home ground here, soldiers of Islam – the Koran and the Kalashnikov – fanatics who killed without compunction, who called Muslims who would not kill *Chocolate Muslims* because they melted to please the West.

FIS or perhaps Gama'a.

No, he shouldn't have let Vronwy come.

He looked across the wadi, at the darkness under the rocks, where the Land Rover was parked.

At least helicopters would not find them, not in this broken country, not in these narrow defiles.

26
Jaha's Return

Two orbs were in the sky – Horus descending and Thoth, the God of Night, rising – when the ravine suddenly widened out into a broad open space and there, in the setting sun, was her *bedu*. He was sitting on his donkey, on a rocky ledge, watching the Simeonites, just as he had watched them all those days ago, at Raha.

'It's your *bedu*,' said Esther, coming up behind her, amazed.

Ruth said, 'My *bedu*? My *bedu*?'

Shelumiel, his face streaked with sweat and dust, came up behind them out of the ravine. He stared at the small black-clothed figure on the rock ledge. Then he looked round the open space with the river running through it and said, 'Get the tent up and the fire made.'

He turned and shouted hoarsely to the shepherds. The sheep were scattering everywhere. Some were climbing high into dangerous places searching for food. Others were slithering down to the deep-running waters of the river, which was still swollen from the storm in the night. They were looking for mountain watercress, and in their hunger their noses were snuffling under the green waters – they were turning

431

into fish sheep, diving like otters in the pool under the rocks. 'Ho, ho, ho,' Esther chortled, easily amused.

Then she sat down and groaned. They had been climbing all day. In the morning they had toiled up through a ravine with high red walls and a floor that had been polished black, like the marble floor in the temple at Migdol, and the river had been a stream of translucent green water, running silently over it, or tumbling over little waterfalls. At midday the sun had sent beams of rose-coloured light down into the gorge, and they had sat on rocks, in the cool shade, to eat the small – oh, so small! – barley cakes, and cold gristly meat. But they had been happy, contented. A shepherd boy had been berated by his father, and Shelumiel had made Zuri's old joke about a boy's ears being in his bottom: he only listened when he was beaten. 'Ha, ha, ha,' Esther had laughed. She had had an amusing day, even though she was tired out.

Shelumiel had gone back down into the ravine, looking for stray sheep, or for the cattle perhaps, or offering to help the harlots. Ruth watched him go, then climbed up to the rock ledge, to Jaha. He was sitting on his donkey, staring out into the blue distance like some sort of mystic. Behind him was a shelter, a sort of cave. After a moment he said, 'O daughter of Egypt', politely, not looking at her.

'O slayer of Hittites,' she said ironically.

To the east, the small plateau extended into a broad, wide valley of broken rocks that led upwards towards Ti. To the south was a vast desert; beyond it were distant mountains, black peaks towering above a yellow, mouse-grey ridge. She looked at the ridge in loathing and fear. It was a long way off, a day's journey perhaps, but on the far side of it was the

432

valley of Khadem, the valley of slaves.

'May your prosperity and the prosperity of your household, your sons, your wives, your horses, your chariots and your old donkey be very great,' she said, showing her manners, her upbringing.

She sat on a rock that was still hot from the sun. After a moment Jaha dismounted from his old donkey and sat on the rock beside her. She smiled to herself and lay back and closed her eyes. She could smell sweet thyme and hear a low, rhythmic chanting – 'Praise to thee, praise to thee, praise to thee' – which puzzled her, but not enough to make her open her eyes. Like Esther, she was tired, tired to the bone. She heard a voice call to her. It called again, a voice at once timid, outraged and anxious. It was, of course, Rebecca. *Mouse*.

She sat up and looked down at the camp. Rebecca was staring up at the ledge reproachfully. If she had a husband, her look seemed to say, *if she had a husband she wouldn't abandon him*.

Ruth looked away. On the other side of the shelf was a natural amphitheatre, full of little sandhills and Benjaminites. 'Praise to thee, Praise to thee, Anubis,' chanted the Benjaminites, whiskery and strange. They were gathered round a tethered ox. It was a thin, starving ox, and the God of Moses only knew where it had come from. It stood with green garlands round its neck, its muscles shivering, content not to be pulling things, happy to stand and be chanted over, a poor beast that did not recognize the soft death-hymnal of the abattoir workers. They were good butchers, the Benjaminites; it was their madness made them good with animals. As Ruth watched, a long knife was drawn and the animal's throat was quietly, silkily, cut. The ox stood, unnoticing, enjoying the sweet music as its blood splashed down on the sand of the amphitheatre, into the pot dishes and over the arms and tunics of the Benjaminites, who collected it and drank it. Slowly the blood ceased to gush and the ox gave a small, puzzled groan and fell to its knees. Already the Benjaminites were piling dry thorn twigs round it and were calling out for Esther, Esther the Simeonite, to come running quickly, quickly with her pot of fire!

Soon smoke drifted up, smelling of singed, burning hair and of desert thorn as the ox was shrived.

'Well?' she said, tired of saying nothing. 'Did you and your kinsmen go, perhaps, to Nakhi?'

Yes, he and his kinsmen had been to Nakhi.

'And this Nakhi,' she said, 'is the Nakhi that is called the centre of the world?'

Yes, he agreed, Nakhi was certainly a great way-station, a most important oasis, standing as it did at the point where the Way of the Hajji crossed the ancient road to Kadesh-Barnea and Ashdod. It was certainly the centre of the world.

'Well!' Ruth rolled her eyes. 'Well! Did you see the King of Egypt sail to Nakhi in his great royal barge? Did the King, the Pharaoh, bring gold and lapis lazuli to this new centre of the world? Did he bring a tribute of beautiful cup-bearers, maybe, of Egyptian slave-girls, all the way from Memphis?'

Jaha said nothing. He had never, as they both knew full well, been to Memphis. Sometimes he pictured it as a larger Baal-Zephon, the frontier town of mud. Sometimes he saw it as a city of white tents, filled with beautiful Egyptian women like the wives of the military governor of Gaza.

'Well, what then,' asked Ruth, wanting him to speak, to say something foolish, 'did you and your kinsmen find in Nakhi?'

They had found merchants travelling with a pack train from Midian to Egypt. They had found sea merchants from Sirbonis, who had come inland from the Great Sea. They had found seal-cutters and minstrels from Assyria. In the tents of Nakhi, he told her, the talk had been of an Egyptian war.

'In the *tents* of Nakhi?' queried Ruth. 'Ho! And what did they say in the houses? In the priest-temples? What did they say in the chambers of the scribes, and in the marble bath-houses of Nakhi?'

She was chuckling to herself. She was an Egyptian, and behaved like an Egyptian, like a true sophisticate, but he was quite aware that she knew far less than he did. She got up, wandered to the back of the cave, looked at the drawings, the pictures of animals, which were terribly primitive, some type of bedouin art she assumed.

'The world is moving,' Jaha said.

'The world is moving,' said Ruth solemnly, scratching a picture of her own, wondering what he meant. She came back to the ledge and looked down at the camp. Zuri was sitting outside his tent, mumbling and sucking away on a biscuit. She thought how scraggy he looked. His beard was long, he looked like a Moabite. All the men had beards now, which would have been a shocking thing in Egypt.

She glanced at Jaha's pannier bag. Her stomach was crying out for nourishment. What would he say if she asked for food?

'But you did not stay in Nakhi?' she said finally.

No, he had followed a group of his kinsmen who had

decided to return to the south, back to the wandering tribes of Israel. He had got up early one morning and had followed them back across Ti, across the desert.

Ruth pictured him leaving Nakhi in the dawn, a boy on a donkey. Despite her irony and sarcasm (a true child of Egypt), she imagined Nakhi to be a city of substance, a sort of Goshen but set in the grey Ti mountains rather than the green, cobra-filled fields of the Delta, and populated by rather more interesting and colourful people than shepherds and brick-makers. There were no sea merchants, no rollicking sailors, in Goshen; no seal-cutters in a thousand years, no camel trains of Midianites from the mysterious East.

'Did you have enough food to eat on your journey?' Her eyes flickered hopefully back to his skin pannier bag.

Each day he had shot birds, and one day a young desert pig. At night he had lit his fire and made his cake, and had lain wrapped in his cloak, sleeping badly, worrying about leopards and lions eating his donkey.

One day he had seen nineteen eagles over the mountains of Ti.

'How did you know where to find us?'

He looked at her, amused.

'Will your kin not wonder where you are gone to?'

They would assume that he had gone to the Egyptian garrison post, to watch the soldiers at their drill. They would expect him to reappear in the course of a moon. The bedouin nation were famous wanderers. In four moons they might travel from the land of the Hittites to the frontier station at Stile. They might set up their black tents in the mountains of Edom or on the salt marshes of Gaza. They grazed their flocks and were gone. Nobody could tame them, nobody could pin them to the land.

'No,' said Ruth delicately. 'I know.' The bedouin were held in contempt in Egypt; they were savages, the true *hapiru*.

She wondered why he had come back. She wondered if he would perhaps say, 'I came back for you.'

She said, teasing, trying to make him ashamed, 'When you went to Nakhi . . . you had *belongings* to sell to the merchants?'

Jaha looked uncomfortable.

'Perhaps you sold *belongings* to the merchants, to the Midianites?' she persisted, wheedling faintly.

The boy said, 'There were *belongings* brought by others to Nakhi.'

Bales of rich dyed cloth, a gold pot filled with incense worth fifty silver shekels – gold spoons, amulets by the score, linen kilts. There had been a flock of sheep driven inland by marsh bedouin – Amorite sheep, Israelite sheep, he told her, looking out over the valley – that had been found in the sand dunes of the Way of the Philistines.

He looked at her slyly. Her smile had gone. The dancing lights had gone from her Egyptian eyes.

She said, 'Did they say, did they say in the tents of Nakhi, what happened on the Way of the Philistines?'

Soldiers of the Frontier Division had caught the Israelites. They had caught them and had driven them back to Egypt, whipping them back along the military road to Stile. Another 600,000 Israelites (Jaha spoke the Egyptian numbers impressively but uncomprehendingly) had taken the Way of the Hajji, and had perished.

Their *belongings* had been found in the desert.

'Found?' cried Ruth. 'Found?'

It was these *belongings* that were for sale in the market of Nakhi. There was more Egyptian stuff on the market, said the Nakhi merchants, than there had been for years.

A bird raced across the sky, speeding south from the Ti plateau, gliding suddenly down into the deep shadows of the valley, seeking its nest. Then the sun fell behind the far hills, and darkness came down over Elim river, and all the valleys.

Ruth knew now why he had come back. He had come back, just like his kinsmen, for *belongings*. The markets might be overflowing with stuff stolen from the dead of Israel, but Jaha would like a new amulet, a silver Egyptian earring, a spoon of beaten gold filled with incense, for himself.

She looked at him with hatred. She stood up. She said, *'Shalom'*, which was the Upper Egypt, upper-middle-class way, of saying 'Amun', meaning 'Amun go with you.'

She went down, stumbling down through the broken rocks, through the scree.

She remembered watching the folk of Dan and Gad depart from Raha, on that fine, crisp, winter's day, their sledges and litters and herds moving north-east towards Bahah and the Great Sea. She remembered the blueness of the great northern sky, and the men on donkeys, in their cotton padded jackets, their faces muffled against the wind. She remembered the out-riders shouting, 'See you in Canaan!' and Rebecca weeping over some boy who had gone and who had been kind to her.

She remembered watching their distant campfires, after their first day's march, the tiny flickering lights already a vast distance away. She remembered wishing she was with them.

Esther was making cakes. There were only bitter mountain herbs to spread on the barley dough, only a little fat and goat's milk to make them with. Zuri was mumbling into his beard about cucumbers and garlic.

Shelumiel said, 'Why does one bedouin come back to us?'

Ruth shook her head.

At the next campfire the Benjaminites were eating the heart and the liver and the tongue of their ox. They were eating it hot from the bubbling pan. Ruth could hear tambourines; hear laughter – Miriam and her dancing women, invited to the feast. She raged inwardly. Shelumiel was forever with the harlots. Sometimes he worshipped at the house of Asher, tumbling a priestess and saying his prayers.

She said, stuttering in her rage and fear, 'The families who went north were caught by Egyptian soldiers. They were driven back to Egypt. Those who went along the Way of the Hajji have been killed by the bedouin.'

Esther and Giliad looked at her, frightened. Shelumiel said nothing. He sat staring into the fire until Zuri had taken Giliad into the tent to study his sums, and until Esther and Rebecca had curled under their skins.

Then he said, 'Who told you this?'

'The bedouin.'

Shelumiel looked silently into the flames.

'At least,' she said bravely, hopefully, 'the families who went along the Way of the Philistines are back in Egypt!'

'Yes, they are back in Misri. But they were from Pi-Ramese and had worked on the corvée. For running away they will be declared state servants. They will spend their lives working on the irrigation canals, or building granaries, or labouring at the royal tombs, and their children will be state servants, and their children's children; slaves to the fourth generation.'

Ruth said, 'None of our house worked on the corvée.'

'No. We paid the Benjaminites to take our place.'

Under the cliff the timbrels of Miriam played, the Benjaminites danced in the firelight.

Shelumiel said, surprised, 'So Moses was right. This Kenite and his God were right to bring us south along the Yam Suf.'

'Yes, yes, we have the Kenite and his God!' said Ruth.

'Don't talk to the bedouin.'

'Shelumiel, you are not my husband.'

He got up.

She said, 'Shelumiel, what will happen to me when he dies?'

He looked down at her in the firelight. Then he walked away, towards the distant fire of the family of Reuben.

He wanted her for a concubine! He would dissolve her marriage contract and take her for a concubine, and her widow's portion would be gone, and though she was only fifteen, no husband would ever come seeking her again! She sobbed quietly, in self-pity. Suddenly, she remembered the wedding present Zuri had given her, when she first came to the house by the canal, the bronze looking-glass with a long handle of ebony.

How she had laughed! How she had bubbled, and chortled, admiring her smooth, round, dimpled face in the shining metal! But in the panic of their flight her looking-glass had been left in Goshen, in the little house by the canal.

She sobbed afresh.

After a while she went and crawled under her skin, up against Esther. From the Benjaminites' camp she could hear Miriam's girls singing. Nearer, in the tent, she could hear Giliad memorizing phrases from his *kemyt*. In Egypt, he was to have been the first of Zuri's family to be a scribe. After another year at the scribe school he would have completed his *kemyt* primer, and would have moved to advanced texts. He had wanted to be a scribe of ritual and magic, but Zuri intended him for a tax assessor and had insisted that he learn mathematics.

'What if there are no taxes in Canaan?' Ruth now heard him ask.

'There will always be taxes,' said Zuri.

'Won't there always be ritual and magic?'

'Not always the same ritual and magic. Four hundred scribe priests of Amun were killed in the temple of Thebes when Akhenaten abolished their god.'

'And were the scribe priests of Akhenaten killed,' asked Giliad, 'when the priests of Amun were restored?'

'The priests were killed and the people suffered; we are suffering now,' said Zuri. 'Why do you think we are brought to this Wilderness? Why do you think I was brought away from my house in the paddy swamp?

You will be a scribe to the tax office. The first tax official of Canaan. You will impose a tax on the milk and the honey.'

Zuri snuffled noisily, the old humorist.

Ruth curled herself against Esther and slept.

Another man was snuffling. He was snuffling noisily about the rocks and terrifying Jaha. Earlier, Jaha had watched a vulture fly into the western sky and had uneasily touched his scarab amulet, because at nightfall the Vulture Goddess, Mut, hunted, and was not choosy about her prey. Then he had watched the moon rise over Ti. It was a full moon, milky white; then, as the sky darkened to a royal blue, it had become bright silver. Below him the campfires of the Israelites had flared in the night. He had made his bed and securely tethered his donkey. He had no fire, but ate the raw meat of the badger he had killed two days ago. Then he went down, cautiously, to the plateau and filled his skin sack with water from the river, easily evading the shepherds watching over their flocks.

On his way back he heard the sound of gasping and snuffling, and stopped, terrified, thinking that the Egyptian Gobbler had come to eat his heart.

It was the Israelites' Lawgiver. He was scrabbling up through the rocks, gasping, grunting and muttering.

Jaha froze. The Lawgiver scrambled past. After a moment Jaha followed him up the hillside – though at a cautious distance, because he was wary of Amorite magic, frightened of spells. The Lawgiver, after all, was an Egyptian scribe who had turned into a mystic; he was a great *hawi*.

He was the man who had made fire burn on the Yam Suf.

Was he going to talk to his God?

What would Hathor, Goddess of Sinai, make of that?

Jaha crept carefully up the hillside. In the darkness lizards slithered softly away, out of his path. He peered cautiously round a huge boulder.

The Lawgiver was sitting on a rock.

He was sitting as still as a statue.

There was no sign of Isis; but above him was the Eye of the Thoth, huge and silver and cold.

27
A Bedouin Feast

A sudden flash of light – but it came from the distant south, a beam as from a lighthouse thirty kilometres away – a car, perhaps, on the Watia Pass.

'Richard?'

Vronwy was calling softly in the valley below, worried about him. He stood up and found his way carefully down the scree. She was standing by a limestone rock, her face pale and ghostly in the moonlight.

'Did you find him?'

'No.'

She looked round. 'I can't believe I'm really here. I keep thinking it's biological warfare – anthrax or something.'

'No, it isn't anything like that.'

'See those white stones. Don't they look like bleached bones to you?'

'Vronwy, this place has only been a restricted area for a few months.'

'And how long does it take for the flesh to fall—'

'Hush.'

He hugged her; the first time since they had been in London. She was shivering, chilled.

'Are you OK?'

'I think I've got a cold. I don't know.'

'Come on.'

They walked back to the Land Rover.

'I think we can make our way through Wadi Wutah tomorrow. Then through Umm Dud. Tomorrow night we'll be at El-Garf—'

A sharp intake of breath. She stopped suddenly.

Richard said, '*Salamat.*'

The two men standing by the Land Rover nodded politely and returned his greeting.

Cartwright, coming out of nowhere, said, 'I promised these lads a cup of tea.'

The two bedouin sat and drank politely, delicately, though when Vronwy produced sugar lumps they dipped them in their tin mugs and sucked them with sudden relish. They were Azazimeh bedouin, the poorest inhabitants of Sinai, on their way south to camp by the oilfields. They sucked their sugar and shook their heads in despair over the bedouin of the south. The elder of the two shouted loudly, and the younger one, whose name was Ayish and who was the sheikh's son, gave a great wail. Vronwy, hunting through the groceries for cocoa-butter cookies, said, 'What's the matter with him?'

'We're disapproving of the happy-go-lucky bedouin of El-Tur,' said Richard. 'They like to throw all-night parties, with dancing and hash-smoking.'

'Now those,' said Vronwy, trying to be jolly, 'sound just the bedouin for me.'

'We're invited to eat. Their camp is further up the wadi. A meal is being prepared.'

'How did they know we were here?'

Nobody bothered to answer that one.

They went in the Land Rover, all five of them. Richard drove without lights eastward through the

Wadi Wutah, which was narrow and winding, its bed filled with the debris of *seils*, of previous flash floods. At one point rocks fifteen, twenty metres high almost met on the wadi's bed, and the Land Rover only just managed to scrape between them. They passed a spring on the right-hand bank, pouring from a narrow ledge of rock, and water suddenly tumbled down on the car's roof with drumming noise that made Cartwright stiffen in surprise and the bedouin laugh. Richard turned on the vehicle's lights. Vronwy saw stunted palm trees and in the mist of water a face, hands cupped – she even saw the water pour down between the fingers – then the image was gone, the ghost banished by the wiper blades. It was a face, a figure from her dreams; she was dreaming now while she was awake, and always the same images, the same faces.

The wadi widened. A huge, circular space had been washed out by countless *seils*. In the moonlight they saw the tents ahead, heard the dogs bark.

'Well, that's saved us a bit of our journey tomorrow,' said Cartwright comfortably. 'We'll be able to have a lie-in.'

There were three large, extended families. Children peered at them, women, veiled, turned away in confusion. They sat in the sheikh's tent and Vronwy shivered, despite her thick jumper. Outside, at the fire, a bedouin was stirring a blackened brass cooking pot.

'Gosh, a man cooking,' she said, 'a new man, a new bedouin. Fancy that, Corporal Cartwright.'

'Bedouin men often cook,' said Richard. 'The women are off with the flocks all day, looking for pasture. If the men didn't cook, they'd starve.'

'Yeah, right. What is it?' asked Vronwy doubtfully, looking at the cooking, the stirring of the pot. She was a well-travelled girl. She had eaten frogs legs from tiny silver dishes in the Rue St-Honoré when she was eight; she had eaten rice and stewed mutton in Arab cafés when she was eighteen; but these things had not been done from choice.

'A fodder-fed goat,' said Richard.

'Bloody marvellous, eh?' said Cartwright. The SAS trained in the Malaysian jungle, where they lived on raw snakes.

Ayish, the sheikh's son, filled their glasses with a thin fruit cordial. He was about sixteen. He had played their Led Zeppelin tape repeatedly in the Land Rover. Now he piled their plates high with rice and goat meat running with grease. There was a stew of canned meat and beans, steeped in livid, fatty sauce; and there were pitta bread and cucumbers. Richard and the sheikh talked. It would take the Azazimeh bedouin a week to ten days to travel to El-Tur. They had no Peugeot cars, no motorbikes, they had their camels and their flocks of goats and sheep, and they followed the old paths that they had followed since time began, and their life was as it had always been.

Richard said that nothing changed.

The sheikh said that his people had tried to change. They had made small pots of beaten brass to sell to the tourists who in recent years had started to come to the Azazimeh's ancient home, the Wadi Shei-ger, to photograph its incredibly steep sides, its dark columns with huge elephant-feet bases, its massive and fantastically shaped rocks gouged out by the winter rain – white calcareous rocks and red sand-stone rocks, rose-red walls and white crystal floors –

its desolation, its awful beauty. For 2,000 years the Azazimeh bedouin alone had pitched their tents in the Wadi Sheiger, but now the place had acquired a new name, and in a million tour brochures from Hamburg to St Louis it was known as the Coloured Canyon, the *ultimate desert adventure, the true taste of the Great and Terrible Wilderness*'. The Azazimeh had welcomed their new guests. They had offered them camel-rides and souvenirs, but their visitors had shown little interest. They had come in 4×4s and thought of themselves as superior, sophisticated *travellers*, not vulgar tourists. They did not want their picture taken on a camel, and did not want to buy cheap bedouin pots. What they did want to do was to photograph the bedouin girls – but the Azazimeh girls were shy and would not be photographed, and ran away squeaking like mice.

Last year, in the summer, the Egyptian army had come in and cut the wadi off from tourists. The Azazimeh had moved further south and tried to sell their little brass pots in Dahab, but the crazy bedouin of Dahab (who were more dissolute and lost to Allah than even the bedouin of El-Tur) would not allow them to pitch their black tents in the Dahab hippie village.

The sheikh ate his rice and meat, his long brown fingers shaping riceballs that were flicked neatly into his mouth. Dogs sat round the entrance to the tent, groaning and scratching their fleabites.

And as for the Towarah bedouin of Sharm el-Sheikh! Why, they were an even greater scandal than the crazy bedouin of Dahab. They made their living smuggling hashish into Sinai – bringing it over from Iran, in fishing boats, wrapped in watertight plastic bags. If the boats were stopped by the Egyptian navy the Towarah bedouin dumped the bags overboard, weighing them down with bags of salt. The salt dissolved in a few days, the bags bobbed up to the surface and the Towarah bedouin collected them up at night and became rich.

Last winter the Azazimeh had gone north, climbing up to the plateau of El-Tîh, to the poor, desolate country that they knew so well. But even here they encountered the Tiyaha bedouin, ancient enemies who stole their goats and sheep, and on one occasion raped one of their women in daylight, which was most serious.

'I suppose rape at night isn't serious?' asked Vronwy, when Richard had translated.

Certainly not, said Richard. Among the bedouin rape at night was a misdemeanour. A bedouin woman of virtue, after all, would be in the tent of her father or her husband by nightfall. But rape during the day was a terrible crime because it distracted the women from tending the flocks.

'Yeah, right,' said Vronwy.

Everything was bad! cried the sheikh. Nothing was as it was. The bedouin of the north drove red Toyota trucks, and charged extortionate prices for Time cigarettes and tins of meat, and cassettes of music, and batteries for the stereos.

Ayish, who one day would inherit this dismal state of affairs, sat and looked angry and upset.

The food was eaten. Tea was drunk. There was a small silver plate of sweetmeats – old and musty honey jellies taken from a tin. The cooking pots were put down for the dogs, and the dogs cleaned them, and the pots were stored away until the next meal.

The women sat in the back of the tent, a million miles away, dark eyes shining over their veils, children peeping out from round their feet.

Richard said, 'It may be that the Azazimeh bedouin are the original inhabitants of Sinai. They and the Tiyaha tribe are the only people who can scratch a living from the edge of the plateau. It's a place so barren that in three thousand years nobody has ever disputed their territory. These people may well be the descendants of the bedouin who lived here at the time of the Exodus.'

Vronwy shivered. She said, 'I'm not going to offer up some terrible insult, am I, the sort of insult that will make them slit our throats in the night, or rape me, or do something really serious like letting down the tyres on the Land Rover, if I get into my sleeping bag and go to sleep?'

Richard spoke in Arabic; the men nodded sagely, and the sheikh spoke softly. Vronwy said, 'What did he say?' and Richard said, 'He said that his house was our house.'

Vronwy stood up and said, 'Good-night', and the bedouin men nodded, and mumbled and the sheikh said, 'Leltak sa'ida we-mubaraka.'

'May your night,' Richard translated, 'be happy and blessed.'

'Ah,' said Vronwy. 'He said that, did he?'

The sheikh spoke again, nodding mournfully at Vronwy.

Richard said, ' "The feaster makes merry, the wolf prowls, and man's lot is still the same." '

'Yes,' she said, believing it.

She went out of the tent. An old bedouin woman was crouched over the fire, dragging goat entrails

451

through the bright red embers, then placing them in
the hot ash next to the roasted heart, lungs and
kidney. Cartwright, who had vanished some time previously, either to have an extended piss or to send a
vital signal to London that would stop the End of the
Word by Mad Muslim Scientists, was crouched by
the fire watching her. Vronwy said, 'When shall we
three meet again, ha, ha.' Then, to the woman, 'Thank
you. Thank you very much. Good-night.' The woman
nodded several times, agitated and alarmed.

'And you do that to sear the meat, do you, mother?'
Cartwright was saying, interestedly, as she left them.
'There's a terrible prejudice against offal where I
come from.'

Vronwy took three aspirins, washing them down
with bottled water, got into her sleeping bag and
curled herself into the sand, behind the Land Rover
and next to the camels and the goats. She prayed
that scorpions and snakes would not sting her or
bite her this night. She fell asleep instantly. Richard,
when he came some time later, looked at her sleeping
bag, Velcroed and zipped up tight, and sighed; then
he got out his own bag, lay down next to her and
looked up at the stars until Palmer's voice said: *The
ingenious stupidity of the Bedawin is often very per-
plexing. Not feeling certain as to the particular form
of the interrogative particle "when" employed by them,
I enquired of an intelligent Arab with whom I chanced
to be walking. To make the question as plain as possible, I said, "Supposing you were to meet a man with
an ibex on his shoulder, how should you ask him when
he shot it?" "I shouldn't ask him at all," he replied,
"because I shouldn't care."*

It was ironic, thought Richard, that it had been the

Towarah, the only tribe that Palmer approved of, the tribe he described as being entirely free from the *lawless predatory instincts which distinguish other Bedawin tribes*', that had killed him.

For 20,000 pieces of gold, each stamped with the head of the queen, those happy-go-lucky, party-loving Towarahs had slit his throat on the plain of El-Tur.

They woke to the hacking of smokers' coughs as the bedouin men sat over their tea, and the women and girls tended to the animals, and the dogs ate the camel dung for their breakfast.

They sat in their sleeping bags drinking bottled water. Richard said, 'Did you know, the earliest known coin-operated vending machine for water was invented by the ancient Egyptians? It was in use in Alexandria in about 300 BC.'

Vronwy did not reply. Richard said, 'The bedouin believe that when a man rises from sleep in the morning, the spirit of God sits upon his right shoulder, and the Devil on his left. To rid himself of the Devil he must wash himself with water and say, "I seek refuge in God from Satan accursed with stones." '

Vronwy said, 'Why do you keep telling me things? You're forever telling me things I don't want to know. Anyway, do you believe them when they come out with that sort of stuff? For Christ's sake, they haven't washed in years.'

Richard said, 'Are you feeling any better?'

Vronwy said, 'No.' She wondered if she should tell him about her dreams.

They drank tea, boiled up in the blackened brass pot.

A helicopter was moving slowly across the sky to the south.

Cartwright said, 'They won't bother about a few bedouin. They know better than to try to keep bedouin out of their grazing lands. We'd do well to stay with this lot, if we can.'

The bedouin were not moving from the Wadi Wutah for some days. They knew of several passes called Nagb el-Mirad. They wished that Allah would lead Richard to the place he desired to go to.

Richard said goodbye. Vronwy gave gifts of cigarettes, tinned mackerel.

They got into the Land Rover and set out up the Wadi Wutah. The pass was seven metres wide, running between jagged sandstone rocks. After an hour they reached the head of the wadi. They stopped to check their position. The track wound round the mountains into the Wadi Umm Dud. They could see the entrance, the tall, red sandstone cliffs. Somewhere beyond Umm Dud was the wide, long valley of El-Garf, the place old bedouin still called Debbet el-Ramlch, the land of stones.

Beyond that was the cliff of El-Tîh and a small forgotten pass, a pathway that Sayed el-Prince had tried to use in October 1973, to take the tanks of Egyptian Third Army up to the plateau.

Cartwright said, 'That lad's still there.'

Vronwy and Richard looked back. In the distance a bedouin boy was following them on a camel. They waited for him. It was Ayish, the sheikh's son. He spoke loudly and earnestly. Richard said, 'He knows of a pass called Nagb el-Mirad where there is a cave with ancient writing. It's in the cliff, pretty close to where El-Prince came to grief. He wants to be our guide.'

Vronwy said, 'We need one.'

Richard said, 'He wants five US dollars a day.'

'I'm sure your paymasters can squeeze that much out of Fort Knox,' said Vronwy. 'Three quid a day? It's not much more than a corporal in the SAS gets.'

'Now, now,' said Cartwright, listening to the radio, his eyes on the sky for helicopters, 'we get our food and accommodation, remember.'

Richard said to Ayish, 'OK. Five dollars a day.'

Ayish smiled; a broad grin, showing white teeth uncorrupted by the sugary Western confections he so longed for.

28
The Valley of Stones

She was picking her way through the sharp stones, a
sack over her shoulder, her hair sodden with sweat
and thick with insects. Behind came Giliad, with his
quernstone, which he carried slung in a net; Esther
and Rebecca. Zuri was supposedly being helped along
by the oldest of the Ethiopians, a slave who had been
bought as a boy by Zuri's father's father, on the day
he was made assistant registration clerk to the tomb-
makers at Thebes, but the old Ethiopian was hardly
able to help himself. At one point Shelumiel had
raised his whip to beat him, but Ruth had cried,
'No!' and Shelumiel had dropped his hand, shaken
his head wearily and turned away. The old Ethiopian
was a sorry sight, almost blind as he stumbled along;
he had not even noticed that he was about to be
lashed.

There was no water. What vegetation grew – shriv-
elled acacia, desert thorn – was stripped to the bark
by thin, feeble animals who cut their mouths trying
to nuzzle in the roots for moisture. At night the Israelites ate the animals that had died. They were satiated
on fresh meat. In Egypt the poorer families ate meat
four times a year. Many were now ill with dysentery.
Ruth saw with despair the number of sheep that

were lying down, too exhausted to move, or even to find shade. The shepherds were wearily hauling them to their feet, forcing them onwards for a few steps until they collapsed again. Shelumiel was everywhere, shouting though his voice was cracked and parched.

The cattle were dead, all but four oxen that pulled the sledges. The herdsmen whipped them over the rocks, but every few minutes the sledges caught in the stones.

Esther said, 'Carry me, Ruth.'

Ruth stopped to wipe the sweat from her eyes. Esther knew that she could not be carried; she was making a point, that was all.

They were in the Valley of Stones.

Across the wide valley, under the harsh sun, other families, other flocks, were moving like snails.

On a distant hill, a dozen bedouin sat on their donkeys and watched and waited. At dawn, Shelumiel had said, 'The first bedouin to come near our tents, I will kill him.'

Now Ruth saw Jaha, away from the other bedouin, waiting for her. She said, 'Come on, Esther, come on!' and Esther followed her, because even as a child she knew that if she was in a burning clay oven she must try to get out, even to her last breath of consciousness.

They climbed to the place where Jaha was sitting by his donkey. Then Ruth put down her sack and lay on the hot rocks.

The sun was white in a white sky.

She had been brought up to believe that there was one God, that he was the Sun God, that he was, somehow, the spirit of Akhenaten, whose very name meant 'the solar disc is content'.

The Egyptians, though, knew differently.

The sun was a venomous snake, perched on the forehead of the Sun God; a cobra spitting fire down at the Sun God's enemies.

The sun was a ball of flame held in the horns of the Cow Goddess, Hathor, who was supported by the Air God, Shu.

The sun was a falcon in brilliant plumage.

The sun was a ball of dung being rolled across the sky by the Scarab God, who was a dung beetle.

Beside her, Rebecca, Esther and Giliad also lay in the heat. A woman of the shepherds shouted at them angrily. They would die on the rocks!

Yes, the sun was a ball of dung. Her eyelids were closed; the heat beat through them in an orange glare.

Ruth sat up.

She said, 'How far to water?'

Jaha said, 'A little while.'

In truth, he guessed it would take them another five hours, and when they reached the wells there would be less water than they needed. The bedouin had camped there the night before and discussed poisoning the wells with carrion meat before the tribes arrived, but in the end had done nothing. It could only be a matter of a few days, and the bedouin could wait easily enough.

Esther and Giliad were lying on the stones as if dead.

Zuri was plodding up the valley, his head bent, his old servant behind him.

'Husband!' Ruth called, 'Zuri-shaddai!' but he did not stop or turn his head. He was putting all his strength, all his will-power, into placing one foot in front of the other.

Jaha said, 'You have been too slow. Why are you so slow? Why are your slaves taken from you?'

'The army of Israel,' she said, 'has need of food and of slaves.'

In truth the army of Israel was tending the cattle and shepherding the flocks. Only the Spies were free to range along the high red ridges.

'Was that the army of Israel,' said Jaha, 'that fought with the Dinkas?'

'No. It was the men of the families of Manasseh and of Amram that fought so bravely, oh so bravely, against the Dinkas.'

'So where then was the army of Israel?'

'The army of Israel, O slayer of Hittites, has not yet fought its first battle.'

She shaded her eyes against the white glare. Shelumiel was standing with the flock, watching her, watching her talking with the bedouin boy. She could feel his anger. He was blaming the bedouin for all the horrors that had befallen them.

'Get up,' Jaha urged her. 'You must go forward. Go up the valley. It is just a little way. Hurry, hurry!'

Ruth said, 'Help me, *bedu*.'

He stared at her.

She stood up and tried to lift her sack. After a moment Jaha grabbed it from her and put it on his donkey. And then he put Esther up on his donkey, in front of the sack, and Esther sobbed for tiredness and relief, and wound her fingers tightly into the rough hair of the donkey's mane.

Ruth thought, 'Today he helped me, although on the day at Marah, after the people of Manasseh and Amram were slaughtered, he would not help me.'

Jaha said, angrily, 'Come on. Come on!'

Ruth took Giliad's quernstone. He tried to refuse to give it to her, but she took it, and after a moment Jaha said, 'Here, give it to me', and took it from her himself and slung it over his back.

'Move!' he said. 'Move, move!' and he hit the donkey. She did not look round to see if Shelumiel was watching.

For four hours Jaha led them up the valley. She did not believe they would ever have reached the top without him; they would have collapsed, the men would have had to leave the flock of sheep and the cattle to help them, and even more of the sheep would have died, and the goats would have scattered.

They reached the top of the valley. They could see now that the mountains they had passed through were not a separate group, with the high cliff of Ti rising behind them, but were in reality part of the Ti plateau, which fell by broken steps down into the plain beneath. The air was fresher. Ruth turned and saw Rebecca coming up behind them. She had not complained, and had not sat down in five hours. Her skin was grey. She did not seem to see anything or know where she was.

'Look,' she said. 'Look, Rebecca. Look!'

'Look, Rebecca! Look, Mouse!'

The view was immense. Born and raised on the flat Delta, they had never been so high before, so close to the sky. Far to the south were other mountains, black distant peaks that looked higher than Ti even. To the west, across the empty desert of Ramilsh, was the long ridge that the Spies watched so anxiously. There were tiny figures moving on the distant mousy-brown, yellow hillside.

Jaha said, 'Khadem.'

461

Khadem!

'This way, this way!' He pointed to a faint track
that went round the eastern slopes of Ti. They moved
forward, round the southern edges of the cliff, climbing gently. An hour later, in the distance, Ruth saw
a glimpse of dusty green. Then she saw the palms
and tamarisks and acacia trees, the green haze of
mountain broom; and she blinked tears from her eyes,
and held the tail of Jaha's donkey and let it pull her
along.

They had travelled four days from Elim.

They were arrived at the wells of Reph-i-dim.

That night Ruth doled out the flour to the women of
the shepherds and herdsmen. Then she put eight
handfuls of flour on the heated stone, with the water,
and made the cakes for the family. The barley sack
was lighter. In five days, perhaps, the sack would be
empty.

Jaha had disappeared. What did the bedouin have
to eat?

Hopes of *belongings*, she thought, to keep them
alive.

Shelumiel said, 'Listen. Do not talk to the bedouin,
or accept any food from the bedouin. I've told you
before that if I find a bedouin near this tent I will
kill him.'

She did not reply.

He said, 'Tonight you will come to me.'

Ah, well, he had wanted her since the first day she
had come to her husband's house, since the first day
she had been a wife, or what the city folk called a
child-wife, in the time before Zuri gave her her marriage contract for fear of the Gobbler.

'The nakedness of thy father's wife thou shalt not uncover,' she said softly, not unwilling to tease him with the Kenite's laws. 'It is thy father's nakedness.'

She went away from the tents, to the fig trees beyond the herd, curled in the sand in the darkness and slept.

When she awoke it was dawn and there was excited shouting, and the mad Benjaminites were dancing in the antelope pen. The Spies, they said, had found a spring in the hills that bubbled up like green wine; a spring the bedouin had known of but had kept secret until the Spies nosed out the running water and killed the two bedouin who guarded it.

She got up and ran after the other women. She climbed after them, up a small gorge overhung with desert mimosa and rock-sage, smelling of badgers. She could smell water now and hear it tinkling over stones. Two Levites stood by the thin stream of liquid that bubbled out of the rocks.

It was not true, they shouted, that the bedouin had first found the spring.

It had been Moses! Moses had gone up into the mountain and had struck the rocks of Ti with his staff, and God had made the water burst from the barren rocks.

That was the truth! Even the Spies, when asked, would say that it was the truth!

At dusk there was a feast of roast sheep, and for the priests the flesh of a young milk kid, and Miriam and her musicians played their instruments and danced bare-breasted, as they had for rich Egyptians back at home. Ruth and Esther laughed to see the shepherds' wives scandalized, and their uncomfortable husbands cry 'Shame'; but were quiet when they saw the priests looking hard and cold at the dancing of Miriam in the firelight.

Moses had gone into the hills again. People looked to see a pillar of light over Ti, but there was only the black cliff against the stars and the rustle of acacias and date palms in the night breeze.

Shelumiel said, 'Come.'

Ruth looked into the fire, into the smouldering dung.

Shelumiel said, 'Come with me.'

He had been watching the dancing girls.

'Come with me.'

She went with him, into the tamarisk bushes, behind the tent in which Zuri lay eating a dish of kid flesh in milk that had been sent to him by Miriam. As Shelumiel took off her tunic she said again softly, 'Thou shalt not uncover the nakedness of thy father's wife. It is thy father's nakedness', but Shelumiel ignored her, so she lay back, naked, and hoped he would not find her too thin.

Jaha was a boy; no older than she was. Shelumiel was a man. And it was not the first time.

29
Sandstorm

There was a near-vertical ravine with red sandstone cliffs and a narrow passage with hard, black granite walls, then they were out into a wide valley that stretched upwards towards El-Tîh, bare of vegetation, strewn with huge, ugly boulders. They crept out, over the stones, the Land Rover rocking from side to side, occasionally crashing down on the suspension. Ayish's camel swayed smoothly, sedately, behind them. There had been bedouin coming this way since the first of the *hapiru* spread south from Canaan in the Early Bronze Age, to take Egypt by storm with their terrible pony chariots.

When they stopped for tea Vronwy gave Ayish the loan of her personal stereo; thereafter the camel, which was called Moses, swayed to the tinny tones of Led Zeppelin.

Slowly, painfully, the Land Rover moved forward up the valley. The noise of the engine would travel for a mile or more, but the sound would be unfocused, and there were no seismic intrusion detectors here, not according to Cartwright. Vronwy was driving. She sweated, her muscles tense, as the vehicle jolted, its chassis grating over the rocks.

'How much further, do you think?'

'It can't be much further.'

On the map it was an hour, at most, from the sandstone ravine of Telat Umm Rutheh to the plain of El-Garf.

They came to a steep incline, a stretch of sand baked dry with a crust like concrete. Cartwright took the wheel. The others stood and watched as he revved the engine and pressed hard on the accelerator. The Land Rover was almost at the top of the slope, its turbo howling, when it hit a patch of loose gravel and skidded and spun round and came to a standstill with its side against a rock.

'OK, let's clear a path,' said Richard. They all climbed up and started to pull stones away from the front of the vehicle.

'Oh, Richard, your hands . . .'

His hands, so recently cut open in a back-street of Cairo, were puffy and grazed. Vronwy bent down her head and kissed them. Cartwright was examining his own hands. 'Dear, oh dear,' he muttered hopefully.

They cleared stones. They made a path, a short length of road. The Land Rover scraped along the rocks until it was free. They stood for a moment looking at the deep scratches gouged in its metallic paintwork. 'Poor bloody Worboys,' said Vronwy, thinking how he would have to take it back to Jerusalem and account for its condition.

They moved forward again. Ten minutes later the vehicle smashed its chassis down on the rocks for perhaps the thousandth time, and this time it stayed down, its near front wheel jammed against the suspension.

They unloaded the boot. They jacked it up. They discovered that a pin had snapped at the bottom of the hydraulic shock absorber and was wedged in the spring.

It took them three hours to free it. The shock absorber was damaged beyond repair. They could move forward at five kilometres an hour, maximum, and now they swayed like the camel swayed, but without a camel's grace.

It was late afternoon when they reached the top of the pass. The weather was changing. A storm was blowing up, sweeping along the plain below the cliff of El-Tîh, from the east, from the Wadi Biyar. Cartwright wanted to look for shelter under the rocks, but Ayish had found grazing for his camel and pleaded with them not to go further.

They camped out in the wadi, by the dull-green herbage. There would be no helicopters flying, not in this weather.

Cartwright lit the spirit stove and Richard made a fire. They ate the last of the pitta bread, with tinned sardines, trying to shield their food from the wind that was already laden with flying grit. When they had eaten, Vronwy and Richard walked to a small rise. A sidewinder viper shimmied away from them with its continuous, sinuous double-movement and buried itself. 'Oh, God,' said Vronwy, her heart thudding.

The cliff of El-Tîh stretched far into the distance. Beneath it was a world of stone rubble, the plain of El-Garf, with the ridge of Sarabit el-Khâdem to the south. Small whirlwinds chased themselves across the desert. The old British army road that came up from the Gulf of Suez and skirted El-Khâdem before curling south towards the Watia Pass was invisible: an unmetalled track used nowadays only by the Egyp-

467

tian army, and by the scientists, presumably, at the research station.

There was nothing in this landscape to show the hand of man, not in the last 2,000 years, not since the Pharaoh's copper-smelting furnaces at El-Khâdem were finally extinguished.

They went back to the Land Rover. Ayish sat by the fire, his back to the wind. He was watching a scorpion frantically trying to escape from the stinging grains of sand by burrowing a hole. Each time it made progress, the sand collapsed and it had to start again. Soon its legs moved more slowly. Its poisonous curved tail was no longer erect and threatening, but lying flat. Vronwy — hater of snakes and creepy-crawlies — leant forward and made it a hill of sand with her tin mug, a wall against the wind. But the scorpion had given up. It lay still.

'Don't touch it,' warned Richard.

The fire billowed clouds of fragrant smoke. They drank tea that was smoky and thick with sand. Cartwright went to the back of the Land Rover to check on his monitoring equipment. Richard and Ayish talked in low tones, leaning forward, their backs to the wind. Moses also sat with his back to the wind, his head high like a sphinx, his huge lids closed over his eyes, his mouth rhythmically chomping.

Richard said, 'He says he knows of three caves near Et Rakineh, close to where several Egyptian tanks were burnt out by the Israelis. *"Tili al gush wa pasha khush."* '

'What?'

' "The paper tigers have left, and the pashas have come in." The bedouin prefer the Israelis to the Egyptians. The Israelis give them motor vans and television sets. The Egyptians don't give them anything.'

'The Egyptians don't try to make them live on a reservation.'

'No, well. Anyway, he says the tanks were still there a couple of years ago.'

Cartwright came back. He said, 'These caves. When we get there I'll set up an OP, somewhere on the cliffside. I should have a visual range on the objective.'

Vronwy said, 'Good-oh, Corporal Cartwright. We'll soon need water. Does Ayish know where we can find any?'

Richard spoke to Ayish.

'*Themail.*'

Ayish scooped out a hole in the sand at the bottom of the wadi, where the vegetation was its sickliest green.

'*Themail,*' he shouted.

Around them the wind blew. They watched the hole. In time a thick, yellow, creamy liquid started to collect in the bottom.

'Yeah?' said Vronwy doubtfully.

Ayish grinned and nodded.

They used a large spoon to scoop the liquid into a flask.

Balls of grass appeared out of the blowing sand, tumbling across the dunes. Richard said, 'Fear and tremble, you violent ones who are in the storm clouds of the sky. On the day that he chooses, he will split open the earth with his knowledge.'

'What's that?'

'A spell from *The Book of the Dead.*'

'Christ, Richard!'

The sand against Vronwy's face was numbing her skin. She leant forward and covered the dead scorpion, then she went back to the Land Rover. Cartwright was sitting crouched in the back. He had the GPS out of its case, and the other instrument, the small black unit. For the first time she saw that he also had a gun, a rifle with a magazine attached. She pointed to it, and said, 'What would you say if we were stopped and searched?'

'If I got the chance, love, I'd chuck it away.'

'What if you didn't get the chance?'

'I'd say it was to protect our two noted academics, our two archaeologists, against terrorist attack.'

'You wouldn't, well, sort of shoot anybody with it?'

'Not if I could help it.'

'Not a lot of point in bringing it, then?'

'No, not really.'

Condescending bastard. She got out her sleeping bag. She rolled herself up in it, pulling the hood over her head. Her bag smelled nasty and sweaty.

Only the desert, she thought, was clean. Dangerous, unforgiving, but always clean.

She was asleep when Richard came and shook her and said, 'The fundamentalists have taken over in Cairo. The president of Egypt's dead. Cartwright wants us to move before dawn.'

30
Somerset

WDC Henry was punching in the number to open the door when a detective inspector in traffic division came out into the sharp March morning and said, 'The Met are after you again', and looked at her curiously. She went up to the Crime Squad's temporary office. The clerk said, 'Thank God you're here', and grimaced. Before she had got her coat off, her boss was looking out of his cubbyhole, a sulky, injured, immense bulk of aggression and resentment. She said, 'Morning, sir', brightly, and a vein on his forehead started to pulse. That was the trouble with George; his terrible temper, for which he was always sorry afterwards. He said, 'Come in here.'

She followed him into his office and closed the door. He said, 'It's getting bollocking ridiculous. They want you tomorrow and they won't even say how long for. I've told them no way – they can get on to Portishead if they want to. Portishead are as pissed off as I am. Christ Almighty, who do they think they are?'

He went on for a bit longer. Whiskyish red eyes. He'd been at the Bells again. How many CID officers were dipsos? She said, 'Sir.'

He came alive. His voice came alive.

'Well, what the hell, what the fucking hell, do they need you for?'

She looked at him.

'What job was it? What were you doing?'

'Come off it, George. Let me have my coffee?'

'I have told them, told a certain DI Elsworth of Scotland Yard, that you cannot be released. Is that OK with you? Is that all right?'

'I don't know anything about it.'

She went outside to her desk. He was stressed. Come lunchtime he'd tiptoe off for a massage at the Avalon Whole Life Therapy Centre, and then he'd come shambling back in, the great bear, stinking of aromatherapy oils. He was overworked. He'd toiled through four nights in the last two weeks, nights that had been fruitless and pointless, nights of boredom and failure, and nobody in Scotland Yard or anywhere else cared a shit.

The job was bogged down. She sat and worked, sifting through reports of drugs brought in through Poole Harbour, through West Bay on the Dorset coast. When this job's over, she thought, she'd leave Crime Squad. She'd put in for a transfer, work for some other bastard in some other place.

George's door slammed open, slammed back so hard it nearly broke the glass. He said triumphantly, 'Portishead have told the Met that they can sod off.'

Everybody in the open-plan office looked at him, then at her.

She opened the *Express*. She started to read:

Cairo Falls to Islamic Terror

Islamic fundamentalists have taken over the centre of Cairo. On the palace steps leaders of the terrorist Hizb ut-Tahrir organization declared the dawn of the 'Khalafa' – the Islamic state. Police units armed with automatic rifles watched without attempting to interfere. In scenes reminiscent of the last days of the Shah's rule in Iran, wealthy Egyptian families in the exclusive suburb of Maadi are barricading themselves into their luxury villas and pinning their hopes on the armed forces, which have been largely kept free of fundamentalist influence. A businessman said: 'Only the army can now save Egypt from the rule of the Mad Mullahs.'

She was conscious that George was still standing in his doorway, staring at her. After a bit, though, he went back into his office. He'd be phoning, she thought; phoning his massage lady.

She got herself another cup of coffee. Already the air-conditioning was giving her a headache.

Something else, though, had been giving her a headache, these past few days; keeping her awake at nights, alone in her tiny rented cottage on the Somerset plain. Something that had nothing to do with her loneliness, her sad longing for companionship, her mourning for her dead fiancé.

She had been having nightmares about the collapse of time.

She knew that the universe – or the region of it that this world, this little world, occupies – is governed by three spacial dimensions, together with the dimension of time itself.

What would happen if a fifth dimension were to be brought into being? A sixth dimension? A seventh dimension?

What would be the result if through the physical experimentation of string theory and super-string theory, and super-gravity, or whatever else those scientists might be dabbling in on the plains of southern Sinai, it were possible to extrapolate a Closed Timelike Curve from a particle, to *uncurl* other dimensions from their tight little ball?

What would happen if Elizabeth St George had not been crazy?

At lunchtime she went out, out into the brisk fresh air. Round the church there were hundreds of crocus, deep yellow and mauve against the vivid green, their hearts open to the sun. She went into a café in the pedestrianized shopping centre, bought a sandwich and coffee and sat by the window.

She sat, the sun striking warm through the glass, pondering on a world with more than four dimensions.

A Closed Timelike Curve would release mankind from the confines of the four-dimensional world. It could, conceivably, bring the ultimate triumph of good, or of evil. It could mean the end of suffering and of pain. It could mean that lovers never parted, that loved ones did not die.

Tears swam for a second into her eyes, and she blinked and looked out at the precinct, at the daffodils in containers, their heads dancing in the wind.

A controlled Closed Timelike Curve could mean that children were never orphaned. It could mean the banishment of famine, of drought and disease. *Cinéma vérité* would really be *cinéma vérité*. There would be no need to watch *Gone With the Wind* to see the fall of Atlanta; you would be able to watch the fall of Atlanta as it happened, or the battle of Agincourt, or of Trafalgar. You would be able to watch Cleopatra die while the Roman legions sacked Alexandria; watch and be there when Shakespeare took the part of Rosencrantz at the opening of *Hamlet*.

A couple of middle-aged ladies sat down next to her. They spread butter on their scones and travel brochures on their table. 'We thought that this year we'd go and join Ted and Mildred at their gite in the Ardèche –'

A Closed Timelike Curve would allow travel into other universes. It would bring the gift, or the poisoned chalice, of everlasting life. Ah, but would it?

She shook her head. In truth it would not have time to do any of these things. In truth, gravity would be fatally weakened by the existence of a CTC. And the more dimensions that came into play, the weaker gravity would become, and before the holidaymakers of Somerset could even book their tickets (not to the Ardèche but to the parallel universe of their choice), the world would be destroyed.

This had been her nightmare, lying in the dark, in the low-beamed bedroom, in her tiny cottage on the Somerset plain.

Through her head, as the vixens barked in the night and the owls hooted, had run the theory, the formula: *If you double the distance between two bodies in the three-space-dimensional world, then the gravitational pull drops to a quarter of what it was. The universe we occupy is used to this, it can cope with this. But if we suddenly had four space-dimensions, the gravitational pull would drop to one-eighth. In five dimensions, gravity would drop to one-sixteenth. In six dimensions, it would drop to only one-thirty-second of the gravity that governs the world as we know it today.*

A Closed Timelike Curve, if string theory is consistent, would have ten or even twenty-six dimensions. Before the cork was out of the champagne bottle, before the revisionists had started on their journey back to strangle Hitler at birth, mankind would be spinning through its last, doomed, blistering or freezing seconds on a planet spiralling away from or into the sun; and the sun itself would be falling apart or collapsing into a black hole – and nothing, nothing would survive, not life, not even the dead, inanimate stones.

The door opened. It was George. He got himself a sandwich and a coffee. On the tray, when he came over, was a small chocolate-fudge nest containing three small, brightly coloured chocolate eggs.

She said, 'You'll get fat.'

He said, 'It's for you.'

'Ta,' she said, eating the cake, bearing no animosity.

She really was quite frightened, because there were various experiments going on all over the place, and not just Muslim scientists in Sinai, or people messing about with particle accelerators. At the European Synchrotron Radiation Facility at Grenoble they were producing X-rays a million million times brighter than the last generation of X-rays. There was a potential for disaster in all this, a potential for destruction; scientists meddling with things they could not fully understand. The unification of physics, long predicted to come by the millennium, might bring with it the unification of many other things; the unification perhaps of matter, of flesh and blood and bone.

A uniformed policeman was hurrying down the precinct. He vanished into Boots.

'What was it like up there, then?'

'Pardon?'

'Working with the Met.'

'No different, George, from working anywhere else.'

'Anyway, you can't go. It's not on.'

'Don't worry about it.'

'Life's a bugger,' said George.

Life had at most 1.1 billion years left to bugger about in. The work had been done at the California Institute of Technology and the University of Toronto, it had been done by the best of the boys and girls working in theoretical astrophysics. Life on earth was 3.5 billion years old, and the hand on the earth clock pointed to nine. When it strikes twelve, she told herself, the earth will be just a frozen cinder, after first having been cooked until the oceans evaporated, then melted into a blob of larva, and then put out to cool – a rock cake made of rock, wandering aimlessly through a dark universe, the sun itself having died of old age.

She wondered whether to tell all this to George. Whether it might put his problems into perspective.

'Yes,' George sighed, a coded apology, 'life's a real bugger.' He wasn't the one who had flown off the handle, dear me no, it was life that was; life that had him helpless in its grip.

The policeman had come out of Boots. He was peering into the poster shop, where there were often girls in miniskirts to be seen. He turned and saw them both in the café window and came over at a fast walk.

'Oh, buggery, buggery,' sighed George.

The policeman came hurrying in. He said, looking at her, 'Can you come back to the station?'

George said, 'What's happening, lad?'

'The Met, sir.'

'Yes, lad' – a grim, humourless smile. 'The Met want her, but the Met can't have her.'

'The Chief Constable's been on.'

George's smile vanished. It would be the massage lady again after work tonight, even at twenty-five quid a throw, which was a lot for a poor policeman.

'There's a helicopter coming for her.'

George said, 'A helicopter?'

She watched the daffodils as they danced.

'They're sending a chopper for my WDC?'

She sympathized.

'A bleeding bollocking helicopter?'

'It's nothing to do with me,' said the copper, frightened.

'Christ!'

The policeman said it would be a Navy helicopter from Yeovilton. It was a priority job, this, a VIP job; it would pick her up from the helipad behind the police station at fifteen hundred hours.

George was looking at her. He seemed bewildered, puzzled. 'What the hell,' he pleaded, 'is going on?'

The earth, at the end of the day – *Don't say at the end of the day* – the earth, when all is said and done – *Don't say when all is said and done* – the earth in reality – *Reality? Reality? Whose reality is that then?* – is a small planet orbiting a star on the edge of a spiral galaxy.

The weak anthropic principle states that although the universe might be infinite in space or time, it contains regions (like that occupied by the earth) in which time and space are not infinite but are strictly limited. In these regions, dimensions other than the four dimensions we know on earth are *curled up tight*. Because they are curled up tight, conditions for intelligent life can be met.

The weak anthropic principle says that there cannot be workable Closed Timelike Curves because if a workable CTC were created, a CTC capable of transporting matter back through time, into the past, then the dimensions would no longer be curled up tight but would be flattened out, just like the four dimensions we have already, and that clearly cannot happen because if it did happen the conditions necessary for intelligent life would cease to exist.

Who said the conditions for human life had to exist?

Or, to look on the bright side, who said the weak anthropic principle had to be right? It wasn't one of the Ten Commandments, was it? It wasn't brought down from Mount Sinai on a slab of stone?

31
Reph-i-dim

There was a law pronounced against the slaughter of breeding animals. It was written on a clay tablet and fired in the kiln by scribe-potters who had worked at the Pharaoh's foreign office. It was set up, on the rocks behind the tabernacle, next to the law against buggery. A joke was that a poor shepherd from the hills beyond Succoth, who had never seen writing before, believed that God had thrown the clay tablet from the sky and Moses had caught it in his arms.

Each day the Levites held a court of judgement.

Ruth went up the cliff of Ti, taking Esther with her. Esther was afraid of lions and leopards, and of camels that lived in the rocks, and she would not let Ruth take her far. They climbed high enough, though, to see the black mountains far away to the south, and the smoke from the furnaces of Khadem.

Ruth looked round for Jaha, but Jaha was nowhere to be seen. Zuri had said to her, the night before, 'Shelumiel says he will take you for a wife.'

'So, Shelumiel wants me for a wife?'

'When I am gone it will be his duty.'

And his pleasure, she thought.

They climbed for an hour. Esther said, 'We must go back.'

Ruth looked round, searching the slopes for Jaha, her *bedu*. Esther sat on a rock and ate the small piece of cake she had brought with her. She had been resisting eating it for three hours.

Birds, small and sand-coloured, appeared to beg for food, which was something that neither girl had seen happen before in their lives. Whoever gave food to birds, except to fatten them in cages?

They lay on their backs. They were starving to death; slowly, day by day. The sheep could no longer be killed. The oxen were gone; the goats were gone. The gazelles and four of the milk-fed hyenas remained; nobody liked to interfere with the Benjaminites, who would, at the smallest provocation, set their Wolf God to tear the bowels from their enemies. Ruth closed her eyes, then opened them again quickly in sudden alarm, looking up, sensing something in the air, something with beating wings.

Two eagles were lazily circling the summit of Ti.

Esther was asleep by her in the sun.

'What's that?' asked Ruth.

'What?'

'Nothing,' said Ruth, confused, blinking at the bare, dry hillside.

They were starving to death on the slopes of Ti.

Jaha did not appear. Was it because two bedouin had been caught stealing sheep and had been killed? Had the bedouin, Jaha with them, gone back to Nakhi?

A man of Korah stood before the Tabernacle and shouted, 'Is it a matter of no interest, O Kenite, that

482

you brought us out of a land that flowed with milk and with honey just to see us die in the Wilderness?'

Hungry people laughed at his wit.

'Has any good come of this, O Kenite, other than that you, a scribe to the subprefect at Migdol, are now turned into a prince?'

The Levi priests told him to be quiet or they would put his eyes out.

'I will be quiet,' he shouted, 'when I get my inheritance of vineyards, when I get to this land flowing with milk and honey. I will be quiet when I get some food for my family, for my little children, my tiny little children.'

People sobbed; they were a sentimental people, a hungry people; they sobbed for their children, for themselves.

'Would to God we had died by the hand of the militia in Egypt, when we ate bread to the full! Would to God we had died in our homes!'

The people cried and groaned.

The Benjaminites set up an altar to their Wolf God.

The Asherites set up a tabernacle to Ashtoreth, their Mother Goddess, and hired six new priestesses, not all of them women of the house of Asher. Their religion demanded priestesses of maturity, but experience had shown that the Asher cult thrived and gained converts when the priestesses were young. 'Did you bring us into the Wilderness to go with the whores of Asher?' roared the wits, drunk at night outside the tabernacle of Yahweh, calling for Moses the magician. 'Did you bring us to the wilderness to sleep with a three-shekel whore in the temple of Asher?'

Aaron, the priest again, came out of the tabernacle.

He shouted, 'This is the law given to Moses by God. Yahweh the Thunderer will go before us! He will cut down the Hittites, and the Perizzites, and the Canaanites, and the Jebusites! The Lord Yahweh will show us the way and will destroy our enemies!'

Then Moses himself came out. He threw down his rod, and his rod turned into Nehushtan, the Serpent God of Egypt, and wriggled away under a bush.

'Lo!' cried the scribe-priests, raising their arms.

But the people were too hungry for magic. They were no longer amused by tricks. They chanted, 'Give us bread! The Lord Yahweh, give us bread!'

Others shouted, 'Take us back to Egypt!'

Moses picked up his rod and went back into the tabernacle, where only the priests of Levi were allowed to go, into the inner sanctum where Yahweh sometimes lived in a wooden box.

Outside, the people sat and waited.

When Moses came out again, he had Aaron by his side, and Aaron was wearing a robe that none of them had seen before. It was of the deepest blue, and round the hem were pomegranates of light blue and purple and scarlet, and there were gold bells embroidered between them.

And he cried, 'Behold the Ark!'

He held up a wooden box of shittim wood. Bezaleel had covered it with hammered brass and fashioned on it two gold figures, representing Osiris with wings.

'Behold,' Aaron cried again, 'the Ark of the Covenant.'

Again he held up the Ark.

Bezaleel stood, red with pride and embarrassment.

The people wondered if Yahweh was inside it. They wondered what would happen next.

Moses stared out over the tamarisks. He mumbled so quietly that nobody could hear him. It was Aaron who shouted, 'I, Yahweh, will do marvels such as have not been done in all the earth or in any nation. You will all see the work of Yahweh!'

The people watched and waited.

'I will drive before you the Hittites, and the Perizzites, and the Canaanites, and the Jebusites! You will worship no other God but Yahweh! Hear me, I am a jealous God! You will not go whoring after other gods!'

There was a buzz of excitement. Everyone turned to stare at the tent of Asher.

'You will not whore after strange gods!' cried Aaron again.

Two young priestesses, who were hoping for passing trade, hid themselves behind the curtain in confusion.

The men of Korah laughed. Everyone laughed.

Moses fell to the ground, foaming at the mouth. People looked at him with interest. After some moments the Ark was taken back into the tabernacle, and the crowd dispersed.

Ruth and Esther went up into the hills again. This time Giliad went with them. At dawn Ruth had baked cakes, using the last of the barley grain. Eight cakes, each one scarcely a mouthful, smothered in herbs.

They had one cake each.

Jaha was waiting, sitting on the ground by his old donkey.

Esther and Giliad sat and talked, and looked at him slyly, and pretended that he was not there. Ruth pretended to be cold and Egyptian, although to be Egyptian was never to be cold, never to be melancholy like a Nubian.

Jaha said gloomily, 'Your men have killed two of my family.'

'Your family?' she said, taken aback.

He nodded.

She said, 'Ho! So your family are sheep-stealers?'

He sat by his old donkey, looking down at the oasis of Reph-i-dim, the oasis that belonged to the bedouin, and that had been taken over by these Egyptian Amorites while its true owners sat in the waterless mountains.

'Or perhaps,' she said, 'they came creeping into our tents not to steal sheep but to offer themselves as guides?'

She looked round, smiling happily at Esther and Giliad.

These Amorites, these Israelites, would drink the wells dry, the wells of Reph-i-dim, the only wells in two days' hard riding on a donkey; they would drink them dry and their sheep would destroy the pasture and even the date palms would shrivel and die. They had killed his family at the spring. They had killed his kin, and tossed the bodies away for the vultures, which was not the way of the bedouin. These Amorites knew nothing except how to wail, and complain, and kill.

'Listen, did they tell you that you would eat a milk-kid that night, or a sheep? And listen, what about the *belongings*, eh? What about the *belongings* you sold in Nakhi?'

486

'Egyptian soldiers are coming,' said Jaha with certainty, 'and now there is no one who will guide you to the Wells of Ophir.'

'We do not want guiding to the Wells of Ophir.'

'You will never reach the Wells of Ophir.'

'Then we will go somewhere else.'

She laughed. Giliad's and Esther's eyes flickered towards her, alarmed. Had her *bedu* got food to eat?

Her head ached. She felt faint. She sat down.

Did Jaha have dried porridge in his sack? Would he want her to lie with him? She had the sophisticated city-dweller's view of such things; she had been made a child-wife at fourteen to a man of 120 even by his own reckoning (certainly he had, as a youth, seen the Pharaoh-God on the steps of the temple at Memphis, certainly this had happened, because he had talked of it ever since) and she had slept five times with his son.

Giliad and Esther had taken out their cakes. They were wondering whether to offer cake to Jaha. They were terrified that he might accept. They did not dare to take the risk. They ate. Instantly the cakes were gone.

Ruth took out her own cake. It was so small. Her mouth ran with saliva; her hand trembled. She held it out to Jaha.

He took it and slowly ate it.

She wanted to cry. She wanted to cry because she had been saving the cake for hours, and it was the last food in the world, and she was starving, and it was useless to look forward to tomorrow's cake; there would be no cake. She wanted to cry for the disc of blackened barley flour and chaff.

She sobbed quietly.

Jaha said, 'You would like to see Nakhi.'

'The centre of the world? Oh, who would *not* like to see Nakhi.'

He snorted, pleased.

'Oh,' cried Ruth, her head pounding, 'oh for the gold-filled tents of the merchants of Nakhi! Oh, for the green dates and the bread of Nakhi! Oh, for the pleasure gardens of the sheikhs of Nakhi!'

He looked disconcerted.

'Oh,' she cried, 'for the peacocks of Nakhi!'

Esther was laughing.

Ruth laughed. She cried and laughed. If she saw a peacock of Nakhi she would eat it.

'We are dying, *bedu*.'

The bones on her fingers were like skeleton bones. Her arms were skeleton arms. The bones stuck out from her hips. Her head pounded; there was a buzzing in her brain. Her stomach hurt, pain tearing through her gut. She doubled over, her face against the hot sand.

Esther was looking at her and snivelling. Giliad looked frightened.

Jaha stood up. He climbed on to his old donkey. It, also, looked too thin and starved to live.

'*Bedu*?' said Ruth, crawling to her feet.

She watched him ride up into the wastes of Ti, towards the eagles.

'Jaha!' she cried when he was almost gone.

They sat in the shade. Flies tormented them. Giliad had brought a skin of water, but Ruth refused to drink. She did not need to drink, she said. Esther said, weary but frightened, 'The slave of Ocran said that when he was dying.'

So, perhaps she was dying.

Perhaps she would not live to see Zuri dead before her. Perhaps, in death, she would rob Shelumiel of a wife, or a concubine.

The shadows lengthened. Osiris fell over the Civilized Lands.

The night was mauve and the rocks the colour of deep rose. 'We must go back,' said Giliad. 'It is time to go back to the tents.'

Ruth did not move. She was a dark, dense shape under the rock.

Esther slowly got to her feet.

'Come on, get up,' said Giliad. 'Perhaps there will be food! Ruth!'

Ruth did not stir.

Giliad said, 'Something is coming. Quickly! Come on, come on! Get up, quickly! It is a leopard coming. It is a lion.'

The noise might have been leopard, although he was more in fear of jackals that hunted in packs and killed men who were weak.

It was a somebody on a donkey. Man and beast were silhouetted against the purple sky. It was Jaha. He was weary and sweating. He brought with him a badger, newly killed. He threw it down and Giliad took out his flint dagger with the ivory pommel and in the near-darkness sliced open the animal's belly.

They stuffed themselves on the liver, and gnawed furiously on the heart. Jaha watched, then said, 'I will make fire', but Esther, her face a mask of dark blood, said, 'I am the fire magician of the family of Zuri.'

Giliad fetched water, slipping down to the spring

and creeping back. Esther made a hearth in the desert sand and her agile fingers spun the dry wood while she mumbled and muttered: *Hail, you monkey seven cubits tall, whose eyes are made of gold and whose lips are of fire and whose words are like flames* ... And the tinder burst into fire and Giliad threw on handfuls of knotgrass, and broom as kindling, and Jaha kept a nervous watch in case the smell of the roasting meat brought men up from the camp to kill him.

Jackals came, the little foxes of the desert; prowling, yelping as they fought each other, their eyes glinting yellow.

Jaha sat on one side of the flaming broom and Ruth sat by him. He took the badger from the wooden spit and they watched; and dared not touch it, because it was his meat, his to give or to withhold. He tore off a haunch and tossed it to Esther and Giliad and they fell on it, using Giliad's flint knife to hack it into chunks. He pulled meat from the badger's back and tore away the bits of fur that still clung to the flesh, and took the hot strands of steaming white meat in his fingers, and held them up in the firelight, and Ruth leant against him and he fed her, poking the bits of meat and slippery, still bloody tendon into her open mouth.

Giliad and Esther sat and watched, shocked and fascinated.

'You would like to see Nakhi,' he said insistently, holding up a morsel of congealing fat, and this time she did not mock; he was, after all, offering to take her away from death. She did not reply, but she put out her tongue to take the fat.

The stars were out. The Eye of Thoth was bright

490

as glass. Shooting stars fell into nothingness from the roof of the world. From directly above them, the Bear God looked down on the dark mountains of Sinai. She leant against Jaha. She licked the fat from his fingers.

32
Warwickshire

Armed police around a park laid out by Capability Brown. Patrol dogs in the Victorian walkways, upsetting the deer. A lake with swans and an elegant, eighteenth-century bridge. A Georgian mansion house, now a gallery of contemporary art.

A good meeting place for physicists from Oxford and Birmingham. A few minutes from the M40. A smooth emerald lawn for the helicopters.

In the Visiting Exhibitions gallery a huge projected map of central Sinai. Satellite photographs of a white, single-storey building in a rocky landscape, the photographs blown up God knows how many times.

About ten men sitting round a long ebony table; behind them, like frozen onlookers from another planet, white, modernistic sculptures on plinths. Light filtering down through skylights.

A young man wearing a khaki pullover without regimental insignia: 'The army moved shortly after midnight, Central European Time. The presidential palace has been retaken. The headquarters of Gama'a al-Islamiya were stormed with considerable bloodshed, but loss of life elsewhere is described as minimal. Paratroopers have retaken the airport and have dropped on Luxor, where Western tourists were holed up in the Hilton. French Intelligence says that Libyan troops are moving up to the border in the Western Desert. We expect satellite confirmation shortly. All activity has been in Egypt proper; nothing has happened east of the Delta. Militia heavily infiltrated by Gama'a are in the central Sinai region, the so-called Science Nature Park, but the garrison at El-Tur and Sharm el-Sheikh will obey orders from Cairo.'

A middle-aged man, a civilian: 'Nevertheless it would be a mistake to believe that fundamentalism is entirely an urban phenomenon.'

Val Henry sat at the table. She was introduced. There was coffee but she did not like to help herself. Biggin said, 'Miss Valerie Henry was part of the police team responsible for surveillance on Dr Corrigan. Miss Henry, please tell us, what exactly does Dr Corrigan think is happening in central Sinai?'

She said, 'He believes that scientists at El-Garf have succeeded in manipulating a particle in such a manner as to produce a Closed Timelike Curve.'

The ten men round the long, polished table looked at her.

She added, remembering Richard's words in the secure room at Guildford, 'A tear in the fabric of time.'

A physicist from Cambridge, she had once attended his lectures: 'He really believes this?'

'He did not believe it at first. But he believes it now.'

A man from M16, a man she recognized, who probably disapproved of her being there, despite the intensive twelve-month investigation before she had been given her security clearance: 'You are confident that you know what he believes?'

'About this, yes. Not about everything.'

At first she had believed that Corrigan loved Elizabeth St George. She had thought that grief was fuelling his anger – that in his frustration he was blindly seeking a world where Elizabeth was not dead; and she had felt sorry for him, so sorry for him; because for two years now she had herself cried nightly into her pillow, seeking in dreams a world where Andrew was not dead, a world in which they spoke together, made love together, led their lives in each other's company. Corrigan, she thought, was seeking a way back to yesterday. She had not dared to hope, not consciously, that he would succeed.

But in her dreams a way had been found.

'Does he believe' – an American voice from out of the air, and she realized that the room was linked acoustically to another place – 'does he believe that the scientists at El-Garf are deliberately trying to produce a Closed Timelike Curve, or does he believe it to be a by-product of other research?'

She said, 'It is not relevant.'

Biggin said, 'It may be relevant. You are not qualified to say that.'

'It is not relevant to the existence or otherwise of the Closed Timelike Curve. In his view it is therefore not relevant.'

'OK, does he think' – again the voice from the ether, fractionally delayed, coming from a long distance – 'that this CTC is being deliberately used by the scientists to convey matter through time?'

She said, 'I don't know. But he believes that time travel has occurred. A German tourist in Sinai went missing for several hours. Dr Corrigan thinks he was caught up, during that time, in a Closed Timelike Curve.'

'Can we have this very clearly. Dr Corrigan believes that, by uncurling a particle as you put it, to release additional dimensions, these people at El-Garf have created a CTC capable of transporting matter – of transporting people?'

'Yes.'

Another long pause. They must have known what she was going to say. They must have known why they had been called together, from Oxford and Birmingham and Cambridge, called to secure rooms in California, Washington or wherever.

An English physicist: 'You realize the increase in size involved?'

'A million, by a million, by a million, by a million, by a million.'

Another voice, another American: 'OK, but is there any sort of equation here?'

She did not speak. She did not know.

The second voice again, 'I'll try and get one worked out.'

She said, after a moment, 'The German who disappeared in Sinai. Although missing for only a few hours his body suffered from a degree of dehydration which could have happened only if he had not taken in fluid for several days. There is also a corpse in a morgue in Cairo that Dr Corrigan believes was brought from the past into the present.'

'From where in the past?'

'From 1300 BC. Perhaps 1400.'

A long pause. She waited for Biggin to say that the corpse was a fake, that the levels of lead in Elmer's bones, established by the University of Pennsylvania Medical Centre, had been conclusive. Biggin said nothing. She thought, 'They've been lying after all.'

The second voice from America, drily: 'Anything else?'

She said, 'Not that I know of.'

The first American voice: 'The dehydration can be explained. There's no great mystery about Gabriel. We sent a memo about Gabriel three days back. I don't know what the security level was.'

The army officer who had been speaking when she arrived said, 'A minibus, a small coach full of tourists, has disappeared.'

'What? Into thin air?'

'It is believed that they ignored the warning signs and tried to visit the Coloured Canyon, which is now inside the Exclusion Zone.'

'So they might just have been arrested?'

'Or killed.'

Biggin: 'There's nothing showing on the satellite. I think we should move on. El-Garf has been operational for almost a year. We know it's funded by something calling itself the Islamic Science Foundation. We believe money is coming from Iraq, from the sale of oil that was permitted by the UN on humanitarian grounds. We have identified some of the physicists working there – you have a list of names. NATO Intelligence believes that research has involved electromagnetic fields, microwave-systems technology, the destabilization of weapons-guidance systems. But is it possible that something we don't know about is happening at El-Garf? Something we might want to preserve, learn more of, rather than destroy? Events in Egypt are moving very quickly. Israel is not prepared to wait. We need an answer.'

They discussed possible side-influences of electromagnetic-field experiments. They discussed the quan-

497

tum effects of microwave research. They discussed time travel in the quantum world. Midnight brought them to parallel universes and the classic Young two-slit experiment in optics.

'Explain again' – an army officer, tense. 'And please simplify if you can.'

An English physicist, patiently: 'You direct a weak beam of light, one photon at a time, towards a screen containing two slits. According to quantum theory some aspects of this photon – the wave function – *must* pass through both slits simultaneously. Yet a detector placed close to either of the slits will show that the photon has come wholly through either one slit or the other as a particle.'

'So quantum theory is proved wrong?'

'No. This is quantum theory – wave-particle duality.'

'But if your detector has shown the photon to come one hundred per cent through either one slit or the other—'

'It is the wave-like nature of the light that requires it to pass through both slits simultaneously, and the wave-like function cannot be measured by the detecting equipment.'

'Why not?'

'The very act of measuring or observing what occurs influences the results.'

'Then how do you know that it has occurred? How do you know that any part of the photon has passed simultaneously through both slits?'

'Because, when the photon is observed afterwards, it has properties which show it to have been impossible for it to have passed one hundred per cent through one slit or the other.'

'And how does this relate to parallel universes?'

'The Everett interpretation is that two universes come into being a moment before the photon reaches the screen. In one universe the photon passes through one slit, in the other it passes through the second slit. At this point, there are two quite separate worlds. Later the two universes come back together again. One universe, one photon.'

'Summarize, please.'

'The coming together of universes does happen. It happens on a small scale. It's been observed.'

'Is there agreement on this?'

Silence.

'Parallel universes, groups of universes, not forming part of our space and time, but observed to communicate at the level of atoms?'

A voice from America: 'I'm not saying the parallel-universe idea is wrong. I am saying it's a very elaborate structure to solve a philosophical problem, to find a way that little Johnny can go back to the time of his great-great-grandfather and murder him, perhaps. OK, let's buy Everett's theory. Let's move on. It's not the philosophical argument we need to address. Let's ask the question: if we want to build a Closed Timelike Curve, a time machine, how do we go about it?'

At one a.m. they were building a time machine at a point beyond the event horizon, beyond the membrane covering a black hole, the boundary of the region of space-time from which nothing could ever escape.

'We know that within a black hole there is a singularity of infinite density where the laws of science break down. We know that close to one of these singularities it is possible to travel into the past because of the space-time curvature. Now, OK, let's look at "naked" singularities – singularities that are not decently hidden inside black holes, shielded by event horizons. It has been known for more than twenty years that there are solutions of the equations of general relativity which would, in theory, allow a time traveller to avoid a naked singularity and pass through a wormhole and emerge into a different region of the universe.'

'Alive?'

'Why not?'

The voice from the States, that she knows now is in California: 'The presence of the time traveller would destabilize the solutions. Gravitational forces would tear him apart. This is all highly theoretical. I do not believe there is any practical application.'

An English physicist: 'I agree with Hawking. Quantum-mechanical effects would destroy any time traveller approaching a CTC. Either that or they would prevent a CTC from forming.'

'Anybody disagree?'

The physicist in Washington: 'Hawking had to ignore the gravitational effects of quantum fields. Fluctuations would approach infinity near a CTC. We can't apply quantum theory to gravity; we don't know how. You can't apply the techniques we have available today to space-time containing CTCs. You are pushing us beyond the limits of our knowledge. Hawking's calculations showed only our inability to deal with the problem.'

'You are saying that quantum mechanics would not prevent time travel?'

'On the contrary, there are quantum-mechanical effects that would make time travel possible.'

Biggin said, 'I want us to break for thirty minutes.'

It was one a.m. The American voices were still lively enough, but then it was only eight p.m. in Washington, and six p.m. in LA.

Time was manmade after all, reflected Biggin, walking out for some fresh air into the cold, dirty March night.

In Sinai it was three a.m.; two hours before dawn.

And the sandstorm had passed, and the heavens were filled with stars, more stars than Vronwy had thought possible; and in the starlight the mountains were frozen waves – Serbal and Tarbush, and all the valleys and ridges and wadis in between, and the broad, flat valley of El-Garf was a white frozen crystal sea, and beyond it, clear in the pale light, was the distant black loom of the ridge of Sarabit el-Khâdem.

A serpentine head – huge, a Loch Ness monster – moved in the stillness; Moses, looking down at her with deep hooded eyes; black sockets to infinity.

She lay back and stared upwards at the heavens.

Cartwright had disappeared. He was always going off, prowling about, doing the things a corporal in 22 Regiment SAS felt he ought to do.

Richard said quietly, 'You see the South Star?'

She looked to the southern horizon; to the pale light. She saw the star, bright over the Jebel Musa.

'Yes.'

'You can see it only from October to March, and it goes two hours before the dawn. Now, the ancient Egyptians called the Plough the Daughters of the Bier. And there is a sad story about the Daughters of

501

the Bier, and about the South Star.'

'I don't know that Moses and I want a sad story right now.'

'It's not that sad.'

'You say that now, but I'll bet it is.'

'The four main stars of the Plough are the bier of a murdered man, in some stories a murdered god. And the stars that form the shaft of the plough are his weeping daughters.'

She looked up at the galaxy – at the Milky Way that the bedouin called the Way of Dates.

'And the daughters of the dead god carry the bier to the South Star,' whispered Ruth, 'because they believe that the South Star is the murderer of their dead father – for why else should the South Star flee? Why else should the South Star disappear when they draw near? But it is not the South Star that is the murderer, it is the North Star; the North Star that hangs always from the roof of the world and remains cold and silent. The North Star is the murderer, but the South Star never has the time to prove her innocence.'

It would soon be dawn. The star in the south was fading.

The light round the rim of the world was brighter.

Naked under Jaha's cloak, she huddled against him for warmth.

'Did you know that story, my *bedu*?'

Val Henry wrote on her pad:

i. In principle it is quite possible to construct an artificial time machine.

ii. This machine would rely on the fact that massive rotating objects distort space-time. This distortion would be utilized, adapted, to change the dimension of TIME into a dimension of SPACE.

iii. Thus, to move forward in space – to physically move the machine in a forward direction – would be to move forward in TIME.

iv. Thus, to physically move the machine backwards would be to move backwards in TIME.

v. This activity would take place in the distorted region of space-time. It would not violate the rules of relativity.

What would you need to construct such a time machine?

According to Tipler of Tulane University, New Orleans, you would need a cylinder as dense as a neutron star. In size it would have to be ten kilometres across and 100 kilometres long. If you then spun this cylinder twice every milli-second so that the rim of the cylinder was moving at half the speed of light—

'You would have a machine that could reverse the roles of time and space.'

'You would have the equivalent of ten neutron stars joined together. We don't have time for this stuff.'

A young Cambridge physicist, who had become progressively more impatient: 'Has it never struck you as remarkable that some considerable time after Tipler came up with his time-machine blueprint, astronomers discovered that the universe already contained machines built almost exactly to his specification?'

'Write it up in *Scientific American*. This is populist garbage. Pulsars have a similarity to the relativistic

503

properties needed by a time machine, that's all. We're wasting time.'

'It could be that something we don't understand is happening in this Sinai Science Nature Park. It may be we're going to have to open our eyes, take off our blinkers, use our imaginations just a teeny little bit here.'

'Write it up in *Scientific American* . . . And don't tell me I'm blinkered, OK?'

Dawn. She left the conference. She passed the black-bereted policemen, the rain dripping from their camouflage jackets, the rain running from the greased stocks and barrels of their submachine-guns. She turned out into the park and walked down to the lake. The rain was on her face and she was crying.

For every universe in which the spark of life dies, in which a human spirit passes into the unknown, there is a universe where it does not. They are there, all there, in the quantum world. But the only experiments in which other universes can be detected are indirect. You can tell the interior temperature of a planet by its exterior temperature, but you cannot take the temperature at the centre.

Other universes are paper universes. Universes of the imagination. You don't need quantum physics, you need William Blake:

> *To see a World in a Grain of Sand,*
> *And a Heaven in a Wild Flower,*
> *Hold Infinity in the palm of your hand,*
> *And Eternity in an hour.*

On an atomic level the other universes are there –

504

just as on a physical level the earth is moving, round and round its centre, round and round the sun. But our brains cannot detect, cannot feel the presence of other universes, any more than our bodies can feel the earth rotating.

The quantum computer will detect these other universes, these universes that are identical to ours but different from ours, these universes with their galaxies, their black holes, their suns and moons – these universes in which Andrew may not have died, in which he may still be alive.

Paper universes. Universes of the imagination. Fantasy.

But the quantum computer is not science fiction and it is not science fantasy; it is not the arid theoretical computations of the physicists. It is almost with us. Even now, at the Max Planck Institute in Munich and the California Institute of Technology, a machine is being built that will solve virtually impossible problems – problems that would take conventional computers thousands of years – in a few minutes, by breaking the problems into an *unlimited* number of smaller tasks and solving them simultaneously in parallel universes.

By the year 2005, perhaps, the machine will be with us.

Already, the banks are worried that criminals will use it to crack their RSA cipher, the super-code they use to send cash across the world. Already, at Oxford, theoretical physicists are working out how to stop a money order being sent from London to Sydney being stolen by rogues in a parallel universe.

Do the laws of England extend to roguery in a parallel universe?

Will the Fraud Squad be dispatched to track the villains down?

She laughed out loud, but without joy.

She was sick of being lonely in bed at night; she was very sick of talk, of no-hope talk.

A policeman was following her, a chap in uniform, a West Mercia constable, chubby-faced, getting on for middle-aged, the sort you expect to go home to kippers and a mug of tea for his supper. He'd forgotten his cape – either that or somebody said, 'Get after her', before he had had a chance to grab it. Andrew must have done his time in uniform, on the beat, although he was already in CID when she met him at a Golf Club dinner dance. It was New Year's Eve and she'd been dragged there by her golf-crazy parents.

Should old acquaintance be forgot . . .

She turned and walked back towards the mansion house, and said, 'Morning', and the copper said, 'Bloody awful, eh?' and she said, 'Bloody awful, I'll say.'

Biggin was walking round the formal gardens. He was watching two cats, one white and fat and English, the other small and beautiful with Egyptian eyes. The cats were sitting on a wall in the rain, which was unusual behaviour for cats, looking at each other steadily and with cold dislike, ignoring Biggin. Behind the cats there was a coach house, large and impressive, converted into flats and houses. A woman in a dressing gown was staring out of a window, a mug of tea in her hand, watching the policemen with their guns. Two papier-mâché geese stared out of the window next to her, their dead eyes fixed on the lake, with its moorhens and swans.

'It can't be done, you know,' said Biggin. 'Not using

any technologies available now or in the remotely conceivable future. The harnessing of a pulsar, extrapolating a CTC from an elementary particle – it's just not on.'

'No, sir.'

'They've got a dozen of the best physicists from Pakistan at El-Garf. They've developed an electromagnetic beam that can distort the instruments of a Phantom at 20,000 feet. That's what they're about, that's what they've always been about. It's always down to air power, has been since 1940. It was air power that won for the Israelis in '67, it was air power that saved them in '73. The break in the Egyptian SAM shield south of Chinese Farm, that was what let through the Israelis and buggered Third Army. That's been the scenario. The Egyptian government overthrown, the fundamentalists taking over – then a new Holy War.'

'So why did the Egyptian government let them build El-Garf?'

'Because even though they were pro-American to their last Big Mac, they couldn't turn down the chance of a super-weapon against Israel. A re-run of Yom Kippur has always been on the cards. The Egyptians wouldn't need a parallel universe if the Israeli air force was powerless to operate over Sinai. The Egyptians let the building go ahead, thinking they could control it. They couldn't.'

Val put her hand out to the forsythia, vivid yellow, wet with rain. She was crying again, soundlessly crying, the tears falling slowly down her cheeks.

He said, 'I'm sorry.'

He knew what she had been through, had seen the police psychiatrist's reports. She was a physics undergraduate, in Cambridge, engaged to a lad in the West Mercia Crime Squad. After he was killed, when she was still in her third year at university, she applied to join the Force. The psychiatrists were doubtful about letting her in, but eventually they said yes. She got a good degree, to the surprise of her family, though not to her professor. She had a sharp, analytical mind, a maturity of judgement. She was in Crime Squad within two years. Her good physics degree brought her to the attention of SIS. Security screening had taken twelve months. She was processed by the unit that cleared staff for GCHQ at Cheltenham, and was aware that screening was taking place. She was not aware that she was to be offered a job with MI5 as soon as the current SIS operation in the Middle East was over.

Biggin knew. He had seen the file. WDC Henry had a future. She would be a thief-catcher in the quantum world, a world where physicists, not Scotland Yard coppers, would be employed to track down evil-doers.

He said, 'They're still at it. They're busy trying to decide if the moon's really there when nobody's looking at it. They're having a wonderful time.' He paused. 'You know a CTC cannot extend back beyond the moment when it was first created. It's the one thing that everyone agrees. A CTC created now, in Sinai, could not conceivably send anything – information, matter, anything – back beyond the moment of its inception. If it was first built six months ago, then it could send people back to that point, but no further.'

'But a natural CTC, a natural CTC that has been there, dormant perhaps, for centuries?'

He wanted to be kind. 'I don't know. You're the physicist.'

She said, 'No, no, I'm not a physicist, and things have moved on unbelievably quickly since I was at university even. The thing about quantum physics is that we simply don't know how it works. It's the central part of physics itself but it's a bizarre, illogical mystery. There's an aspect, a primary, all-important aspect – rule, law, call it what you will – that we have not yet managed to comprehend. Listen, they were talking, back there, about the classic Young two-slit experiment in optics, about the behaviour of a photon of light. Well, there was one aspect of this that they did not go into. If you fire a photon of light on to a screen through a pair of slits you will get a pattern of bands showing that the light has behaved as a wave. But if you close one slit off, the light will go through the remaining slit in a direct line and hit the screen as a particle. All right? Well, if one of these slits is opened or closed *after* the photon has been fired at the other slit, the photon will somehow, apparently, *know what has happened.* If the other slit has been opened, it will behave like a wave; if it has been closed, it will behave like a particle.

'The Copenhagen theory to explain this states that the photon will behave as a wave or a particle depending on whether or not it is being observed. Our looking at something, measuring something, determines what will happen – determines what *has happened in the past*, because we can use a light source from five billion light-years away and observe it at the end of its journey, and thereby influence not only what it is now but what it was when it started out.

'By measuring, by quantifying, by observing, we are

creating the present and shaping the past – or what we call the past, because the past is not really the past until it has been measured, quantified, by us now. The logical extension of this theory is that reality is something that exists only in our minds. That's why they're talking now, in there, about whether the moon really exists when we're not looking at it. We sing, 'Should old acquaintance be forgot and never brought to mind', and the truth is, according to the Copenhagen interpretation, that if we forget our old acquaintances, our old lovers, then they never existed in the first place.'

He listened and sympathized. If the past could be changed by quantum measurements in the present, then there were things in the past that Val Henry wanted to change.

'Yet the alternative theory,' went on Val, lost in the quantum maze, 'is in many ways the more startling. This theory requires us to accept that the photon hitting the screen somehow sends a message *back in time* to its previous self, before it went through the slit, telling its previous self whether or not the other slit was going to be opened or closed. This theory requires us to accept that information can pass through the universe at speeds greater than that of light – Einstein wouldn't have it, but the experiments have been done and they work – and this, of course, is a way of saying that *time can travel backwards . . .*'

She talked on, pouring out the arguments that had gone through her mind, night after night as she lay in her bed in her cottage in Somerset, arguments she had not been able to share with anyone, because even to hint to George that she was obsessed by the Einstein-Podelsky-Rosen experiment into the uncer-

510

tainty principle rather than drug-smugglers in Poole Harbour would have sent him running to the massage lady before you could say Schrodinger's Cat.

Biggins looked back at the mansion house. In an hour the helicopters would come in, and the communications equipment would be taken down from the roof, and the Visiting Exhibitions gallery would be restored to the modernistic statues. The decisions had been taken. In an hour they would be processed, through the CIA at Langley, through Northwood, through NATO Supreme Command in Berlin. In an hour the Israelis would know.

'They made some models at Washington University in the mid-nineties, it makes a very elegant and powerful solution. It's not the way-out stuff Elizabeth St George was mixed up in. Now, if the physicists at El-Garf have been experimenting with particles and have unknowingly triggered a reaction—'

He said, 'It's too late.'

She stopped.

'It's too late, and from the start it was an arid discussion. You know this. You know it's fantasy. You know what would happen, in reality, if they uncurled an elementary particle.'

She looked shocked. After a moment she said, 'What did the tests show, the tests on the boy soldier?'

'There's a problem with the results. Nobody's denying that there's a problem. It's being worked on.'

She looked out across the lake. A small car, its lights on in the dirty morning, was making its way from the coach house down to the bridge. Somebody who had to get to work early.

'What's going to happen?'

'The Egyptians are dealing with El-Garf. We've

offered them the SAS, but they aren't interested. The Americans could do it, or the Israelis – we've had a job holding the Israelis back – but the Egyptians want to do it themselves. They're going to send paratroops in to take the research station.'

'Where is Dr Corrigan?'

'Somewhere south of El-Tîh, together with our bloke on the ground. Things have moved faster than we expected. We're trying to pull them out.'

33
An Army of Egypt

Zuri said, 'I will not see the olive groves of Canaan. I will not see the cities of the plain.'

Ruth lay on the goat-hair carpet. Her head buzzed. Her scalp crawled with bugs. In the lamp the rancid oil burned. There was a fire outside and shadows danced on the tent walls.

'Wife?' said Zuri feebly.

Where were his other wives? Why was she the one looking after him in his terrible old age?

'If you carry my bones to Canaan, wife,' said Zuri, 'it will be in a casket, as Moses the Kenite carries the bones of Joseph.'

Ruth said nothing.

'I am dying,' Zuri said.

She thought that yes, he was dying.

He cried out, 'I would be reconciled with the King! At your feet, O my King, my lord, my pantheon, my sun god, seven times seven I fall.'

She sat up wearily. He was lying there, on his wooden bed with the gilt cobra feet, holding up his amulets depicting Hathor, his bracelet of green scarabs. He waved his thin, muscle-wasted arms. His loose skin flapped back and forth.

'I look here and I look there, but there is no light!

I look to the King, my lord, and there is light.'

There was no food left. He had not eaten for three days; no proper food – only sticky white globules of manna, insect droppings scraped from the underside of tamarisk leaves, which he regarded with loathing but gobbled up all the same; and tiny yellow tubers of wild nut grass.

When the animals died their carcases were given to the fighting men. It was the law of the Wilderness, much older than any law of Yahweh.

Ruth went outside. A cool wind was blowing down from Ti. The fire blazed and filled the air with the scent of the mountains. Shelumiel was sitting with men of Korah. They spoke in low voices, plotting and scheming.

'The Kenite is a fool. We are fools to listen to him.'

'When all is said, it was Joshua who brought us here, Joshua the Soldier.'

'We would be dead long since but for Joshua.'

'And what about all these laws? *Thou shalt not suffer a witch to live.*'

'He hates Miriam because she will not lie with him.'

'He has his Ethiopian whore.'

They saw Ruth and stopped. She sat by the fire. She said, 'The Lord be kind to you and to your families.'

They said, graciously, that the Lord was kind. Let him be kind also, they said, to the house of Simeon.

She said to Shelumiel, 'Your father is dying.'

Shelumiel got up. He went into the tent. Ruth looked away from the flames, to the mountain, though the fire still danced in her eyes. Her head buzzed and she was seeing strange things, strange faces. When the flames faded, she looked up at the canopy of stars over Ti, the million lamps hanging down from the roof of the night world. For a moment she let herself believe she was back in the flax fields of the Delta, in the garden of her husband's house, listening to the lap, lap, lap of water.

'The Lord be kind to your family,' repeated one of the men of Korah, pockmarked and leering, leaning towards her meaningfully. They all knew that soon Zuri would be dead, and that there was a marriage contract that would give Ruth a good widow's portion. She was of marriageable age, the house of Zuri was reckoned rich among the families. Even if their oxen and goats were dead, they still retained two sledges and many *belongings*, as well as the flock of sheep. A widow of Simeon might just fancy a man of Korah, a real man, not an old goat.

'*Shalom*,' she said, to show her superior class, looking up for Isis in the night sky.

She decided that the shapes in her head were the gods of Egypt; the gods come to find her. She was Egyptian; this proved that she was Egyptian. It was true that for seventy years her family had officially worshipped only one God, the God that Moses now called Yahweh or Thunderer – but that did not mean they were not Egyptians, it did not mean they had no respect for other gods. There were Egyptians who worshipped only the Crocodile God – they were not threatened with the corvée or sent out into the Wilderness! They worshipped a Crocodile God called Sobek, and lived in a city called Crocodilopolis, and for ten generations they had kept a tame crocodile which they adorned with earrings of molten stone and gold, with bracelets on its forepaws, and every day they gave it bread and human flesh; and every time the tame crocodile died they embalmed it, and tamed a new one.

No Amorites, no Israelites, had done anything as bizarre as that!

Yes, she was Egyptian, and of good family; she was not going to marry a brigand, a brick-maker.

Shelumiel would have to marry her; Zuri had said it.

She looked up for the dark shape of Isis as she flew the night skies, seeking the fourteen parts of Osiris, who had been torn apart by his brother Set, and was now King-God of the Dead. Soon, she thought, Zuri would appear before the terrible court of Osiris, to account for his sins.

What would happen when she, Ruth, died? When her own heart was weighed on the scales against the feather of truth? She who had slept with her brother, with her husband's son, with a bedouin?

Shelumiel came out of the tent. The elder of the Korahs said, 'Listen, we're all God's people. What makes Moses the Kenite think he can make the law? Why does this scribe from the subprefect's house tell us what the law is? The true prophets, the true leaders went along the Way of the Hajji. This Kenite will take us to a land of milk and honey, will he? Well, listen. He brought us *out* of a land of milk and honey.'

'Yes, yes,' laughed the other Korahs.

'I heard you before,' said Shelumiel. 'I was before the tabernacle. I heard you then.'

'He brought us out into the Wilderness and for what? To make himself into a prince to rule over us?'

'I have already heard all this,' said Shelumiel, tiredly. The men of Korah were not naturally men of wit; when they found a good joke they stuck with it.

'Can you see green pasture? Can you see waving corn? Can you reach up your hand for figs, pluck vines, eat the flesh of pomegranates?' The speaker looked at Ruth, and she shook her head: no, she could not reach up for figs or pomegranates.

'We don't believe we will ever see the Springs of Ophir, or the King's Highway, and we don't believe Yahweh comes down to Moses the Kenite in a pillar of fire.'

There was silence. There was doubt. Everyone had seen the pillar of fire. Everyone had seen it flickering over the Yam Suf.

The elder of the Korah said abruptly, 'We want a captain to take us back to Egypt. We want a captain who will speak for us to the viceroy at Baal-Zephon. We have spoken to the Soldier, but he will not help us.'

Shelumiel said nothing for a long time. Then he said quietly, 'No. Like the Soldier, I have set the Kenite's yoke upon my neck and I must bear it.'

They all sat round the fire. There was no wine to drink. Eventually, the men of Korah stood up.

'Peace be upon your house.'

'Peace be upon your house.'

The pockmarked man with hopes leant towards Ruth and said, 'Peace be upon *your* house.'

She turned away. She would not marry a man of Korah; she would not marry a brick-maker. She would rather be Shelumiel's concubine.

She looked at Shelumiel, hesitantly, shyly. Her breasts, which had been plump and round in Egypt, were so thin; she worried about them.

Later there were cries from the watchers at the campfires. When Ruth ran out from the tent, she saw lights flickering in the distant hills, on the ridge of Khadem.

A star shot up into the sky and exploded in a burst of light. There were flashes that were like lightning – though it was a clear night and there was no sound of thunder. Rebecca was crying out for Wolf, Wolf, to save her, though nobody had caught sight of Wolf for days.

A messenger came from Joshua the Soldier. Shelumiel was called to the barricade, with the men of Simeon. The herdsmen and shepherds went with him.

Later still, though no one slept and the lights still played over the distant hills, there was a sweet, soft noise of bells that mingled with the sound of the crickets, and then Miriam was there, standing by the fire. Giliad looked at her with awe and wonder. The witch who was saved from death only by the power of the Soldier, here at the tent of Zuri-shaddai.

Miriam's eyes gleamed. Round her neck was chainmail of gold, given to her by a king – a lesser king, maybe, a tribe king of Migdol, but still a king. Her white kilt was as tight on her body as on the dancing girls of the Pharaoh. One of her breasts was bare, in the high fashion of Thebes; it shone with oil in the firelight, the nipple dark as the night.

Two of her dancing girls were behind her.

'Your husband,' she said politely to Ruth. With her hand, she indicated the tent, delicately asking permission to go inside.

Ruth nodded. Yes, Miriam was a witch.

A moment later she got up and followed the witch into the tent. Zuri was lying on his bed, his eyes closed, his mouth open and snoring, his old bones sticking out from under his kilt.

'Oh, my love is like a young hart,' Miriam was saying, ironically, standing looking down at him. 'Sweet is his voice, and his countenance is comely!'

Zuri did not move.

'Oh, his locks are bushy and black, and his eyes are as the eyes of doves by the rivers of waters,' said Miriam, 'and his cheeks are as a bed of spices!'

Zuri's eyes opened.

'Oh, he brought me to the banqueting house, and the banner over me was *love*.'

Zuri's mouth opened. His two yellow pegs appeared.

'Stay me with flagons!' cried Miriam. 'Oh, comfort me with apples; for I am sick of love!'

Zuri cackled.

Miriam knelt by the bed; she leant over Zuri, her naked breast against his chest, and kissed him.

'His mouth is most sweet,' she said softly. 'This is my beloved. This is my friend.'

They were the poems of Akhenaten, the songs of the poet-Pharaoh.

'Thy navel,' said Zuri naughtily, 'is like a round goblet that wanteth not liquor, thy belly is like a heap of wheat set about with lilies.'

'Yes, yes,' said Miriam, laughing.

Zuri said, 'I am dying.'

Miriam said, 'Never. Never, oh never, Zuri-shaddai.'

Yes, he was dying. He was going to Earu, to plough and harvest as he had on earth; to Earu, where the soil was rich and corn grew seven cubits high. In his claw-like hands now he held his two *ushabtis*, little clay men inscribed with the formula that would bring them to life and allow them to work in his fields in the Afterlife.

Miriam was weeping.

He would appear before Osiris and Anubis! He would be taken before the forty-two judges, and judged on the forty-two sins. Was he guilty of lying? Of slander? Of heart-eating, which was useless remorse? Had he been guilty ever of damming up running water, or of hindering the gods in their revenues? Well, he had never dammed up water without permission, and you never hindered the tax man, even if you wanted to.

Osiris. He'd come face to face with Osiris! The man-God who had been the first to take fruit from the trees and to train vines from the poles. God of the Underworld, perhaps, but you could have confidence in a god who first trained vines.

'Husband,' Ruth cried, from the curtain of the tent, 'you are not dying! Never, oh, never, Zuri-shaddai!'

After the trial his heart would be placed on the scales by Anubis, the jackal-headed God of the Underworld, to see if it was lighter than the feather of Maat, the feather of truth.

If the scales weighed against him, his soul would be devoured by the Gobbler.

Miriam held him in her arms and wept.

Ruth turned and went outside. Giliad was crouched by the fire, looking in awe at the two bare-breasted dancing women. One of them was painting the other's eyes with a pencil, dipping the reed into an alabaster pot and applying it by the light of the fire. The woman whose eyes were being painted said, 'So, Giliad of the family of Zuri, which is the girl that is spoken for on your behalf?'

'That we may tear her into tiny shreds,' said the other.

Giliad's eyes widened. It was Esther who said, 'He is betrothed to Sarah, of the house of Dan.'

Ruth sat by the fire. She was sitting staring into the flames when the silver trumpets sounded.

A Benjaminite came running through the darkness. Esther looked for his Wolf God, bounding ahead, seeking bowels to eat. The Benjaminite shouted as he ran.

The Spies had returned! The Spies had found a path to the east, across the desert of Ti, to a valley that flowed towards the sea!

But then came further news.

Other Spies were also returned.

The lights on the ridge to the south were the camp-fires of a vast Egyptian army. A Pharaoh's army.

The Soldier said, 'He'll put the Fourth Division of Seth on the right flank. It's where they've fought since Seti's time. If he follows the same plan as he used against the Shawi, he'll put the First Division of Amun in the centre, with the Pharaoh's Own Regiment in the van. I thought I saw light reflecting on their breastplates, just before the sun went down.'

He turned to Giliad, who was, with a boy from the house of Asher, his runner. 'What did you see, young eyes?'

'I thought I saw eagles,' said Giliad, puzzled, because the eagles he had seen had been like huge dragonflies, and had moved faster than any eagle in the world.

'Carrion crow,' said a Spy, softly.

Beneath them, in the gorge, they could hear men working in the darkness to build a wall of stones and wattle sheep-pens.

The Soldier peered out into the night. 'Knowing

Amarek, the Second Division of Pre will be in reserve. But the chariots, what of the chariots? In my view they will sweep out to the east in the hour before dawn, and come in with the sun behind them.'

Giliad thought, 'There are 2,500 chariots in the division of Pre, and each chariot has three spearmen.'

'If the chariots get through the line, we are dead,' said a captain of Gershon. 'They'll bring the heavy infantry through behind them. Stiff-armed buggers – they chop with their axes as if they're slicing melons in Fayum.'

Giliad thought, 'They will slice through the heads of Ruth and Esther, but not through my head because I will be already dead.'

Giliad could see Shelumiel's face, pale in the starlight; he was one of the few men still stubbornly shaving in the Egyptian fashion.

'The fires are out,' said the Soldier, staring out towards the distant ridge, now in darkness. He sounded puzzled. 'They're under battle orders. The Dinkas won't like that, they like their porridge.' A moment later he said, 'They must have been behind us on the road to Khadem, the whole lot of them, though I could have sworn there was only a regiment of militia between us and Etham . . .'

Then he said, decisively, 'Watch for the commandos, watch out for the Ne'arim, those boys are murder.'

The Spies slipped quietly away down the path. They were the Soldier's best men; the men with coolness and resource. They ranged over vast distances; without them the tribes would never have got this far through the Wilderness. As the other captains turned to go, the Soldier called back the chief of the men of Korah.

'You must hold on if all else fails. If all is lost, you must give us time. Trust in the Lord.'

The chief of the men of Korah laughed. They were brick-makers and tomb-makers, and they trusted no one.

'Trust in the Kenite's God,' said the Soldier again. 'Or in your own God.'

'If we had trusted our own God,' said the man of Korah, 'we would still be in Egypt.'

He embraced the Soldier. He turned and went in the darkness. Soon after, his breath rasping, Moses came up the path, helped by the innkeeper Hur, and behind them Aaron.

'So, Joshua. The Pharaoh has at last brought his army to destroy us.'

'Us? If it was for us, he'd have sent a company of border guards. If it was for us, he'd have sent the chuckers-out from the brothel at Migdol. If it was for us, he'd have sent his Dinkas on a sporting expedition, a change from boar-sticking in the barrack square at Tanis.'

Aaron said, 'If they are not come to destroy us, why are they here?'

'I've been trying to work that one out. Maybe it's Muwatallis they're after. I reckon they're marching round the back of Edom. Not that old Muwatallis won't give them something to think about, he's a cunning old bugger, and those Hittites are nasty fighters.'

'Why do you not put out the campfires?'

Aaron itched to be a soldier.

'In the first place because it's too late, he's seen us. In the second place, they're decoy fires. If you notice, they're out beyond the pale. They're there to draw in the enemy if they send out the Ne'arim during the night. Boy! Where's that boy? Where's the lad?'

'Sir,' said Giliad, pushing back the boy from house of Asher.

'Go down to the picket lines. In front of the decoy fires, you understand? Tell Eliab I want men thrown out twenty paces, one man in four, tell him. They're to keep as still as stones, then when the Ne'arim come crawling towards us, they're to scream out before their throats are cut. No, don't say that. Say if the Ne'arim come, they're to give the alarm and retreat.'

'Sir.'

'Retreat in an orderly fashion.'

'Sir.'

'Then tell those fat harlots of Miriam to get off their plump arses and bring me some wine.'

'Sir,' said Giliad.

'Then come straight back, and without helping yourself to a trollop. I know what you lads are like.'

'Yes, sir,' said Giliad, slithering away down the hillside.

'Fires,' said the Spymaster softly.

Lights were again flashing on the far ridge.

'Egyptian sorcery,' said Moses, in a dismissive voice.

He was, after all, a magician who could summon up Yahweh in a pillar of fire.

All night they watched the lights.

Moses leant against a rock. From time to time his head slipped, and once he began to topple over, and only a warning shout from Pagiel, the boy of the house of Asher, jerked him awake.

'Stay by him. Help him,' said the Soldier.

524

Gingerly, Giliad and Pagiel helped up the Lawgiver. He was thin, terribly thin – they could feel his bones through his linen dress. 'Thank you,' he said humbly. His breath was low but laboured. They tried to persuade him to lie down, but he refused.

'Sir,' said Giliad, 'sir, you must eat.'

'Yes, give him food,' said the Soldier.

But Giliad had no food. Pagiel slowly, reluctantly, produced a piece of bread. Moses looked at it unseeing for a moment, then shook his head. Pagiel ate it quickly. The Soldier said, 'Well, Moses, we are far today from the wine shops of Migdol.'

'Where you always drank too much,' said Moses.

'Ah! We're here because you thought to cure me of drinking the wine, eh?'

Moses laughed, a thin, uncomfortable laugh. Giliad looked nervously at the Lawgiver's staff, that turned into a snake at his bidding.

The Soldier said, 'You've done well, my friend.'

'Well? To bring you all from the fleshpots where you did eat bread to the full?'

The words of the leader of Korah had struck home.

An hour before dawn the Spies came sliding back through the picket lines. They reported that there were no troops on the plain between Ti and the ridge of Khadem. They had ventured to the lower slopes of the ridge itself. There had been no sign of Egyptian pickets, no sign of the Ne'arim commandos.

The decoy fires were burning low.

Moses said, 'I did not bring you here for this, Joshua. I did not bring our people here for this.'

The Soldier said, 'Go and pray. Go and pray to Yahweh.'

A faint light appeared in the east. Moses, who had been leaning back against the rock, stood upright. From the tabernacle a horn sounded. Pink light spread out from the east, and caught the white linen hangings of the tabernacle. It turned the white sheets red.

Moses went slowly down the path. He was weak with hunger. He was a scribe, when all was said, a scribe in the subprefect's office, not a man who had ever got his hands dirty, or walked the dust road from Migdol to Succoth feeling on his back the whip of the overseer of the corvée.

Some of the women and children were gathered round the tabernacle. Moses spoke quietly. Aaron cried out his words.

'In your mercy, O Yahweh, you have led forth the people which you have redeemed. You have guided us. You have brought us to your holy habitation. You will protect us from the host of Egypt.'

Up on the rocks Giliad stood by the side of the Soldier.

'You have a family?'

'Sir, I am grandson of Zuri of the house of Simeon.'

'And your father?'

'In Egypt, sir.'

The Soldier nodded. There were many orphans among the families; there would be many more before the sun was high. He turned and raised his arm. The silver trumpet sounded; the quickened notes of the assembly. Men who had been stood down during the early hours to drink at the buckets or snatch what food they could find were moving back towards their posts.

'Would you go to your regiment?' asked the Soldier.

'I would stay with you,' said Giliad.

After a moment the Soldier nodded. Pagiel said that he too would stay. 'It's better on the staff,' he whispered to Giliad, 'for a man of ambition. Well, grandson of Zuri, who today leads the host of Simeon?'

'The prince Shelumiel,' said Giliad.

The men of Israel were in two phalanxes, standing out in front of the wall of stones and thorns. The right flank was protected by the cliff face, with men on the ridge to stop Egyptian javelin soldiers from seizing the ground; on the left flank were boulders rolled down from the slopes of Ti, strewn to stop chariots. Behind the defensive wall, in the narrow gorge of the oasis, were the remaining sheep of the flocks, the goats and gazelles, and the women and children.

'Sir, what is your own family?' ventured Giliad.

The Soldier, Joshua, smiled faintly. 'I am of the family of Nun, of the tribe of Ephraim, who have been soldiers of the king of Egypt for five generations, since the days of Joseph and the dawn of the New Kingdom. You ask me my family? My family is a *word*. You ask me my regiment, my regiment is the *world*.'

He looked at Giliad.

'And the *world* of Joshua is the Pharaoh's Own Regiment, of the First Division of Amun.'

'You served in the First Division of Amun?'

'Yes, I served in it,' said Joshua heavily. 'By all the Gods! Herdsmen and whores, soldiers and scribes, the mad fools of Benjamin and the brick-makers of Korah – what brings us here, dying in the Wilderness? What brought you, Pagiel? What brought the fat farmers of Asher to Sinai?'

But Pagiel did not know. One day he had been tending the oxen that turned the water wheel, the next he had been tramping the road to Baal-Zephon.

'Giliad? What brought Zuri of the tribe of Simeon to Reph-i-dim?'

'We dared not stay behind, sir,' said Giliad, 'when the Benjaminites fled with so many *belongings* and all our family were called to the corvée. My father would have died carrying stones to Pi-Ramese.'

'No, no, you think that is why you came, but you are wrong. It was Moses, little Moses the Kenite,' said Joshua. 'The scribe of the wine shop, who used to write our love letters for us, on bits of papyrus he pinched from the subprefect's office.'

He looked at Moses, still standing before the tabernacle, a scraggy-bearded figure in a dirty Egyptian dress.

He raised his arm. From high on the slopes of Ti the silver trumpets sounded. At the head of each phalanx a standard was raised.

The standard of the left phalanx was white, which in the Egyptian army represented the crown of Upper Egypt; and the right standard was red, which corresponded to the crown of Lower Egypt. The field commander's standard was of blue and yellow stripes, which represented the battle helmet of the Pharaoh. It was ironic to use the battle signals of the enemy, the Soldier admitted, but they were standards that would be understood by every man on the field.

The tribes also had the banners of their own Gods. The yellow woman-headed Lion God of Judah; the fire-spitting Dragon God of the Reubenites; the Bull God of Joseph; and on the banner of Dan – the banner under which no other tribe would serve – the Snake God Nehushtan, the sworn enemy of Yahweh, the God of Moses.

A Spy raised his arm and pointed.

The Soldier looked out over the plain. Two snakes of dust were writhing down from the far ridge. There was a distant glint like the sun on a reptile's back; swords and javelins flashing in the dawn light.

34
The Pass of the Watering Place

A cry in the night woke him, breaking through into his dreams and jerking him awake. He opened his eyes and thought it was the dawn, but it was only starlight that bathed the plain of El-Garf. Shooting stars were falling – a dozen or so of them, one after the other – bright meteors in the heavens. He listened again for the cry, and then heard something rattling round the Land Rover, snuffling around the empty aluminium water containers. He unzipped his bag and put on his boots. Vronwy was curled in a ball, asleep, her face in deep shadow. On the far side of the dead fire Ayish was sleeping peacefully. There was no sign of Cartwright. Richard moved quietly. He reached the back of the vehicle. The rattling stopped.

Was some creature sitting there, round the far side of the Land Rover, frozen, its senses alerted?

He moved forward suddenly, round the vehicle, towards the containers, the cooking gear. Nothing. Whatever it was, it had melted away into the night, into the deep shadows of the limestone rocks.

He walked out into the desert. He found his way through a clump of desert thorn, then sat down on the desert floor. The distant cliff of El-Tîh was a long black coast rising from the sea of moonlit sand. He

531

looked up at the sky, at the glittering canopy of stars and planets. Nothing here could have changed, not in 3,000, 4,000 years. This was the Wilderness, unchanged and unchanging, this was where Israel was made, this was where Christ fasted.

After a while he saw shapes, moving shadows – things that had been made worried, or curious, by his presence. They were there for a moment, then softly disappeared into the darkness.

He stood up. He was alone in the sea of sand, and rocks, and thorn bushes. He went back to the camp. Vronwy's eyes peeped out from the opening of her bag. She had zipped it up over her chin, almost to her nose; she looked like an Arab girl, a bedouin girl, as dark and mysterious as the night.

'What's the matter?'

'I heard something.'

'What was it?'

'I don't know.'

He got back into his sleeping bag. It was bitterly cold. On nights like this, in the high desert country, he had known a bucket of water be solid ice by morning.

'I hope it wasn't a snake.'

She had a terrible fear of snakes, a miserable phobia for an anthropologist who liked to work in the field, studying the nature of man in ancient civilizations, rootling about in stone ruins where scorpions and reptiles lurked.

'No, it wasn't a snake.'

Snakes did sometimes rattle water containers about, for they got as hungry and thirsty as anything in the desert, but they did not make a snuffling noise, and they did not like to slide around in the cold – although once, on a dig out in the Arabian Desert, he had known a snake crawl into a girl's sleeping bag. It had crawled into her bag seeking warmth, insinuating itself down her body; she had woken in the darkness to the feel of its coils wrapping themselves round her feet. A bright, sensible girl reared in a small town in Custer County, Idaho, she had quietly woken the girl sleeping next to her, and then lain still, without moving by a fraction, for five hours until a medical team arrived by helicopter from Cairo. When the bag was carefully unzipped the snake had revealed itself as a cobra, the asp of ancient Egypt, the god snake that had fatally poisoned Cleopatra.

He decided not to tell Vronwy the story. He said, 'It was more like a possum.'

'Yeah? You know about possums?'

He knew about possums. In his life as the husband of Melanie, he had lived for a year in north Florida, where possums rattled round the garbage bins every night.

He said, 'But it wasn't actually a possum. Possums, in my experience, don't run away. They either lie down and pretend they're dead or they stand absolutely still and look through you. They think they're being extremely clever.'

'Oh, well, night-night.' Vronwy was zipping her bag right up again, curling herself into a little ball.

He stared up at the stars. The cry that had awakened him had been the sound of jackals, the cry of desert foxes, the *little foxes* of the Song of Songs. But there were no jackal packs hunting in Sinai, not now. And there were no gazelles either, not that he knew of – but he would swear the dark shapes melting into the night had been gazelles. And the stars above had never been so bright, he thought, not on this earth, not in this age.

There was a sound on the wind that could have been the sound of a trumpet, or the distant horn of an army truck on the winding road from Gharandal to El-Khâdem.

Vronwy slept. The shooting stars fell.

Another sound; a black shadow, but this time it was Cartwright.

'There's something wrong. I was through to base. I got a signal to pull out, then the link cut dead. And stay close to the vehicle; there's a wild animal out there.'

'Moses,' said Vronwy.

'It's probably eaten fucking Moses.'

He was lying on his back, reaching under the side of the Land Rover. He pulled out his rifle.

Vronwy said, 'You do know this is a Science Nature Park? They've been reintroducing native fauna. I hope you're not going to shoot it all.'

Richard was already out of his sleeping bag, pulling on his jacket. 'This animal, what was it?'

'Some kind of big cat.'

Vronwy said, 'No way.'

'Yeah, all right, love, no way.'

'Sand cat, perhaps. Did it have furred soles and a ring tail?'

'I didn't hang about to look at the soles of its feet.' Cartwright was already throwing stuff into the back of the Land Rover, scooping up their cooking gear, chucking it in.

Vronwy said, 'It may have been a Caracal lynx. They've got tufted ears, but I don't suppose you hung about to check its ears either.'

Leopards had been here, *Panthera pardus*, in Sinai, in the late Bronze Age. *Can the Ethiopian change his skin*, the Egyptians had asked themselves, despairing of their attempts to civilize their southern neighbours, *or the leopard his spots*? There had also been wolves in Sinai, though never in Egypt proper, never in the Delta, and it was many centuries now since they had inbred with the northen jackal.

Vronwy said, 'Perhaps you can track them on your equipment, corporal? If they've reintroduced wolves or leopards they'll have given them radio collars.'

Cartwright said, 'Can we get a move on? I want to be down in the Wadi Gharandal by dawn. At least into the sandstone ravine, where the buggers can't see us.'

'Oh, baby,' said Vronwy, 'if it's a big cat it won't need to *see* us— '

'The choppers, arsehole!'

'Well!' Vronwy looked shocked.

Richard said, 'We're not going back to Gharandal.'

Cartwright stopped throwing gear into the back of the Land Rover. He said blankly, 'Oh, bloody hell. Oh, Christ. Listen, now listen, *sir*. When they say pull out, get away from the target, you have to be bloody mad to take no notice. There's weapons research going on here that would make your hair fall out just thinking about it. Tell him, miss.'

'Tell him? Me? Me tell him?'

'Acoustic bombs. Why do you think you've had the shits for three days?'

'Are you saying I've been bombed?'

Richard said, 'OK, you get out of here. Take the Land Rover, take Vronwy.'

535

'Richard!'

'I'm going to Nagb el-Mirad.'

Ayish would take him. They would make the journey by camel, slowly, sinuously swaying across the sands in the dawn. A bedouin on a camel, under the cliff of El-Tîh. They had never seen camel here, of course, not in 1300 BC, though they must have heard of them, for in the time of Rameses the Great they were spreading westward from Asia Minor. Yes, he and Ayish would go to Nagb el-Mirad by camel, the first camel in the western world.

Vronwy was arguing with Cartwright, swearing at him. 'You know he's been ill, you know he's stressed.'

'Yeah, love. Well, I'm stressed. I'm dead stressed—'

Richard spoke quietly to Ayish. When they found the cave of Nagb el-Mirad, he would give Ayish enough dollars – US dollars, not Egyptian – for a personal stereo, a good stereo – not the sort that the bedouin of northern Sinai sold from their red Toyotas – no, a Western stereo costing a hundred dollars.

Cartwright said, 'I know what he thinks, miss' – his voice urgent. 'They told me what he thinks. I know he's a nutcase, but I still can't kidnap him.'

Vronwy said, 'Look, corporal, we've got to sit down and talk this through.'

Cartwright said, 'No, love, no talking.' He picked up her sleeping bag and threw it into the back of the Land Rover.

Vronwy said, 'I'm not leaving Richard.'

There was a red light on the ridge of Sarabit El-Khâdem. A red light rising in the sky, winking.

The stars were fading. It was less than an hour to daylight.

Cartwright said, 'We've had it. That bastard'll see us. We'll never get back as far as Gharandal, not with the suspension packed up.'

The high whine of the helicopter settled to a low drone. The red light winked its way across the plain towards El-Tîh. It was a spotter helicopter. They had watched it all the previous afternoon. It had appeared at midday and had steadily patrolled the boundaries of the Science Nature Park, forcing them to stay hidden under a ledge at the head of Telat Umm Rutheh until six p.m.

Cartwright said, 'These rocks, this pass, how far is it? Is it the sort of place we can disappear in?'

Dawn. The Land Rover rocked across the desert of the Debbet el Ramlch, throwing a cloud of dust up into the pure crystal air. Moses the camel trotted behind them, his reptilian neck throwing long, prehistoric shadows.

Fifty thousand feet above, the satellite's camera eye spotted the movement, the shutter clicked, the images sped through the blue ether to the CIA in Langley, to GCHQ Cheltenham, to NATO's central intelligence unit in Berlin.

The Land Rover reached the long grey cliff, bumped along under it, eastward. A fissure, a small gorge – no different from a dozen others. Richard leant out of the window, glimpsed a patch of dusty green in the lemon light.

A gun emplacement with old sandbags splitting open, a battered aluminium ammunition case, an old MINISID sound surveillance microphone set up by the first Sinai Peacekeepers after 1973; an imaginary voice in his head, a Texan voice from Red River calling

They drove the Land Rover as far as they could under the rocks. Cartwright jumped out and grabbed his black case. Richard stared at the small rock-strewn opening, at the Nagb el-Mirad itself, the Pass of the Watering Place.

Four red date palms, the fruit even now swelling. Acacia in the hollow by four ancient wells – pre-Byzantine by the look of them, whatever Palmer might have thought. The cliff high on either side. Crumbling ledges. A pathway, a track, up the narrow ravine.

So this was the pass that had been held by an Israeli guncrew; this was the place where El-Prince's tanks had been destroyed, where Egyptian Third Army's attempt to probe the southern flank of the Israeli Sinai defence forces had been turned back. This was the place where El-Prince had seen ghosts from the Late Bronze Age, travellers through time and space.

'Richard!'

'Yes, I heard.'

It was the helicopter they had seen take off from Sarabit el-Khâdem in the hour before dawn.

Cartwright had linked the surveillance unit in the black case to the GPS. He pressed the tit. 'Christ,' he said, surprised, looking at the electron counter, turning it off and then on again.

'It's coming closer.'

They could hear it somewhere behind El-Tîh.

'There it is.'

A silver speck over the cliff, a tiny glittering fish in

538

the deep blue yonder. Cartwright was talking quietly now, on his high-frequency radio. 'Low directional beam. You won't pick it up on the intell sats. Ultrasonic standing wave at about twenty-five MHz using oppositely directed transducers. All right it's impossible, I'm only telling what I'm getting, I'm linking it into the NavSat now.'

Richard went over to the wells. Moses was standing looking down at the stones. They had long since dried out – 1,000, 1,500 years ago, maybe – when the climate had changed and the water table had fallen. Perhaps, Richard thought, Moses had a vestigial folk memory – perhaps the electrons in the rocks contained encoded information that still batted back and forth in a *wave-like manner*, to be picked up by supersensitive beasts of the camel kind.

He knelt down next to a large stone half-buried in sand. It was shallowly hollowed out on one side – the indentation might have been natural but wasn't. It was an ancient stone trough – Late Bronze Age, Early Roman – once used for watering flocks and herds.

'Richard!'

'Look for a boulder, a large shaped boulder,' he called.

Vronwy was giving mugs of water to Cartwright and to Ayish. She shouted, 'Come and have a drink. You haven't had a drink since last night.'

'I'm OK, I'm not thirsty.'

'You must drink, Richard. You know you have to drink.'

He was examining boulders, moving from one to another. 'Look for a round stone, something spherical' he shouted, jumping down into a dry gully.

'Richard! Richard, please!'

'And it came to pass,' he shouted, his voice echoing round the opening of the gully, startling a desert partridge so that it flapped up out of the palm trees with a wild beatings of wings, 'when Jacob saw Rachel, the daughter of Laban, his mother's brother, and the sheep of Laban, his mother's brother, that Jacob went near and rolled the stone from the well's mouth and watered the flock.'

She said, 'Ayish, Ayish, make him come and drink.'

Ayish grinned in delight, as he did every time she spoke to him; not understanding a word.

'Corporal Cartwright? Tell him he's mad not to drink.'

'He's all right.' said Cartwright, meaning that it was a bit late to start worrying about Richard's mental state of health.

But she knew that he wasn't all right. She knew that once people had passed a certain stage of dehydration they no longer wanted to drink, and that this could be a very serious thing.

'Richard,' she shouted, 'Richard come and piss.'

'What?'

'Piss, for Christ's sake, piss!'

Ayish looked troubled. Cartwright stared at his small screen, still talking into his radio. 'Yeah, yeah, switching from transmission to reflection conditions at each half-cycle, in other words at around fifty MHz. No, this is not in a laboratory, this is in the open over five kilometres. I'm going further up the cliff to take another reading.'

Richard came back, jumping over the stones. He said, 'OK, anthropologist. The stones, what do you make of them?'

She said, 'Cattle or sheep were always collected in

one place. They were gathered in one spot and the tents of the tribe were then pitched around them. Then they made a circle of stones and thorny acacia – they call them *dowars* today, but they're no different from the *hazeroth* of the Old Testament. Richard, what colour is your urine?'

Dark yellow would mean he was approaching the danger point, that dehydration was approaching eight per cent of his body fluid.

He said, 'I'm OK. Stop worrying.'

She held up the aluminium water container. 'Please drink.'

'Later. Ayish?'

Ayish nodded. Vronwy said firmly, triumphantly, 'Well, I'm not having a drink till you have one. I've not had a drink and I won't until you—' but they were already setting off up the path behind the acacias. Vronwy called after them. 'I'm making tea. You're to come back for some tea. And where are *you* going?'

Cartwright was also heading up the gorge, not stopping for tea, not that she cared about his level of hydration. His radio and surveillance equipment were slung over one shoulder, his rifle over the other.

Richard climbed upwards. There were tamarisks growing under the cliff. In the dry soil was a Jericho rose, the bulbous plant of Sinai that could lie dormant for ten years until revived by rain – this one was in full bloom, its scarlet flower a vivid gash. He turned and looked back down into the gully. Already he could see, in the distance to the east, the Wadi el-Biyar.

He looked the other way, out over the broad rock-strewn plain of El-Garf. In the far distance he could see a white building on the ridge of El-Khâdem; the weapons research station. Four tiny shapes were descending the ridge. He watched them reach the base of the escarpment. They spread out, each one seeking the best path through the rocks, the long, flat dunes of sand.

'Bastards.'

Ayish looked round, startled. Cartwright was above them. The soldier was cradling his rifle in the crook of his arm. He was looking at the small dust clouds through binoculars.

'Ferret scout cars, mark fives, with Swingfire missiles.'

Richard said, 'They're coming this way. Was it the helicopter?'

Below, Vronwy was sitting under the young date palms – descendants, perhaps of date palms that had grown here since the Bronze Age. He shouted, waved at her. She came slowly up the path. The sun was getting hot. He shouted to her to hurry, his voice echoing round the gorge. He said again to Cartwright, 'Well, was it the helicopter?'

'Must have been. Unless they've got seismic intrusion detectors here, in this gully, or down by the palms, and I can't see any, only the old Yank stuff from the seventies.'

'What do you suggest?'

'Play the mad archaeologist, if I were you, sir.' It wasn't a role, his tone implied, that Richard ought to find difficult. 'Tell them you've found Tutankhamun's holiday cottage. Show them a bit of wood from Queen Nefertiti's sun lounger.'

Cartwright was a humorous cove. He wouldn't be staying around to play at mad archaeologist himself; that went without saying.

The scout cars were finding the going heavy. It would take them half an hour, perhaps longer. When he turned round again, Cartwright had disappeared; Richard did not suspect the workings of quantum mechanics so much as SAS training.

Ayish tugged at his arm, pointed upwards urgently, bad-temperedly. He had been watching the Egyptian scout cars. He wanted to secure his hundred dollars before the tide of history swept onwards, impervious as ever to the needs of the poor bedouin, and the American professor was arrested, beaten up or shot.

It was a natural cave, like the cave in the Wadi Wutah, but lower, its entrance less than five metres high. As they stood by the low black hole, Vronwy came up the path behind them. She insisted that Richard drink from a bottle of water. Then she gave it to Ayish, who grinned and drank gratefully.

Richard crawled into the cave's entrance. It was bigger inside that he had expected – this was the work of man, chiselling away with flint axes in prehistory, or in the time of the Old Kingdom. He stood upright.

'U'a!' said Ayish softly.

Richard saw it. It was slowly sliding behind a small rock: a carpet viper – its venom would kill a pigeon in sixty seconds, humans had died after five days. He saw another snake, further back, only a fraction of it was visible – moving, sandy red, glistening skin, gliding between two stones.

Sunlight, bright sunlight behind them, pouring in through the low entrance, and at the back of the cave – or as far into the cave as they could see – were tiny reptile eyes. Wasn't the carpet viper virtually blind?

Perhaps these were burrowing vipers, found only in Sinai, supposedly very rare, snakes famous for the poison fangs protruding from their cheeks, so that they could use them even when their mouths were closed.

Vrowny was standing beside him, petrified, not breathing.

'Palmer,' he said conversationally, 'used to chase carpet vipers over the rocks, throwing stones at them.'

She said, 'Fuck Palmer.'

Then she said, 'Richard, what do I do?'

'Just stand still.'

Ayish was standing uneasily in the entrance. The bedouin hated reptiles. There were no bedouin professional snake-charmers – at least not among the Towarah. The nearest they came to snake worship was through the *hawi* of the tribe, the wise man who was venom-proof and could cure hurts and staunch wounds by the power of his breath.

Ayish was no *hawi*.

Richard held up his torch. There were inscriptions on the far walls. Figures of animals, a procession of what looked to be the ibis of Egyptian hieroglyphics. He remembered the ibis scrawled in the cave in the Wadi Wutah; these looked similar, possibly drawn by the same hand. Engravings – proto-Sinatic, alphabetic, the link between hieroglyphic and Phoenician.

They were well preserved. There was no wind in here, no driving rain. Even the desert sand that blew in during a storm would fall gently.

A movement. The rattle of small pebbles.

'Christ, Richard,' Vronwy said, shakily.

His torch was following the inscriptions. 'How well up are you on the proto-Sinatic alphabet?'

'I know the Canaanite word for house began with a b sound,' she said, clinging on to her sanity. 'And so, in the proto-Sinaitic alphabet b was represented by a house. Can we go now?'

'They won't hurt you if you keep out of their way.'

He moved over to the wall. There were inscriptions made over many centuries. There was medieval Arabic. There was early Roman graffiti. There was stuff from the Middle Kingdom, proto-Sinaitic.

Her voice tense, unnatural: 'What does it say?'

'I don't know. It's very difficult. There were no vowels. Bd might be bad, bid or bud.'

He walked further, following the torch beam. He was almost at the back of the cave. There was a dry shivering sound, scales scraping together, the carpet viper's warning to its enemies. The carpet viper, he remembered, could leap from a coil, strike a man's face.

More hieroglyphs. More proto-Sinaitic scrawls. Then, clearly sculpted, cut with a tool in the rock, late hieroglyphics, words he could read:

My face grew frightened now at the work. I toiled in misery; I brought abundance, yea abundance of turquoise and obtained yet more by my search. The mountains burned like fire; the vein seemed exhausted; the overseer questioned the miners. The skilled workers who knew the mine replied, 'There is turquoise to all eternity in the mountain.'

The miners of El-Khâdem recording their story, their misery, their pride. They must have come to El-

545

Tîh in search of fuel for the furnaces, seeking out new veins of turquoise or copper.

He reached the back wall. He examined the walls, the roof. He made the snakes rattle and slide, and felt one dart a venomous bite against his boot. In a dark recess he found more inscriptions – New Kingdom, written with a childish hand, the sign of a door bolt that meant 's' and the twisted flax that represented 'h' in the phonetic language of the Late Bronze Age, followed by the determinative for 'man' with the royal cartouche – king, prince, leader. Next to it, as if to reinforce the message, was the sign of 'h', which had the transferred meaning 'majesty'. By these signs was the hieroglyph for a mouse, with the tiny figure that represented a female, and a wolf with the male symbol.

He stared at the inscriptions. He felt a terrible disappointment.

There was nothing new here – nothing that had not been found, photographed in all probability, many times before. Ayish had claimed that this was a secret cave known only to the bedouin, but Ayish had been anxious for his reward. Next to the inscription denoting a female called Mouse was graffiti by Eddie of Dallas, a remembrance of a visit in March 1976. 'Home in July. Roll on, baby!'

His disappointment was intense but irrational. What could he have expected? The Ten Commandments, carved on a pillar of stone, leaning against the cave wall? Exodus graffiti? 'Moses, Miriam and Aaron the priest were here. Home to the Promised Land in May. Roll on, baby!'

He stared at the idle scrawlings, the row of little ibex, carved by some ancient Egyptian traveller, some bored child. He felt weary and embarrassed. This place was no different from a dozen other sites of minor archaeological interest in central Sinai. He had come on a long journey, and not just a physical journey but a journey of experience; he had anticipated, against all judgement, he had anticipated . . .

What? A Closed Timelike Curve that would clang its doors behind the cave's entrance, carrying him into the vortex of time?

Suddenly he was thirsty.

He turned to Vronwy. 'Vronwy—' But Vronwy was no longer there; she had fled from the snakes, and Ayish had gone also, and he was alone.

Cartwright lay with his sniper rifle watching Vronwy go back down the path. He watched through his telescopic sights as she waved nervously to the men getting out of the first Ferret scout car. They were not regular Egyptian soldiers but members of Gama'a, the most fanatical of the Muslim fundamentalist groups. They were wearing black uniforms, carrying Benelli M3 semi-automatics. He saw her walk towards them and shook his head, as if in pain.

She said, 'Hi. Look, I think we're lost', and tried to give the militia men a helpless sort of grin, and shook her head ruefully, and got ready to plug the British Museum line or perhaps she'd try *American University, Cairo? Say, what kind of jeep is that? You don't have any water you could let us have, do you?* Then she saw the look on their faces, and the expression in their eyes, and knew it for what it was, even before the first man raised his gun.

And Cartwright was not going to fire. He was not going to reveal his presence up in the rocks, even though the man was dead in his sights, even though he had a bead on the man's brain. He sighed, but very gently, as the man casually aimed the barrel at Vronwy's stomach. He was not going to do anything, partly because, if he did, the other militiamen, in the other scout cars, would call up helicopter gunships and hunt him down and kill him, and he had no means of escape, waterless as he was in the rocks. Then again, he felt a certain resentment at being sent into a combat situation with two civilians. Then again – though this was possibly the least of his motives – he was a soldier working undercover, with a duty not to be caught, not to be killed, not to be identified.

The Gama'a militiaman flicked off the safety catch. A second man was raising his weapon. A huge black shadow flickered down first over Cartwright's head, then over the small oasis. Two planes, Israeli markings, swooping down from El-Tîh. In a split second they were past the Land Rover and the scout car, out over El-Garf, a blur of speed, skimming the ground to avoid radar. A second later came the thunder crack of their massive Rolls-Royce jets, but by this time they were curving up over the white research station, and the rockets they had loosed were snaking down, leaving writhing trails of white smoke. There was a massive plume of flame as two rockets exploded on the ground short of the weapons research station and two others smashed directly into their target.

Cartwright reached for his radio to send a signal, then he saw that the Gama'a leader's gun was still pointing at Vronwy's stomach, and she was wisely not moving an inch.

Cartwright saw no reason at all now not to kill him.

He shot him carefully through the head.

And he killed the second militiaman, also through the head, counting calmly *one two three* to control his breathing as he moved the telescopic sights from one target to the other. And he got the third man in the base of his spine, as he scuttled in panic back to the jeep.

He looked round for the fourth. He felt comfortably sure that there'd be no official inquiry on this job. This wasn't Gibraltar, this wasn't a Belfast roadblock. There'd be no whining bastards demanding to know: *Was his life threatened*? No dry judges asking: *Had he used minimum force*? and sending for psychiatric reports before banging him up in prison for twenty years.

The fourth militiaman was trying to crawl behind a rock, trying to merge himself into the scenery. After a moment he stopped moving and froze, a bit the way hares froze in the winter wheat round Brecon, where Cartwright had done his field training. Cartwright watched him for a minute, establishing that he had no submachine-gun. He decided to let him be.

It wasn't that he enjoyed killing, he told himself.

But then he had second thoughts. The man might have a pistol. Or he might jump up and run back and grab one of the semi-automatics lying in the sand.

Cartwright shot him. Three rounds. After the second round the man's body jerked up into the air, and the third round went through his head.

Out on the plain the other scout cars had stopped. Their occupants were looking back at the smoke rising over the weapons research station. If they could hear the crack of Cartwright's rifle, they ignored it.

Cartwright saw Vronwy walk over to the dead men and bend down. He wanted to say, 'Leave them be, love.' She turned, went to the palms and sat in their shade; being sick, probably, he thought.

He sat in the shade himself, listening to the tiny HF transceiver that was now picking up messages. He sent a brief signal. It was acknowledged. In a little while the first of the helicopters came slowly over the escarpment of El-Tîh. He was about to switch his rescue beacon on when he saw that they were not UN Peacekeepers but had Israeli markings.

She came up the path. She said, 'Was it you? Was it you that killed them?'

'Yes.'

'What, all four?'

'That's right.' No point in false modesty, though his hands had started to shake, and he badly wanted a cigarette. She wasn't falling over herself to say thank you. She looked the type to start writing letters to her MP; he sometimes wondered why he bothered. She'd certainly been sick. She looked terrible. She was stressed out, more stressed out than the Yank. He wondered if he ought to tell her about the therapy counselling they'd have laid on back in UK. He'd killed four men. He'd need some therapy counselling himself.

'Where's Richard?'

'I don't know.'

'Where's Ayish?'

'Buggered off. The bedouin always do, you'll find.'

'Richard?' she called, looking round the rocks in the bright sunshine, climbing up to the cave. 'Richard?'

She went down on her hands and knees and crawled into the cave. She was blind, the sun still dancing in her eyes. She had no torch. She went further in, blinking round her. She was terrified that he might have been bitten, might be lying in the dark with vipers crawling over him.

'Richard?' she said quietly.

She stumbled. She heard the dry rattle of the carpet viper.

'Richard!' she shouted, and the snakes scurried, startled, from behind her and before her.

'Richard!' She stood up and yelled, 'Richard, Richard!' and the panic-stricken vipers slithered at huge speed down into crevices and holes, her strong, violent voice pursuing them into places they had not known for a century or more.

She searched around, her hands feeling over the rocks, over the sand, feeling for his body. She felt a sudden sting of pain in her hand and jerked back, and saw, at the back of the cave, by the scrawled graffiti of ibex, two children quietly intent on their drawing; children with huge eyes in skeletal skulls, thin emaciated arms, pot bellies. Then the children were gone. She stumbled back to the cave's entrance. She crawled out. Her hand was bleeding from where she had cut it. All she could see around her was the glaring hillside in the white light. She scrambled up, over the dry stones. Her eyes searched the soaring limestone pillars, the stone screes that tumbled down into the gorge.

There was nothing. Nothing but a great emptiness. She cried out, but her voice was swallowed up by the heat, by the vastness.

Eventually she lay down on the rocks.

The sun was massive. There was a helicopter, a black silhouette in the sun's eye. Then she saw that it was not a helicopter at all, it was a flock of exhausted quail driven south by Mediterranean storms, and the noise she could hear was the fluttering of their wings as they tried to reach the waters of the Yam Suf.

35
Reph-i-dim

The Soldier said, 'If you ever command a regiment, remember that a phalanx will always drift to the right as it marches.'

'Yes, sir,' said Giliad. Pagiel, the boy from the house of Asher, asked keenly, 'Why does a phalanx drift to the right, sir?'

'Because a soldier's shield is on his left arm, and in the phalanx it is held to protect his neighbour on his left – and the neighbour looks for as much protection as he can get. See those men? Mycenaeans from over the Great Sea.' The Soldier pointed to the first column of men approaching across the plain. 'The Northern Corps has been using them against the Libyans. They're in barracks at On, or they were. And there's Sherden among them – you see their leather helmets, with the spike and the curved horn? I heard the King had recruited ten regiments of Sherden. He'll need them if he's going to take the Empire back to the Euphrates.'

Pagiel asked, 'What, sir, of the Second Company?'

'Ah, now they're the lads,' said the Soldier, his eyes on the bronze standard at the head of the second column. 'The Second Division of Pre – the *numerous of heros* division. The commander will hold them back. He won't want to have to account to Amarek for dead heroes, not in a petty skirmish like this. He'll send in the Mycenaeans and the Sherden. When a mercenary's dead you don't have to pay his wages; dying's what those sods are here for.'

The two columns were approaching the cliff. There were perhaps two hundred men in each. Behind them, out on the plain, were a dozen chariots – not the lumbering ox carts of the Asiatic mercenaries, but lightweight Egyptian chariots, each one pulled by two horses.

The chariots were here for sport, they were here to hunt down the *hapiru*. It was a pastime they had grown to enjoy, ever since the order had gone out, nearly a year ago, to clear the eastern Delta of Asian interlopers and drive them back to the Wilderness.

Aaron was climbing up the path. He called out, 'What now of the Pharaoh and his army?'

The Soldier said, 'What Pharaoh? What army?'

The great army, seen in the night, had disappeared. Perhaps it had never been there. Perhaps it had all been Egyptian magic.

'The Pharaoh is in Memphis,' said the Soldier, 'drinking the wine of the Theban vineyards, eating pomegranates and shagging the willing daughters of the nobility. Perhaps when the chief deputy of the Northern Corps sends his monthly report on military activities in the borderlands of the Empire, the Pharaoh *might* read about a minor punitive raid against a few rebels. But it won't detain him for long. Would you spend your time worrying over a border raid in the Wilderness, when some virgin with pouting breasts was lying on her back with her legs open?'

Pagiel snorted with delight. He was an Asherite; the Asherites were lewd.

'A soldier's language is not shocking,' said Aaron smoothly, 'from the lips of a soldier. I would be more shocked,' he went on, 'to hear you speak like a scribe-priest or a family man.'

'Sir,' said Giliad.

The column of Mycenaeans and Sherden had halted. An order was shouted, the sound carrying across the desert. The soldiers stood at ease, their shoulders bowed down by the weight they carried on their backs. Another order was shouted. They shuffled apart, sat down in the sand, drank water from their skins.

The Soldier smiled faintly. He remembered an evening spent long ago in the barracks at Menzelah. The standard-bearer – an idealistic young Nubian aristocrat, a court favourite, a Child of the Kap – had insisted that the Egyptian infantryman fighting foreign wars was a most noble figure. The Soldier remembered how the assemblage scribe – a great wit – had stood swaying on the table, drunk as Old Moab, and shouted: 'The infantryman? The *much exerted one?* (They roared at that!) Why, as for nobility, a *painful* blow is dealt to his body, a *savage* blow is dealt to his eye, and a *splitting* blow to his brow. ("Yes! Yes!" The distribution scribe had beaten his shoes on the bench.) His head is split open and he is laid down and pounded like a piece of papyrus! (The distribution scribe had choked.) His bread and water are carried on his shoulders like a donkey's burden, and the arches of his back are bent! (The distribution scribe had slid under the table.) If he ever succeeds in returning to Egypt, he is like a stick that the woodworm has eaten, and his clothes have been stolen and his retainer has run away.'

They had cried with mirth.

'And his girl, his girl in Egypt, has run off with a *scribe!*'

God, he wondered he hadn't died!

Egyptian officers on horseback were looking at the barricade of rocks and thorn, at the Israelites who were defending it. Then they cantered round the western flank, looking at the boulders thrown down from the cliff. The sun shone on the silver buckles of their kilts, the clasps of their cloaks. They were almost within javelin range. In the clarity of the morning Giliad could make out the gold rivets that held the bronze armour to the linen of their dress.

'A long javelin shot?' said a Spy, perched above the Soldier in the rocks.

'Not unless you want to give the Second Division of Pre our javelins to throw back at us.'

'We could kill the bedouin.'

A small group of bedouin was high on the cliff, on the other side of the gorge of Reph-i-dim. Waiting for *belongings*.

The Soldier shook his head impatiently. 'The Mycenaeans and Sherden will come straight into the gap,' he said. 'They won't waste time on the cliff, and they won't want to come through the boulders where they can't bring the chariots. They'll come straight into the gap.'

'And we will kill them,' said Aaron.

'With luck we will hold out until nightfall,' said the Soldier. 'If we manage that much, they might decide we're not worth the bother. It depends on their orders. They might feel shame to send the Second Division of Pre and the chariots to deal with a gang of *hapiru*.'

He looked down at the defensive wall, the tangle of rocks and thorn bushes lined with javelin men. Archers were positioned behind them on the cliff. It looked well defended. A tough nut to crack. But the javelin men were only shepherds and brick-makers; the archers were only herdsmen.

Well, there was nothing more he could do. He had brought them thus far. He had shaken off the Egyptian chariots in the tidal flats round the head of the Yam Suf. He had taken the panic-stricken families out into the Wilderness of Shur, away from roads used by the traffic of the Empire, away from tracks frequented by royal messengers. He had stopped them – some of them at any rate – from trying to make a quick journey along the Way of the Philistines, or the terrible dry journey through the Wilderness of Paran. He had taught them to fight. Moses the Kenite, a more sensible priest than most, had kept a cool head, said the things he was told to say. Yes, he, Joshua, had brought them thus far, and in fifty days there had been only one encounter with royal forces, and that only with Dinkas.

An order was shouted in the desert. The Mycenaeans and Sherden were getting to their feet. To them this was just another job, just another day's work; while they waited, they had been sitting in the sand throwing knuckle-bones, to see which landed face up.

The platoon leaders moved ahead of their men.

In the desert the men of the Second Division of Pre beat on their shields, half mocking, half encouraging their mercenary allies.

The bronze trumpets of the Egyptians rang out. The noise echoed round the gorge. The Benjaminites' antelopes came running through the camp in panic, darting between the tents, skidding round the second and third lines of defenders, jumping the thorn bushes, fleeing out of the gorge and running like the wind across the plain. Three chariots moved to intercept them, and two gazelles fell to Egyptian arrows.

Again the bronze trumpets sounded. The Soldier raised his arm. The silver trumpet of Israel answered the harsh, powerful voice of the Empire. The first two ranks of Red Phalanx and White Phalanx stood forward, in front of the barrier of thorns, out in the desert, facing the enemy. Those under the red banner were commanded by Shelumiel the Simeonite; those under the white banner were commanded by Eliab of the house of Zebulun. The field commander was Elizur of the house of Reuben.

'The Lord is our strength and song,' said Aaron quietly.

'Yes,' said the Soldier. Today he himself stood under the standard of the Moon God, though at other times, in frivolous mood, he prayed to the woman-headed Lion God of Judah.

There was a roar from the Mycenaeans and Sherden. They were moving slowly forward towards the Israelites.

The Soldier wore his blue officer's cloak, the cloak he had worn when he served the Pharaoh's Own Regiment of the First Division of Amun.

There was a mighty yell as the Mycenaeans and Sherden fell on the defenders of Reph-i-dim.

The sound made Ruth's head jerk round. Zuri seemed not to hear, although his eyes were open, his hands clutched his little clay men. Sunlight shone into the tent, though oil still burned in the copper lamp.

Ruth sat trembling. She did not know whether or not she should leave him and go up the cliff. Rebecca had gone. Wolf had appeared and dragged her away. The two surviving old Ethiopians had also gone – trying to escape, to clamber up the cliffs and find a hiding hole. Well, if the Egyptian soldiers did not kill them, and the serpents did not sting them, she, Ruth, would certainly make them wish they had. She repeated the thought to herself, refining it, savouring it. If the serpents did not sting them or the leopards devour them—

'Wife?' said Zuri anxiously.

She would strip the flesh from their bones.

'Yes?'

'Did I care for you?'

She thought for a moment. Yes, she decided judiciously, he had cared for her. Even though he was so terribly old – 150 at least – he had married her when he could have kept her for a concubine or given her to one of his sons. She had been bitter at the time – married at fourteen to a man of 150! – but she was a year older now, more mature, more knowledgeable about the way the world wagged. What if she had married that boy from the scribe school who wanted to lie with her (had, indeed, lain with her twice)? What if she had been left behind in Egypt? Would her scribe boy have saved her from the soldier's spears? She doubted it.

'You cared for me.'

Ah . . . another sin avoided.

'Sing me a song,' said Zuri.

She wondered if he thought she was Miriam. There was a strange noise from outside now, mingling with the yelling and the screaming and the battle trumpets. It was a *thump, thump, thump* sound, like that of 1,000 staves cracking down on the skulls of 1,000 men.

'Sing for me,' said Zuri.

She sighed. She sighed for her home, for the land of Misri.

'Sing for me,' said Zuri pathetically, 'a song of old Egypt.'

She wept then for the sound of the nightingale in the pomegranate groves, for the murmur of doves in the flower gardens.

A song for old Egypt . . .

She sang. She sang of the deep flowing Nile, the colour of molten bronze, with its yellow-flowered banks and the red-sailed lateens. She sang of the sun-dappled vines in the garden of the little house by the dyke:

> *The beams of our house are cedar,*
> *And our rafters are of fir . . .*

She wondered if Zuri, lying with his eyes closed, was back in his vineyard, talking to Renenutet, the slow-slithering Cobra-Goddess who guarded his crops, or was he back – she smiled inwardly, her heart welling up with affection, for he was surely dying, even after being 150 years, and it was to Osiris he would have to answer now, not to her – was he back with his two slave-girls, those lissome, naked Nubians with plaited black hair whom he so delighted to please? Was he giving them hand mirrors of polished bronze so that they might decorate themselves with black kohl and with scarlet pencil?

Oh, I have gathered my myrrh with my spice,
Oh, I have eaten my honeycomb with my honey,
I have drunk my wine with my milk.
Behold, thou are fair, my love,
Behold, thou are fair, my love,
Oh, I am sick of love . . .

She sang the poem of Akhenaten, the Pharaoh-God.

Zuri cried suddenly, 'Glory to thee, thou who risest in the horizon. Praise to thee, thou beautiful child.'

Esther came into the tent. She stared at her father, trembling. She began to cry.

'Hush, hush,' said Ruth.

But Zuri did not hear either of them. Already he was being guided by Horus along the path to the Underworld; already he was crawling past the monkey that crouched with its net to snare him, past the serpent that was as long as life itself; in his hands were the *ushabtis* that would work his fields in paradise; on the amulet round his neck the seventy-five secret names of the Sun God Re that would buy him passage in the Sun God's boat.

Ruth had stopped singing. Esther's eyes gleamed black through her tears. She was looking for Zuri's soul, the ba that would come fluttering like a bird from his mouth and would return every night for as long as his body remained uncorrupted. Her eyes probed also for the unseen, invisible ka that would also live on, in his corporeal shape, if his heart truly weighed as light as a feather and was not eaten by Ammit the Gobbler.

Outside, there rang out the harsh notes of the battle trumpets of the Second Division of Pre.

Ruth cried out, 'Oh, my father, oh, my brother, oh,

my mother Isis! Release me, look to me, for I am one of those who should be released!'

They saw Zuri's ba leave his body, flutter from his mouth . . .

After a moment, from under his arm, from under his cloak, Ruth took the silver statue of Ka-nefer, the priest of Ptah.

They ran out of the tent. Ruth turned to look at the barricade, at the wall of stones and thorns with its thin line of defenders, the men of the third rank, the old men and boys. She wondered if Shelumiel was alive, and if he was alive, would he now marry her? She thought he would. She thought he would, even though he was so remote and unfriendly.

Esther was crying out to her, shaking her arm.

They ran up the path under the tamarisk bushes. Wounded men, trying to escape, cried out to them, for help or for water, but they dodged out of their way and scrambled up the cliff, looking for the old Ethiopians, whose job it was to look after them.

Shelumiel was in the thick of the men of Simeon. Muscle and sinew, the Soldier had said, but the men of Israel were half starved and exhausted.

'Hold your position! Cover your neighbour! Hold your position!'

Thump, thump, thump . . .

The Mycenaeans were coming again; coming to destroy Red Phalanx. Through the glare and the dust he could see their leather tunics, their boar's-tusk helmets, their swords beating rhythmically on their wooden shields. He could see their Egyptian officers running alongside them, yelling and swearing.

Thump, thump, thump . . .

The Mycenaeans crashed into the Israeli fighting rank, spearmen thrusting forward between the defenders' shields, Sherden swordsmen moving through to support them, their swords – made out of iron, a metal scarcely known in Egypt – jabbing upwards, seeking unprotected bellies to slash.

'Second rank! Second rank!' cried Shelumiel.

The second line of men of Red Phalanx moved forward. They took their places among the fallen. They raised their spears and their bronze swords, now pitted and broken, and at a yell of command smashed back into the wall of Mycenaeans and Sherden.

The men of Israel cried out, 'Shelumiel! Prince of Simeon!'

Ruth had cried out the words once, mockingly.

At other times she had said, 'The nakedness of thy father's wife thou shalt not uncover. It is thy father's nakedness.'

He had never been able to match her irony and wit.

Thump, thump, thump . . .

A new wave of Mycenaeans was being thrown into the gap.

The Mycenaean shields were cheap wood, painted to look like ox-skin, but their beating echoed round the gorge, and far behind the barricade the remaining gazelles leapt in futile blindness at the rock walls.

Now came Sherden, with their iron swords.

The men of Israel could not hold the line.

There was no more ground left to yield. Their backs were against the piled up stones and broken sheep-pens, the desert broom bushes and thorns.

The standard was down.

The Sherden were coming through, slashing through the dead and the dying. Shelumiel's back was against the thorns as they came at him, a solid wall of shields and flashing swords.

There would be no palm wine to rinse his corpse, no bruised myrrh to fill the orifices of his body; there would be no funerary prayers; no clay men to till his fields. He was going naked to Osiris.

He was dead. He felt the tearing, pitted knives rend his flesh and the flint axe of a Mycenaean smash through his skull, and the heels of a Sherden grind into his face and trample his body while the desert grit filled his mouth and eyes. He was dead. For the first time in a hundred days he was no longer thinking of Ruth, his father's wife.

'Sir, I will rejoin my regiment,' said Giliad, standing under the moon standard, but Joshua was not listening; his eyes were everywhere, peering out through dust that glinted with red and silver motes, peering at the left flank, where the tiny remnant of White Phalanx still held the wall of boulders; at the cliff where Egyptian javelin-throwers were almost at the summit and only a handful of Israelite women were left to throw stones on them; then down in the gap, the yawning gap where he had always known it would be decided.

'Sir,' shouted Giliad, thinking of Pagiel, dead an hour ago, his skull smashed by the sword of a Sherden as he carried a message to Ellisur. 'Sir,' he shouted, fearing the Soldier would not let him go. 'Sir, I would rejoin my regiment.'

The Soldier was not listening. Giliad saw from his face that the end was very near.

Harshly the bronze Egyptian trumpets blew. The noise soared over the field of battle and now the silver trumpet of Israel was faint. Through the dust Giliad could see the Mycenaeans preparing to attack again. All that opposed them was the third line of men of Red Phalanx.

'Sir,' he cried. 'Sir!'

The Soldier was looking at the tabernacle, where Moses was still being held up by Hur, on a rocky outcrop, and where Aaron was standing in front of the scribe-priests.

'Sir,' said Giliad, 'sir, I would rejoin—'

'Go to the tabernacle. Tell them to go. Tell them to go now.'

He watched Giliad scramble down the path.

So, it really was going to end here, in the Wilderness, in a dry valley under the wall of Ti. Well, the priests and some of the women might escape. And other tribes would find their way to Canaan. Not all the families who took the Way of the Philistines or the Way of Hajji could have been killed. Some must have slipped past the army posts, survived the terrible dryness of Paran. And other groups of families – from Pi-Ramese, from Zarw – were pushing their way east through the mountains, led by their priests, their own Kenite prophets. In the night a Spy had brought word of tribes who had reached the eastern side of Ti and formed a Confederacy of Nomads – 'embracing the Midianites!' said the Spy, which was one way to describe raping the women, enslaving the men and stealing the flocks. Israel would fall on the rich pastures of Canaan; it would happen one day, whatever might happen here at Reph-i-dim. But it would be a great pity if Moses the Kenite did not survive; he was a man of ideas, a man of vision even. He was better than most of the snake-charmer politicians handing

out God's laws and ordinances to the Children of
Israel.

Thump, thump, thump . . .

Only the third rank, the old men and boys, were
left to face the Mycenaeans. And behind the Mycenaeans and Sherden, the men of the Second Division of
Pre were marching towards the gap.

Yes, the end was very near.

Giliad ran through the camp. He passed small
children who had been abandoned in the panic, and
now played happily in mud made by water that had
spilled from the leather buckets carried to the soldiers. He ran past the sheep that were stampeding
in every direction; past the temple prostitutes of
Asher, who were helping wounded men towards the
rocks. He reached the Levite guards, and passed
through them to the tabernacle. He blurted out the
Soldier's words, and Aaron ran up to Moses and
embraced him, then jumped down and looked up
through the haze to the rock where the Soldier stood,
then nodded to the scribe-priests to take up the
wooden box that contained the tribes' covenant with
God.

Giliad turned and half ran, half staggered back
down to the camp. A child screamed. Giliad turned
towards the barricade. The wall was crumbling.
Stones were falling, the thorn bushes being scattered.

A Mycenaean soldier staggered into the camp,
through the curtain of dust, his kilt covered in blood,
his sword arm steeped in blood to the elbow. Others
appeared behind him, closing together into a group.

And now the last defence of Israel was moving
into place; the line that was to hold firm while the

shattered remnants of Red Phalanx and White Phalanx fled up into the barren reaches of Ti, to cower in caves or behind stones, perhaps to be hunted down and slaughtered, perhaps to be driven down from the hills and across the plateau to the slave mines, but perhaps to survive.

It was down to the men of Korah, to the brick-makers and the tomb-builders of Karnak, to the *hapiru* from the crumbling, deserted slums of Amarna. They let the remnants of the Red Phalanx and White Phalanx through their ranks; they moved forward slightly and closed ranks themselves. Their three captains – Eliab, Dathan and Abiram – moved five paces to the front.

Giliad stood in the middle of the fleeing men of the Red and White Phalanxes. He shouted, 'To me! To me! Men of Simeon! Men of Benjamin!' but his voice was lost in the victory yells of the Mycenaeans and Sherden. He looked up at the rocks, searching for the Soldier, but the moon standard of Joshua no longer flew. He looked round for Esther and Ruth, but the tent of Zuri was abandoned, half flattened under the tamarisks.

He heard the harsh cry of the bronze trumpets of the Second Division of Pre, and waited in vain for the silver trumpet of Israel. Beyond the men of Korah, in the exposed torn gap in the barricade, he saw Egyptian infantry officers yelling orders to their men, and the Mycenaean and Sherden foot soldiers clumsily moving to one side.

Then, through the gap, he saw the chariots. The horses' blue and yellow livery was bright and clean, their plumed headdresses nodded and waved; the charioteers – those aristocrats of the chariot corps –

stood on their platforms, their archers already drawing their short, deadly bows.

The first volley of arrows was loosed. The men of Korah raised their shields. The charioteers whipped their horses forward, forward into the gap, into the oasis of Reph-i-dim. Giliad, with a weariness he had not thought possible, took his short sword, his bronze falchion, from its sheath. Then he walked towards the barricade, towards the men of Korah. He walked towards his death, and his head was filled with the heady scent of desert poppy, and there was the spinning of chariot wheels, and there was a terrible choking storm of dust, and again the *thump, thump, thump* of swords on shields, and the cries of the doomed men of Korah ('The Earth opened her mouth and swallowed them up,' wrote the Levite propaganda scribes, and also, 'There came out a fire from the Lord') and thirty centuries of hot desert dust separated into motes and specks, into atoms and subatoms, into particles and electrons all around Giliad's burning flesh.

36
Night at Nagb el-Mirad

The Israeli helicopter that had spotted Vronwy hovered over them as they carried her down the path. Ayish brought water. Cartwright pumped liquid into her – fixed some sort of saline drip to her arm. Now she lay in her sleeping bag, under the date palm, looking up at the dancing leaves. Richard said, 'I'm sorry.' She shook her head weakly. Ayish murmured softly in Arabic, a prayer perhaps. Cartwright chattered away on his radio.

Richard fed her water slowly, terrified that he would kill her. But her temperature dropped, and after an hour she drank more liquid.

In the afternoon different Israeli helicopters came overhead, flying low over the plain towards El-Khâdem. Cartwright watched them through his binoculars. They landed on a distant ridge. It was a task force of commandos, but there were also civilians who would be Israeli Mossad Intelligence agents, scientists. The Gama'a gunmen had long since disappeared; presumably down the mountain track to El-Tur, or down the old road to Gharandal. Ayish made a fire and boiled up tea. Towards evening a helicopter flew back across the plain and landed at Nagb el-Mirad. Four Israeli soldiers, relaxed but wary, carrying guns. Their officer said, 'OK, we'll take you to Taba.'

Cartwright said, 'Don't worry about us, mate.'

The Israeli officer frowned. 'No,' he said, 'no, you have to leave here.'

'Oh, yeah? This your country, is it?'

There was a brief flare-up. Cartwright explained that he was not a poor sodding Egyptian who could be pushed around. The Israeli officer looked at him with distaste, then went back to his helicopter, spoke on his radio. He came back. 'Don't try and go over there, over the desert to Sarabit el-Khâdem.'

Cartwright said chattily, 'I don't know what it is about me. I don't know why it is that everybody thinks they can order me about. It's been like it ever since I can remember. Even when I was in nappies, there were officers in romper suits saying, "Don't do this, Cartwright" and "Don't do that".'

'El-Khâdem is not safe. This desert is not safe.'

Cartwright said, 'Never mind about us, chum. We know all about the tiger.'

The Israeli officer looked baffled.

Cartwright said, 'Well, cheerio then.'

He had been told by an American voice (Christ knew who he was really working for) to monitor the research station until UN Peacemakers moved back into the Exclusion Zone, which was expected to be the following morning. He had been told that the Israelis had pre-empted agreed action by the Egyptian Air Force, that there was a huge diplomatic row going on.

The Israeli soldiers gave them water but refused to give them food. Cartwright watched uneasily as they took away the bodies of the four Gama'a militiamen, his imagination conjuring up a court in Tel Aviv and some bearded Israeli judge demanding to know if he'd shown his yellow card and given the bastards three warnings to stop.

Just before nightfall the helicopter returned. A doctor examined Vronwy. Richard said, 'If there's any question about her being in danger—'

'She's exhausted. Has she been exposed to the effects of an acoustic device – an acoustic bomb?'

'From very long range. Several days ago, on the plateau. She didn't even know it had happened.'

'She ought to be in hospital for tests.'

Vronwy said, 'I'm OK. I'm going to lie here.'

The helicopter departed, this time flying back towards the border at Taba. The other helicopters at Sarabit el-Khâdem also rose into the sky and went slowly towards the border. The sun went down over Egypt.

Darkness fell.

They listened to the radio. There was no mention of the bombing or the Israeli helicopter intrusion into Sinai. There was martial law in Cairo, a plea for calm.

Richard cooked the remains of their food supply. He sat next to Vronwy, put an arm round her. She told him she had hallucinated as she lay on the hillside.

'Don't go to the cave again,' she said.

'No.'

'Promise.'

'There's some interesting graffiti.'

'There's some deadly snakes.'

He felt a shudder, her skin crawl. 'Don't think about it. Hey, stop, stop. . . . I'm not going near the cave.'

'So why don't we leave this place?'

'I've been a long time getting here.'

And others had been a long time on the journey, and had not got to the Pass of the Watering Place, and never would.

Darkness over the desert. A new moon, a sliver of palest cream.

Vronwy said, 'Richard?'

'Yes?'

'You know what a wise man once said to me about the desert?'

'What wise man?'

'Never mind what wise man, a wise man.'

'Yeah, OK, go on.'

'The desert, he said, knows the answer to questions we have not yet learned to ask.'

They sat in silence. Then he said, 'These hallucinations . . .'

A pause, then she said: 'I thought I saw two children in the cave. Some birds in the sky.'

And the lower slopes of the hillside had been clothed in desert thorn, picked out with the scarlet flowers of the Jericho rose. And the air had been thick with the scent of desert poppy.

'Was that all? Children and birds? Vronwy?'

She said, 'Children and birds. What more do you want?'

There were moving shadows again, shy and subtle, out in the rocky sands. Gazelles that were never seen during the day. He saw the huge, bulging, indignant eyes of jerboas. Snakes would be slithering through those rocks; hunting before the temperature fell. The Turks swore that the Sinai desert at night was full of *djinn*, of wicked lost souls in torment.

A distant howl. Moses tossed his head in the dim starlight and snickered nastily. Cartwright said, 'It's that fucking lion.'

Vronwy said, sleepily, 'Piss off.'

'You wait till it comes and eats you.'

'There were lions here, and leopards,' said Richard, 'in Pharaonic times.'

Vronwy slept. Richard wondered what had happened to her as she lay on the baking rocks.

He said to Cartwright, 'I'm going up the path.'

'Right-ho, squire.' Cartwright had shut down his receiver, and was quietly smoking; a soldier taking his ease.

Richard disappeared into the gorge, a ghostly figure, his desert boots silent in the sand. Some time later, around midnight, when the sliver of the moon had almost gone and stars were bright, Vronwy woke and said, 'Where's he gone?'

Cartwright was peering out into the night through his binoculars. 'Just be quiet for a minute.'

Lights exploded on the ridge about Sarabit el-Khâdem.

Cartwright, now speaking into his radio, said, 'They've blown it up. I repeat, the Israelis have blown up the laboratory.'

Another explosion. For a split second the entire plain was bright as day.

Vronwy saw Richard.

He was standing on a ledge, up on the side of the cliff, looking out over the plain.

Explosion followed explosion on the distant ridge. Rockets of light rose high in the sky. She watched

573

Richard stand on the ledge and stare out at El-Khâdem.

Over his shoulder, although she knew that he was unaware of it, a Spy was saying softly, 'We could kill the bedouin.'

37
Ti

At night jackals snuffled round the tent, howling in torment. Once there was the chilling, snickering laugh of a hyena – one of the Benjaminite milk-fed hyenas perhaps, turned vicious and wild with neglect – and Ruth and Esther clung to each other in terror before tumbling out of the tent and throwing more wood on the fire. Red, unblinking eyes shone all round them in the darkness. Then the red eyes disappeared, and the night was quiet for a few moments until, suddenly, yellow eyes shone – yellow eyes with black pupils: the eyes of a wolf.

They had screamed then. Screamed for the night guard.

It was Shelumiel's body that drew the jackals, and hyena, and the wolf. It was the smell of rotting flesh underlying the sweet spices. One morning a four-toed jerboa was found eating Shelumiel's stomach, stuffing its mouth even as Esther cried out. Its huge eyes were petrified and it sandy-furred ears flapping with alarm, but it was reluctant to leave its meal, even when a pot was thrown at its head.

It was then that Ruth despaired of ever taking Shelumiel's body to Canaan.

On the sixth day after Reph-i-dim she bound his

corpse in linen. Over his chest she placed a bronze javelin and a bronze amulet of a falcon. She ran her fingers over his face, with the terrible gash from scalp to chin, now black and purple. Her fingers touching his three gold earrings, his black, curling hair. On his finger was his gold scarab ring that depicted Akhenaten the Pharaoh with Nubian prisoners.

It was Miriam who sent gold stalls to place on Shelumiel's fingers and toes to protect them on his journey to the Underworld. Round his neck Ruth hung three amulets depicting Hathor; they were the only amulets she possessed. The men of Simeon, those that had survived, cut a grave in the soft rock, by an ancient burial place on a hill next to where they were camping. She lined the grave with Phoenician purple cloth, a gift from the house of Gad.

They buried Shelumiel at dawn. At the last moment, in a sudden impulse, she placed in the grave the silver statue of the priest Ka-nefer: a talisman to protect him, a great gift to show his worth, his nobility, when finally he came before the throne of Osiris.

She was frightened, anyway, of the ka of Ka-nefer, frightened of what it might do to her if she melted its statue down into silver shekels.

Esther wanted to put into the grave her wooden hippopotamus with jaws that opened and closed when a string was pulled, but Ruth said no.

Esther said, 'I want it to fight the crocodile for Shelumiel.'

'The Prince Shelumiel,' said Ruth proudly, tears falling silently down her face, 'will not be frightened by any crocodile, or any serpent, or any jackal god.'

She turned and went, down the hill from the burial place.

She felt pleased about saying that. *The Prince Shelumiel will not be frightened by any crocodile.* She repeated it to herself, and the tears fell in a deluge, because yes, he had been a prince, and he had died fighting bravely.

When she had gone, Esther put her hippopotamus gently between Shelumiel's hands. A mortuary priest, a confused Levite not convinced by the new burial customs required by the god Yahweh, came with his red seal, the seal of the necropolis with its grinning jackal god standing on nine bound captives. Another Levite priest recited the ancient spells. They tarred the linen to aid mummification, to preserve the body corporeal so that Shelumiel's ba would have a home to flutter home to each night. The gravemen pulled stone slabs as lids over the hollowed-out burial chamber, and piled them with more stones to keep out the *little foxes*.

Ruth looked across the hillside. Greenstuff grew in the shallow wadis, but for the most part this was a stony desolation, hard gravelly sand with small pebbles on its surface, covered in desert thorn. When the wind blew, the dead thorn bushes were plucked from the ground and rolled across the plateau. People had lived here. There were a dozen low mud-built huts, signs of recent occupation by Midianites. The wadi had a trickle of water; there was pasture, though poor enough. There were the beehive houses of ancient savages.

Rebecca and Wolf were standing some distance away. Wolf looked confident. He wore the blue cloak of an office in Joshua's army; a cloak made from the hangings of the Dragon God of the Reubenites, for the men of Reuben now worshipped Yahweh, the God who had saved them by opening the ground and spitting fire on the Pharaoh's army, and had them swallowing the heretical men of Korah. This was what the story-scribe had written on his scraps of papyrus, just as he had recorded the parting of the Red Sea at Elim, and destruction of the Pharaoh's army by the flood. Ruth did not understand why God had taken the men of Korah, but certainly the brick-maker who had winked his eye at her, and would have made her a brickie's wife, was gone, consumed by the monstrous vengeance of Yahweh, who was also called the Thunderer.

For I am a jealous God, a God of vengeance. I am a jealous god and my NAME IS JEALOUS.

Most of the tribes now worshipped Yahweh, whose name, when not the Thunderer, was *Jealous*. The Asherites' temple had been destroyed, and its harlot priestesses taken as concubines. It would be some years before the worship of Ashtoreth revived through the length and breadth of Canaan, its main act of worship being found so attractive that frustrated priests of Yahweh would repeatedly cry down the centuries, 'Thou shalt not whore after strange gods!' and repeatedly the men of Israel would do so.

Ruth looked at Wolf in his blue cloak and thought of Giliad who had died and whose body had not been found. But she did not think about him for more than a passing moment. So many people she knew had been killed since the Pharaoh's militia first swept

578

through the eastern Delta, driving out the Amorite tribes, and he was only a boy, her husband's son, whom she had known for less than a year.

And it was not in the Egyptian nature to repine.

The sun was coming up. Ten more days, the Spies said, to the Wells of Ophir. In ten days they would be next to the Eastern Sea; another ten days beyond that and they would find the King's Highway, the misty road that had been trodden by Abraham and Joseph, and that would lead them to Canaan.

Jaha was sitting on his donkey, waiting for her to come down from the burial ground. She walked over to him. She put her hand round his leg as it hung down the side of his shaggy, skinny beast and leant against him. There was a cool breeze with the dawn but later it would be very hot. They would have to walk for many hours before pitching their tents, and she was thankful that Jaha and his donkey would be with them.

Jaha had stopped saying, 'You will like to see Nakhi.' Nothing had been discussed, but when she said quietly, tentatively, 'You will like to see Canaan', he had not shaken his head, and so it was accepted that he would travel with the Israelites. Already a scribe-priest had spoken to him as the inheritor of her widow's portion, which was one half of Zuri's small flock of sheep. The nation of Israel had to grow, and to grow quickly, if it was to conquer the cities of the plain and defeat the giant Anaks that stalked the land and ate people up; there would be many bedouin and Midianites in Joshua's army.

All along the plateau the families were on the move. The Reubenites were already heading east with their large flock, the Danites following behind them. Mose the magician, now Moses the prophet, was standing watching the families. At times he flapped his arms as if invoking spells. His mouth was working, his stained beard going up and down.

'When God speaks to him,' said Ruth, 'He comes down in a cloud about his head.'

'I don't see any cloud,' said Jaha, still uncomfortable when he was anywhere near the snake-charmer.

'It isn't given for you to see it,' said Ruth, and added proprietorially, squeezing his leg as she walked: 'It's up to me to see these things for both of us.'

She would marry Jaha. She would be his wife. She would bring him ninety head of sheep, a bed with cobra gilt legs and two old Ethiopians, who still had a few years' work left in them. It wasn't bad, she thought proudly, for a bedouin.

'*Bedu,*' she said affectionately.

She pointed to the east. 'I can see the Wells of Ophir! I can see the date palms and the fields of flax! I can see the King's Highway!' She strained her eyes, willing them to see beyond the black, cruel rocks silhouetted against the dawn.

'Ten days,' warned Jaha.

Ten days marching in the heat. She felt her heart fail her, then she threw back her head and filled her lungs.

'Ten days!' she said strongly.

They were going to a land of a million olive trees, to a place where the silver-grey leaves rustled in the wind, and the air was perfumed with the scent of pines. They were going to a country where cedars grew in mighty forests, and the valleys were filled with lemon and pomegranate.

'Will there be camels?' asked Esther, coming up to

them. 'Will there be camels in Canaan?' and Jaha said yes, there would be camels, camels with humps.

They passed Miriam and her dancers, toiling with water skins and tent blankets strapped to their backs, but singing, singing, and soon Esther and Ruth sang with them.

And the ragged band disappeared into the East, and silence fell on the plateau.

And far away, in the course of time, the Pharaoh Merneptah fought a new enemy in Canaan, and defeated a new army, and proudly inscribed on his victory stele ISRAEL IS LAID WASTE — not for the last time misjudging his new eastern neighbour — and as the words were carved in the black basalt of the stele, the nation of Israel emerged from the mists of legend and song, and entered recorded history.

And there were battles at Al, and at Gibeon. And Jericho fell, and the Canaanite kings were imprisoned in a cave at Makkedah. And the descendants of Simeon settled, at last, in the mountains west of Hebron, and the Reubenites (Esther had married a rich though elderly Reubenite) settled east of the Dead Sea, and the Danites, including the descendents of Mouse and Wolf (he had become a great commander in Joshua's army) along the coast of the Great Sea.

And during this time families of bedouin occasionally camped by the prehistoric beehive dwellings on the plateau of Ti, on the southernmost edge of the Wilderness of Paran, and grazed their sheep on the thin grass of the wadi. In the last days of the New Kingdom Empire, when David sat on the throne in

Jerusalem, there was a small Egyptian military way-station here, and brick foundations were laid over the grave of Shelumiel, so that it was no longer surrounded by hot, baking sands.

Then the Empire collapsed, and the Egyptian soldiers departed, and there was silence for a while until Jeroboam the Second was king of Israel and a small Iron Age village was established, occupied by Midianites, and an outer mud wall was built over the Egyptian bricks that covered Shelumiel's tomb. In the time of the Persian Empire the village was burnt down – and then rebuilt; and the mound grew a few centimetres higher. And it was abandoned again, during the wars between Ptolemy IV and Antiochus of Syria, and a layer of wind-blown sand covered the crumbling mud walls, and the only visitors were again passing bedouin or occasional cohorts of Roman soldiers who crouched for shelter against those walls that remained. Then, in the time of Augustus, when Cleopatra was dead and Egypt was a Roman province, and Herod the Great sat on the throne in Jerusalem, it was briefly occupied for the last time.

It was a ruin, almost obliterated by the shifting sands, when Joseph led the donkey bearing Mary and her child westward along the wadi of El-Arish.

And another two thousand years or so passed, and the mound assumed the character of the small hill that rose behind it, and a thin layer of sandy soil covered it smoothly, and desert thorn grew. And by the time of the Afrika Korps and El Alamein, of the Six Day War and the Yom Kippur War, it had become part of the hill itself, its origins revealing themselves only coyly to the eye of an archaeologist (it was marked 'Tell?' on the maps of the American Research Center in Cairo).

It was just part of a hill on El-Tîh, though it carried the bones of Shelumiel, Prince of Simeon, deep in its core.

38
The British Museum

A huge blown-up photograph of an open grave. Contours of bones; ribs making sharp ridges like desert dunes. Black, dry, brittle scraps of fossilized skin, the skull still showing wisps of hair. Sand in the eye-sockets. Sand in the mouth. The skull not staring up but turned, wearily, on its side. A corpse, resting.

Grave goods. A pot – recognizable as Egyptian, nineteenth dynasty. Small objects that might have been amulets. An object – scarcely noticeable – black and almost covered by sand, nestling under the ribcage, next to the beaten-bronze bowl that protected the dead man's genitals on his journey to the Underworld.

A second huge photograph. The blackened object from the first picture – now blown up to twenty times its true size – cleaned, artistically lit, revealing itself as a silver statue of a fifth-dynasty high priest of Ptah.

Saltman said, 'Look, is there any way you can make Worboys act a bit more reasonably?'

Richard said, 'You upset him.'

'I upset him? *I* upset *him?*'

'You know you did,' said Vronwy.

They were sitting at the back of the basement theatre, holding glasses of white wine, waiting for Worboys to give his lecture.

'Listen, I said the stele at Medinet Habu shows a sea battle from Rameses the Third. No sane man, sane person' – quick uneasy glance at Vronwy – 'could go along with the stuff about it being a covered Mycenaean battle chariot. You've seen it. It's down there now, in Gallery One. Those guys are Sherden, and they're not captives – you know they're not captives. They're waving *khepesh* daggers, for Christ's sake. Worboys must have been taking some sort of pill.'

Vronwy said, 'Leave Worboys alone.'

'Leave him – how about him leaving me alone? Have you heard the stuff he's been spreading around?'

'This is his big day. Have another drink.'

'I can't have another drink, baby. This is the BM; they give you one glass and that's it.'

Anyway, it was too late. Worboys was marching into the theatre, Di and Jo flanking him on either side like bridesmaids. There was a polite round of applause, a shuffling in seats. Worboys stood in front of the blown-up photographs and looked out in satisfaction over the sea (well, not sea perhaps, but definitely pond) of faces. So many of these people were the Great and the Good. Colleagues from Edinburgh, from Liverpool, from Chicago House, from UCL. Wittich from Berlin in the third row, smiling his encouragement; Claudel from Lille; Holman from the American Research Center in Cairo. Sitting in the front row were three Trustees from the BM. Next to them, roseate with pride, was Marian, and next to her his two small daughters, neat and solemn in matching frocks with velvet bows.

'The joint British Museum University College expedition to El-Misheili,' he began, his smile turning to a cold accusatory glare as he spotted Saltman – Saltman of Pittsburgh, who was beaming desperately with bonhomie and goodwill.

'Excavations at El-Misheili started during Ramadan – unusual, but we were concerned by the political situation in the area and the need to make haste. First examination showed that many of the graves had been either robbed or severely disturbed through intensive reuse. Those reasonably well preserved, however, showed the variation of construction and burial practice one might expect in a site occupied from the Stone Age to Roman times. A lamp from the time of Herod was the last evidence of occupation found on the mound, leading us to believe that the site was probably deserted sometime in the period 37 to 4 BC. . . .'

Worboys spoke with authority. He was noticeably more confident ever since his profile in the *Observer*, his photo in the *Daily Express* (holding the fifth-dynasty silver statue like a ballroom-dancing trophy), the *Sunday Mirror* story, THE MAN WHO BEARS THE CURSE OF KA-NEFER, PRIEST OF PTAH, which had secretly delighted him, although Marian had been most upset, and his two little girls had cried.

'You can imagine our excitement when my assistant Miss Diane Fitzgerald reported to me the discovery of a grave that in stratigraphical terms belonged to level four – the Late Bronze Age IIB or III – a level that represented a very sparse settlement, nucleated, in fact, towards the east of the tell's surface – and in a context which must be seen as having been extra-mural, no regular burials apparently having taken place in that area.

'This grave was apparently undisturbed. We moved the CAT-scanner into place. As you know, in conventional X-ray scanning the structures through which the waves pass are superimposed on each other. In CAT-scanning, however, X-rays pass through the object at different angles, allowing us to draw a three-dimensional picture. We are all of us, I am sure, familiar with the CAT-scan of the mummy of the Chantres of Amun, Tjentmutengebtiu, which even showed the wax figures of the four Sons of Horus within the visceral pack. The other feature of the CAT-scanner is that it detects differences in the density of structures observed, and can be programmed to ignore the presence of sand or similar material. This, of course, is what accounts for its enormous value to the archaeologist in the field.

'To continue. Once we set up the CAT-scanner we found ourselves looking through the tomb wall at a most remarkable sight. In the grave was a body that was clearly undisturbed. The arms were drawn across the chest, the feet were crossed. We could see the shape of the bowl placed over the genitals. We could see the grave goods and the outline of what was to prove to be a bronze falcon-amulet on the breast. We could see a bronze javelin head, and what appeared to be the remains of its wooden shaft.

'There was evidence of flesh and hair, indicating that this had been a shallow burial in hot sand, leading partially, at least, to natural mummification.

'Next to the grave goods was a dense metallic shape some fifteen centimetres long and five wide, which puzzled and excited us greatly. By this time, however, it was approaching dusk, and despite the most frenzied pleas from Miss Fitzgerald and Miss Ward' – a jolly grin at Di and Jo, who chuckled sheepishly, for this was Worboys's finest hour and they were good-natured girls who knew that they must play out their allotted parts – 'I decided that we must control our curiosity as best we could until the following morning. I therefore went back to the camp and made a vast pot of "Beefy"-brand beef stew for us all.'

Laughs.

In fact, he had not slept a wink that night on the windy plateau. He had felt like Cortes on a peak in Darien – or like Ahmed Abdel Rassoul, the Arab who had chanced into a rock crevice at Deir al-Bahir in 1871, and by the light of his candle found the coffins, canopic jars and libation vases of Rameses the Great, Seti and Tuthmosis the Third. All night he had tossed and turned. Long before the dawn he had been up, plying his badger-hair shaving brush by the light of a lamp, brewing a kettle of tea, making a vast pot of sustaining porridge while Jo and Di were still deep in the refreshing slumbers of youth.

'At first light the camera was rigged directly over the small stone tumulus that had been exposed. We waited until around eight o'clock when the sun was fairly high in the sky but still low enough to throw distinctive shadows. The stone slabs were raised, revealing the sight which you can see on the photograph behind me.'

The lights in the theatre slowly dimmed, except for a spotlight on the blown-up photograph of the grave.

'The body had been wrapped in Egyptian linen, traces of which remained. You can see how the shoulders were tightly drawn up, the feet crossed. The Egyptian character of the burial hardly needs to be pointed out. Strands of another material, possibly coloured, were also found, and traces of a black bituminous material which may indicate an attempt at mummification. The body was male, and he had died violently, almost certainly in battle. You can see where he had suffered a fatal head wound, and where three of his ribs were smashed very probably by a blow from an axe. Examination of his teeth shows that the roots of the third molars, which commonly erupt around the age of eighteen, are open, but those of the first and second molars are closed. This together with a calculation of the bone mineral density of the vertebrae, suggests that our warrior – for the javelin makes clear his war-like status – was aged twenty-three or perhaps twenty-four when he died.

'Among the more unusual grave goods was a pot containing traces of opium and gold finger stalls, normally only provided for kings, princes or high officials. There was a ring portraying Akhenaten – this foxed us for some time, and led us to wonder if the grave did not in fact belong to Late Bronze Age IIA, and even now there can be no certainty on this score. An oddity, an Egyptian child's wooden toy, was placed next to his heart, next to the seat of truth.'

A slight pause, then: 'And of course, the most important of the grave goods, a silver statue of an Egyptian priest of the fourth or fifth dynasty that some of our friends in the media have chosen to believe is the long-lost effigy of Ka-nefer, the high priest of Ptah.'

Next to Richard and Vronwy, Saltman was making a small choking noise that he intended to imply hilarious disbelief. 'Chosen to believe?' he said in a low, strangled voice. 'Chosen to – he was the one who told them!'

'Hush!'

Worboys went on. 'It was Herodotus who recorded the ancient legend, about the silver statue of Ka-nefer, the fifth-dynasty high priest of Ptah. He wrote that it had been stolen from the temple at Thebes, and later taken out of Egypt when the Hyksos were expelled in the days immediately prior to the founding of the eighteenth dynasty. Many people have searched for the statue, not for its monetary value – it is, of course, priceless – but for its magical-religious connection, the statue having supposedly been empowered with supernatural formulae making it possible for Ka-nefer's ba to return to it and live on after the mortal remains of Ka-nefer had corrupted. You might well say that this kind of religious theological experimentation, this desperate dabbling in magic, was more practised in the New Kingdom than in the fifth dynasty, and that Herodotus was falling, like so many after him, particularly in the cinematographic industry, under the spell of Pharaonic religious mumbo-jumbo. That is as may be. If this is indeed the effigy of Ka-nefer, and if it does have paranormal properties, I can at least take comfort from the fact that the ba of Ka-nefer is now haunting the Cairo Museum, and not my own small house in Epping.' A shared laugh with the audience, a reassuring look at Marian and the girls, who smiled back, brave but unconvinced.

'But I would suggest to you that our primary

interest is not in the statue itself, important as a find though it is – and indeed, colleagues have been kind enough to call it the archaeological find of the decade—'

'Hush,' said Vronwy, even though Saltman had not opened his mouth.

'Our primary interest must be in the man who was buried with it, the man whose skeletal remains we see in this photograph, caught by the camera at the moment they were first revealed after some three thousand five hundred years of darkness. Who was this man, this young leader killed in conflict, so revered that he was equipped, like an Egyptian prince, with gold finger stalls for his journey to the New Life, with pots of myrrh and opium, yet who was buried in a rough-and-ready grave on the desolate plateau of El-Tîh? Where did he come from? What was he doing wandering in the bleakness of the Wilderness of Paran?'

'He's going to say it,' breathed Saltman in awe. 'He's really going to say it.'

'And I cannot help thinking not of the expulsion of the Hyksos – Semites though they were – but of another expulsion. Of an expulsion which perhaps this discovery at El-Misheili can, for the first time, attempt to date. An expulsion of Amorite tribes from the eastern Delta. A clearing of raiders and of wandering bands of *hapiru* either in the reign of Akhenaten, the Late Bronze Age IIA, or by the frontier militia of Rameses the Second. An expulsion that also swept up, in its wave of xenophobia, Semitic tribes who had lived in Egypt for perhaps two or three hundred years. An expulsion known to us as the Exodus.'

'He said it,' said Saltman, stunned. 'He goddamn said it.'

Vronwy managed to get another two glasses of wine by squeezing herself close to Worboys to offer her congratulations. She looked round for Richard, to give him a glass, but he had gone. She drank her own wine, then went out of the theatre looking for him. She went up the west stairs, then, instinctively, up again to the Egyptian galleries. Only the dim security lights were on. She looked into Gallery 19: the Mummies Room.

'Richard?'

She drank her wine and put the glass down on a mummy's case. She turned and walked down the long procession of Egyptian galleries, past the fresco that showed the magic spells needed to perform the Ceremony of the Opening of the Mouth, the spells that would bring the dead to life.

'The Cult of the Dead was misnamed.'

'Christ!' she exclaimed, her heart thumping.

'It was in truth an attempt to cheat death.'

He was staring into a glass display case. At samples of barley and dates and pomegranate that had been taken from tombs 3,000 years old, at alabaster jars that still contained traces of eye make-up.

At a bronze, ivory-handled looking-glass.

'At a time when the most advanced civilization in northern Europe was a Stone-Age axe factory in Great Langdale, the Egyptians had achieved everything a civilization can hope to achieve. The provision of food and shelter, the inventions of fire, the discovery of the wheel, the development of an oral a a written language, a social framework and a civil service. That was when the priests of Misri set out to conquer death.'

'Yeah, right. Look, it's just gone nine. I vote we go to Luigi's and eat.'

'The Ceremony of the Opening of the Mouth was performed to restore the senses of the deceased – Ptah, Creator God of Memphis, did this for the gods at the time of their creation. It was as his substitute that priests of Ptah performed the rite on the dead of the New Kingdom. I am alive. O Horus, son of Isis, make me hale as you made yourself hale. Release me, loose me, put me on earth—'

'Richard!'

'Cause me to be loved.'

He was staring into the bronze as Elizabeth had stared into the bronze. *Wouldn't you just like to see the face that first looked back from this metal? Wouldn't you like to be able to recover it, to call it back? Her image is there, you know. Some rich man's daughter from Thebes or Memphis, looking at herself on her fourteenth or fifteenth birthday; her image is in the metal, a pattern of displaced electrons.*

Vronwy said, 'This has all got to stop. This has got to stop or you'll blow your mind. Quantum mechanics, retrocognition, parapsychology, New Kingdom mystical mumbo-jumbo—'

'What did you see, Vronwy?'

'Oh, God, Richard!'

'What did you see?' Richard repeated, peering down again into the bronze mirror, yearning for an image. What did you really see when you collapsed?'

'A flock of birds. I hallucinated about a flock of ⌐ds.'

'And?'

'Some children. I saw children in the cave.'

It was always the same answer.

'Yeah,' he said, 'right.'

'Anyway if I had seen things, imagined I had seen things, it would not be altogether surprising. The amount of auto-suggestion required, in the given circumstances, would hardly have been great. A person with only a small amount of imagination could fancy tanks and chariots and missiles coming down. You'd been banging on about it enough.'

'What the world might call retrocognition, or the operation of a quantum mechanical Closed Timelike Curve, is what a Shropshire girl would call the fancy of a lively imagination?'

'That's it,' she said stubbornly.

He smiled faintly.

'I'd been accoustically bombed, you bastard!'

'Ah, yes, of course.'

She thought how much he had changed since that night at Nagb el-Mirad. He'd been spending hours on the phone to a woman police officer – not an ordinary police officer, a woman who was connected with M15 and had her own reasons for believing in Closed Timelike Curves, in the transference of matter in the quantum world. He'd been to Cambridge to meet an angry young physicist who claimed that the Western scientific establishment was hidebound by convention, blinkered from seeing the true logic of the quantum mechanical world.

He was giving up his job at UCL.

She suspected he was planning to return to Sinai.

'Listen, Elmer was a fake,' she said loudly. 'A Cairo inner-city corpse. A desperate attempt by an obsesse

American PhD student to keep the funds coming in. The autopsy reports were forged, the sending of bone and flesh samples for analysis a charade – all designed to fool the CIA, who weren't fooled at all. And the insignia of the Kap on Elmer's arm came from an article you wrote yourself in *Egyptian Archaeology*. Right, Richard?'

'Perhaps.'

'No! No way perhaps—'

'OK, let's say Elmer was a fake,' he said. 'And Herr Gabriel died because he wandered into the Exclusion Zone, into a place where scientists were testing an acoustic bomb, a device designed to kill human and animal life without destroying property. He was caught by the blast; his internal tissue half cooked, his blood half evaporated. What do you reckon? Did Gama'a agents find him and carry his body back to the chapel of St Onuphrios? Or did he somehow manage to crawl back himself? Did he see the torches of the New Zealand Peacekeepers? Did he try to cry out?'

'I don't know. Why are you doing this? Why are you behaving like this?'

She was frightened. 'Is this what Elizabeth was like?'

No image appeared in the bronze. Nothing took him back to the Delta, to the golden land of Misri; no face smiled out at him in delight.

'You worry too much,' he said. 'Let's eat.'

They walked back down the galleries and down the main stairs. People were still leaving after Worboys's lecture. Saltman was saying heartily, 'And these are our kids, Worboys? Hi, kids,' and Worboys was saying, 'Suggesting I look at the Uragit stele of Baal in the Louvre, Saltman, had a certain malice, a certain unpleasantness—'

'Oh, for Christ's sake, Worboys, you have to take a joke—'

Vronwy went to get her coat. A young woman came pushing through the front doors, ignoring the indignant yelp of the attendant.

'I'm looking for a man who claims he's found Moses' body in a grave in Egypt. Is it true or has somebody been having us on?'

The attendant sent her back out again. Richard looked at the display in the foyer, which included the Medinet Habu stele frieze that Worboys though was a Mycenaean cart and Saltman a Sherden boat. The stone was smoothed and worn, the figures indistinct after more than three thousand years. But it could, he thought suddenly, just as easily be an Egyptian stonemason's representation of a different kind of vehicle entirely.

A minibus, perhaps. Entering Thebes in 1500 BC, its occupants waving not khepesh daggers but video cameras, the strange, puzzling devices on their heads not the spiked helmets of the Sherden but the baseball hats of a quite different, though equally ubiquitous people.

The search for the missing tourist bus in Sinai had been long since abandoned. It was presumed lost in the harsh mountains; the authorities were waiting for bedouin to come across the wreckage, the bones.

'You know, I really thought you were going mad,' said Vronwy, coming out of the cloakroom. 'I thought you were becoming obsessed, just the way she was obsessed.'

He wondered how Celia was getting on, showing her punters the sights. He wondered if they were complaining about the food and the bedbugs. He thought what a pity it was that Eloise wasn't on this particular trip, wowing the Pharaoh in her little yellow top with sunflowers. He wondered mostly, though, about Celia. He wondered if she was missing Morecambe.

'Timetravelers of Baltimore,' he said. 'A firm that delivers the goods.'

'What?' she said, suddenly wary.

'Nothing. Listen, I'm not going mad, OK? I'm not obsessed, right?'

'Right.'

'Let's eat.'

'Luigi's?'

'Luigi's.'

They went out.

Maybe he, one day, would make the journey that Celia had made. That Professor Palmer had made. That Herr Gabriel had unwittingly attempted.

'I was going to put you down,' said Vronwy, 'for Obsessives Anonymous.'

'Idiot.'

A sparrow, perhaps the ba of an Egyptian corpse in the Room of Mummies, fluttered softly by their heads as they passed under the rustling trees.

A selection of bestsellers from Headline

STRAIT	Kit Craig	£5.99	☐
DON'T TALK TO STRANGERS	Bethany Campbell	£5.99	☐
HARVEST	Tess Gerritsen	£5.99	☐
SORTED	Jeff Gulvin	£5.99	☐
INHERITANCE	Keith Baker	£5.99	☐
PRAYERS FOR THE DEAD	Faye Kellerman	£5.99	☐
UNDONE	Michael Kimball	£5.99	☐
THE VIG	John Lescroart	£5.99	☐
ACQUIRED MOTIVE	Sarah Lovett	£5.99	☐
THE JUDGE	Steve Martini	£5.99	☐
BODY BLOW	Dianne Pugh	£5.99	☐
BLOOD RELATIONS	Barbara Parker	£5.99	☐

All (*Group Division*) books are available at your local bookshop, or can be ordered direct from the publisher. Just tick the titles you would like and complete the details below. Prices and availability are subject to change without prior notice.

Please enclose a cheque or postal order made payable to *Bookpoint Ltd*, and send to: (*Group Division*) 39 Milton Park, Abingdon, OXON, OX14 4TD, UK. Email Address: orders@bookpoint.co.uk

If you would prefer to pay by credit card, our call centre team would be delighted to take your order by telephone. Our direct line *01235 400414* (lines open 9.00 am–6.00 pm Monday to Saturday, 24 hour message answering service). Alternatively you can send a fax on *01235 400454*.

TITLE		FIRST NAME		SURNAME	

ADDRESS	
DAYTIME TEL:		POST CODE	

If you would prefer to pay by credit card, please complete:
Please debit my Visa/Access/Diner's Card/American Express (delete as applicable) card number:

Signature .... Expiry Date ....

If you would *NOT* like to receive further information on our products please tick the box. ☐